Harrowing

LEGENDARY FARMER BOOK 2

Print book ISBN 978-1-7376510-2-4
Ebook ISBN 978-1-7376510-3-1

First edition, August 2022

This is a work of fiction. Names, characters, places, and individuals either are the product of the author's imagination or are used fictitiously, and any resemblance to actual persons, living or dead, businesses, companies, events, or locales is entirely coincidental.

This book is dedicated to my mother, who never gave up hoping that I'd write down some of my crazy stories. I love you, Mom!

Book Two: Harrowing

har·row /ˈherō/ *verb*

gerund or present participle: harrowing

1. draw a harrow over (land).
2. cause distress to.

Chapter One

Rouge

No matter how you sliced it, office work was more boring than anything else. Zoey had the lunch menu memorized. Toting boxes of 3D reference models for the artists, cleaning Mr. Hamncheese's cage for Harris's team (apparently they'd used it to create models for the Greater Hamster, and it was now the unofficial team mascot), and picking extra pickles off Granny's sandwich just didn't float her boat. Every once in a while someone would take a minute to explain something about their actual job, and that was really cool, but being the department dogsbody? Not cool.

On the other hand, she loved being a guinea pig for Dr. Joe. Take today for instance. She'd just spent half an hour holding a *real life Mambele*! It was exactly like the one she had in game, right down to the leather wrapped handle, the moon-shaped curve into a straight stabby bit, and the spike on the back. The weight of it felt a little different, though, and it definitely wasn't as sharp or pointy as the real thing, though it lodged into the target on the wall of the gym just fine. It smelled like warm metal and leather, and when she touched it with her tongue, she grimaced at the tang of iron.

Now, the warm fluid surrounded her like the coziest blanket she'd ever felt. She looked up at Dr. Joe where he was leaning over the pod. The sound of his voice was slightly muffled by the mask and headset she wore, but she knew what he was asking.

"Everything feel okay, Zoey?" He asked the same thing every time, and he actually waited for an answer., unlike most adults. They might ask, but it was usually pretty obvious they didn't really care about the answer. Even though her answer was always the same, he still listened.

Today, she decided to ask something that had been bothering her for a while. She knew that when she spoke, the pickup in her facemask would carry it loud and clear to his earbud. The cameras and screens in the mask fed audio and video back to her, in turn. "Hey, Dr. Joe. Why don't people use the bathroom in *Veritas*?"

Dr. Joe froze, and a red flush rose up his cheeks. He cleared his throat, and looked up and to the right, avoiding her gaze. "Ah, well, you realized that, did you? Well, the truth is," he looked back and grinned a little, mischief dancing in his eyes, "when we were doing beta testing of the game, we found that the system was sometimes a little *too* convincing. Nobody could agree whose responsibility it was to clean up the resulting mess, so we just took out the option entirely."

Zoey laughed, picturing a bunch of people in white lab coats playing rock paper scissors over piles of waste. She shook her head and held her thumb up. "I'm ready to go, Dr. Joe." He rolled his eyes at the rhyme and the title she insisted on giving him, but returned the gesture, then reached up and closed the lid of the pod. Blue fluid silently filled in the space around her, and she laid back and closed her eyes.

❦ ❦ ❦

Rouge kept her eyes closed for a moment, getting used to the feeling that she had been instantly transported somewhere entirely different. The disorientation was better in that she didn't feel so dizzy and disconnected until she got used to feeling less of everything. It was worse in that she *didn't* feel so much less of everything, so the disconnect her brain had to deal with between where she was a moment ago and where she was now was *fierce.*

She drew in a few deep breaths, taking in the crisp smell of snow. She swore she could almost feel the little hairs in her nose freeze. She opened her eyes as she breathed out, watching her breath puff into clouds in the still winter air.

It was late winter now. Winter was short in *Veritas*, so there was only another week or so until it all melted, and spring would begin. Veritas Corp knew that everybody got tired of winter pretty quickly, no matter how many snow-related events they ran. She was really sorry she'd missed the Snowball Fight event in Bright, but no matter how much she'd prayed to Gina for just a short trip back to join in the fun, she'd gotten no response. So much for having some pull with the Lady Upstairs.

Everybody on the farm was tired of winter, too. Now that everyone who could be was partied, and Aspen's animal companions could use Party Chat, *everybody* got to listen to Khor complain about how the snow got stuck in his fur. Did the little unicorns complain? No!

Not that they could, because apparently, they counted as animals instead of NPCs or something. Aspen said the bat, goat, and spider each had 'part of my soul', so maybe that was it? Though what the rationale was for excluding Sarave and William, Rouge had no idea. Of course, Sarave and Sumi had worked out a complex technique for communicating via web patterns, so it was really only William who was still out in the cold (ha ha), and the vampire didn't really seem to mind.

In any case, the kids were smart enough to spend most of their days inside the house, napping in front of the fire, or causing mayhem as they played by climbing under and over furniture and people alike. Even the duck spent most of his time in the barn, head tucked under his wing as if he were trying to find out if ducks could hibernate.

No, Codswallop and Khor were the only ones who insisted on walking around. Codswallop followed Rouge (or her Zombie) everywhere he could. He would allow other people to feed him, but other than that, he was a one-girl bird. He sometimes got ice stuck between his toes, but he could groom it out himself, unless Rouge was around, in which case he hopped from foot to foot, warbling pitifully, until she did it for him.

Khor, on the other hand, did absolutely everything he usually did, just as if everything wasn't covered in snow and the same approximate temperature as Antarctica. As a result, he got these crazy balls of snow on his fur and ice between his split hooves. Sometimes he looked like a whole city of small animated snowmen walking around complaining about how 'no one ever looks after the goat'. Aspen finally threatened to shave him, which had helped for a day or so, but then the huge beast was right back to his whiny ways.

Now, Codswallop thrust a cold bird head into her hands, and she smiled, feeling like her face would crack in the chill. "Hey, Wally. How are you? Did you miss me?"

The large ostrich rubbed his head against her, leaning into her side so hard that he nearly knocked her down, leaving her in no doubt that he had, indeed, missed her. She opened her inventory and pulled out an Ear of Corn, which she fed to him. As her greedy bird swallowed the cob whole, she looked around, taking in the beauty of winter in the wilderness. The only signs of civilization were her own tracks, left by her Zombie as it wandered around, and smoke rising from the chimney of the house, about half a mile ahead. The snow was only about six inches deep, this time, and while it was a slog to walk, it wasn't anything her high dexterity couldn't handle.

"What was I doing, Wally?" She looked down at her hands, seeing that she wasn't holding anything except a bird head looking for pettings. She pulled up her inventory, sorting by items most recently added, and found a stack of 99 Full Waterskins. "Ah ha. Water run, huh? Good thing I looked. I guess I should take these back before I get to work. I *really* don't want to see Sumi cranky again."

Rouge shuddered and continued on toward the house, enjoying the crisp sound of the snow beneath her boots, though not the chill of her fingers and toes. She had quickly found that deep immersion wasn't always great. She'd never really noticed normal changes of temperature in game, except that you could get debuffs if you stayed in the hot sun too long without a hat, or walked outside in the cold without boots and a coat. Now, though, her toes curled as they tried to warm up by touching each other, to no avail, obviously. She had sewn some Simple Fur Socks a few weeks ago, so at least she didn't think her toes would *actually* fall off now.

She pulled out her Mambele and began tossing it back and forth as she walked, catching the hilt firmly at the end of each throw. The soft slap of the leather against her palm made a pleasant counterpoint to the crunch of her boots and Codswallop's soft, cheerful chirps as he strode beside her. She should probably ride, but the ostrich didn't have his saddle on, and it wasn't in her inventory. Probably stored in the barn, which was fine, but no way was she bouncing her butt on his bony back all the way to the house. Once again, full immersion made things a little *too* realistic.

Halfway back, she chucked her blade toward a distant hillock of snow. It was a little higher than usual when she went on a river-run, so she vaguely wondered if a new tree had fallen and been covered by a drift. Not something she would do with a regular blade, of course, but with the [Return] spell and how the game considered wiping down the blade in any way as 'cleaning' it, she didn't have to worry about it getting lost or rusty. The hillock cursed.

You have dealt 28hp of damage to Player *Po0pHead1*. Player *Po0pHead1* was taken by surprise and is unable to move for 5 seconds. Player *Po0pHead1*'s [Camouflage] was broken.

For a heartbeat, Rouge stood there, wide-eyed, as the 'snow' vanished to reveal a man, dressed all in white from head to foot, crouched along the path

5

broken through the snow by her Zombie's feet. Then Codswallop let out the loudest honk she'd ever heard. The sound echoed across the snowy landscape, and from the corner of her eye, she caught a flash of movement as another player stumbled, startled by the noise, and their knife swiped harmlessly through the air by her head. Instantly, she crouched. Using every scrap of her level 21 [Acrobatics] skill, she thrust herself up, somersaulting backwards through the air. She landed neatly on Codswallop's back, toes curling into his body through her boots as she leaned forward and caught at his feathers with her left hand. She reached out with her right and used [Return].

You have dealt 11hp of secondary damage to Player *Po0pHead1*. Player *Po0pHead1* is Bleeding.

She grinned viciously, and cast [Poof!], followed by the new spell she'd gotten for completing the Training Montage quest: [Repeat]. It forced the target to repeat the last one second five times. It was *amazing*, and she knew she hadn't figured out what all it could be used for yet. It had a cooldown of twenty-four hours, and it would only work right after the one second you wanted to repeat, but if your timing was good...

You have dealt 11hp of secondary damage to Player Po0pHead1. Player Po0pHead1 is Bleeding.
You have dealt 11hp of secondary damage to Player Po0pHead1. Player Po0pHead1 is Bleeding.
You have dealt 11hp of secondary damage to Player Po0pHead1. Player Po0pHead1 is Bleeding.
You have dealt 11hp of secondary damage to Player Po0pHead1. Player Po0pHead1 is Bleeding.
You have dealt 11hp of secondary damage to Player Po0pHead1. Player Po0pHead1 is Bleeding.

Even as her smoke cloud billowed out over the scene, and Po0pHead1 and his buddy tried to turn it blue with their cursing, she and Codswallop were bounding toward the house as fast as an ostrich with a Relationship of 100 could go, which was pretty darned fast, even without breakfast rolls.

Chapter Two

Aspen

A spen was sitting by the fire, toasting his toes, and contemplating the two sharpened sticks he was using to knit some of Sumi's silk into new socks to replace the very well-worn pair currently dangling from a drying line nearby, when he heard Codswallop bellow. He'd only heard the sound once before, when a small hunting pack of Lesser Wolves had come down from the mountains hunting easier prey and thought the ostrich looked like dinner. It wasn't a sound you forgot.

Instantly, he was up, pulling wet boots on his bare feet, even as he sent out a message over party chat. ::Why is Codswallop upset? Where is he?::

Rouge's voice came back, sounding tense and breathless. ::We're headed toward you from the river, top speed. At least two Travelers after us. I hurt one. Gave him a Bleed debuff, too.:: She sounded gleeful. ::But I think we could use some help. Be careful, they use camouflage, so if there are more, they could be anywhere. Be there in a minute!::

Aspen frowned, thinking hard as he grabbed the new staff he'd made to replace the one broken in the battle against the vampires. "Khor!" he snapped.

The goat poked his nose in through the window between the barn and the house. <I heard. I'm ready.>

"Good. Rouge is coming to us, so I want you ready to take down anyone following her. Try not to kill them. I want to know what's going on. Sumi!" The spider dropped down into his field of vision and waved a leg. "Bind them. If you take more than one, you can pick and choose which one to keep, and let the other one see how we deal with enemies." His face was cold, and his voice hard. Rouge would have been very surprised to see her gentle farmer friend at this moment.

"What should we do, Aspen?" Sarave stood near the stove, with Juniper, now a solid toddler already near half her mother's height, standing with her fist in her mouth and huge eyes going from one member of her family to another. The goblin's speech had progressed remarkably quickly over the winter, since she and Aspen spent most evenings conversing quietly while Sarave sat holding her sleeping child in the rocking chair Aspen built for her. Now, only her musical accent and an occasional error in tenses gave away the fact that she wasn't speaking her native language.

Aspen hesitated on his way out the door. "Stay here with Juniper and the unicorns. Bar the door, and exit down into the tunnels if they try to come in. It's not worth risking any of you to protect this place. Thanks to William, we can always start again."

Silus' sleepy voice joined the conversation. <What about me?>

"Use your [Sonar]. Find anything that's shaped differently than what your eyes tell you. I know you have a hard time seeing with the sun reflecting off the snow, but do your best. They may know about you, so be careful. Don't get caught, and don't get hurt. Go!" Aspen opened the door, and Silus and Sumi exited, both vanishing quickly.

Aspen followed, moving more slowly, using Khor's massive bulk as cover. Nuisance was standing on top of Khor's massive head, beady eyes surveying their surroundings intently.

::What's with the duck?:: Aspen sent in party chat.

::He wouldn't get off.:: Khor answered brusquely, his own eyes and nose busy looking for danger.

Just then, Nuisance quacked loudly, the feathers around his head rising as he stared intently at the roof of the house. Khor and Aspen whipped around, looking upward as a mound of snow became a humanoid figure dressed in all white, holding a bow taut with an arrow trained on Aspen.

<Down!> shouted Khor, shouldering his human friend aside. He grunted slightly as the arrow meant for Aspen hit him instead, but he didn't even pause as he raced toward the house. He reared back on his hooves so he could try to sweep the enemy from the roof with the sides of his massive horns. He caught them with the backswing, and the figure went flying with a feminine curse.

::Sumi! We have one for you!:: Aspen yelled, running toward the woman with his staff ready. Before he could reach her, Codswallop appeared, The oversized bird had leapt onto the roof in one mighty bound, and immediately jumped down again, landing next to the woman. Rouge flipped over the ostrich, knife slashing. A flashing red glow surrounded the woman, indicating a critical hit, and red splashes appeared on her white clothes.

Sumi appeared beside them, casting out loops of sticky webbing. The woman's feet and hands pulled together, and she yelped in surprise and fear. Rouge leapt from behind, hitting the attacker hard on the back of her head with the hilt of her Mambele. The woman went limp.

"Good." Aspen gritted out. "Make sure she's not bleeding out, bind her well, and put her in the barn. Close the shutters between the house and the barn so she can't get in if she gets loose. Rouge, you said there are at least two more?"

Rouge's hazel eyes were as huge as Juniper's as she watched how smoothly Aspen's team worked together. It was one thing to know her new friends were former soldiers, and another to see them in action. "Uh, yeah? I got one pretty well, I think, and unless he's managed to use a Bandage to stop the bleeding, he should be easy to see. The other one I only heard. Two guys, at least."

Silus' voice came over the party chat. ::Two. One was bleeding but has stopped now. The trail disappears after that, but I can still tell where they are. They're trying to come in around both sides of the house. The injured one is to the west.::

Aspen nodded, eyes flicking from side to side. ::Khor, you and Nuisance take the injured one. The rest of us will go east. Ready?::

Everyone indicated agreement, and he chopped a hand through the air.

Khor took one large step, then raced toward the west side of the house, lowering his head into ramming position. A man yelled, and then the huge goat was out of sight.

Rouge sank back against the side of the house, taking advantage of the slight shadow there to enter [Stealth]. Even in the daylight, she became difficult to see, though Aspen could still tell where she was because of some magic of being in a Traveler's Party together. She slunk silently along the wall, not even leaving footprints in the snow.

Aspen stepped to the side, away from the house. That arrow had been intended for him, so it seemed likely it was him they were after. It might simply have been that the woman thought if she took out the goat's human handler, he would stop attacking, but Aspen knew from long experience that when faced with a creature as large and menacing as Khor, few people were able to think so logically.

He strode out, making sure he was clearly visible, trying to draw the attacker's attention as he pretended to look around. He heard a flicker of wings, a high pitched sound at the edge of hearing, and then Silus said, ::Duck!::

A bare hesitation as he wondered if she meant he should get down or that Nuisance was coming delayed him in reacting just long enough for a knife thrown at him to clip his shoulder. He hissed in pain and almost dropped his staff, but held onto it through sheer determination. Then Rouge was leaping out from concealment, performing a perfect [Backstab], followed by pulling her savage weapon back and up, tearing it free and releasing a gout of blood. The man screamed and staggered.

::Yes!:: Rouge exclaimed. ::Crit and 87 damage! Bleeding, too! I love this knife!:: She drove the blade into the man again as he struggled to recover, and Aspen ran to help her, not that she seemed to need it. He brought the iron-shod tip of his staff down onto the man's temple, and it crunched under the force. A golden glow surrounded both him and Rouge as the man died.

::Damn it! Khor, is yours alive? Silus, are there any more?:: He watched as Rouge crouched to loot the body, pressing his hand against his wound and flattening his body against the stone wall of the house.

Khor growled. ::Dead. He was too injured to take a hit. Nuisance tried to eat his nose.::

Silus' serious little voice responded, ::Not that I can tell. I found their tracks coming from the pass, before they started using [Camouflage]. I only see the tracks of three. There are some horses tied up here, too. Three with saddles and a pack horse.::

Rouge squealed excitedly. ::Nice! The mounts are Soulbound, so they'll find their owners when they respawn. The packhorse can be stolen, though.::

Aspen frowned. ::I hadn't thought about them respawning. Can you tell where they'll be?::

::You can only respawn at a spawn point. The closest one, besides your little shrine to Gina, is back in Vargo. They'll have to cross the mountains if they want to try again.::

Aspen nodded, lowering his staff. "Good," he said, finally feeling safe to speak out loud. "You and Silus go see what you can learn from the horses. I'm going to have a little chat with our prisoner."

Rouge's eyes widened again. "She's still alive? Yes!" She made a strange movement, pumping her fist up and down as she danced a few steps. "She probably won't tell you much, since it's not like threatening to kill her will really do much good, but bribery might be worth a shot. If you have something she wants." She looked a little dubious.

Aspen smiled at her. "I think I can figure something out." Silently, he sent, ::Silus, come get Rouge. You two have a mission!::

::Yay!:: came the bat's response, and he could practically see her puffing up with pride. ::I'll be right there!::

Sumi had patched Aspen's shoulder and gone off to check on Khor by the time Silus returned, and the bat and girl went off together, Silus riding on Rouge's shoulder, while Rouge rode on her freshly saddled ostrich. Codswallop looked wary, and his big brown eyes darted around in search of any further danger.

Aspen waited until the girls were out of sight before turning back to the house. He rapped on the door. "Sarave?"

"Is it over?" The goblin's muffled voice answered, but there was no sound of the bar being lifted. Aspen nodded in approval.

"The fight is over. I'd like you to stay inside for a while longer, though. We have some… business to attend to, and it'll be best to keep the little ones inside." Aspen's voice was colder than the frigid air surrounding them.

"I understand." Sarave had grown up during the war, and came from a people who were not known for their gentleness. He knew she did, indeed, understand.

Aspen turned and opened the door to the barn. He stepped into the dimness, leaving the door cracked behind him. On the ground, he saw the woman, her face turned away from him. A trail of blood ran down her face from the bump behind her ear, left from when Rouge had struck her. Her hands were still bound tightly, but he could see loose strands fraying from the webs around her feet, so he knew she was only pretending unconsciousness.

Aspen stopped a few feet away. He was too far for her to reach easily, but close enough to loom threateningly. With pale topaz eyes glinting coldly, and an emotionless expression on his lean face, he knew his appearance was frightening.

He heard the creak of the door behind him, and knew Sumi had joined him.

<Are you sure you want to do this?> she asked softly.

His eyes flickered from the arachnid to the silent figure on the floor. He nodded almost imperceptibly, though for a moment he actually hesitated. But his face hardened again, topaz eyes like shards of frozen flames. He stepped forward, and brought the end of his staff down on the woman's hand, where it lay on the ground. He leaned, just enough.

"So," he said conversationally, voice far different from the warm, laughing one that his new family was familiar with. "I've been talking to Travelers a lot recently. They've told me some very interesting things…"

Chapter Three

Rouge

Silus was absolutely, completely, the cutest thing Rouge had ever gotten to snuggle. That totally included the sugar glider her friend Kira had let her hold in fifth grade.

It probably helped that the sugar glider bit her.

Anyway, it was really hard to concentrate on anything except the warm, fuzzy creature tucked up under her chin, so she missed the point where the tracks of the invaders became visible.

::Rouge?:: Silus' little voice over the party chat was exactly as adorable as Rouge would have expected. ::Roooouuuuuge? The horses are that way!:: The little bat wiggled as if she would fly off, and Rouge had to fight not to tuck her chin down over the silky fur in an attempt to keep her there.

"Oh! Sorry, Silus! I was just thinking about, um, something else. Where—" She broke off as she saw the faint trail leading through the gleaming snow.

She crouched down, examining the prints.

"They weren't worried about being backtracked, were they? They walked in a line so that only one had to break the trail, but it doesn't look like they tried anything sneaky."

She touched the marks. They overlapped each other, with the smaller, shallower marks probably made by the woman clearly showing on top of the others. One pair of hard-soled boots, and two pairs of something that let the outline of the foot show through slightly, one larger than the other.

No other prints.

You have gained one level in [Tracking]. It is now level 5.

Rouge sighed and waved away the notification. "Yay, skill up, and all, but not right now! Sheesh!" she muttered.

Silus squeaked softly. ::Skill up?::

Rouge stood, brushing snow off her pants. "Sorry, yeah. I got a level in [Tracking]. I'm always down for better Skills, but I wish the system wasn't quite so in your face, literally. Totally breaks the immersion."

Silus was silent for a moment. ::What did you say?::

The elf girl giggled.

"Sorry, Silus. I just wish the notices would wait for me to look at them when I'm ready."

::Oh.:: Silus snuggled back down, her little body shivering slightly in the chill breeze. ::I wish that we got notices when we got levels and skill increases. We know something happened when we see the glowies, but everybody loses track eventually, and you don't always know what you leveled in, anyway. I don't even know what level I am.::

Rouge stopped dead, Codswallop grumbling as she pulled sharply on his reins.

"Whoa, what! Really? Um, I can tell you that. I can't see friendly NPC's levels usually, but we get a little bit of info for being in a party together." With a thought, she pulled up the party list.

Name	Level	Hp	Mana
Motte Bailey	96	1455/1455	0/0
Rouge the Rogue	27	117/117	100/100
Aspen (NPC)	34	341/523	523/523
Khor (NPC)	53	812/981	0/0
Sumi (NPC)	41	243/243	92/92
Silus (NPC)	19	70/70	10/10

She shook her head again at Aspen's numbers. If it hadn't been obvious before that he was a special NPC, it was clear when you looked at even the limited stats they got in the list. How the heck did he have so much hp and mana at level 34? A player of his level might have those stats, but if they did, they'd have no points left for Endurance, Dexterity, Strength, or Wisdom. Rouge couldn't speak to his Wisdom, but he obviously had plenty of the others, so he had way more stat points than he should. *If* he were operating under the same rules as players.

But as Rouge and Motte had learned in the last month, NPCs had a system all their own. They could gain stats independent of levels, and often did. NPCs 'blessed by the Gods' grew at an increased speed that could create monsters if they were given time. That said, most NPCs who fit the bill were actually Quest or Story NPCs. They needed to be extra tough so when some stupid Player decided to try to kill them, they could kick him or her to the curb. *Veritas* was a game where every action could potentially affect the entire story, so when an NPC was important, the developers didn't want them to keel over in a stiff breeze.

"You're level nineteen," Rouge told Silus, scrootching the tantalizing silver tufts in front of the big ears. "Only one more until you're twenty!"

Silus squeaked excitedly. ::I wonder if I'll get to become a Greater Fruitbat then!::

Rouge froze in dismay. "Will you get bigger?"

::So big! At least twice as big as I am now! Aspen says my mother had a twelve inch wingspan!:: Silus stretched out her wings as wide as they would go. The thin skin was nearly translucent in the sunlight, and her wings almost seemed to glow.

Rouge relaxed. "That would be good. Sometimes I worry I'll hurt you when I pet you."

Silus giggled. ::I can handle it! Aspen used to be so clumsy. He'd even pinch my ears accidentally, so I'm used to it.::

The two fell silent as they entered a small clearing where four animals were tied up.

Now that Rouge was in deep immersion, all she had to do was think about wanting to know more information about the beasts, and tags appeared above their heads. The old pod and headset had never been sensitive enough to pick up on thoughts without a conscious tell of some sort, like squinting for [Identify]. She read the tags: Po0PBucket (Po0pHead1), DancingFire (FlyingFir3), Lamp (R3dLit3), StuffCarrier (Po0pHead1).

"Huh. Wow, that guy sure has a lot of imagination." Rouge cocked her head to the side. "So, Silus, just out of curiosity, did you know this one is a mule?" The thief pointed at StuffCarrier.

::Whoa,:: the bat said, eyes even bigger than usual as she took in the large animal. ::I've heard of those. They all kind of look alike to me.::

Rouge walked over, holding out her hand to the mule and triggering her [Steal] skill. She would have to remain in contact with the mule for five minutes, during which time the owner would receive messages warning them that the theft was being attempted, so they could try to stop it. Since Po0pHead1 had just been killed a half hour or so ago, he'd still be on forced logout, so he wouldn't know until he could respawn in a few hours.

She patted the animal, and it shuddered, leaning away from her slightly. She frowned, and pulled a carrot out of her inventory. The mule's ribs were sticking out, which was a sign that the owner hadn't been feeding it. You didn't *have* to feed any animal associated with your account, but it was a good idea. It would be more loyal, faster, stronger, and have more endurance when it was treated well. Newbies sometimes let their mount's Relationship get down to 0, at which point it would start to misbehave – disobeying or even running away for a day or two. You learned pretty quickly not to do that, and besides, they looked so pathetic that you'd have to be a monster not to feed them sometimes!

The mule inhaled the carrot, and she pulled out the whole stack. She stroked the long, silky ears. "See how long his ears are? Way longer than a horse. Plus, his mane is all short and spiky, instead of long and flowy." The elf girl gestured to the fuzzy crest standing up between the animal's ears.

::Oooooohhhhhh. Got it!:: Silus chirped happily, always excited to learn something that would help her be a better scout. Rouge had noticed that even though the tiny creature took her job very seriously, and everyone else listened to her and counted on her doing her job, she also seemed to be very inexperienced, so sometimes she missed things.

Congratulations! You have successfully stolen Po0pHead1's Beast of Burden! You have recovered: 10 x Wolf Claw, 22 x Mosquito Blood, 1 x Rotten Bear Fur, 31 x Food Rations, 17 x Water Rations, and 1 x Greater Wolverine Teeth.

Would you like to change the name of this Beast of Burden? Yes/No

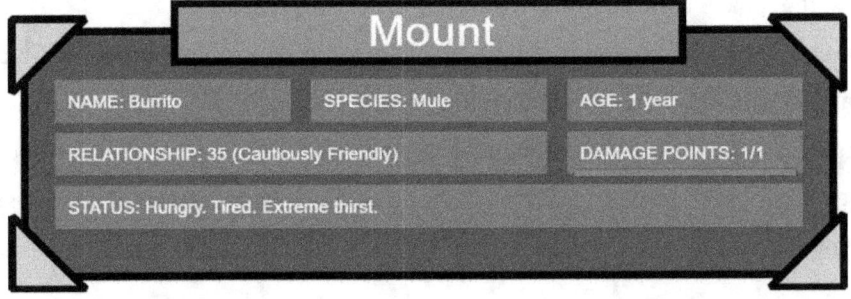

Mount

NAME: Burrito	SPECIES: Mule	AGE: 1 year
RELATIONSHIP: 35 (Cautiously Friendly)		DAMAGE POINTS: 1/1
STATUS: Hungry. Tired. Extreme thirst.		

"Oh, yeah!" Rouge quickly changed the name, then stroked the mule's cheek even as she fed him another carrot. "There. Now you're Burrito! I know you're not actually a burro, but I couldn't resist. It's way better than *StuffCarrier*. Ugh." She rolled her eyes as she rubbed his forehead and pulled up his stat sheet.

Quickly, she removed a Water Ration from the pack and gave it to the poor animal. At least Po0pHead1 got one thing right. He really was a poophead.

She turned to the three horses, tilting her head thoughtfully.

::Do we have to kill them?:: Silus' voice was very small and sad.

"Oh. no!" Rouge was shocked. "Not only would that suck, but it's actually better for us if we don't. They'll automatically return to their riders, but if they've been treated as badly as poor Burrito, they'll take their sweet time about it. A well-cared-for mount will return at its top speed, but given the state of the pass, that'd still take a week or more. Though if these guys are here, I guess that means the pass is clearing. Huh." That realization made her pause for a moment, but then she went on.

"Anyway, if we kill them, they'll respawn in a day or so, at the same place as those jerks. Way better to leave them. No, I was trying to decide if I should cut them free or not." She pointed to the ropes tying the three horses to nearby trees. "I can do it, since I'm a Thief, þut that would let them return to their owners a little faster. If I leave them, they'll get free after two days, and then head home. I know what I *should* do, but I feel really bad letting them just stand there. There's nothing to eat or drink, and they can't run away from predators."

::Then shouldn't we let them go?:: Silus asked sweetly. ::If they get eaten, they'll get back sooner, so it's better not to take the chance.::

They both looked at the animals and came to a silent mutual understanding that they would ignore the fact that their group had cleared the area of predators large enough to kill horses. Rouge summoned her Mambele from her inventory and quickly cut the ropes. Po0PBucket immediately started grazing, seeming in no particular hurry to leave. DancingFire immediately ran off toward the pass, and Lamp followed, though the horse ambled slowly, occasionally stopping to eat .

Rouge watched them, then her eyes widened. "Wait, one of them should be heading for the house, right? That female player is still alive."

The girl and the bat looked at each other. ::I guess she's not? Anymore?:: Silus finally said.

The girl winced. "Oh, man. I guess that makes sense. I mean, she'll respawn, and having her on this side of the mountains would be dangerous. Still, though...."

::You don't leave an enemy alive behind you.:: Silus said, softly, with the tone of someone who was repeating something they had been taught, but weren't sure they believed.

Rouge sighed. Then she spun, staring back toward the house. "They did it again! Just like that old bad-guy, His Librarianness! He sent me out here to get me out of Bright, and they sent me away so I wouldn't argue when they killed that player!"

::Me too!:: Silus sounded as scandalized as Rouge felt.

The two looked at each other again, in complete understanding. Adults sucked, even digital ones.

Chapter Four

Aspen

Aspen tried to ignore the glares Rouge and Silus sent his way, but it was difficult, especially when his neck felt so cold without the warm little bat snuggled up to him. Instead, Silus was on Rouge's shoulder, watching him with large golden eyes that held an accusatory gleam.

He cleared his throat slightly, looking toward Sumi instead of the two young females. "So, Sumi and I learned that the group that attacked us today were given a quest by someone in Bright. Unfortunately, the quest was issued to the leader of the guild, who shared it with the rest of his guild members, so FlyingFir3 didn't know who it came from. She did, however, know that her group was not the only one to receive it, so we can expect more attacks like this one."

He held up an amulet. It was a simple stone needle on a leather thong, but the tip of the needle swerved to point at him no matter how he moved it. "Apparently, they found something of mine, and a mage was able to create a tracking spell with it. FlyingFir3 didn't know if the other groups also had one of these, but it's best to assume that they do. I know someone who can do a cleansing ritual to cleave the link between me and the trackers, but last I heard, she'd moved to Bloodhaven."

He looked back at Rouge, who was slumped in her chair, arms folded, glaring. He sighed. "Rouge, you said you came out here to meet Duke Penbrooke, correct?"

She sat up straight, expression brightening. "Yeah! So, are you ready to admit you're him?"

He paused, topaz eyes widening. "Ah…"

She waved her hand, rolling her eyes. "Come *on*, Aspen. There's no one else out here. You're some big war hero, and you have all these super loyal, super awesome companions. I'd have to be an idiot to think you're a regular old retired soldier turned farmer. I may be 'just a kid', but I'm *not* an idiot." Righteous indignation bled from every word.

Aspen sighed, running his hand through his already-disheveled hair. "I know, Rouge. I don't think you're 'just a kid', either. I do think," he looked at her piercingly, "that you're an innocent, and an idealist. There were choices to be made today that you and Silus didn't need to bear the weight of. Not yet, anyway. I'm sorry if you feel slighted, but your task was also important, and I don't regret sparing you those choices."

Rouge deflated, slumping in her seat again, though this time she just looked rebellious and a little thoughtful. "Fine," she muttered, "whatever. So, you admit that you're this Duke guy?"

Sarave was staring at Aspen, her gaze questioning, and now it was her eyes he avoided.

"Yes, all right. After the Battle of Bright, when Akuji was slain, Geral and King Chester needed someone to pin a 'hero' label on. It couldn't be either of them, because the nobility knew they were in the city at the time. They needed someone weak but believable, with no political clout. I, drained and disliked as I was, was the perfect human sacrifice. While I laid in bed, too weak to move a finger, Chester made me a Duke. Geral claimed credit for the 'plan', though any imperfections were my own fault." He shook his head.

"They were all waiting for me to die. Another martyr to join Lark, this one political instead of religious. When I failed to do so, thanks to my friends here," he nodded his head toward Sumi, Silus, and Khor, who had his nose stuck in through the window, as usual, "they tried to help me along to my final rest." His voice was bitter at these last words, as he remembered the poor, weak king with whom he had shared more than one heartfelt talk over tea and battle maps.

::Three poisoning attempts, a hidden dart trap in his clothes chest, and two arrows 'accidentally' sent his way when he was on the balcony getting some fresh air. All in rapid succession.:: Sumi inserted. ::After that, we started planning to get him out of the city.::

::Chester made him the 'Duke of the North',:: Khor put in, snickering slightly, ::but he didn't say what that meant. So we figured, might as well claim the whole northern area of Quarternell, right?::

::I got to take a message to the King!:: Silus piped up. ::He lives in a really, really big castle! It has *three* kitchens, and seven gardens! It was really hard to find him, but Sumi told me to look for the teeny tiny miniature buildings, and there he was!::

Aspen glanced at Sarave. The goblin looked confused, since she couldn't hear the animals speak. Aspen picked the narrative up again. "Sumi wrote a letter. She said I was dying, and wanted to go somewhere alone to do it. It took some back and forth, but she convinced Chester to make a deed for 'the homestead north of the Whispering Mountains and all unclaimed lands surrounding it'."

Sumi's voice was smug. ::He's rather absentminded, King Chester, especially if you catch him away from all his advisors and ministers. He also forgot to limit Aspen's rights to anything valuable found on or under the land, likely because Aspen was supposed to die.::

"So, here we are." Aspen shrugged. "I always intended to go back for more supplies, if I survived the winter, though not until after summer harvest. It seems that whoever sent these assassins after me isn't content to wait, however."

::I checked the pass.:: Khor put in. ::The snow is still deep. I went halfway up the first peak, and I could barely see above the snow. I don't know how that lot got here.::

Aspen looked toward Sumi. "According to FlyingFir3, they had five [Float] scrolls. They used the scrolls on a hide, and then rode the hide across the mountains. Each scroll lasted one day. She claimed they were a Quest reward Po0...." He grimaced as the spider raised a warning foreleg. "Ah, their leader had in his inventory for some time, waiting for 'something fun' to use it on. Apparently, he decided this was it."

Rouge nodded. "That makes sense. Those guys weren't all that high leveled, so they were probably casual gamers who thought the quest sounded interesting. They were probably in it more for the entertainment value than any interest in whatever the quest reward was." She looked at Aspen. "Did she say what it was?"

His face was grim. "Five hundred gold, three hundred experience, and a weapon of Rare or higher rating."

The elven thief's hazel eyes widened. "Wow. They came all the way out here for that? They must have been bored. Hey, hang on a sec." Her eyes went wide and blank.

Aspen looked at the others in confusion. Five hundred gold was enough for a family to live on for a year! Add in the experience and the weapon, and half the Thieves Guild in Bright should have been knocking down their door. Why did the Traveler girl seem so dismissive?

Rouge's eyes came back into focus. "Yep, that's what I thought. Those scrolls only drop in the Cloud Dungeon, and sell for about 1000 gold each. That's good money, so the five hundred doesn't even come close to making it up. The XP is chump change, and rare weapons aren't that hard to come by, especially if they didn't specify what kind of weapon. I mean, a Rare Simple Iron Dagger sells at auction for about seventy-five gold. Whoever set that quest either wasn't very serious about it, or they didn't know much about Travelers. Or," she paused thoughtfully, "there's something FlyingFir3 either didn't tell you, or didn't know."

Just then, she jumped and clapped her hands over her ears, blanching. "Oh, holy hand grenades! That was my logout alarm! Sorry guys! I forgot I'm at work! I'll log back on when I get home!" Her eyes went blank and her face expressionless once again.

The group looked at each other, bemused, and Aspen went to get the blanket to cover her up.

ễ ễ ễ

The next two weeks were taken up with hurried preparations for an early return to Bright. It was agreed that Sarave, Juniper, and Khor would stay at the farm with William, Nuisance, Kayti, and Kayli. Khor was powerful enough to keep them all safe from any realistic danger, and between Sumi, Sarave, and William, they could take care of the fields, which they would plant right before the others left. In the worst case, they would all escape through William's tunnels and run to the mine to hide until Aspen and the others returned.

At first, Aspen thought the Traveler's magical party chat would allow him to continue to communicate with those he left behind. Unfortunately, Motte and Rouge quickly disabused him of that notion. Party chat would work only as long as the speakers were within a mile or so of each other. Helped keep it 'realistic', apparently, though since it was already real, he wasn't sure what that meant. That meant he would have to hope that his leaving would keep the others safe.

When Silus finally reported that the snow was melting, Khor went to investigate.

::She's right,:: the goat told Aspen, Motte, and Rouge, who were gathered in the kitchen for lunch. ::The snow is barely up to my knees now. I'm sure it's still deeper higher up, but someone could conceivably make it through the pass.::

Aspen looked at the two Travelers. Motte was deep in thought, but Rouge was cheerfully eating the sweet carrot soup Sarave had prepared. Little Juniper, who was now beginning to speak in short sentences, was showing the elf girl the soup in her spoon as if it was the most fascinating thing in the world.

"Will you be ready to leave in a week?" Aspen asked them. "You said it could be difficult for you to travel as a Zombie. Can you make it work?"

Motte nodded, smiling at the two girls as they giggled. "We'll have to take it in shifts. Rouge will be fairly safe while she's on Codswallop, but I'll be on foot, since I left my mount in Bright. I'll call him, now that the snow is melting, and he'll meet us somewhere along the way. You're sure you want to leave the wagon here?"

It was Aspen's turn to nod. "No reason to slow ourselves down with it. I know you said your Zombie could pull it, but there's no need to risk you being stuck if an attack comes. You and Rouge can carry the goods we have for sale in your inventory, and that will leave us ready to fight or run if necessary."

The tank frowned a little. "I appreciate your trust in us, but are you sure you want to do that? You've only known us a short time. We could betray you as soon as we enter Bright."

Aspen laughed a little, and pointed to the tiny bat snuggled up on Motte's shoulder. "Silus knows a good heart when she meets one, and Sumi can see through liars better than anyone else I've ever met. My own judgment has sometimes been less than spectacular, but I've never known those two to be wrong."

Motte's lips twitched. "What about Khor?"

The farmer chuckled. "Khor thinks everyone is out to get him. Fair enough, since usually he manages to antagonize people nearly as soon as he meets them. It's a self-fulfilling prophecy. I remember one time we were getting armor made for him. The smith had seen him from a distance and was looking forward to the 'challenge of fitting such a magnificent beast.'"

He shook his head. "By the time he'd taken all the measurements, Khor had managed to step on his foot twice, eat some of his hair, and break the handle of his favorite hammer. That armor looked beautiful, but the inside had several places where it didn't quite fit right. Just enough off to be annoying, but not enough to do him an injury. It was the equivalent of a little boy putting itching powder in the clothes of a lad he doesn't like." He smiled ruefully. "That goat is his own worst enemy."

Rouge was listening by this time, though Juniper had managed to crawl into the older girl's lap and convince her to bounce her knee as if the toddler was riding a goat. While Juniper squealed happily, Rouge grinned and spoke. "Poor Khor. I'll make sure to bring him back some cinnamon rolls, too." She rolled her eyes in anticipation. "This is probably the first time anyone has ever actually looked *forward* to returning to North Goose. Oh, man, I have dreams of those buns! Though sometimes I'm afraid I'm going to wake up and find out I ate my pillow."

Aspen laughed. "We have quite an itinerary. Cross the Whispering Mountains before the snow has completely melted. Travel to Bloodhaven to get the link between me and any more of those amulets cut. Pass through North Goose for pastries. Then to Bright to unmask the villain who sent killers after me, and convince them to call it off."

Rouge grinned. "Sounds like an adventure! Even Mr. Thrill-seeker over here," she hitched a thumb at Motte, "can't say this is boring!"

Aspen quirked a smile. "Did I mention that we need to plow, plant, and fertilize our fields before we go?"

"What?" Rouge nearly whimpered. "Why?"

Aspen nodded at the little girl now busily stretching out Rouge's curls and laughing when they sprang back up when they were released. "We have mouths to feed, remember? We can probably forage for much of what we need, but this is a farm. That's what we do."

Rouge sighed. "Vegetables?"

Aspen nodded, and then touched the lump of the Goddess' Seed still tightly webbed to his chest. "Vegetables. But we might have a few surprises for you yet."

༘ ༘ ༘

The first task Aspen had to undertake was making a proper plow. The one they had brought with them was a simple wedge of metal with a harness attached. It was difficult enough to pull that even Khor was tired at the end of a day, and the furrows varied widely in depth. It often became stuck on stones or roots, as well, even when they thought they'd cleared an area completely of any such objects. So, Aspen used the axles of the cart to give him enough metal to attempt to create a new one. He had read about it in one of the books the Head Librarian had originally sent with them, and the book contained detailed diagrams. His first step was to make a small, working model out of wood, after spending a full day clearing the area of the proposed new field as best they could, including much smaller obstructions that Rouge and Motte's Zombies had ignored.

Everyone was tired and cranky by the time they settled in around the fire after dinner, and Silus, the only one who hadn't worked all day, was clearly glad to get away from the grumpy group when she left to eat and fly her rounds. Sumi, too, left to help Silus with scouting, while most of the others opted to sleep. That left just Aspen and Sarave, who was sitting near the fire holding Juniper in her lap, in quiet companionship.

Aspen applied his knife to the small pile of wood beside him, while Sarave rocked the toddler, who was drooping inexorably . When the little girl's eyes finally closed, and her steady breaths indicated that she was asleep, Sarave cleared her throat softly.

"You are a Duke, then, friend Aspen?" she asked quietly, not taking her eyes from the tousled head of brown curls resting on her shoulder.

Aspen sighed, plying his knife so smooth curls of wood fluttered to the ground around his feet. He would have to sweep them up before bed, or he'd hear about it from Sumi in the morning. "Aye, I am. Technically, at least. I grew up in a small village and sought youthful adventure. I found far too much, and in the process got a title added to my name."

Sarave's lips quirked. "What is that name, if I may ask? I never heard of an Aspen associated with the war, and while I was never a warrior, everyone knew the names of all the powerful players in that contest of death."

Aspen tested a tiny wheel against the shaft of wood he held, shook his head, and whittled some more. "Iorgas Penbrooke, Duke of the North, Hero of the Battle of Bright, Master Necromancer, Atae's Left Hand. You know that name? Or parts of it?"

Sarave closed her eyes, a shiver running through her body. "*Hozinte ssa'kinte*. Scourge of the United Peoples. This is you?"

Aspen spun the little wheel on a tiny axle, grunting in satisfaction before saying simply, "Sounds right."

The goblin woman held Juniper so tightly that the child protested in her sleep, causing her mother to loosen her grip just slightly. "You could not tell me?"

He began carving another piece. "What would you have done? Run away? You did that anyway. I'm not that person anymore. Iorgas died the day he killed Akuji, and his daughter died with him. Aspen is the name I claim now."

Sarave laughed roughly. "You do not just get to leave everything behind. Life is not that simple."

"I *know*." Aspen put down his knife and gathered up all the pieces of his little wooden model. "That's why I came here. No one was ever supposed to know that Aspen the farmer was more than a retired old soldier. You would have been happy living in this house with Juniper if you didn't know. You are still welcome here, if you can forget you're living under the same roof as a man who killed thousands of your people." It was his turn to laugh, harsh and rasping and humorless.

Juniper snuffled in her sleep, little face wrinkling and eyes blinking a few times before she settled back into sleep. Sarave stroked the down-soft curls away from her daughter's face. She sighed. "Goblins, trolls, and orcs. Yet I would trade every one of their lives for the one I hold in my arms. One you gave to me. Does that give me the right to judge, I wonder?"

Her thin lips quirked, briefly showing the sharp teeth her ancestors had gifted her with. "No goblin ever treated me better than you have. Most of them far worse. Trolls and orcs were our slave masters, though they would claim we were serfs of our own will." Her yellow eyes, glowing faintly in the firelight, flicked toward him. "Would you do me one favor, oh *Hozinte ssa'kinte?*"

Aspen's topaz eyes met hers, straight and clear. "If I am able."

"If you meet a goblin named Nekthadt, spare him unless he gives you no choice. He is my brother, and he tried to protect me when no one else would. He was punished for that, and all I know is that he was in Bright when I was banished. He only has one eye remaining." She touched a finger to her left eyelid, closing it.

Quest: "Wherefore Art Thou, Brother?" begun.
Sarave has told you about her brother, Nekthadt. If you find him, give him news of his sister.
Success: +50 Reputation with Nekthadt, Maximum Reputation with Sarave, which cannot be reduced unless you betray her.
Failure: Variable, but likely Nekthadt's death. -10 Reputation with Sarave.

Aspen sighed softly and nodded. "If I meet him, I will do what I can."

Sarave smiled, and rocked her child while Aspen learned every part of the plow by heart.

ᴇ̆ ᴇ̆ ᴇ̆

The next day, everyone gathered around as Aspen placed the collection of metal parts into a pile. It included two rusty broken axles, an old shovel, and several horseshoes they'd found as they cleared the land. The tall man glared at the crowd, shoving his hat back from his forehead so the full force of his pale glare could touch them. "Don't you all have better things to do?"

A cheerful chorus of "No!" resounded, and Silus and Rouge, now a nearly inseparable pair, began to giggle. Aspen growled slightly, but a small smile quirked his mouth for a moment before he set his hand to the first axle.

Quest: "Plow, Boy" begun.

You've learned all about how a plow is built, and now it's time to put all those smarts to good use. Gina didn't give you those brains just so you could lose arguments with an arachnid.

Success: Experience. A plow of Good or better quality. The goddess Gina will grant a boon and raise the Item Quality by one grade.

Failure: Create a Common or Poor quality plow, or fail to create anything useful. Your metal is too damaged to try again.

Smiling in satisfaction, he drew in a deep breath. Picturing the powerful angled wedge of the share, he fed all of his strength into the spell he could feel forming under his hands. He imagined the weight, the feel, the shape of it, exactly as it was in his wooden model, but full sized. He knew how it needed to curve, how it needed to fit to the mold board behind. He felt the metal soften beneath his hands, becoming a glob of molten ore, then slowly begin to take the form he required of it.

Unlike in Joanna's memories, it wasn't a rapid process. He had to stop and back off several times when he pushed too much magic in too quickly, or his image wasn't clear enough. He felt sweat drip down into his eyes and closed them, finding that it actually helped him bring his desired form into focus.

He didn't know when the onlookers began to disperse. He did feel when someone draped a cool, damp cloth around his neck, but he didn't know who it was. His whole world centered around the plow forming beneath his palms.

Twice, he let the magic drift, and was rewarded with blisters. Once, he felt himself nearly run out of mana, but thanks to many years of practice, albeit in a far different field of magic, he was able to slow the drain to a trickle that his mana regeneration could handle.

Ever so slowly, the metal began to take shape. He saw it sliding through the soil, imagined it lifting the furrow slice, easily cutting through roots and pushing aside stones. Hard earth turned to soft, fertile soil as it passed. The beast pulling it was easily able to drag it through the ground, held back only by the weight of the plow itself. He opened his eyes and watched the color, seeing the color of golden wheat shimmer along the edge. Then, at last, he let it go.

The plow blade dropped to the ground with a thump. Aspen followed, landing on his behind on the cold ground. The blisters on his palms had healed, but they were still tender, and the cold felt good against them, though the rough surface didn't.

He fell back, splaying out his arms. "Only wheels, chains, frog, and shafts left. No… problem…."

A deep voice answered him, and a large shadow fell across his face as someone moved to stand above him. "You did a good job, I think. I'm a city boy, but this looks like what I've seen in books. I'm glad I'm no mage, though. I'd far rather plow my way through things with my axe. No pun intended."

Aspen opened one eye, unable to see Motte against the backdrop of the sun, but recognizing the voice. "Are you sure? It sounded like you intended it to me."

The big man chuckled, dropping down to sit beside his exhausted friend. "Well, maybe a little. Here." He held out one of the ubiquitous poorly crafted clay cups.

Struggling to sit up, Aspen accepted the drink. Water soothed his dry throat, and he sighed in relief. He hadn't even realized how thirsty he was. He raised the cup in salute. "Thanks."

Motte nodded. "Everyone else got tired of watching you stand there with your hands in a shiny blob. I think the kids are playing catch." He grimaced.

"Ah, I mean all the kids, not just the unicorns. Anyway, Sarave and Sumi are getting things ready for us to leave, and Khor is off doing whatever he does. You looked like you might pass out there, a few times, so I figured someone should keep an eye on you, just in case."

Aspen smiled tiredly. "Was it you with the damp cloth, then?" The other man ducked his head in acknowledgement, and Aspen gave him a crooked grin. "Thank you again, then. I needed it." He turned an assessing eye on the large blade now gleaming in the sun. "I think I should have tried something smaller first. I just didn't want to make everything else, and then find out it was all a waste when I couldn't make this. We could have made do with the old one, I'm sure."

Motte shrugged, taking back the clay cup and rising to his feet in one smooth, powerful movement. "You need to practice, or you'll never get better. And you're right. It would have been a waste to spend all day working on something only to find that the key element was impossible. But now you're stuck. You'd better get to work, because there's not much anyone else can do without that plow."

Aspen rolled to his own feet, a movement less powerful but more graceful than the tank had used. "Whoa." He pressed a hand to his head, grimacing slightly. A familiar pain sliced through his forehead. "I must have nearly run my mana to zero. Losing a week to mana burnout would have been embarrassing."

"Like I said," Motte replied, turning back toward the house, "I'm glad I'm not a mage."

Chuckling, Aspen turned back to the remaining unused portion of metal, now a fused lump shunted aside at some point during the process. "Back to work then." He sighed.

ざ ざ ざ

The rest of the process was simple in comparison. The sun was swinging low again when he finally stood, leaning on his staff, staring at the objects in front of him. It looked more like a puzzle disassembled by a gigantic toddler than a farming implement, but all the parts were done and ready to be put together.

Around him, shivering in the chill night air, stood his friends. Everyone who could had taken turns during the day taking apart his little model and putting it back together again. Now it sat, slightly grubby from handling, and bent where Juniper had used it as a teething toy, on the table in front of Gina's statue.

Aspen looked around. "Everybody ready?"

As one, they nodded. Rouge jumped up, pumping her fist. "Let's get it *done!"* She grinned, and then grabbed a chain, hefting it with only a small grunt in spite of her slight stature. Everyone else grabbed hold of the closest piece and set to work.

The process was not without problems. The wooden parts of the harness had to be carved down a little more in order to fit together. The mold board took both Aspen and Motte to get straight. Juniper decided to run off with the smaller wheel, and she was much faster than she used to be. In fact, Aspen was fairly certain he saw the glimmer of a few stat gains, even in the fading sunlight.

Finally, though, it was done. As the last chain was hooked to the harness, Aspen received a notification.

Quest: "Plow, Boy" complete.
You have created a plow of Good or better quality.
Reward: The Goddess Gina is pleased. Your plow is now an Epic quality item. Gina's Plow – A complex plow of a quality never before seen in Quarternell. The blade will always remain sharp. The soil turned by this plow will be more fertile than before. Cannot be placed in Inventory. Rarity – Epic. Value – Priceless.

Rouge whooped when she checked the item description, and slapped her hand against her father's in some form of celebration. Motte grinned, and picked the elf girl up, swinging her around. Everyone else applauded or shrieked in happiness, and Aspen glimmered like a firework in the near darkness as he got several stat gains that had been delayed until he completed his item.

Only Khor shook his bearded head, scraping a large hoof against the ground irritably. His tone was sour. ::Looks heavy. I'm not looking forward to pulling that. Not that anyone asked.::

Chapter Five

Rouge

Farming was boring. Not that Rouge could say that, because that was, like, Aspen's *thing* now. Though how someone as cool as he had been could just up and decide to go live out in the middle of nowhere (literally!) and become *boring*, she didn't know. He was a Duke! He should have a castle or something!

Admittedly, there were all those attempts to kill him, so that was a thing. Maybe if someone was trying to kill her, she'd have run away, too. Plus, the thing with his daughter. That was *sad*. Even for a game, that was dark stuff. She'd put some serious effort into being extra nice to him for a while after all that came out, but there was only so much a girl could take.

Farming. Was. Boring!

In the last week, they had plowed and planted four gigantic fields. With food storage, if the spring crops grew as quickly and plentifully as Aspen's crops grew in the fall, that would produce enough food to feed everyone in Bright for a year. Aspen had been busy planting seeds with a little tool he made that poked a hole into the ground and then dropped the seed in when he turned a knob. This was where Rouge came in, because it was her job to pat the dirt back down, then use water from her inventory to "moisten" it. Just moisten, not wet.

She hated the word 'moist'.

The first saving grace was that on the second day she figured out how to make her Zombie do this task, even though the set of instructions she had to use was pretty complex. She'd known there was an 'Advanced Settings' tab in the Away User Interface, but she'd never used it before. Now she could program if/then instructions, and that helped a ton.

The second saving grace was the Study Room. Dr. Joe had a huge list of things he wanted to research about how immersion affected people, and not all of them were directly game-related. Normally, when you logged in, the game dropped you into your avatar, wherever it happened to be. When you logged out, you went back to your body in the real world. In fact, you were always at least vaguely conscious of your real body, even in the best pod on the market. Apparently, Dr. Joe wanted to see if he could erase that last lingering awareness of the physical body without having to actually put people into long-term immersion.

In order to study this, and the effect it had on the brain while performing everyday functions, Dr. Joe had created a kind of half-way location. Zoey suspected it was the same 'place' you saw when you first logged in, and where you created your character. Emily, the AL (Automated Learning) program that served as the UI for character creation, was even there. Now, when Zoey logged in from the pod at work, she could choose whether to return to her Zombie, or go to the Study Room. When there was farm work to be done, she usually opted for the Study Room. Because duh.

In the Study Room, she had access to literally everything in the public part of the Library of Congress, as well as the actual internet. She didn't have to log out, get out of the pod, and get her screen to check something. Some people, of course, had implants in their eyes, jawbone, and hands to allow them to interface with the world wide web any time they weren't actually playing *Veritas*, but even if they weren't astronomically expensive, her dad was way against implants.

What was the downside to the Study Room? Well, there were two. First, of course, were the tests. She had assigned reading and activities, and then when she logged out, she was tested on what she did. Sometimes she had to answer essay questions! It sucked.

Second was…

"What are you doing, Rouge?"

Yep. Emily.

Rouge looked up from the 'book' she was reading. This time it was *Beowulf*, which was on her optional summer reading list for school. She scowled at the bland, pretty face in front of her.

"What does it look like I'm doing?" She couldn't help being cranky. Emily was *always* trying to talk to her. No matter what she was doing, the Automated Learning Program Interface (ALPI) was there, asking questions. Usually the same one she'd asked this time. Emily herself, of course, never showed emotion, except in a very programmed way. If you smiled, she smiled back. If you got mad, she'd apologize, look sad, and…

"I'm sorry, Rouge. Did I offend you? Is there anything I can do to help?"

Rouge sighed and leaned forward until her face landed in her book with a smack. She could even feel the dry paper against her skin, the pinch of the center crease against her nose, and smell freshly printed paper and ink. She was pretty sure there would be a drool spot on the page when she raised her face.

Seriously, though. She'd never considered how *annoying* NPCs would find it to be asked that question over, and over, and over, and over…. That is, if NPCs felt anything, which of course they didn't, because they were programs. Still, they acted so real! All except, well, *this one*.

Why the program designers had decided to make Emily so fake was a question to which she still hadn't gotten a satisfactory answer. Something about user feedback in the initial testing, and how people kept becoming overly attached to her. Whatever. Becoming attached to her definitely wasn't an issue anymore.

She rolled her face so that one eye could see up, looking at Emily's expression of false concern. "No, thank you, Emily. I'm just reading."

Emily nodded. "It's just that your heart rate had slowed, and you were close to entering true unconsciousness. I wanted to make sure you weren't feeling unwell."

The elf girl sat up in her simulated chair at her simulated desk. She felt more comfortable as Rouge when she was in the Study Room, even though they had made a 'Zoey' avatar for her. It was just too real, and it got creepy. Being Rouge reminded her it was still the game.

"I was falling asleep. I mean, as close as you can get in game, anyway. Working my way through this is hard, and something about being in here just makes me sleepy. Not enough stimulation, I guess." She scrubbed her palm over her face, closing eyes that felt tired and hot, even though they were really closed back in the pod. Ugh. Thinking about this not being real actually made her feel really weird. Like, floaty. Dr. Joe had looked concerned when she told him that, so now when it happened, she kept it to herself, even though she was pretty sure that was exactly the kind of thing he wanted to know.

Emily smiled brightly. "I see. Would it help if we changed the environment? I can adjust it to anything within my databases, and I do have a wide range of available-"

"No!" Rouge was vehement. The first time Emily had offered this, she'd taken her up on it with great enthusiasm. The ALPI was right, though. She really could create anything, and the range was too wide, and too realistic. There was just something eerie about being able to change every aspect of her surroundings. Almost God-like. Rouge felt increasingly disconnected the more they altered her surroundings, and had to log out in order to feel like she was back in her own skin.

"Thanks, Emily. I like this room the way it is. The book is just hard. I mean, the story is okay, but all the Hrothgars and Heorots are confusing." Rouge closed the slim volume on the desk in front of her.

Emily cocked her head, looking at the book. "Hrothgar is the king, and Heorot is the location. I'm not sure I understand the difficulty."

"They're not words I know, and then you add in all the alliteration. You know, all the words start with the same sound, it seems like, and they..." Rouge trailed off and waved her hand, unsure how to explain her meat brain to a digital brain.

Just then, a quiet alarm went off. Emily said, "Your game avatar has completed its task. Aspen is making his final preparations. You wanted to be notified."

Rouge jumped up, shrieking, "*Yes!* Send me in, Emily!"

Emily nodded, and the Study Room dropped away.

⁓ ⁓ ⁓

Rouge's Zombie was standing near Aspen, not far outside of the fruit tree grove. The tall man was holding something in his hand. His head was bowed, and his eyes were closed. Looking around, Rouge saw that they weren't alone. Everybody was here except Motte and William, and they all stared at Aspen with subdued excitement.

Aspen finally looked up, his expression nervous. "The quest says to plant it after the last frost in the spring. We haven't had a frost in more than a week, sheltered as we are by the mountains, but I still don't know. Should I take it with me and plant it on the way?"

::You probably can't leave it behind, and how would you carry a potted plant, exactly? What if something happened to it? What if it got too large for you to carry?:: Sumi's tone was acerbic, but Rouge thought she sounded nervous, too.

::Will we know right away if it worked?:: Silus' voice was soft and concerned. ::Gina would know if there's going to be another frost, right? So if the quest is going to fail, it should happen as soon as he plants it?::

Khor pawed at the earth. ::Just do it. There's no other choice, so just do what you have to.::

Sarave looked at each one as they spoke, and her expression was conflicted. "I know this quest began before you met me, so I do not know what you would lose if you fail, but it seems too much of a risk. Cannot you ask the Goddess again? Perhaps she'll answer if we give her a better offering?"

Aspen shook his head. "No, If she hasn't answered, she's not going to. She told me Virac is fairly strict, and she couldn't help me too much. I'm guessing this is one of those things I have to decide and fail or succeed on my own."

Rouge raised her hand, feeling left out. "I'm sorry, but what quest? I know you guys all know, but could you fill in the new kid, please?"

Aspen quirked a smile, rubbing the back of his neck as he did when he was worried or thinking. "I got a quest from Gina back in the fall. She gave me a special seed, but I'm supposed to 'plant the seed after the last frost in the spring.' The question is, if I do it now, and there's another frost, will I fail the quest? If we were south of the mountains, I'd wait another two weeks at least. But," he shrugged, "even there, we sometimes get frost after this point, and sometimes we don't."

She tugged at a curl, twisting it around her finger as she chewed her lower lip. "I dunno. The Winter Events are all over, and the last patch note said something about a 'Spring Triathlon Event' coming up in Bright, so you're probably safe. Is it a big quest?"

The others exchanged confused glances before Aspen shrugged again. "Pretty big," he admitted.

"Flip a coin," she suggested.

His eyes widened. "What?"

"Sure. You know what they say: 'The Gods don't need luck. They invented it.' Maybe you just need to give it a chance." She crossed her fingers and mentally sent a message to Gina/Bridget to take a hint.

One eyebrow rose, and Aspen gave a half grin. "I suppose it's as good an idea as any." He scratched his jaw. "Ah, do you have a coin? I don't exactly carry a lot of money out here."

Rouge rolled her eyes so hard she thought they'd get stuck that way, but pulled a single gold out of her inventory and handed it to the farmer. "I want it back." She narrowed her eyes at him.

He just grinned, resting the coin on the back of his thumb. "Heads, I plant it. Tails, I wait, and try to figure something out in a few weeks while we're on the road." His thumb pushed the coin up into the air, where it spun, sparkling gold.

Rouge jumped up, somersaulting in midair, and shot out a hand to catch the coin, slapping it down on the back of her hand as she landed. It shone bright against her caramel skin. "Heads," she said.

Aspen drew in a deep breath, then let it out, closing his eyes. He let the breath out in a long exhalation, and nodded. Without a word, he swung toward a mound of freshly turned earth. He clutched the seed in his hand, and then pushed it down into the sun-warmed earth with his thumb. He held that pose for a moment, and Rouge had to suppress an urge to call him Little Jack Horner. She sensed this was a Serious Moment, though, and bit her lip.

Aspen pulled back his hand, patted the soil over the seed, and stood up. A moment later, he was surrounded by a golden light so intense that she had to shield her eyes. Between her fingers, she could see that everyone else was doing the same. Juniper, who had been playing with the unicorns nearby, began to cry, and Sarave turned to find her daughter, blinking her own light-sensitive eyes as they streamed.

The light lasted one second, then two, and then it ended as abruptly as it had begun. When she finally managed to focus her gaze on Aspen, she blinked in astonishment. He'd been in pretty good shape before, but he was solid muscle now. He looked really healthy for the first time since she'd met him, and she downgraded her estimate of his age by several years, guessing he probably wasn't actually much older than her dad, and might even be the same age.

His eyes were bright beneath the brim of his hat. His jaw was firm, and he had that cool square jawline shadow that all the super-hot guys seemed to have. The creases around his mouth and eyes, which she realized now probably came from pain and illness as much as age, were significantly reduced, though not gone. His nose was still a little too big, though.

"Oh my gosh! You're actually good looking!" She clapped her hand over her mouth, feeling her face burn as she realized she'd said that out loud.

He laughed, his cheeks and ears reddening. "Ah, thanks. I think." He tugged his hat down over his face, a smile still tugging at his lips. "I got the quest completion notification, if you hadn't guessed. I got a new quest, though." His eyes flicked up, and he read out loud.

Quest: "Nice to Meta You" begun.

You have planted the seed of the Meta tree. This tree has never before grown outside of Gina's Garden. Predators will be attracted to the power of the tree as it grows, though other creatures may come to defend it when they sense its sacred nature. Protect the tree until the fruit ripens. This tree will grow with magical speed, and fruit will be ripe in two months. You must eat the first fruit in order to complete the quest.

Success: A Blessing of Gina.

Failure: The tree will die, and Gina will be displeased. -25 Reputation with the Goddess Gina and her faithful.

Khor, who would be remaining behind when most of the others left for Bright, and so would have the unenviable task of defending this tree until they got back, groaned and shook his horns.

::Damn it.:: he said.

Why did the goat always get the last word?

Chapter Six

Aspen

A spen stared down into the freshly built well. William had created the stone-lined hole in a little over a night, and Aspen and Motte had built the surface structures in less than a week. Now, a neat round well sat near the center of the new fields. A small windmill drew water up and dumped it into a simple raised irrigation system on wheels that Khor and Sarave could shift to water the different fields.

He was both very proud and very nervous as he looked at the new structures. Reading about building something in a book could be very different from creating useful devices. He desperately wished that he was staying here to fix the inevitable mishaps, even though he knew Sarave was smart enough and could read well enough now to puzzle out how to solve the common problems described in *Well, Now You Have Water* by Art E. Sian.

Rouge, already astride Codswallop, who was prancing eagerly in place, cleared her throat loudly. "Let's go! I only have four hours before work is over, and Motte and I switch places." She hitched a thumb at her father's Zombie, standing nearby in a massive black suit of armor. The combination of his unnatural stillness and the blank black helmet made him seem astonishingly threatening.

Sumi, hanging from the roof covering the well, rubbed her legs together worriedly. <Are you certain I shouldn't come with you, Aspen? Sending you with just Silus and the two Travelers seems... unwise.>

Aspen shook his head, patiently repeating the same argument they'd had since yesterday. "Now that we know there will definitely be attacks on the farm, you need to stay here. When we hoped it was only Travelers who would follow me, it made sense for you to come, but not now. Khor will need someone to keep watch at night. He can't do everything, and the others are emergency support only."

He set his hand gently on Sumi's cephalothorax, carefully avoiding ruffling the sensitive hairs. She shuddered at the unfamiliar feeling, before leaning toward him slightly. "Take care of them for me, my oldest friend," he said somberly, and heard her mental sigh.

<All right.> The spider switched to party chat. ::Take care of *him*, Rouge and Motte. We did not bring him here only to lose him after all.:: There was no overt threat in her voice, but it was cold as an ancient grave.

Rouge saluted jauntily. "Gotcha. We'll protect him with our lives! Like, literally. We both set the farm as our respawn points, using your shrine to Gina, so if things go wrong, you'll have a chance to kill us again yourself." The Traveler girl sounded far too cheerful to be talking about such a grim subject, but Aspen knew she was just excited to get going, and all the optimism of youth was telling her that things would be fine.

Khor scraped his hoof in the dirt anxiously. The huge goat was standing near Sumi, with a duck on his head, and two young unicorns prancing around him as if he were a drab sort of Maypole. ::Hurry up and go. The sooner you leave, the sooner you'll be back.::

Sarave had a smile pasted on beneath her worried eyes, and nodded from her place nearby. "Indeed, friend Aspen. Sooner begun is sooner done, as Jeremy used to say." Sadness flitted over her face, and she clutched a little tighter at Juniper's hand.

Juniper, who clearly didn't understand what was happening, and only wanted to play with the unicorns, struggled a little against her mother's grip. Her big blue irises, surrounded by the yellow sclera of her mother's people, were locked on her furry friends. "Bye bye, Uncle Aspen! Go 'way!'"

Everyone laughed, and Aspen finally turned to face south. "All right then. I can take a hint." He pulled his hat down over his eyes, hiked his pack higher on his shoulders, and took off at a jog, heading for the mountains.

🍂 🍂 🍂

The first four hours were easy, and they made good time. Everyone kept with Aspen's easy trot, and Rouge was too busy looking around and practicing with her Mambele to maintain much of a conversation beyond such things as, "Oh! The spring flowers are sprouting!"

Motte's Zombie stayed a steady fifteen feet behind Rouge and Codswallop. The pack horse, Burrito (which was apparently a tasty meal made with flatbread, meat, and beans back in the Traveler's home dimension, and which Rouge seemed to find inordinately amusing) was tied to Motte, and kept up with them easily. Silus, of course, was sleeping in her basket on Aspen's pack.

When the sun was high overhead, they stopped at the highest point of a large foothill. Beyond this point, they would enter the actual mountains, and the levels of the beasts there were much higher than those of the foothills and flatlands.

Rouge climbed down off Codswallop, wincing slightly and rubbing her behind as though it pained her, which it likely did.

Aspen turned his gaze away politely and dug in his pack for lunch, careful not to disturb Silus' basket. When Rouge felt that her buttocks had been sufficiently restored, she fed Codswallop and the mule, then flopped down on the ground before promptly jumping up again.

"Yuck! I miss the times when I could sit anywhere and only be a little uncomfortable. That dirt is *cold* and damp! I'm glad I'll be logged out while you guys go through the high passes. I bet there's still a lot of snow up there." She toed the frozen ground experimentally, grimacing.

Aspen smiled at her from his seat on a fallen tree, munching his lunch as if he hadn't a care in the world. "When will your father return?"

She wrinkled her nose. "Call him Motte. We don't use 'dad' and 'daughter' in public. Some people get weird when they find out. Most people think he's my overprotective big brother." She grinned. "A few girls not much older than me have even asked him out. It's gross, but hilarious to watch him try to turn them down nicely."

Aspen swallowed his bite. "Has anyone asked that he did accept?"

Rouge cackled. "No! He never dates! He definitely wouldn't start with a little gamer girl young enough to be one of his students. Heck, he's actually met a few of his students in," she flicked her eyes at him, "um, Bright. He didn't tell them who he was, of course. It's part of why he wears a full helm most of the time. I mean, he hasn't lately, but that's because you're his friend."

"I see." Aspen kept his voice neutral, wondering why he felt a little relieved.

"Anyway, he'll be on in about an hour. His class and office hours are over, but he has to get home before he can log in. I have to go now, and his Zombie is linked to me. It'll just be you, Wally, and Silus for a while. Are you sure you'll be all right?" She looked a little worried, and tossed her Mambele from hand to hand as she did when she was nervous.

He nodded. "The higher-level beasts are in the actual mountains. I'm sure we'll meet some as we pass through, but between Motte and I, I believe it will be fine. I made it through last fall with just Khor, Sumi, and Silus."

Aspen neglected to mention the several pieces of long-burning Incense the Head Librarian had given them before they left. It lasted for a day, and drove away monsters of a higher level than your own except for field bosses. It also stank of unclean socks and rotten fish, but nothing was perfect. The worst part had been listening to Khor gripe for almost two weeks about how he'd never get the smell out of his fur.

He looked hard at Rouge, who was chewing her lip and flipping her blade faster and faster as she glanced at something visible only to her. A timer, he suspected. "Are *you* all right?"

She sighed and seemed to deflate slightly. "I have to take the bus all the way home today. Usually, I go to the college and ride home with Motte, but he'll be going home without me today so he can protect you in the mountains. It'll be fine, but I'm a little nervous. I have to make a couple of connections, and I won't get home until after six."

Aspen frowned, trying to make sense of this. "A 'bus' is a public conveyance of some sort?"

Rouge nodded. "Yeah, um, kind of like a really big carriage that picks up anyone who can pay and transports them along a pre-set route. So, you have to go by all the places other people need to go that are in between where you get on and where you need to go."

The tall man scowled, feeling concern rise up in him. No matter how competent and dangerous Rouge was in this world, as he understood it, she was more like a lady of means in her other world. "This does not sound safe. When you leave, you should contact your father," he corrected himself, "*Motte,* and tell him to wait for you at his school. I can remain here until you're both safe at home."

The elf girl shook her head. "No, really, it's okay. Thousands of people do it every day! I'll be fine. Plus, I don't need *two* of you going all protective on me. Seriously, one dad is *plenty.* You just stay here, and Motte will be here in an hour or so." She pointed an accusing finger at him. "Don't move!" Then her eyes went blank, and her arms fell to her sides. Her body, usually constantly moving in some way, stilled.

He shuddered. He would never get used to that. More importantly, though, he was worried for her. He hated how helpless he felt to protect her in that other world. He had come to consider her a friend, if not something more like a daughter. Perhaps if he and Calliope had stayed together and had another daughter, she would have been like the cheerful Traveler girl.

No. He sighed. Truthfully, any child of his would likely have been far too serious, as Birdie had been. The life he had provided wasn't one in which a cheerful and outgoing child would have flourished. He clenched his jaw against the pain that thinking of his lost daughter brought, and pressed his fist over his heart, curling in around the pain, though whether he meant to beat against it or protect it, he couldn't say.

As the pang of loss faded, he stood, brushing his frozen rear with his hands until feeling began to return to it. He'd been a little afraid his pride would cause him to lose his buttocks to frostbite if Rouge hadn't left soon.

Glancing around, Aspen took in the still forms of the two Travelers, a disgruntled Codswallop, who was nuzzling Rouge's Zombie and ignoring Aspen entirely, and the patient mule chomping brown wisps of grass nearby. He scratched his jaw, knowing that if he didn't do something until Motte returned, he would simply dive into a festering pool of self-loathing that could take days to escape.

His eyes caught on his pack, and the long metal bar protruding from it. At the last moment, he had grabbed the bar from the leftover scrap from the plow to use for Mage Smith practice. Ah ha! Now there was a plan!

ĕ ĕ ĕ

By the time Motte blinked his eyes, Aspen was deep in a creative stupor. Under his hands was a rotating curved blade, around two feet long, with a viciously sharp edge. That edge was glowing a soft gold, and heat waves rose from it, oddly disconcerting in the cool air.

Aspen gasped and opened his hands, letting the blade drop, released from his magic. It fell to the ground, chiming like a bell as it hit a rock. He took off his hat, wiped his forehead with his sleeve, and slapped his hat back on. He looked up and grinned at Motte.

"Good timing, my friend! I was just seeing if I could create a farming implement with a bit of, ah, flexibility in its purpose." He smiled wryly. "I failed the first three times, since I kept picturing it as a weapon. Once I started thinking of it as a tool for mowing grass, things went much more smoothly."

Motte's usual solid black helmet vanished into his inventory, exchanged for one that revealed his mature, intelligent face, and he smiled. "No making weapons, eh? I'd wondered why you hadn't made something for Sarave and William to use to defend themselves."

The farmer sighed. "Gina was clear about that. Farming implements only. If I had had more time, I would have left them something besides some axes and a pickax, but I'll be back before harvest, so this," he held up the blade carefully, "didn't occur to me."

Motte cocked his head. "Scythe blade?"

Aspen nodded. "I'll attach it to my staff. I've never had much use for weapons other than magic and the staff, but I know the basics. I was once an enlisted soldier, though I rose up through the ranks rather quickly once they discovered my *speciality*. Necromancy was illegal, you know, but they changed the law when it became clear how useful I could be against Lich Lord Akuji's minions."

Motte puffed out a breath, shaking his head, and busied himself with transferring Burrito's lead from himself to Codswallop. "The more I hear about the human government, the less I wonder how things got so bad. Duke Geral is power hungry, and King Chester is incompetent." He picked up Rouge's Zombie and placed her on Codswallop's back. "I'm amazed humanity wasn't wiped out."

Aspen carefully wrapped his new blade in leather and slid it into his pack, then picked up the pack and slung it over his shoulders. "I am as well. The Duke and the King both tried to get you Travelers involved in the battle, but when you all discovered that Akuji could strip away your skills and levels, you refused to fight any but the lowest of his creatures. If there was any chance of Akuji or one of his Lesser Lichs being nearby, none of you would take a quest for any price."

Despite his best attempt to keep his tone neutral, a trace of bitterness seeped in, and he could see the other man grimace. They began to jog, with Aspen setting a pace he could maintain all day, and Motte matching it easily.

Motte finally broke the silence, his deep voice somber. "I'm sorry, Aspen. It seems cold now, but at the time we Travelers were new to your world. We were having fun discovering new places and learning new things. Few of us were of a high enough level to be of much assistance, and those that were would never dream of risking the results of their hard work on a quest. Honestly, it didn't matter that much to us that Quarternell might fall, except that it was more accepting of humans than the Dark Races were likely to be. Those of us who joined the Dark Races thought it was great fun, and many who chose to be human wished they hadn't."

Aspen's tone was tightly controlled when he responded. "And you? Where were you at that time?"

They jogged a while longer before Motte worked out how to answer. "I was having fun too. I did take several of those quests battling low-level mobs. I even got the Goblin Slayer Achievement. I was only level twenty-three, though, during the Battle of Bright. It was just entertainment. Something to do after Zoey, *Rouge*, went to bed. I started playing a lot more after she told me that all she wanted for her birthday was to be allowed to be a Traveler too. I wanted to be strong enough to make sure she was safe here."

He tilted his head back toward Codswallop, keeping pace a precise fifteen feet behind them as they wound their way through increasingly narrow and rocky paths. "If it helps, Rouge watched the battle on, um... with a magical device that lets us see this world through someone else's eyes. She was really upset that I wasn't helping. She saw all the villages destroyed by Akuji's army as it passed, and she wanted to go help. She knew about how the lichs could steal points and levels, and she didn't care. I finally had to block the streams so she couldn't watch anymore. I only let her join because that was all over."

Aspen felt his heart clench at the thought of being able to send his daughter away, protect her from the horrors of that time. He stared down at his feet, easily traversing the treacherous path they traveled. Left. Right. Breathe. Left. Right. Breathe.

Finally, he nodded. "Though I wish you had made a different choice, I do understand that this country, not even this *world* is your own. Though you try to hide it, I can tell that you struggle at times to even see those of us who are native to this place as real people. Our lives don't, after all, truly affect yours in any way. You can simply decide one day that you no longer wish to come here, and you are done."

Aspen glanced back at the elf girl riding the massive ostrich behind them. His voice barely carried over the sound of their feet and their measured breathing when he continued. "Certainly I am not one to judge you for putting your child first."

Motte smiled slightly and started to nod. Then his eyes flicked past Aspen's shoulder and widened. He jerked to a stop, grabbing the slimmer man and thrusting him behind his massive armored body. The full helmet reappeared on his head, and an enormous axe in his hand.

"Stay back," he ordered softly. "Wyvern."

The Wyvern was the level one hundred field boss for the entire Whispering Mountains range. Its thirty foot long body blocked out the sun as it swooped overhead, silent except for the slow beat of its wings. As the two men watched, it banked as it caught a warm updraft, and then lazily began to swoop down again.

Two men, an ostrich, and a mule held their breaths as the mighty beast stretched out its neck and shrieked a challenge to the sky. Absolute silence was the only answer, and, satisfied, it continued on its way, though it was visible for a long time due to its huge size.

Finally, Motte relaxed. "Damn, that was scary. That thing killed me once when I was only level thirty-four, and believe me, you don't forget a thing like that. I turned that quest back in to the guild, even though I lost credit for giving up, and I was never sorry."

Aspen nodded, tugging at Burrito's reins as he started jogging forward again. "Akuji had two Zombie Wyverns that he used to pull his chariot. He had plenty of magic to fly himself, but he always was a pretentious bastard."

Matching Aspen's pace, with Codswallop keeping a steady pace behind him, Motte grimaced and nodded. "I saw that huge sword he used once. What did he call it?"

Aspen rolled his eyes. "Chaotic Death Eater. At least, that's what our translators claimed it was. In ancient Diomade it was *Bhujaki'h,* or something like that. I should ask Sarave. I'm sure we oversimplified it." His smile was grim. "I killed him with it."

Motte's steps paused for a moment before he sped back up. He was shaking his head. "Every time I think I'm used to the idea that I'm hanging out with the guy who ended the war, you say something like that, and it hits me all over again. I'm sorry. I shouldn't have mentioned it."

It was Aspen's turn to shake his head. "It's... actually okay. For whatever reason, it doesn't hurt as much lately. I think it's been good for me, letting it out. Lark would say 'like lancing a boil.'" He smiled, genuine amusement lightening his expression, "From the time she was a little girl, she could make anything about healing or medicine. She first dosed me with some foul concoction that was supposed to help me sleep when she was only seven. It did make me sleep... for a week."

Motte's deep chuckle was filled with warm, fatherly understanding. "I understand. Rouge started trying to help me prepare dinner when she was around that age. She wanted to do it all by herself, so I gave her a box of mac and cheese – ah, pasta with a cheese sauce, but all you have to do is cook the pasta and add the ready-made sauce – and told her to go for it. I worked at the kitchen table so I could keep an eye on her, but she was really careful. Unfortunately, she didn't read the instructions well enough, so she didn't drain the water off the pasta. We had overcooked cheesy pasta soup, and it was… not good."

The two men laughed, and Aspen glanced back toward the elf girl sitting on her devoted bird. The world these Travelers came from was strange, indeed, but family was family, no matter where they came from. Rouge and Motte were fortunate to have each other.

He was still smiling as Motte gave a strangled cry, and his metal shod feet swung across Aspen's field of vision. Aspen whirled around, hand going to his staff, strapped across his pack. The Wyvern was back, and it had swooped down to pick up a tasty snack in a surprisingly hard and heavy shell.

Motte was lifted through the air for several yards, and then the scaly monster let out a frustrated growl and dropped him into a lingering snowbank in the shadow of a cliff. The snow crunched, and Motte vanished.

The Wyvern, deprived of its first choice of prey, turned back toward Aspen. Its vicious red eyes flicked over the group before settling on Rouge, sitting up high enough to be easily snatched and carried away. Aspen turned and ran back toward the girl, waving his arms.

"Codswallop! Flee! Find some trees or someplace to shelter! Go!"

The ostrich, his eyes rolling frantically, bobbed in place for a heartbeat. Then he ducked his head and dashed forward, taking Rouge's Zombie away down the path just as the Wyvern's great claws closed on the place she'd been a moment before.

Again, the creature screamed in anger, and its eyes focused on Aspen this time. He swallowed, and gripped his staff painfully, until he reminded himself that a strong grip was a flexible one, and relaxed his fingers slightly. He settled into a fighting stance, and waited.

The Wyvern stretched out its wings and neck, settling close to the ground.

A cloud of dust rose from the road that made it difficult to see. He was barely able to dodge as a lightning-fast jaw snapped at his head. Almost instinctively, he thrust the staff under its jaw and up, forcing the mouth closed. He could feel and hear the snap as the monster's teeth crashed against each other. A waft of breath rolled over him, reeking of rotting meat.

The dust swirled, and the beast grunted, followed by a furious roar of pain. Aspen heard Motte's shout of triumph. "Two hundred ten HP! Take that, you bastard! Teach you to eat people when they're weak! Guess what? Weak Travelers get stronger even if you eat them a few times!"

The reptile thundered to the ground, and as its wings stopped, the dust settled down. There, at the base of one wing, lodged in the joint, was a huge war axe, still quivering. Thick, crimson blood ran from the wound, and the Wyvern pulled the injured appendage close to its body.

Motte appeared; his black armor covered in filthy slush. He was holding a huge shield in front of him as he ran, putting the full force of his strength behind the solid mass of his armor and body. "[Battering Ram]!" he bellowed.

With racing steps, he barreled past Aspen, and ran hard into the Wyvern, focusing the main force of his strike on the axe already embedded in the creature's wing. With a sickening pop, the axe cleaved through the joint, leaving the wing dangling by a strip of skin. Motte shouted in triumph again, then in pain as the monster's jaws snapped shut on his helmet, left exposed by his nearness and the aftereffects of his attack.

The big man's eye glared out from between the six-inch teeth, his helmet cracked and straining. His gauntlets slipped futilely as they tried to force the mouth to open again. The muscles the beast used to bite down were much stronger than those that held the mouth open, though, and his efforts were in vain.

::Go, damn it!:: Motte's voice echoed in Aspen's head. ::This thing will pop my head off in a minute, and you have no chance. Find Rouge, and I'll rejoin you when I respawn back at the house.::

Aspen's hands trembled on his staff, his mind filled with visions of battlefields strewn with death, picked over by the macabre creatures who always followed wherever blood was spilled. He'd slain far too many of those who had lain dead and dying on the field of battle, and nearly as many were his former allies. Once all the fighting was over, he'd run away as soon as he could, swearing he'd live a quiet life and die a quiet death.

But this was too much. He was no longer a rook in someone else's game of war, and Motte wasn't just another soldier, facing inevitable death while Aspen waited for the moment he breathed his last so that his body could be turned into a different kind of weapon. This was his friend, and Aspen was through watching his friends die.

He dropped his pack from his back, careful even in his haste to avoid damaging the woven cage in which Silus slept. *How* she still slept, he had no idea, but he would make certain she was safe. He pulled the scythe blade from its makeshift sheath, and, with steady and rapid fingers heated the heel and tang of the blade and brought it together with the metal cap on the end of his staff.

A crunching of metal made him look up, to see that Motte's helmet was beginning to buckle beneath the fierce pressure of those vicious jaws. The other man still struggled to free himself, but he was clearly growing weaker even as he bashed his gauntleted fists against the teeth and jaws of the Wyvern.

Aspen stood, braced himself, and swung for the huge creature that towered over him.

The scythe screeched as it stuttered and skipped over the dense scales of the animal, and it snorted at his pathetic effort, shaking its head. If Motte hadn't been clinging to the beast's head now, his neck would likely have snapped from the movement.

::GO!!:: Motte roared in Aspen's head. ::I'll be back in a day! Don't die here, you idiot!::

Aspen felt this description was unfair, though probably accurate, but he drew in a deep breath and pulled the scythe back for another swing anyway. This time, he focused on the tattered strip of skin where the wing dangled, and the raw muscle showing through the blood. The tip of the scythe caught in the ragged edge of the skin and pulled at it hard enough that it tore a little more.

The Wyvern opened its mouth to roar a protest, then seemed to remember it was in the middle of something and closed its jaws again. This time, the helmet crunched beneath its bite, and Motte's body fell limply to the ground.

Aspen howled with rage, wrenching the scythe from the Wyvern's shoulder. He remembered what Gina had told him. *I've been stretching it a little to let you do the magical smithing, since it has to do with farming implements, but don't let it wander too far, or I can't be sure how well it will work.* He was holding a farm implement, not a weapon. He needed to…

"*[Mow]!*" He shouted, throwing all the strength of his Goddess-enhanced body into cutting at one particularly dense piece of grass that just happened to be on the other side of the monster standing before him.

The Wyvern gurgled, and its head slowly toppled from its neck, neatly severed just under the jaw at the thinnest point of the serpentine neck. Aspen fell back in the dirt, landing on his rear next to his pack. A golden glow shrouded him as he leveled, the coruscating brilliance almost blinding him.

"Holy crap." A deep bass voice came from the dirt beside him, and he turned, squinting through his blurred vision. Motte lay there, head still attached to his body, though rather the worse for wear, if the blood streaking his dark skin was any indication. Which it usually was.

Aspen choked out a pitiful excuse for a laugh. "I thought… you were dead."

Motte rolled his head so he was facing the sky, wincing as he did so. "Damn close. I have about two hundred HP left. I managed to pull my head out of my helmet when that boss yelped after you poked it with your overgrown knife. Just in time, because I don't think I'm going to be able to recover that helmet. It was my favorite one, too. Part of the set."

Aspen leaned over shakily, resting his hands on Motte's chest. "[Heal]," he murmured, and his hands lit up again. Motte groaned in relief.

"Ahhh, that feels better. I love having a healer in the party." After taking in the full effect of the spell, the big man levered himself to a sitting position. The two men sat, staring at the huge corpse, steaming slightly in the chill air.

Finally, Aspen reached over and tapped at Silus' basket. "Wake up, sleepy head. You missed all the excitement." There was no response, and he frowned. "Silus? Silus!" He tugged the container from its straps and looked inside. It was empty. A hundred scenarios flew through his head, each worse than the last. Then his eyes narrowed, and he looked over at Motte, who was watching with a concerned expression.

"Your daughter stole my bat!"

Chapter Seven

Rouge

Zoey popped out of the pod so quickly that it barely had time to start draining before she was under the shower, rinsing off. She snagged the towel a bemused Sara offered her, and dashed out to change, not even bothering to pull socks onto her wet feet before she stuffed her toes into her shoes. She was heading straight home, so who cared, right?

In the month plus since Zoey started her job, she'd fallen into a routine that matched her first day pretty well. The main exception was that Georgia McKeene was never again on her bus, for which she was profoundly thankful. She'd asked Nina, who seemed to know everything about everybody, if she knew why Ms. McKeene was riding in the first place, and found out that the older woman's car had been in the shop for nearly a week. No further info, but Zoey assumed it needed deep cleaning to get rid of all the poisonous slime.

Zoey's time in Design was always interesting. The errands (which she tended to think of as 'Reputation Quests' and 'Fetch Quests', with an occasional 'Escort Quest' thrown in for variety) ranged from prosaic to deeply bizarre. The pickle sandwich, it turned out, was *not* a prank, but the near-daily order of an older woman named Dot, who insisted on being called Granny by absolutely everybody.

The time Zoey spent in Research and Development with Dr. Joe and Sara, though, was amazing. They had developed a pod that allowed for long-term immersion. Like, not even needing to eat or drink or pee or *anything*. Well, the body continued to perform its basic functions, but some tubes took care of that. (Though, ew. She was glad she hadn't signed up for that.) The user just laid down in body temperature blue goop, and forced themselves to breathe it in. It served as food, water, and air, so off you went!

She didn't know what it was (proprietary information) or how it worked (proprietary information), and she got a full-face mask instead of having to do the drowning thing anyway, since she wasn't actually going to stay in more than a few hours (because her dad wouldn't give his permission, not that she *really* minded) but it was a-maz-ing!

After monitoring her as she did various activities in real life, Dr. Joe and Sara had her enter *Veritas* and repeat the same activities. When she logged out, she answered a bunch of questions about her 'experience'. That part was like the most boring test ever, and it happened *every day*. Today, for example, there were questions about how realistic she felt the cold weather was. The answer, of course, was *way too realistic*. Still, she hurried through the questionnaire at record speed and thrust the tablet at Sara, who received it with a bemused expression.

As she raced down the stairs toward the bus stop (the elevator was too slow), she wished she had a pod like the lab one back home. When she was submerged in the goop, everything she felt in the game really was almost like real life (at least as far as she knew - she'd never actually ridden an ostrich before). Something about the goo let it give her a much more realistic experience than just the haptic feedback of the gel bed in her pod at home. They told her that if she ever got to do the whole shebang with breathing in the stuff, she'd even smell and taste things 95% like real life, instead of the 60-70% most people got with the bed and the headset. Sometimes, she thought it would be worth it just to get the full experience of eating that last cinnamon roll. Mmm….

It was thinking about the taste of that cinnamon roll that made her realize that she'd been so distracted by her hurry to get home and meet up with her dad and Aspen that she'd left her lunchbox back in the lab. Not for the first time. In fact, she'd managed to leave it at least once a week since she started work, and usually she just left it there until the next day.

Today, however, was Friday, and her dad had wrapped up a big slab of lasagna for her, along with a piece of cake. She hadn't been able to eat it all, and there was no way she was leaving cake and lasagna behind. She screeched to a halt just before she exited security, and headed back to the lab.

The door was ajar, and the lab was silent when she entered. Dr. Joe and Sara were probably back in the pod room, cleaning up after the day's work. However, as she bent over to take her lunch out of the refrigerator, she heard the murmur of raised voices coming from Dr. Joe's office. She glanced around, feeling her still-damp skin shiver, and suddenly felt naked without Rouge's [Stealth] skill.

Silently, she crept toward the door, continually looking around as if she could somehow prevent anyone walking in from seeing her. As she drew nearer, the voices became clearer, and she recognized them. It was Joe and Bridget.

Bridget sounded frustrated and angry. "What do you mean there's no one else? You know she didn't… *doesn't* like Veralt. She specifically requested he not be her team lead!"

Joe's voice was soothing. "I *know*, Bridge, but there's nothing we can do. Veralt is senior on the medical team, and he was furious when he was passed over for the job. With Dr. Perez in the hospital, and then in physical therapy for possibly months, we can't-"

"You can *too*! I know you lost a lot of influence when Amy-"

A loud thump stopped the words, and Zoey's eyes widened as she realized it was Dr. Joe's fist hitting the desk. She hadn't thought he had it in him!

Bridget sighed, and her voice dropped, too quiet to hear for a few moments.

When it rose again, she was saying, "...get someone else in. Anyone. I just don't trust Veralt."

Dr. Joe's voice was heavy when he said, "I'm truly sorry, Bridget. I can't even get in to talk to Carl without an appointment anymore. He still blames me for what happened to Amy. Hell, *I* blame me. If this quest doesn't go our way..."

Unfortunately, before she could hear anything else, the door to the pod lab opened, and Zoey could see Sara's back emerging, straining as the woman pulled a cart like the one Zoey used to deliver food from the cafeteria after her.

Zoey stood up straight, abruptly realizing that she was crouched down like she would if she was trying to be sneaky in the game. Which didn't look suspicious at all, of course. She took two huge steps back toward the hall door, hefted her lunchbox, and tried to look innocent.

Sara finished backing out of the room, and turned to enter the code. The pretty Indian woman froze, and her eyebrows shot up as she caught sight of Zoey.

Zoey smiled brightly, making sure to speak clearly, and not at all in a guilty whisper. "Hey, Sara! I forgot my lunchbox! Didn't want to leave it here till Monday, so I just ran back in to grab it. Sorry I startled you, but I have to go or I'll miss my bus!"

Then, hoping she'd left the impression that she'd hurried in as fast as she was now hastening out, she opened the door and took off down the hallway. She had a bus to catch!

ᖗ ᖗ ᖗ

Rouge blinked open her eyes, expecting to see Aspen and Motte walking ahead of her. She had hurried home as quickly as she possibly could, and she'd peeked in to see that her dad was still safely ensconced in his pod, so she logged in as quickly as possible. After peeing. Because needing to pee *all the way home on the bus* was quite possibly one of the most painful things she'd ever experienced.

Anyway, here *she* was, but where were they? She was sitting on Codswallop under a tree. He was rather mournfully pecking at the grass, looking for anything good to eat. When she shifted in her seat, his head popped up, and swiveled so that he could look at her with one of his huge brown eyes. He chirruped inquiringly, and then rammed his head against her with all the force of a fuzzy bowling ball.

She hugged him, rubbing around his ear holes until he crooned happily, relaxing. "There ya go, Wally. It's okay. What's going on?"

She pulled up the party list:

Name	Level	Hp	Mana
Motte Bailey	96	*Maximum distance exceeded*	
Rouge the Rogue	27	117/117	100/100
Aspen (NPC)	34	*Maximum distance exceeded*	
Khor (NPC)	53	*Maximum distance exceeded*	
Sumi (NPC)	41	*Maximum distance exceeded*	
Silus (NPC)	19	70/70	10/10

As with party chat, the party list wouldn't work when the members were over about a mile away. The conditions (whether they were in battle, if there was bad weather, etc.) made a difference, but if she couldn't see their info, it was good bet that they were at least a mile off.

"Darn it! How did that happen?" She did a one-handed flip off Codswallop's back, landing solidly even as she pulled up her Away Log.

"Nothing, nothing, nothing…" she muttered, flipping notifications away with deft flicks. Then, "What? Party entered combat with a Wyvern? Holy mini-dragons, Batman!" Her Away Instructions contained a clause for emergencies:

IF party enters combat THEN mount (Codswallop) can be instructed to Flee by Motte Bailey OR Aspen (NPC)

In retrospect, adding a clause to limit the distance her big chicken would run might have been a good idea. Codswallop could run very quickly when he was properly motivated, and she was guessing that a giant, flying, two-legged Gila monster had probably been pretty inspiring. Note to self.

So, Aspen gave the flee command, and the ostrich took off. According to the log, he ran for exactly thirty minutes of game time, and had stopped in this lovely frozen stand of sticks about twenty minutes ago. So, not quite an hour ago, Motte and Aspen had fought the field boss of the Whispering Mountains.

And won.

At least, if the fact that her dad was still in-game meant anything. If he had died, he would have been force-logged out for at least two hours real time, and he would have been mucking around in the kitchen grousing about not knowing what happened. Ipso facto, he survived, and so did Aspen, because if Aspen died, Motte would have logged out so he could tell her in person.

She breathed out a deep whoosh of breath. "Okay, Wally. No problem. We crossed these mountains all by ourselves just a few months ago. Now, all we have to do is head back until we get close enough to Motte and Aspen for the party chat to connect. Right? Right. Now, buddy," she looked around, "which way did you come from?"

The bird stared at her and blinked his eyes.

"Nothing?"

More blinking, and then he tilted his head inquisitively and began pecking at the pouch at her waist, looking for food.

A tiny voice entered her mind. ::Are we there yet?::

Rouge nearly jumped out of her skin, and activated [Sneak] almost instinctively. It failed, of course, since she was in broad daylight, but it was a good try by her subconscious to keep her from being murdered. A tiny head poked up out of the pouch Codswallop had been pecking, blinking sleepy gold eyes.

"Silus?" Rouge broke her own [Stealth] by nearly shrieking the name. "What are you doing? How did you even get in there? That pouch isn't-" She pulled open the flap of the pouch, which was one of several non-soulbound bags she used for inventory management. It could be dropped or stolen, so she didn't keep anything important in there, but it certainly wasn't a *real...*

She stared down into the perfectly normal leather pouch, partially filled with a tiny, adorable bat. Silus' big ears were swiveling almost independently of her head, and it was so cute that Rouge squeed, scooping the fluffball into her hand. Immediately, the pouch appeared to fill with an impenetrable darkness, which was its default appearance.

::I'm mad at Aspen. I don't think he should have sent us away when he talked to that Traveler lady. We deserve to make our own decisions. We're not babies!:: Silus' squeaky little voice was such a counterpoint to her words that it was all Rouge could do to keep a straight face. She was in complete agreement, though, so she choked down her mirth and nodded instead.

"Right! I'm super glad you're here, too, because I have no idea where we are. Motte and Aspen were attacked – they're okay! – but Wally ran off with us, and he doesn't know how to get back. I don't even know if we're on the same road anymore. I'd log out and check in with my dad, but my last Tent is on Burrito, and..." Her words started tumbling over themselves, and she stuttered to a stop.

Silus, who had at first gone still and big-eyed (even more than usual), flapped her wings a little. ::I can do it! Maybe we can track Codswallop back, like we did with those mean Travelers, and I'll fly ahead looking for Aspen! And Motte,:: she added belatedly, but Rouge understood.

Rouge nodded, starting to pull herself together after her moment of panic and the mini-meltdown she'd had when she realized she wasn't alone after all. Well, there was Codswallop, but, awesome as he was, brain power wasn't his greatest strength. "Okay. Yeah. My [Tracking] is only level 5, but it's not like there are a lot of other giant two-toed birds out here, right?"

It didn't take long for them to realize that tracking over frozen ground wasn't nearly as easy as tracking in snow. Everything was hard, so there were no muddy, snowy prints, and the grass was brown and scrubby, so they couldn't find convenient stray feathers or bent stalks. Rouge finally stopped and checked the party list again. No change, so they weren't within a mile yet.

"Should we just stay here?" Rouge asked, looking up at the sun and trying to judge where they might be. She knew the sun rose in the east and set in the west, just like in real life, and since it was after mid-day, *that* way had to be west, so…. Yeah, that told her nothing.

There were a ton of smaller trails and larger roads that meandered through the mountains. They all eventually dead-ended or joined back into the main road, but she sure didn't want to spend hours on one, only to end up at an unscalable cliff.

Silus looked around. ::You stay here,:: she said. ::I'll fly north along the road unless it splits. Then I'll try going as high as I can and hope I can see something. I'll come back here before dark, with or without them. I'm sure they know which way we went, so they're coming for us. Right?:: Her piping little voice wavered on the last word, and Rouge snuggled the small creature reassuringly.

"They are. I know they are. Motte can't stand it when he doesn't know where I am. Worst case, I'll find a hole to hide my Zombie in and log out so I can go ask him in our world. I'm more worried about you."

She looked down into Silus' big golden eyes. "Shouldn't you wait here with me? This is no place to be little. I saw a lot of hawks and other big birds on the way out to find Aspen. I don't think you should be flying off alone during the day."

Silus rubbed her head against Rouge's thumb. ::I'll be all right. That's my job! Besides, I'm really fast, and I can hide almost anywhere."

Rouge frowned in concern. "Just come back if you see anything scary, okay?

Don't take any chances you don't have to. Keep trying the party chat, too. I know you can't see the party list, but if you get close enough, they'll hear you."

::Ohhh, yeah! I didn't think of that! I'll be really careful, and try to talk to them all the time.:: She climbed up onto Rouge's thumb and spread her wings, then glided off, quickly rising above the trees as her tiny wings lifted her easily. A steady stream of consciousness entered Rouge's head. ::Look at those trees! No bugs in those trees. I don't like winter because there aren't any bugs or fruit, and even the water freezes. Who decided that water should freeze anyway? Was it one of the Gods? I should bite them. Frozen water is stupid. You can't drink it, and it isn't strong enough to…::

The little voice faded quickly, and in just over a minute, Rouge was left alone again with only herself and a starving ostrich.

🍎 🍎 🍎

Rouge set out a heavy fur that she pulled from her *Body Bag* (skin was definitely a body part!) and sat down on it. She pulled several carrots, some cabbage, and a stack of broccoli out of her pouch. As Codswallop ate the cabbage, she munched her way through carrots and broccoli. She'd never really liked broccoli, but Aspen's broccoli wasn't woody and bitter, and she could eat it all day.

She was just starting to think that she might lie back on the soft, warm fur when she heard a sound. It wasn't much. Just a slight crunch. It could have been a rock knocked loose by some scurrying animal, or a twig breaking under Codswallop's feet. But it wasn't, and she knew it. She froze, and clamped her hand over the ostrich's beak as he pecked at the leafy greens piled up beside her. He rolled an eye at her indignantly, but didn't pull away.

A voice drifted through the chill air, coming from where the road wound off to the south. "…on, R3dLit3! You don't even have the quest anymore. Just forget it and let's go back to Bloodhaven. This is lame, man!"

The voice of an angry young man responded. "Forget you, Hulk. You can go back if you want to, but I'm gonna kill that NPC. Fire won't even play anymore. She says she's gonna sell her stuff and delete her account. I sent a message to the devs about this messed-up mob, but they said he didn't do anything Players don't do to NPCs. It's BS!"

Rouge silently pulled the food and fur into her inventory, then flattened herself back into the shadows under the trees, triggering [Sneak] and pulling her Mambele out of her inventory.

Codswallop, whose intelligence she clearly underestimated, quietly sank to his knees and stretched out his neck flat to the ground. With his dark plumage, he looked more like a shadowed bush than a bird. His white tail was even tucked under so it wouldn't give him away.

She made a mental note that he had definitely earned a treat.

With the silent glide of a stalking cat, Rouge crept from the shadow of one slender tree to another, never quite leaving the darkness enough to break her [Stealth]. When she could finally see the oncoming Players, she froze.

In front was the Player who had died before anyone could even really get a look at him. He was short and skinny, with a faintly Asian cast to his features. He was some kind of archer class, with a bow and quiver over his shoulder. She squinted, and the tag above his head leapt into sharp relief. It read 'R3dLit3: Level 52', and it was bright red, indicating that he was inclined to attack first and ask questions never, as if she hadn't guessed. She had to hold back a grin as she noticed that he was walking. His horse was obviously taking its sweet time going back to him.

Beside R3dLit3 rode a guy named 'UmberHulk6: Level 47'. His horse, at least, looked well cared for. UmberHulk6 was definitely a tank. Not as big as Motte, but heading that way. He had a mop of shaggy blonde hair and blue eyes in a round face. His armor was a mishmash of styles, and he clearly wore whatever worked best, without worrying about how it looked.

There was one group of people who had that patchwork look: PvPers, especially lower-level ones. They wore whatever their victims dropped, as long as it was better than what they had before. They rarely had very much money, but they had a surprising array of equipment.

Finally, bringing up the rear, was someone else Rouge recognized: Doom Bloom.

Rouge froze, eyes wide and locked on her estranged step-sister. The last time she'd seen her, Doom had been protecting Zombies traveling from Bloodhaven to Vargo, Quarternell's last outpost south of the Whispering Mountains. This was one of many ways people had come up with to make real money from playing *Veritas*, and Doom was one of the best.Strangely, Doom had refunded most of Rouge's payment for that trip, even though they hadn't even spoken for close to a year before that.

What was Doom doing with these lowlifes? She knew her step-sister was a mercenary, but surely, she could tell these guys were scum? Doom was a well-known PvPer in and around Bloodhaven, but rarely strayed much further, since her Guild, Angelic Embers, was based out of the free-trade city.

As the three Players walked by, with the two men (boys, really) still bickering and Doom walking silently behind them with a face so completely blank it was a statement in and of itself, Rouge stayed stiff and silent in the shadows. Once their backs were to her, she crept forward, listening intently, even as she started sending messages through party chat just in case Silus, Aspen, or Motte came near enough to receive it.

R3dLit3 was still whining about 'Fire' (presumably FlyingFir3, the archer who had shot at Aspen), and UmberHulk6 was whining about having to walk so far. Then, R3dLit3 said, "…and if I catch that little elf brat who ruined our ambush, I'm gonna kill her nice and slow. I bet she found someplace out there to respawn, and once she tells me where it is, I'm gonna spawn camp her until she quits the game just like Fire did."

"Come on, dude. You didn't even see her tag. How will you know who she is?" UmberHulk6 whined.

"She was riding a freaking *ostrich*, man. Have you ever seen an ostrich mount before?" R3dLit3 sneered.

"I dunno. Maybe there's a whole village of, like, ostrich-riding Amazon elf chicks out there. It's not like anybody has really gone that far north to explore. The mobs are too low level for grinding, it's hard to get to, and even NPCs say it's just empty land. Just let it *goooooo*...." The last word trailed off into a whine that would have made a five-year-old proud, and UmberHulk6 crossed his arms and actually sniffled. She revised her estimate of his age sharply downward.

Doom Bloom spoke for the first time, her voice ice cold. "You should listen to your buddy, R3dLit3. This is a waste of time and money. You had to hire me just to get you through the mountains, and it's going to take at least another day to get there. Then, they'll probably kick your ass again anyway."

R3dLit3's scowl deepened, and he crossed his arms, unconsciously copying his brother's defensive posture. "Shut up, DB. I would've gone whether you came or not. FantumHat was willing to come with us if you weren't. At least he wouldn't constantly complain about the trip. He *likes* killing NPCs."

Rouge gulped. FantumHat was a name even she knew. He was the head of a PvP guild in BloodHaven. A high-level assassin class, he could one-shot-kill almost anyone as long as he got the drop on them. If he had actually come hunting Aspen, their favorite farmer would be dead, no matter what Rouge and Motte did to protect him.

Doom rolled her eyes. "Whatever. Like FantumHat was going to leave BloodHaven for your stupid grudge job when the Murder Hobo Fest is about to start in Bloodhaven. He won it last year, and I don't think he intends to give up the title, or the boons that come with it."

The archer pulled at his stringy brown ponytail and growled. Like, actually growled! "Oh, he would. I know who he is in real life. He may be a rockstar in the game, but in real life, he's just a shut-in who lives in his mom's basement, and I can tell his mommy what he's really doing when she thinks he's 'working from home.'" He finger-quoted the last, as if anyone didn't know what he meant.

Just then, Silus' piping little voice entered Rouge's mind. ::Rouge? Are you there? I'm coming back. I found Aspen and Motte and they were hurt because a big lizard attacked them, just like you said, but they're okay now, but they went down a different path, so they'll be a half hour or so, even though they're running this way as quickly as they can, and they're already out of range, so I'm just going to keep repeating this until you answer. Rouge? Are you...?::

::*Silus*!:: Rouge practically yelled in party chat. ::Enemies! Three... Well, maybe two? One of those guys who tried to kill Aspen before, and his friend. Levels 47, a tank, 52, an archer, and 121?:: Rouge squinted at Doom Bloom. ::Make that 124, some kind of sword warrior type. Also, my step-sister, so maybe she won't try to kill me?::

Silus squeaked. ::*Maybe*? What kind of family do you have? No, never mind, I'll come in and get a look at them.::

::Be careful! Remember R3dLit3 was watching us for who knows how long. He might know about you.::

Silus sounded confident. ::I'm very sneaky.::

::Silus,:: Rouge sent, ::you're a bat. Flying around in the daytime. They might be a little suspicious.::

There was a long silence. ::Oh. Yeah. Okay, well, I'll stay up high then. I'll just look like a bird from down there.:: More silence. ::I see them. Where are you?::

::In the trees. Which is a problem, because they're about to go out into the open, and my [Stealth] isn't good enough for that.:: Rouge was both scared and excited, because once those idiots left the area where she could hide, she'd have to make a decision. ::I'm going to-::

::Wait!:: Silus interjected before Rouge could move. ::If you sink back in the trees a bit further, you can follow the cliff wall just out of their sight. There's an overhang a quarter mile or so ahead, and no branches off the path. If you can get ahead of them, you can wait there and get the drop on them.:: Pause. Paaaaause. ::Get it? *Drop* on them? Because you can get on the overhang and drop down from above.:: Silus sounded like she was giggling like a maniac, but

Rouge had to settle for an eye roll even as she suppressed a grin of her own.

::Yeah, I get it, you goofball. Okay, Let's do that.:: Putting action to words, Rouge watched to be sure the three players were still embroiled in their petty argument, and then crawled slowly backward, deeper into the stand of skinny trees and low-lying bushes. As she passed Codswallop, she touched his back, and he lifted his head from the ground, blinking at her with his huge brown eyes.

"Let's go, Wally," she whispered. "Silus says we can stay out of sight and follow the cliff over there." She tugged on his reins gently. "We have to be fast, but that's what you do, bud."

The ostrich chirruped once, then lifted his wings so she could vault onto his back, tucking her knees in the soft, warm fluff under his wings. She patted his shoulder, leaning forward to hug him. "You're the best, Wally."

Silus swooped down from the sky, flapping her wings almost silently as she led the way. ::What am I?:: The little bat asked, ::Fermented grapes?::

Rouge giggled as Codswallop settled into a ground-eating run, heading further from the trio ahead. The elf girl trusted Silus though. If the bat said this would join back up with the route the Travelers were taking, then it would.

::No, you're definitely fresh grapes. In fact, you're fresh Aspen peas.:: Rouge grimaced. ::That didn't sound right.::

Silus wobbled in the air as she giggled. ::I get it. Thanks. I think you're Aspen peas, too!::

Bat, girl, and ostrich continued to follow the cliff face. Occasionally, Codswallop leapt over fallen rocks and debris, once only barely keeping his footing because of his agile two-toed feet. After a few minutes of running, Silus turned abruptly to the right, leading them up a steep, sharp rock towering nearly fifty feet in the air.

::This way. Watch the ledge. I think it's wide enough, but sometimes it's hard for me to tell how well you grounders walk.::

::Grounders?:: Rouge asked as she dismounted from Codswallop and began creeping up a narrow ledge that was really little more than chips missing from the main body of the outcropping. Codswallop watched after her mournfully, but even his dexterity wouldn't allow an eight-foot-tall flightless bird to use a two-inch ledge. In fact, she was pretty sure it was taking all of her [Acrobatics] and [Climb] skills to stay stuck to the wall like some kind of suicidal spider monkey.

::Oh. I probably shouldn't say that. Aspen says that calling groups of people by names that they didn't pick can be mean. Was it mean?:: Silus swooped in and landed on Rouge's shoulder, her weight so slight that she didn't even disturb the young thief's precarious balance.

::You didn't mean it as anything bad, right? What do you call flyers?:: Rouge made her way up and over as quickly as she could, holding on with just her fingertips and toes.

::Flyers.:: Silus' tone said 'duh' without actually having to say it.

Rouge giggled silently. ::Yeah, it's okay. You fly, and we, um, ground. Right?::

::Right!:: Silus dropped off of Rouge's shoulder, winging her way up and around the front of the rock. They were now about ten feet above the earth. It wasn't far, really, but considering the effort it had taken to get there, it seemed like a huge accomplishment. ::The ledge is just up and to your right. You should find a handhold.... There!::

With great relief, Rouge felt her hand get a good grip for the first time since she left the ground. Once her other hand joined the first, she tested the ledge, then pulled herself silently up.

Your [Climb] skill has increased by one. It is now level 19.

Rouge grinned to herself at the notice, even as Silus settled down on Rouge's shoulder again, rubbing her soft head against the elf girl's throat and blinking her big eyes sleepily. ::I wish I was this strong in my world,:: Rouge thought, not even realizing she'd sent it in party chat until Silus responded.

::You're not?::

::No way. I'm just a normal kid over there. Well, maybe kind of a weird kid, but normal physically. I don't really like sports, and I definitely can't do a pull-up that easily.:: Rouge positioned herself on the ledge facing the path she could now see down below.

She pulled her Mambele out, coating it with some Dwarven Kombucha with a thought. The blade instantly glimmered a sickly green to her sight. She laid another knife, also poisoned, on the ledge beside her, ready to go. She triggered [Stealth] and [Sneak], then tensed and froze as she heard voices coming down the path. Those two morons were still arguing.

"If you don't shut up, I'm going to tell Mom you've been paying Julie Messer to do your math homework." It was R3dLit3's voice, frustrated and irate.

UmberHulk6 sounded sullen when he replied. "You better not. I know where you keep your stash of-"

Doom Bloom finally cracked. "If you two overgrown babies don't *shut the hell up*, I'm going to kill you both!"

As the two males turned toward Doom with matching expressions of affront, Rouge took her chance. She hurled her Mambele at UmberHulk6. As the tank, he would have far more HP, and thus be harder to kill. If she could get in a surprise crit, she needed it to be on him. Archers, though, were usually pretty squishy. Rouge swept the second knife up and flung herself down onto R3dLit3's shoulders, landing feet first and swinging the knife hard into the side of his skull. Without pausing, she flipped backwards, calling the Mambele back to her hand.

You have dealt 47 points of damage to player *UmberHulk6*. Player *UmberHulk6* is Poisoned.

CRITICAL! You have dealt 197 points of damage to player *R3dLit3*.

Player *R3dLit3* is Poisoned.

You have dealt 30 points of secondary damage to player *UmberHulk6*. *UmberHulk6* is Bleeding. *UmberHulk6* is Poisoned.

Instantly, she cast [Repeat] on R3dLit3. If he took that much damage five more times, he'd definitely go down. UmberHulk6, on the other hand… Well, that would be a battle of attrition. Would he be able to catch her before her Damage over Time (DoT) effects killed him? If he caught her, she was dead, so she just had to keep dodging and hope.

CRITICAL! You have dealt 197 points of damage to player *R3dLit3*. Player *R3dLit3* is Poisoned.

CRITICAL! You have dealt 197 points of damage to player *R3dLit3*. Player *R3dLit3* is Poisoned.

CRITICAL! You have dealt 197 points of damage to player *R3dLit3*. Player *R3dLit3* is Poisoned.

CRITICAL! You have dealt 197 points of damage to player *R3dLit3*. Player R3dLit3 is Poisoned.

CRITICAL! You have dealt 197 points of damage to player *R3dLit3*. Player *R3dLit3* is Poisoned.

You have slain player *R3dLit3*. You are now level 29.

"Yes!" She yelled, as she flipped herself backward again, easily staying away from UmberHulk6's flailing axe. Of course he was an axe guy. All big, slow, idiots had to be axe guys. Just once, she'd like to see an axe guy who was actually good at wielding the axe. Just not today.

She ran toward the tall stone she'd just jumped off of, running up the sheer wall and pushing off with her feet when she felt herself begin to fall backwards. She twirled, using her momentum to twist around and face UmberHulk6. She touched down on the top of his head, hearing him grunt slightly as she did so.

He used his axe to strike at her, but she was already gone, somersaulting through the air to land on her feet just out of range.

UmberHulk6 forgot there was an axe in his hand. As he slammed his fist toward his head, trying to swat the pesky insect that was buzzing around him, he clubbed himself in the ear with the butt of the axe haft. He grunted, and then stopped, swaying in his tracks. The idiot had actually Stunned himself!

Taking advantage of the moment, Rouge hurled her Mambele toward the big man, aiming for the narrow slit in his helmet where she could see dim little eyes peering out at her. He shifted at the last possible moment, and the blade screeched off, sending sparks flying. He rushed toward her, arms wide, suddenly looming as big as a Mack truck.

Rouge swore. She had planted her feet too firmly. She had been sure she could make the throw, and she just wasn't ready to recover quickly enough. She called her blade back to her hand, gathering herself to move, already knowing it wouldn't be enough.

Just before he reached her, UmberHulk6 grunted. He slowed, stopped, and toppled to the side. His armor was sliced in two from his shoulder through to the center of his chest.

You have assisted in slaying player UmberHulk6. You are now level 30.

As he fell, Rouge saw Doom Bloom standing behind him, already sliding her gleaming sword back into its sheath. Doom glared at Rouge. "You couldn't aim a little to the left? If you killed him, I'd be in the clear. Now, though, if he caught a glimpse of me, his log may show that I finished him off. If it does, my name is mud in Bloodhaven. A merc who turns on her employers is one that no one will hire. You owe me big, Zoey."

Rouge scowled. She relaxed slightly, since it looked like Doom wasn't planning to attack right away, but she didn't put away her Mambele. "Nobody asked you to help, *Doom*." She emphasized the other woman's nickname to remind her they were in game, not hashing out real-life grievances.

Doom Bloom sighed, pushing her golden blonde hair back behind one graceful, pointed ear. "Yeah, fine. It's just, these morons were going around talking about how they were going to massacre some NPC and his ostrich-riding elf girlfriend, and I've only ever seen one ostrich in *VO*, so…." She trailed off, shaking her head. "Look, it doesn't matter. It's done. More importantly, what are you doing here? They said you were way over north of the mountains, living on a *farm*. You told me you had a quest in Vargo!"

Rouge sighed and flicked her wrist (entirely unnecessarily) to put away her Mambele. Stuff like that ticked up her [Sleight of Hand] skill ever so slightly, and every bit counted. Plus, she could see Doom Bloom roll her eyes at the theatrics, and that made it double worthwhile.

"No, I said I was going to talk to an NPC. I did. He just wasn't in Vargo." She crossed her arms over her chest, daring her step-sister to make something of the omission. She could practically hear Doom Bloom's teeth grinding from here.

::This is your sister?:: Silus' little voice interjected. ::She's not very nice, is she?::

Rouge snorted mentally. ::No, she's not. My mom married her dad when she was nine and I was five. We never got along.:: That was an understatement, but she wasn't going to get into it right now.

Abruptly, a very welcome voice filtered into her mind. ::…hear me yet? Rouge, hang on. We're on our way. Can you hear me yet? Rouge-::

Her eyes widened, and she shouted mentally. ::*Dad!* Um, I mean, Motte! We're here! We're waiting for you!::

Silus spread her wings and flapped away from the shadow of a small overhang where she had been waiting since Rouge jumped down from the ledge. ::I'll guide them here!::

Rouge nodded, but caught a flicker of movement from the corner of her eye. She spun, knocking up her step=sister's hand, and the arrow Doom had been about to loose flew wide. The string of the bow snapped the half-elf's fingers, and she shook them, growling.

"What did you do that for? That thing is-"

"My *friend,* and you almost killed her because you couldn't wait a half a second before going all aggro. Cut it out, or *go away!*" Rouge's tone left no doubt which of those options she would prefer.

Doom Bloom's lips clamped shut, but she stubbornly didn't move. Rouge grunted, and then put her fingers in her mouth and blew sharply. A moment later, Codswallop came barreling around the side of the tall rock. When he saw Doom Bloom, he screeched to a halt, stretching out his neck and hissing at her while fluffing his feathers until his body almost doubled in size.

Rouge stepped in between the two, even as Doom-Bloom's hand twitched at her side. Turning her back on her step-sister, Rouge soothed her agitated bird until he rested his chin on her shoulder, glaring at Doom Bloom with the full force of his loyal avian soul.

Doom Bloom shook her head, whistling for her own steed. It joined them; a standard horse mount, though it was pure white and wore heavy armor that jingled as it pranced beside its mistress. When Rouge squinted at it, the tag above its head read *Oleander (Doom Bloom).*

As the two girls fussed over their mounts and tried very hard to act as though it was completely coincidental that they had met up in the middle of nowhere, Aspen, Motte, and Burrito came into view, led by Silus. Silus, the traitor, swerved upon sensing the tense atmosphere, and headed back to land on Aspen's shoulder, nuzzling in as if she'd always meant to do that. Zoey saw the tall farmer's face soften as he reached up and scratched the little bat's ears, and knew he must have been worried.

As soon as Motte saw Doom Bloom, she could practically see him brace himself for battle. Possibly *actual* battle. She bit her lip as she realized she should have given him a head's-up about the other woman's presence.

Aspen reached them first, his expression wary and puzzled as he looked back and forth between them. Rouge didn't fail to see that he placed himself so that he was slightly in front of her, and his hand was gripping a rather intimidating looking scythe. Where did he get *that*, anyway?

The farmer looked at the fallen corpses of their two opponents, still present because they hadn't yet been looted. His eyebrow rose, and he nodded his head slightly to Doom Bloom. His light baritone was curious but polite when he spoke, and a slight country accent lengthened his vowels and softened his consonants. He sounded like a hick.

"Who's this now, m'lady Rouge? A friend?" That raised eyebrow invited a full and complete answer, even though he tugged the brim of his ratty old hat down over most of it. The shadow of the hat fell over his topaz eyes, rendering them an unremarkable light brown.

Rouge nodded toward Doom Bloom, then felt silly. Like he was talking about one of the *other* random half-elves in a lonely mountain pass that nobody had any good reason for traipsing through. "This is Doom Bloom. She's a merc from Bloodhaven. She was escorting a couple of," she glanced at Motte, "not very nice Travelers across the mountains so they could kill us."

::She's also Rouge's sister!:: Silus put in helpfully.

::*Step* sister.:: Rouge hissed mentally, all the while trying to keep a bored look on her face.

Motte stepped forward, sighing. He held out a large hand. "Nice to see you again, ah, Doom Bloom. I hope you're doing well?"

Doom Bloom shook the proffered hand, her slim fingers completely vanishing into Motte's grasp. Aspen watched, clearly completely at a loss as to what his own response to this should be.

"Nice to see you again, Motte." Doom Bloom actually sounded sincere, which nearly made Rouge's jaw drop into the dirt at her feet. Lily had been trying to ignore the fact that her stepmother had ever been married before since the day her father, Ken, brought his new girlfriend home for the first time. A step-sister was on the bare edge of acceptable, but a big male stranger who had once *known* her mother had no place in her life.

Doom Bloom turned to look at Rouge. "I heard that someone was coming up here to kill an NPC and an ostrich-riding elf girl, and I convinced them to hire me as escort." Her voice turned sardonic. "As far as I know, there's only one person matching that description running around, and I thought it might be worthwhile to go check it out. Good thing, too, because Rouge was about to get herself squished to jelly by that big idiot over there."

Rouge flashed a glance at Motte, but he didn't even look disapproving when Doom Bloom called UmberHulk6 an idiot. It was so unfair! Now even her estranged *step-sister* got more leniency than she did? She crossed her arms, tightening up her scowl to epic new levels.

Aspen dropped back, clearly deciding that Motte could handle Doom Bloom on his own. He pressed a hand to Rouge's shoulder, throwing a supportive half smile over his shoulder as he stepped over to Burrito. He started tightening straps and buckles, and checking in the saddlebags. All completely unnecessary, but in keeping for the kind of default NPC he was pretending to be.

Meanwhile, Motte and Doom Bloom were exchanging pleasantries in blandly non-committal tones, as if they were nodding acquaintances who happened to end up standing next to each other in the check-out line at the grocery store.

Doom Bloom filled Motte in on R3dLit3 and his vendetta, ending with, "It wasn't even that big a deal. Fire got a little freaked out when your pet NPC killed her, and decided to take a break. She wasn't that into R3dLit3 anyway, and she'd been saying she wanted to try one of the new half-breed races, so she deleted her old char and started a new one without telling that jerk." She hitched a thumb at R3dLit3's corpse.

Motte shook his head. "I'm sorry to hear that. I hope she's enjoying her new character more than the old one."

Doom Bloom shrugged. "Only reason I know is because she was in my guild. When she deleted her character, she left the guild, too. She just wanted us to know the real deal, in case she decided to rejoin someday."

"I hope someday she'll be able to tell a bad boyfriend the truth, instead of running away." Motte's voice held a bit of an edge, though his face remained relaxed and friendly.

Doom Bloom shot him a look, but shook her head. "Yeah," she said, "A lot of things would be better if we could all just talk about our problems, instead of ignoring them. Anyway," she smiled a little, "I'm ready to head back to civilization. You guys on an Escort Quest?" She nodded toward Aspen, who was repeating the actions he'd already taken, looking completely engrossed in his pointless task.

"Um. Yeah." Rouge shot a look at Doom Bloom, who was acting very unlike herself. The Lily she knew would have found a reason to feel offended by now and left in a huff. "It's kind of a, um, chain Quest. I guess. We're going to Bloodhaven, then North Goose, and then Bright."

Doom Bloom made a face. "You accepted a Goose Quest? Why? It takes a week to clear that Stench Debuff if you stay more than a few hours."

Rouge tugged a curl, but made herself stop when she saw Motte's eyes flick to the gesture. She knew it was a tell that she was making something up, though she didn't think Doom Bloom knew her well enough to know that. Though, judging by the slight narrowing of the dark blue eyes, she could be wrong.

"OkayfineIwanttogetsomemorecinnamonrolls," she muttered finally, fast and low.

Both of the pale blonde brows shot up, and Doom Bloom looked at Motte. "What?"

He chuckled, the warm, deep sound rolling over all of them. Rouge felt her shoulders relax a little. That sound was a reminder of all the best moments of her childhood, and she couldn't help but feel better when she heard it.

"There's a native in North Goose who makes really good cinnamon rolls." He shrugged. "Apparently, she promised to buy some more for the ostrich, and she doesn't want to let him down."

Rouge felt her cheeks burn hot, but thankfully Doom Bloom latched onto a different part of the statement than she expected. "Native?"

Motte tilted his head toward Aspen, who had to be so incredibly bored of looking into the same bag over and over. "The people who were born in this world. Not Travelers."

The high elf's face grew confused. "The NPCs? Why-?"

Rouge growled fiercely. "Would *you* like it if someone called you something that you didn't understand, but that sounded like an insult? Like you were stupid, or your life had no meaning? I don't think so! We're here in their world, and the least we can do is offer them some respect!"

She saw Aspen's eyes flick to her, widening slightly, and he was smiling as he dropped his gaze back to the saddlebag.

Doom Bloom looked flustered. Her high cheekbones flushed pink. "I... I mean, of course not. But it's not like it's the same thing. They're just-"

Rouge stomped over and stood in front of her sister, glaring up into the taller girl's eyes. "It. Doesn't. Matter. It doesn't hurt us *at all* to treat them like, like *we'd* want to be treated. I, for one, like *myself* a lot better when I'm not a... a beezie!"

"Rouge!" Motte snapped from behind her, but she just whipped a glare back at him, then sent a matching one to Doom Bloom. She turned around and stomped back to Aspen, who was peering into Burrito's bag as if it contained the answer to the question at the end of the universe.

Doom Bloom's voice was dazed when she spoke again. "She's right. There's no reason *not* to be polite. I just... I guess I've been playing in Bloodhaven for too long. NPC's – natives, if you like – are valued less than pets there, unless they provide a service. Even then, someone could decide they don't like their prices, or their cooking, or just the way they're dressed, and try to kill them. If I were you, I'd avoid taking your, uh, *friend* there if you possibly can."

Motte shook his head, still a little disgruntled. "Not an option. We'll just have to make sure he stays safe. You know how much fun Escort Quests are."

Doom Bloom's voice was thoughtful, even as she went over to loot UmberHulk6's corpse. "Sounds like you guys could use a mercenary. I happen to know one who's at loose ends at the moment." She passed her hands over UmberHulk6, and his body flickered and faded. Looking over at R3dLit3, she continued, "I'll help you out for whatever you find on his body. Take it or leave it."

Motte and the slim elf swordswoman looked over at Rouge, who froze with a steaming chicken leg she'd taken out of the saddlebag halfway to her mouth. She scrubbed at her mouth with her sleeve, glanced over at Aspen, who was still being silent and as unobtrusive as six-foot plus of well-muscled yokel farmer with a seven-foot scythe could be.

"Fine," she muttered. "Whatever."

Chapter Eight

Aspen

The next two days of travel were a lot easier with three Travelers, two of whom were high-leveled. They were attacked three more times, but each time they were able to kill or drive off the monsters with relative ease. Aspen gained four more levels, Rouge gained three, and Motte one. Even Silus reached level twenty, though, much to her disappointment, she didn't ascend to become a Greater Fruitbat.

By mutual agreement, the original group didn't invite Doom to join the Party. If she didn't know that Travelers and (some) natives could speak in this manner, there was no reason to tell her. It allowed them to continue acting as if Aspen was little more than a simple farmer, uninterested in the personal activities of the helpful Travelers. Plus, none of them was quite certain how far to trust her, especially since she made no pretense of wanting more than the minimal relationship expected between two members of peripherally related families.

They made excellent time through the mountains, since they were able to ride and run for all but the six hours or so that Aspen had to rest at night. Rouge and Motte tried not to leave Aspen alone with the half-elf swordswoman, but there were times when it couldn't be avoided. Most of this time was spent silently jogging, Doom in the lead, while the two silent Zombies and their mounts brought up the rear. Doom felt no need to speak to or even acknowledge Aspen when the other Travelers weren't around.

The morning of the third day, however, turned out to be slightly different. Motte was present when Aspen awoke, stirring a small pot of steaming oatmeal. Rouge and Doom's Zombies laid with now-familiar stillness in their blankets.

Motte looked up and smiled as Aspen sat up and stretched. "Good morning. I was about to wake you. Silus just went to sleep a little while ago, and Doom is due to come back any time now. Unfortunately, I got a call from a colleague last night. She's sick, and needs someone to cover her lectures today, so I'll have to leave earlier than planned."

Aspen looked down at his hands, carefully pulling on his boots. "Oh? A good friend?" he asked, noncommittally.

Motte chuckled, deep and warm. "The assistant chair of my department. She's forty years older than me and due for retirement any time. I plan to apply for the position, and being in her good graces can't hurt."

Aspen smiled wryly. "My mother was in somewhat the same position when I left home. There were only three teachers in Jumping Hollow, but one of them taught almost all of the wealthier students, including the lord's children. He was much better paid and more respected than my mother and the other teacher. He was planning to retire the next year, and there was a fierce competition to see who would get the position. As I recall, he had somehow convinced my mother to grade papers for him, and the other teacher would polish his shoes every morning."

He shook his head. "I wish I could remember his name. The other teacher. He was a kind man." He sighed, climbing to his feet and going over to accept a fresh bowl of oatmeal from Motte. "It seems like the older I get, the longer it takes for my memories to respond when I knock on the door."

Motte laughed. "I think my memories stopped answering when Rouge was born. Something about having a child tends to drive everything but the present from your mind. 'Yea from the table of my memory I'll wipe away all trivial fond records.'"

He was obviously quoting, but Aspen didn't recognize the phrase. He tilted his head in inquiry, since his mouth was full of molten breakfast grains.

"Shakespeare. I teach literature, and sometimes I feel like I have to drop other people's wisdom into my conversation, if only to prove that I actually do something." The big man grinned, white teeth flashing.

Aspen shook his head, about to respond, when some shift in the atmosphere warned him that something had changed. He glanced over to the bedrolls, and saw that Doom's eyes were open and watching him, a quizzical expression on her face. He ducked his head down, concentrating on his food.

Motte followed his glance, and, seeing Doom was awake, stood and brushed himself off. His smile was a little forced when he said, "There's hot oats for breakfast, Doom. I set some aside for the animals, as well. It should be cool enough by now, and they'll probably appreciate a warm meal. Rouge will be on this evening, but I probably won't be back until late, or even in the morning. 'Without labor, nothing prospers.'"

He waved, and his face went blank.

Aspen shuddered. That was still, and likely would always be, creepy. And this was coming from a man who used to turn his own countrymen into ravening hordes of undead zombies on a regular basis.

Doom sat down and picked up a bowl. Her cool blue eyes were still watching Aspen as if she were trying to figure out a particularly irritating puzzle. She continued to watch him as she ate, saying nothing, so he finally went to the nearby stream and washed his and Motte's dishes. Then he took the rest of the now only slightly warm oats and fed them to the horse, mule, and ostrich. All three animals ate gratefully.

By this time, Doom had finished her meal as well, and gone to the stream for a drink and to wash her dishes. When that was done, she came back, and the two of them began to silently prepare the animals for the day's travel. They should arrive in Vargo shortly before dark that night, and the nearing end of the journey lent a sense of urgency to their preparations. Aspen, for one, was eager to be done with this leg of the journey, and back in a Non-Combat Zone again.

As Doom mounted her white steed, presenting a lovely picture with her long golden braid and slim silver armor-clad figure, she did something she hadn't done before. She spoke. To him.

"What do you need in Bloodhaven, Farmer Aspen?" Her voice was as cool as her eyes, and it took a moment to realize that she was actually expecting an answer.

He cleared his throat, trying to bring back the accent of a childhood spent in a rural part of Quarternell that had been overrun by the Dark Races over ten years ago now. "Need to visit a friend, m'lady. Hear she has a shop there now. Sells magic items."

"Hmm." She made a noncommittal noise, facing forward.

Doom mounting her horse was apparently the signal for Rouge and Motte's Zombies to join them. Rouge's body stood smoothly, though with none of the effervescent energy her soul brought to it, and gathered up her things with a pass of her hand. She was already fully dressed, so it was only a matter of a moment before she was mounted on Codswallop, who made a dissatisfied noise as he gobbled the last few bites of his breakfast.

Motte's Zombie gathered up all the items they'd used in the camp, storing them in his inventory. Then he stepped over into line, three yards behind Codswallop, who was three yards behind Doom. Doom usually rode at the front of the small column, but today she moved her horse beside Aspen.

Only when the small group was moving did Doom Bloom speak up again, startling Aspen out of the reverie in which he usually spent the long, silent hours."What's her name? I've spent a lot of time in Bloodhaven. I can probably tell you if she's still there. NPCs," she paused, shaking her head, "I mean, natives, don't tend to stay there long, unless they're protected by a Traveler's Guild." She nudged her horse into the moderate canter that Aspen had found he could now maintain all day.

Aspen fought to keep his face bland. He knew exactly why few of his people stayed in Bloodhaven. The murderous Travelers cut them down with all of the emotion of a man swatting a pesky fly. By his best estimate, the city population was three-quarters Travelers, and the natives who stayed were mostly criminals of one kind or another, who had nowhere else to go. Some few people managed to make a living as shopkeepers and servants, but it was a risky proposition.

Oddly reluctant, he said, "Her name is Manuela."

There was a long silence, and then Doom said, "That's it? No last name? No job title?"

"No. She works there. Rouge said she'd find 'er for me."

Doom rolled her eyes and muttered, "One of *those* quests. That girl never changes."

Aspen returned his eyes to the road, as did she. He knew that showing any further interest in the Traveler's lives would mark him as something unusual. Most people didn't much care what the Travelers did when they were in their own world, but Aspen found himself irresistibly curious. Now that Doom had actually spoken to him, it was hard to keep from…

"You're Rouge's sister?" The words emerged almost against his will, and he mentally cursed himself.

Doom's eyebrows shot up, and she looked at him, blue eyes calculating. She seemed to be deciding if she should answer or not, which was fine, because he was certain he shouldn't have asked.

"I'm her step-sister," she said finally. "Her mother married my father. My mother died when I was a baby, and I don't remember her at all. So Rouge's mom is the only mother I know."

He hesitated for a moment, but decided it was too late to stop now. "Rouge said she hasn't seen her mother in a long time."

Doom sighed, eyes flicking to a small stand of scrubby trees, as if some enemy might be lurking there. "Dad got a great job in… Well, a long way away. Too far to travel easily. Mom and I went with him. Mom is a history professor, and she got a position at a university near our new home. She's… busy."

Aspen kept his gaze resolutely on the narrow dirt track they were following. "Rouge said she gets vacations during the summer." He realized he had slipped out of his accent, and swallowed his consonants back down where they belonged. "Guess she must need to help out with the crops, or summat." He refused to look over and see if Doom had noticed the change.

The half-elf was silent for several minutes, and he had just decided, with mixed relief and frustration, to let it be, when she finally spoke again. Her tone held more emotion than he'd given her credit for, and it was all he could do to keep his own expression blank and listen.

The half-elf spoke for a long time. The words came out in bits and drabs, painting a picture of a clueless father, a sharp and demanding new stepmother, and two young children caught in the middle. Doom's voice trailed off as the last of it tumbled out, and she glanced over at Aspen as he jogged effortlessly beside her. She straightened up, shaking off the anger and sadness. "Anyway, I guess I feel like I owe her, a little. Because I was too caught up in my own life, and didn't see how much she was struggling. So, I'm helping her now. It's not much, but at least I'm trying."

The slender figure of alabaster and gold and silver shrugged. "I don't even know why I'm telling you. You're just a piece of code, though you seem to be a well-written one. Most of you 'people' do a good job of acting like you're real, but if I watch, I can see your algorithms kick in. Only a few of you are as complex as you seem to be, so Rouge must have found herself a pretty good quest."

Doom's cerulean eyes flickered over to Aspen. "Anyway, you won't tell her what I said. Not unless she asks, and there's no reason she'd ask you about me. NPCs don't volunteer information that isn't related to their quests or their backstory, if they even remember anything else. I've never really talked to one enough to figure it out. I guess I needed to tell someone, and talking to you is like writing it in my diary or something."

The tall farmer continued to jog, his face blank and his conscience writhing. He knew most of his people didn't speak to Travelers more than they needed to. The strange visitors seemed entirely focused on quests and fighting, and though they could be polite when they wanted something, they were just as likely to attack you or try to steal something if they could.

Now, though, he felt like he was betraying both Rouge and Doom. Doom thought he was stupid, and Rouge was his friend. The story was certainly personal, but if Rouge knew, she would be less angry at her step-sister, and possibly even open herself to forming a relationship with the older girl. He frowned down at his feet as Doom kicked her horse slightly, pulling ahead so they were no longer close enough to converse.

For now, at least, he would hold his peace. If something happened to change the situation, or when Doom left the group, then he would reconsider. Right now, he just needed to survive Vargo and Bloodhaven.

Chapter Nine

Rouge

When Rouge dropped into her Zombie, she thought she was prepared to deal with spending time with Doom Bloom. No. She most definitely was not. For one thing, the atmosphere between Doom Bloom and Aspen was so... *weird*.

Doom (because if she was going to spend that much time with her stepsister, something needed to give, and shortening her name was a start) spent her time totally ignoring Aspen, which was rude, but also kind of what they were going for.

Aspen, on the other hand, seemed to find the whole situation a little bit funny, but this time when Rouge blinked her Zombie to life, the look of gratitude he shot her was downright pathetic.

::What happened?:: she asked him in chat.

::Nothing. Why?:: If his guilty tone hadn't told her something was off, the fact that he couldn't meet her eyes was a dead giveaway.

Right. Nothing. If that was true, she'd eat her Mambele. With Dwarven Kombucha. Or brussels sprouts, which was worse. But, speaking of her

Mambele... She pulled her blade from inventory and triggered the item information. Because gloating never got old.

Gina's Mambele of Return – a star-steel blade with a curved back section and rearward spike. In battle, it can be used as a knife or thrown. This one has a spell on it so it will return to the wielder after being thrown. Soulbound to Player Rouge the Rogue. Weight – 2 lbs. Rarity – Unique. Value – ??? Cannot be sold, stolen, or traded.

She grinned, tossing it from hand to hand. She'd been a little worried, because the item description hadn't changed even after she made her deal with Gina. Then, once Rouge reached level 30, and shouldn't have been able to use it any more, TA-DA! It was like the best birthday, Christmas, Hanukkah, and Kwanzaa gift ever, all rolled up into one pointy little package. She didn't even know what star-steel *was,* but her blade now had a matte black look with wavy rainbow colors on the edge like it had been dipped in oily ink. So. Cool.

She wished she could thank Bridget directly, but obviously that was straight out. In fact, the other woman had made an effort to ensure they'd never again been alone together, so she figured Bridget probably had a really good reason for that. What Rouge *could* do, though, was bring in a pan of home-made lasagna big enough for everyone she knew in the department, and then make sure Bridget got an extra big slice.

Doom noticed she was there after she tossed the Mambele twenty-three times. Not that she was counting. But geez, situational awareness much? Rouge was definitely never trusting the half-elf to escort her Zombie ever again.

Doom smiled a weird, tight smile, blue eyes flickering to Aspen. "Oh, good. We're almost to Vargo. You said there wasn't really anything we need to do there, though, right?"

Rouge nodded, glancing between Aspen and her step-sister. "Yeah, we really need to head to Bloodhaven, but since it's late, it seemed like a good idea to stop in Vargo and gather some intel. Then we can rest in an NCZ and let everyone get a good night's sleep before heading out in the morning."

The other woman nodded stiffly. "Fine. NP- Natives can't enter the Dead Tent, so let me arrange for some rooms at the Inn. Unless one of you has a [Barter] skill higher than eighteen?"

Rouge's was seventeen, but she wasn't even going to say anything, not only because it wasn't higher, but because she didn't want Doom to have a reason to make fun of her. [Barter] was a skill few non-Trader class Players leveled over about ten. It only grew if you continually haggled for every little thing. It was actually pretty impressive that Doom had it up to eighteen, even though she was level one twenty-four.

Most Players stopped haggling for basics like buying food and selling rodent tails after about a week in game. The prices for those items weren't that bad, and the gain from haggling wasn't really worth it. People who actually liked that kind of thing generally went Trader, and got a different skill that was more effective (usually [Cheat], though some people got [Bargain] instead).

Rouge, of course, got a Quest. It was a Quest that no one else would even have accepted, but she had a blast doing it. She met a little old man named Grandie in the cloth market of Bright. He had laryngitis, and couldn't bargain, and he was about to lose his stall. She spent twelve hours in-game haggling with everyone from NPCs to Players, and power-leveled [Barter] to level fifteen in one day. Now, vendors offered her .51% better prices than they would a Player without [Barter].

Yay.

In any case, she just shrugged acceptance at Doom, who nodded an acknowledgement, then turned back to face front again, leaving Rouge looking at Aspen's back.

::No, seriously, what's up? You guys are, like, totally awkward. Did she make a pass at you or something?:: Rouge smirked, imagining the look on Aspen's face in such an unlikely scenario.

::No! She *talked* to him!:: It was Silus, who was riding in Codswallop's saddlebag again.

::Silus! It's not polite to eavesdrop!:: Aspen's voice was dismayed. ::You were supposed to be sleeping anyway.::

::Oooo,:: Rouge sent. ::Tell me more! This sounds good!::

::It's not my fault!:: Silus squeaked. ::She was really loud, and she woke me up! I didn't hear the whole thing. Just that her parents don't love her and she feels sorry for you because they didn't love you either.::

Rouge's eyes widened, and she stared at Doom's stiff back. ::Her parents don't love her? That's a bunch of poop! My mom loves her more than she ever loved me!::

Aspen sighed. ::I didn't understand it all, because she was talking about your world, but I got enough. I was *going* to let you two work it out yourself, but now that we're this far, I should probably tell you the rest...::

It took until they could see Vargo, but he did tell her. She asked him some questions, and he basically had to tell her again. By the time they crossed from the dull red stones of the road outside town to the soft bluish stones inside, Rouge was silent and thinking. Thinking really hard.

She thought about all the times she'd gone to visit her mom and Ken and Lily. How Lily had always seemed to be involved in some activity when Zoey got there. How Lily had rarely even been around during the years Ken and Karen had tried to obey the shared custody ruling. How Lily's parents gave her lots and lots of stuff, and enrolled her in all kinds of sports and classes, but never really spent time with her.

And Rouge could see it. Something solidified inside her. Something that had been a kind of a hazy, sad feeling, preventing Zoey from really being angry at or jealous of Lily once the initial misery of her parent's divorce dulled. The thing that, in the end, had led to Zoey telling her mom that she wouldn't be going with them to Seattle, even for the summers. Was it pity? Empathy? Maybe just a simple recognition of shared suffering?

When their entire group had crossed into Vargo, Doom turned to Rouge, startling her from her own inner turmoil. "Do you have a preference on where we stay? The Hairy Lemon is all right, in spite of the name, but it can get pretty rowdy at night. It's hard to sleep there, so you might not get the Well-Rested buff. The King's Crown is pretty classic, but it's where visiting officials stay, so it's expensive, though they do have a really nice private bathhouse. I usually stay at the Cow and the Moon. You have to use the public bathhouse if you want the Freshly Cleansed buff, but it's quiet and insect free, and the price is reasonable."

Rouge glanced at Motte's Zombie. She knew he wouldn't be on until later, if he made it at all tonight, but she felt weird making decisions for him. "Um, okay. Why can't we stay in the Dead Tent?"

Doom glanced at Aspen. "*We* can, but your native friend there can't. Traveler's Guild members only."

Oh. Yeah. All Players were automatically members of the Traveler's Guild, no matter their race or starting location. Part of the starter equipment was five tickets for a free stay in the Dead Tent, and one of the first quests was taking the initial rank test. Needless to say, NPCs were not members of the Traveler's Guild because duh, not Travelers.

Rouge cleared her throat. "So, the Cow and the Moon is okay then, I guess. Though I'm broke, and Motte didn't give me access to his money in his Away Instructions."

The half-elf rolled her blue eyes so hard they should have gotten lost in the back of her skull. "Fine. I'll pay for it, and your dad can pay me back later." She picked up her reins, ready to head further into town.

"Motte."

Doom turned back, confused. "What?"

"His name is Motte. We don't talk about being related in game. I used to call him Dad, and it really weirded out some people in a few pick-up groups we were in. It's just easier not to talk about it. So, call him Motte, okay?" She drew in a breath, then said, "Please?"

Doom's slim golden brows instantly drew together, and she shot a look at Aspen, who was standing next to Codswallop, digging his dirty pinky into his ear, looking innocent and more than a little dumb. "Uh, yeah. I can do that." With that, she led the way further into town.

The Cow and Moon wasn't far from the center of town. Rouge could see groups of soldiers marching in straggling lines as they entered a long building that seemed to be the mess hall, judging by the scent of under-cooked meat and over-cooked vegetables wafting from it. Nearby was a squat and unimposing two-story building with a thatched roof and a sign depicting the round posterior of a well-fed bovine hanging over the door.

Doom handed Oleander's reins to Rouge. "Wait here. I'll make the arrangements, and then we can take the animals to the stable." She nodded toward an attached building with wide double doors and a watering trough outside.

As soon as her step-sister went inside, Rouge turned to Aspen. "Oh my gosh, Aspen! I wish you hadn't told me! I knew how to treat her when we both disliked each other, but now I don't know what to *do*! Like, I actually said *please* to her! I never would have done that before! She's totally going to know you told me!"

The tall farmer pulled his hat down over his eyes, smiling wryly. "Well, that's part of why I wasn't going to tell you. At least not until she left us when we got to Bloodhaven. I'd just like to point out that I'm not the one with the big mouth."

Silus grumbled, ::How was I supposed to know it was a secret? *I'd* want to know if someone was talking about me when I wasn't there.::

Aspen shook his head. ::What's done is done, as Sumi says. Just, next time, maybe ask first?::

::Fine.:: Rouge knew without looking that the little creature was puffed up and pouting. She wiggled her hand into the pouch where Silus rested and scrootched her soft ears. Just to let Silus know there were no hard feelings.

After that, they just stood there silently for a few more minutes. Rouge was just starting to get worried when Doom came back out of the inn. The stormy look on her face told Rouge that the news wasn't going to be good.

"I don't know what the hell is going on, but the Innkeeper says they just got orders that no non-humans are allowed to use any facility also used by members of the Quarternell military. He says letting us stay would break his contract with them, and he'd lose his license. Apparently, it's the same everywhere here. No one will feed us, no one will let us stay, and no one will stable the animals. Every business in Vargo is now humans only." The half-elf's voice was furious, but she kept it low, glancing around as if she was suddenly re-evaluating how safe they were.

Rouge stared. "What? Weren't you just here a week ago with Hulk and R3dLit3?"

The other woman nodded. "We spent the night here, in fact. Now the Innkeeper is pretending he's never seen me before and threatened to call the guard. I don't know what happened, but I think we need to get out of here. Maybe Aspen can stay here with Motte and the animals, but you and I will have to sleep in the Dead Tent after all."

This was *not* in the plan. She had no idea what Motte would want her to do. Obviously, she couldn't leave Aspen here alone, which he basically would be while Motte was Away. Equally obviously, he couldn't stay in the Dead Tent with the rest of them. Her mind whirling, she stared from Aspen to the inn.

::It's all right. I can stay here tonight. Once you and Doom leave, I'll arrange everything. But how will you get Motte's Zombie to stay here? I thought he would only follow you.:: Aspen's calm baritone soothed her thoughts, and she took a deep breath.

"Okay. I have a plan. Doom, I'll tell you on the way." She looked at Motte. "Motte, follow Aspen."

Motte's Zombie turned its blank eyes from Rouge to Aspen and shifted a step closer to the other man. Doom stared in amazement, and Rouge shrugged. "It's an emergency backup in case there was a battle, or I needed to go check something out without a lumbering barrel of iron following me."

DB opened and closed her mouth. "But, he's an NPC-"

"Native!"

"*Fine!* Native. Whatever. You can't set your Zombie to follow a *native*, either!"

"It's. Part. Of. The. Quest." Rouge set her jaw stubbornly and glared at her step-sister, daring her to argue any more.

The half-elf just threw up her hands. "Fine! Whatever crazy hack or glitch you guys have figured out, I don't even want to know. When the GMs lock your accounts for not reporting it, you can tell them I had nothing to do with it! I'm going to the Dead Tent." With that, she climbed back up in her saddle and started off down the road.

Rouge bounced up into Codswallop's saddle and clucked at him to follow. He rolled a long-suffering eye at her, but obeyed.

::I'm sorry, Aspen.:: Rouge sent. ::She's still kind of a butt. Just go ahead and get a room, and put Burrito in the stable. When you get to your room, open the shutters and put your hat in the window. I'll leave Wally at the Traveler's Guild and come back. I'll [Sneak] in, stay with you until Motte wakes up, and then leave.::

The farmer was no longer visible behind her, but they were still close enough to communicate in Party chat. ::A good plan. Just be very careful. If anyone catches you using a Thief skill in a military outpost, they won't give you the benefit of the doubt.::

She nodded, then remembered he couldn't see her. ::I will. Just take care of yourself, and I'll see you in a half an hour or so.::

::See you soon, my friend.::

She couldn't help but smile. He might be an NPC, but it still made her happy that he considered her a friend.

🦃 🦃 🦃

Rouge and Doom Bloom were silent until they crossed out of Vargo and into the Non-Combat Zone around the Traveler's Guild desk. Then they exchanged a glance, and both started speaking at once.

"What the heck-" Rouge said.

"We need to find out-" Doom said.

They blinked at each other, and Doom smiled a tiny, tentative smile, and Rouge laughed a little. "Think the person at the desk will know?" Rouge asked.

The other elf scowled. "They'd better."

They turned to look at the desk, and both sighed. An NPC was manning the desk. It made sense. Vargo was way too far north for most people, and the Guild had to offer quite a nice fee for working up here. Right now, with the Murder Hobo Festival coming up, most of the Players who would have been grinding experience in this area were probably in Bloodhaven. The problem was, NPCs were… not helpful. They could do all the tasks required by the job, of course, but they didn't gossip like Players. Players talked like fishes swam. It was a constant flow, whether it was in game, on forums, in person, via chat, or on social media. The only way to keep a secret in a game was to *tell nobody*.

All of which boiled down to one fact: they'd have to be patient. Rouge was many things, but 'patient' wasn't one of them. She grumbled under her breath.

Doom cocked an arching eyebrow at her. "What was that?"

Rouge gritted her teeth.

Doom smirked.

"Fine," Rouge mumbled. "When you log off, would you find out what's going on and send me a message? *Please*? I'll have to stay on for a while longer, but this is going to *kill* me."

The smirk got bigger, and for the first time ever, Rouge could see that her step-sister had a dimple. Just one, in her right cheek. It made Rouge feel bad, because they'd been sisters for eight years, and she'd never seen the older girl smile big enough to show that dimple.

"Yeah," Doom said. "I can do that."

Rouge smiled. A real smile. She felt the bottoms and corners of her eyes crease, and saw Doom's eyes widen a little. "Thanks, Doom," she said.

Doom waved a little and turned to walk away. Rouge stared at the other girl's back, armor gleaming softly in the light of the moons and the lingering traces of the sunset. Then she swallowed and said, "Lily?"

The half-elf turned and looked at her, raising her golden brows in inquiry.

"What.... What did you talk about with Aspen today?" DB's brows drew down, and suspicion seemed to darken her blue eyes. Rouge quickly waved a hand. "He's my Quest NPC, you know. I just noticed that you were treating him a little oddly when I logged on. I wanted to make sure, um, that he didn't say anything weird to you. Or, um, anything. So... did he? Say anything?"

The blue eyes narrowed, and Rouge inwardly cursed her complete inability to lie, at least when it really mattered.

"What did you ask him, Rouge?" Doom's tone was level.

Rouge sighed. "I asked him what you said to him. You know how NPCs are. They log the weirdest things, and then they spout it straight back. I guess since you were talking about me, and we're traveling together, his program thought it would be okay. I don't know how this stuff works!" She tugged at a curl and stared down at her feet, wishing the ground would open and swallow her up.

"He said Mom and Ken stored your stuff when you went to college. That they basically told you not to bother coming home for the summer. That you, like, haven't even talked to Mom in months." She huffed a breath, tugging at her hair until a twinge of pain got through the 'Minimal Pain Input for Minors' block. "That they were doing the kind of crap they used to do to me. Make you feel unwelcome. Like you're a piece that doesn't quite fit in their little puzzle. Like they only paid attention to you because they were *supposed* to, and they didn't want to look bad."

She stared at her feet, digging in the dirt with the toe of her boot. "That you figured out that it wasn't my fault that I always left almost as soon as I got there, and stopped calling after you guys moved because I finally *took the hint*. And," she looked up, catching Lily's blue eyes with her own, letting her sister see the tears that she couldn't hold back anymore, "that you blamed yourself for not seeing it sooner. For not helping me."

The other girl opened her mouth, but Rouge held up her hand. She drew in a shaky breath.

"Just, let me finish, please? Then I promise I'll listen to whatever you have to say, too. And I won't bring it up ever again, if you just want to keep going on the way we have been. But, Lily…. It wasn't your fault. Any more than it was mine. Well, after that first Christmas, anyway. I really am sorry about that, by the way." She made a face. "I was just so *mad*. But the truth is, we were just kids. In the end, I think I'm the luckier one of us."

She smiled a little, glancing back in the direction of the inn. "My dad can be a pain sometimes, and he really needs to figure out that he's taught me how to take care of myself pretty well, but he *loves me*. I never doubt that for a single second. It took me a long time to admit it, but I don't think Mom did. Does? At least not since I can remember. So don't feel sorry for me, okay? You don't owe me anything. So if you want to leave us, and head back to your life, I'm cool with that. But," she chewed on her lip, "if you want to stay…. I could always use another friend. Maybe," she blinked to clear her vision, "maybe even a sister."

The down-turned corners of Doom's mouth trembled suspiciously by the time Rouge finally finished talking, and she was silent for what seemed like forever. Her expression was softer and more vulnerable than Rouge had ever seen it, and when she spoke, her voice was hesitant.

"I'm sorry, too. I was too busy being my parent's perfect kid to notice that you couldn't. You were never good at hiding how you really felt, even when you were five." She smirked a little, her voice still soft, but gaining confidence. "No matter who our parents are, we're sisters. You were always my little sister; the one I begged my dad for for years."

She paused, and pulled in a breath before plowing on. "I was so happy when dad married your mom, and part of that was *you*. I've never seen a kid as cute as you were. So little, with those fluffy curls and huge eyes. No matter what you think, I *did* let you down. I'm sorry."

Doom closed her eyes and breathed, smiling a little. "I've been wanting to say that for *months*. I'm so sorry, Zoey. And," she offered carefully, "if you'd like to be friends, I'd like that, too. If you'd like to be sisters.... Yeah. I'd like to try that."

Rouge grinned the biggest grin *ever*. "So, you know my Dad and I are a package deal, right? He's a pain in the behind, and he can't make up his mind if he wants me to grow up, or stay his little girl. Whenever I make a friend, he makes them part of the family, too." She rolled her eyes. "He took Jace to buy a jockstrap when he tried out for baseball last year. Oh. Em. Gee."

Doom's eyes widened. "You have a boyfriend?"

Rouge waved her hands wildly. "No! No no no no no! He's my best friend. I'm super awkward in school, and I just don't do that thing where you switch from being an acquaintance to being friends very well. Or at all. You know? But Jace just wouldn't give up, and now," she shrugged, "BFF. Anyway, just be warned that when Dad can tell someone is important to me, he just sucks them into our family. I think it's another weird way of keeping me safe."

The older girl laughed. "Yeah. I can see that. But I think," she, too, looked back toward the inn. "I think I wouldn't mind that."

Rouge sighed. "You think that now."

After that it got a little awkward, but fortunately Doom said she had to go or she'd miss her afternoon class. It didn't take long to get Oleander fed and tied up outside the Dead Tent. Rouge was glad that the developers had made it so that when a Player entered their Dead Tent instance, their mount 'vanished' with them. The idea had been to keep hundreds or thousands of mounts from stacking up outside the Tent, but it also meant that no one knew which Players were inside. Doom vanished into the tent with a little wave, almost smiling.

Unfortunately, Codswallop was Rouge's mount, and Rouge wouldn't actually be entering the Dead Tent until Motte logged on and she knew Aspen was safe. Thus, she had to hide the ostrich somehow, or any Players trying to find Aspen would at least know that Rouge was here. Unless they also believed in a hidden village of ostrich riding Amazons, which was an idea she could totally get behind.

In any case, once Doom was safely tucked away, Rouge took a look around. As much as she wished the ostrich could just hide his head in the dirt and vanish, like people said real ostriches tried to do (which wasn't even true, because she looked it up) he couldn't.

She eyed the bird, who was happily gobbling the High-Quality Mount Feed she'd gotten for him from the NPC. He *had* done that cool thing where he laid down and looked like a bush. Maybe he could do that again?

Rouge looked around. The Guild area consisted of the Teleport Circle, the desk, the Dead Tent, the bulletin board, a few hitching posts, and whatever miscellaneous objects the devs had used to decorate the area; usually some trees, bushes, maybe a bench or two, some big rocks-

Ah ha! To the east of the Tent was a small area that no one would really need to enter. The road passed through from north to south, crossing between the Tent, desk, etc. to the east, and the Circle to the west. The area west of the Circle was clear, and if someone fast traveled in, they'd be able to see everything over there. Behind the Tent, though, were some rocks and scrubby bushes that still fell in the Guild Non-Combat Zone, but were just there because the Zone had to extend that far so that Player-killers couldn't lurk there and murder other Players from outside.

She whistled for Codswallop, and he pranced over, obviously feeling quite cheerful about being saddle free and full-bellied. "Hey, Wally," she crooned, as she stroked his head near his funny-looking ear holes. "I have to go back into town to watch Aspen. It should only be another hour. Maybe two? The class Motte's covering should end any time, so he just has to head home, and then he'll be on. He'd better be, anyway, because I'm going to have to log out to do my daily Feedback Regarding My Experience." She rolled her eyes.

"Anyway, I need you to lie down here and pretend to be a bush for a while. It's getting dark, so if you snuggle up to a bush and take a nap, I'll be back before you know it. I just need you to hide while I'm gone so no one knows I'm here." Rouge pointed to a spot nearby, where the shadow cast by a good sized bush made the ground hard to see, and even a very large bird might become some particularly leafy vegetation for a while.

Codswallop tilted his head one way and then the other, examining the place she'd pointed at, and then looking at her. He leaned into her, chirruping sadly.

Rouge gave him a hug. "I'm sorry, buddy. I wish you could go with me, too, but I have to be super sneaky, and you're just not a town kind of sneaky. Could you please just do this for me? There's a cinnamon roll in it for you!"

A big brown eye examined her, and she had the distinct feeling that the ostrich knew that she was already in way over her head on her pastry promises. Nonetheless, he huffed a breath and flopped down in the grass, fluffing up and tucking his head beneath a wing.

She smiled. "Thanks, Wally."

🐦 🐦 🐦

The moment Rouge's soft-soled sneaking boots touched the bluish stones of Vargo's streets, a Quest popped up.

Quest: "Cat on a Cold Stone Road" available.
Sneak through town on kitty feet. Don't let anyone detect you. Don't use any Thief Class Skills until you reach your destination.
Success: 500 Experience. +1 level in [Sneak].
Failure: If a Citizen catches you, you may attempt to flee. If a Guard catches you, you will be incarcerated for a minimum of 24 game hours. Only time spent in-game will count toward your sentence.
Accept: Yes/No?

Rouge grimaced. Normally, she accepted almost any Quest that she thought she could complete, and that wouldn't take her away from whatever she was doing at the time. That Failure effect was pretty brutal, though. Under other circumstances, it could be interesting to see what would happen if she was actually arrested. There were probably some fun 'Prison Escape' Quests she could trigger.

Right now, though… She was about to mentally select 'No' when she paused and reevaluated. Frankly, she suspected that being sent to jail would be the least of her problems if she was caught. If she accepted the Quest, the system would presumably make the Guards try to catch her so that she could receive her punishment. Or maybe just teleport her straight to a prison cell? Which would be bad, except that without that system prompt, they'd likely just kill her outright. But you can't incarcerate a corpse, right?

So, hoping that she wouldn't have to test her theory, she chose 'Yes', and stepped into the shadows.

The military outpost wasn't that large, and most of the buildings were small and close together. All of the streets except the main north-south thoroughfare were also straight and narrow, presumably so that enemies couldn't get large siege engines or monsters through them, which would force them to travel along the main road, where the army could focus their defense.

In any case, it made sneaking through the town surprisingly easy. The patrols were loud, with heavy boots, and they weren't very alert, so as long as she slipped into a shadow and held still, she might as well be invisible. For a military force that was supposed to be on the forefront of Quarternell's northern defense, these guys were pretty terrible.

It was awesome. Way, way easier than in Bright, where the guards walked lightly and kept one hand on their swords.

Easier though, was not the same thing as *easy*. There were patrols everywhere. It seemed like there were dozens of two-soldier patrols marching loudly over the stone streets. Each time one passed, she would dart out from the shadow where she knelt, laid, or hid behind something, and almost instantly had to find another hiding place because here came *another* set of guards.

She even considered taking to the roofs, like in a Ninja RPG she'd played in middle school. The story was terrible, but jumping across the rooftops was fun enough that she'd spent several nights just doing that and ignoring the actual plot.

Unfortunately, whoever designed the buildings in Vargo seemed to have played the same game. The roofs were incredibly steep, with slippery flint tiles instead of shingles. To add insult to injury, there were even *spikes* around the gutters. Who did that?

Even so, she stuck with it, creeping through the dim back streets as swiftly and silently as she possibly could. She even had to hide behind a stinking barrel full of fermented fish for nearly two minutes while a particularly slow patrol ambled past. As they went, she could hear them murmuring to each other.

"...can't just make us walk all night, can they?" The big man was grumbling.

The woman, who looked like she was several years older than the complainer, said, "Yes. They can." Her voice said that she was very tired of hearing the other's complaints.

"It's not even like there's anyone here to catch! We're all just going to be exhausted tomorrow when they expect us to start riding double patrols outside the walls!"

"Suck it up, Wilbur. This is the easiest station in the army. The milk and honey had to stop flowing someday."

"No it damned well didn't! If we just..."

Then they were too far away for her to hear their quiet conversation, and she peered carefully around the barrel, trying to see clearly with eyes that were watering from the pungent stench. She shook her head. What in the world was happening in this town?

When she finally made her way to the inn, dodging between more patrols filled with increasingly cranky Guards, she looked and saw no window with a hat hanging outside of it. Then she heard a soft murmur in her mind. ::Rouge. Rouge. Rouge. Rouge. Rouge,:: and she realized she'd been hearing it for a while now.

She nearly smacked herself in the face. What had she been thinking with the hat in the window business? They had Party Chat! ::Um, Aspen?:: she asked.

::Rouge! You're back!:: The relief in the older man's voice was heart-warming, and she smiled.

::Yeah. Where are you?::

::East side, southern corner. I have a candle lit and the shutters cracked. You should be able to see the light.::

::Coming!:: She edged around until she could see the east side of the building. Sure enough, the corner room on the second floor had light flickering between the shutters, which were slightly ajar. Conveniently, the building was made of brick, probably so that it wouldn't burn easily, and she could climb that like a gecko with toes dipped in maple syrup. Mmmm. Maple syrup.

She was so hungry.

She shook her head. Focus! She triggered [Stealth] and [Sneak] and began to climb. It was a matter of moments to reach the window, pull open the shutter, slip inside, and close the shutter behind her. Aspen sat on the bed, freshly bathed and in clean, though often mended, clothes. He smiled at her.

Quest: "Cat on a Cold Stone Road" complete.
Reward: You have gained 500 Experience. You have gained +1 level in [Sneak]. [Sneak] is now level 18.

::Well done,:: Aspen said. ::We'd probably better continue speaking like this. We don't want anyone to hear a girl's voice coming from the room. I think the Innkeeper doesn't entirely trust me, even though I'm obviously human. Consorting with criminals, as it were.:: He smiled wryly, but there was sadness in his eyes. ::Did you find out what's going on?::

She shook her head. ::Nothing. There was a native at the Guild desk, not a Traveler, and we didn't even bother to ask. If it's not Quest or Guild related, those guys never know anything.::

::Ah.:: Aspen's voice was thoughtful, but he made no comment. He glanced over by the door, and Rouge noticed the tower of blankets there for the first time. She blinked as she realized what it was. She almost giggled, and had to clap a hand over her mouth to stop the sound.

Aspen had covered Motte's Zombie the same way he covered Rouge's when she logged out suddenly. A flush rose in Aspen's tanned cheeks. ::The staring is… disconcerting. It was bad enough he followed me to the bathhouse, but then he watched me the whole time. I couldn't get him to bathe, either, and he's getting a little, um, ripe.::

This time a choked giggle escaped. Rouge knew that over time Players would develop an Unclean or Stench Debuff. How long it took, and how bad it was, varied depending on what they'd been doing. When everyone around you had the same debuff, it didn't affect you, but when one person was gross, and other people were clean (or even just a lot *less* gross), it would cause a temporary Relationship drop.

::Yeah, he'll have to do that when he gets here. You couldn't wait?::

Aspen's nose wrinkled. ::No. I really couldn't. Sumi has me trained pretty well.:: He glanced around. ::Speaking of, where's Silus?::

She shook her head. ::Not sure. She said she was going to go eat and scout, and meet us back here. Didn't even let me answer, just took off.::

Just then, the piping little voice entered their minds, and a tiny scraping came from the shuttered window. ::Took you long enough.:: The bat definitely sounded disgruntled. ::I've been listening to you two talk for ages. Could you let me in, please?::

Aspen had the shutter cracked open before the bat could finish speaking, and scooped the tiny creature into a protective hand before firmly shutting and latching the window again. ::Silus! Don't just leave! What if something had happened to you?::

The little animal hugged his thumb with her wings for a moment, before remembering that she was still supposed to be mad at him. She stopped hugging, but didn't leave his hand.

Rouge made a mental note not to do anything to make Silus mad at her, because the bat could hold onto a grudge like nobody's business.

::So you don't want to hear what I found out?:: Silus sounded smug, and used one thumb to preen the silver tufts in front of her ears, which were visibly larger. Rouge checked the Party List, and sure enough, Silus was now Level 21. How had that happened?

::Yes, please, Silus. And, once again, I'm very sorry for sending you away when we interrogated the prisoner.:: Aspen sounded like he was about done apologizing, and about ready to start getting cranky. Silus could probably tell too, because she leaned into his thumb again.

::I flew around catching bugs for a little while. There are lots of nice big flies down by the midden pile, and-:: Aspen's hand twitched, and the bat veered back on subject, ::Anyway, just as I was getting full, I got a quest. It was a funny one, and it said that I should 'drop' from the 'eaves' of some big house in the middle of town. Is that what eavesdropping means?::

Rouge could hear Aspen's teeth grinding together, and would have sworn he said something under his breath. Maybe "Gina", but if so, he said it the way Motte said Rouge's name when she ate all the pumpkin pie without asking if he wanted to split the last slice.

::So, of course, I went and listened in," Silus continued. "There were a couple of humans in there talking, and one of them said something like, 'You're sure these orders came directly from Duke Geral?' and the other one said 'Yes, sir!':: The bat even did the voices, and hearing her squeaky voice imitating a gruff soldier was nearly enough to send Rouge into another fit of giggles.

::Then the first guy said, 'We'll put up the posters first thing after breakfast, then. Let the men know we'll be increasing security, and no one who doesn't have a military ID tag can use the facilities for the foreseeable future.' The second guy said, 'Yes, sir!' again, and...:: Silus stopped as the sound of Aspen gritting his teeth became loud enough they could both hear it over her voice.

::You know,:: Silus said reproachfully, ::Sumi says if you keep doing that, you'll crack your teeth.::

Aspen closed his eyes, which were nearly as golden as the bat's in the flickering candlelight, and breathed out slowly before opening them again. ::Could you see the poster, little one?::

::No,:: Silus sounded sad. ::And I would have gotten almost another level if I had. But they closed everything up after that, so I couldn't even hear them anymore. I did hear the first man say one more thing, though.::

::What was that?::

::Iorgas Penbrooke.::

Chapter Ten

Aspen

Rouge stayed with Aspen for as long as she could, but when he saw her glancing with increasing frequency and concern at what she said was a countdown timer, he finally kicked her out. ::Go! It's long after dark, and Motte said he would be back late. I suspect he'll be here at any moment. Do you think I cannot protect myself?:: He raised an eyebrow and gave his scythe a meaningful glance. It leaned against the wall near where he sat on the bed, blade glimmering in the dim candlelight.

Rouge set her jaw, even as she gave the invisible timer another concerned look. ::Look, I have it on good authority that the soldiers here are all at least level 50. If they decide to come get you, they're going to win.::

Aspen sighed, and gently asked. ::If the soldiers here decide to come get me, will your presence truly change the outcome? I respect your will and bravery, but the fact remains that they will take us both, and if we put up a fight, all we can do is die. We will depart before dawn, but for now, we must rest. If we leave now, we will have to go without the protection of either Motte or Doom Bloom, and the beasts outside these walls are too strong for us to defeat.::

Rouge pinched her lips together, and then blew them out in frustration. ::Fine! I'm already overdue to log out, and if I don't go soon, they might bring me back whether I like it or not. I need to be in the Dead Tent before that happens, or you'll have two Zombies to cover, and run out of blankets.:: She smiled a little as she crept silently over to the shuttered window, pushing it open before leaning out slightly, already seeming to fade into the woodwork as she triggered her Thief skills.

::I'll keep watch outside!:: Silus piped up. ::I can let Aspen know if anyone is coming, and we can try to run.::

Aspen glanced over at Motte's mummified Zombie. ::What about Motte?::

Rouge hesitated, and then her shadowy figure slipped out of the window as noiselessly as she had entered. ::Leave him behind. I turned off his Follow function, so he'll stay here. No way you can get away with him clanking around. Hopefully, they'll just leave him alone, once they realize he's a Traveler, but… well, he'll understand.::

Aspen nodded, even though he knew the girl couldn't see him. ::Very well. Though it pains me to leave a companion behind. He will respawn, if things go… badly?::

::Yep!:: The girl's voice was quieter already, as she raced through the streets, rapidly moving away from the inn. ::Don't worry about him! He'll be cranky, but he'll catch back up with us in Bloodhaven. Good night, Aspen!::

Aspen shook his head at the elf girl's cheerful lack of concern over her father's potential impending death. "These Travelers are strange creatures, are they not, little friend?" He scrootched Silus' ears, and the tiny bat leaned into his hand happily.

<I'm still mad at you,> she sent, even as she tried to wiggle closer.

"I know," he murmured. "I just need you to realize that I would do it again. I'm sorry that I hurt your feelings, and made you feel that I didn't value your input, or thought you couldn't handle it. It's just," he looked down, "I had hoped that this world could become a place where our children don't have to learn to be hard. You and Rouge are so filled with joy, unlike us tired old soldiers. I will never choose to burden you with the things that broke us."

Then he yelped slightly, flinching away from the suddenly pointy puffball he'd been holding. <You're not broken!> Silus almost shouted. <Stop saying things like that! You're not old, and you're not defeated! You're just tired!> Silus zipped around the room a few times before diving out of the narrow opening between the shutters over the window. <I'm going to scout. Because I'm part of your team. Part of your *family*! It's okay to let me grow up!>

Aspen stared after her, nursing his wounded hand, which had two small puncture marks on the thumb, which oozed a single drop of blood each. He put his thumb in his mouth. "Good thing she didn't use her [Bite] skill. With my luck, I'd get a Disease debuff," he muttered to himself around the tender digit.

A deep chuckle came from beneath the blanket by the door, and Aspen nearly fell off the bed, fumbling for his scythe. A big hand emerged from beneath the blanket, and pulled it off. A wry grin showed beneath his half-helm. "Sorry," the big man rumbled. "It sounded like you two were having quite a conversation, even though I could only hear your side of it."

He looked down at the blanket in his hand. "I got the Rouge treatment, huh? Sorry about that. I wanted to be back sooner, but every time I tried to sneak out early, someone else would show up to office hours. Sometimes I sit there for two hours answering mail and playing solitaire, and other days…" he shrugged, tossing the blanket on the bed before sitting down himself, making the bed creak alarmingly.

"What did I miss? Did the girls get their own room?" The half-helm disappeared, and Motte rubbed his hands over his short, tightly curled hair tiredly.

Aspen frowned, caught by the desire to offer some comfort to his obviously exhausted companion. Unfortunately, he had nothing to offer; not even some plain tea. He spoke reluctantly. "It seems that things have changed since Doom Bloom was here just a week ago. Non-humans are no longer welcome, and the threat level seems to have been raised. Silus said she also overheard some soldiers talking about how Duke Geral has sent out new orders. It is likely that they are to start looking for Iorgas Penbrooke in the morning."

By the time he finished speaking, Motte was sitting up straight on the bed, eyes alert and wary. "Where are Doom and Rouge?"

"Doom Bloom is at what you Travelers call the 'Dead Tent'. An ominous name, and one that we once used for a far different purpose." Aspen shook his head, pushing away the memory of a tent soaked in blood where the corpses of allies and enemies alike were brought so that he could resurrect them into horrors under his own control. "Rouge was here until just a few moments ago. She stayed as long as she could, to make sure that I would have support if the soldiers came sooner than we expected. She eventually had to head for the Dead Tent herself. I believe Silus may follow, since I managed to say the wrong thing. Again. Those two have formed quite a close attachment."

Motte blew out a breath, the crease of concern between his eyes lightening. "Yeah. I think they're bonding over their dislike of over-protective fathers." He shook his head. "I just want to make sure Rouge doesn't have to deal with the things I have. I've had too many times when someone I thought I could trust turned out to be an obstacle in disguise. This *world*," he waved vaguely around, "was supposed to be something fun we could do together, where I knew she'd be physically safe, at least."

He looked down, sighing deeply. "It's hard to let them grow up, you know?"

Aspen smiled ruefully. "I do. Twice over, at least. Lark, too, refused to let me keep her a sheltered child, and," he lifted his thumb, which was now fully recovered from its meeting with Silus' teeth, "Silus has reiterated her dislike of being treated like a baby."

He flopped back on the bed, staring up at the knotted ceiling planks. "It's just so *hard*, after everything that I saw, both in the war and after, to believe that they can learn to swim without me there to break the waves."

Another warning creak from Motte's bed indicated that the big man had also laid back. There was a long silence before Motte said, "When I was seventeen I had my…. Well, my carriage driver's license, I suppose. That just meant that I could drive a carriage without an adult around to make sure I did it correctly. It was a big deal, because now I could go anywhere I wanted. I felt really grown up.

"In my family, the only parent was my mom. She worked two jobs, and she was gone more often than not. My big sister and I had our licenses, so Mom trusted us to drive around our two younger siblings. My little sister was fifteen, almost sixteen, and I had been teaching her to drive for a while. She was good. She was careful, and drove the speed limit. Followed the rules, you know? A good kid."

He sighed deeply, and there was a catch in it that tugged at Aspen's raw emotions like a pick on guitar strings. "One day, she wanted to go hang out at the market with some friends. I had just gotten a new game. I was playing, and I didn't want to take the time to go with her. It was just me, Kiara, and our little brother, Milo, because Mom and Danika were working. I told her no, and she was furious. She told me I was selfish, and slammed the door on her way out of my room."

Motte was struggling to breathe evenly now, and the strain was audible. "I didn't even know she'd left until the police - the city guards - knocked on our door. Apparently, she decided to drive herself. She was in an accident, and she was dead. Just dead. No chance for a doctor to save her. No chance to tell her... how sorry I was… how much I loved her…"

His voice choked off, and without even thinking about what he was doing, Aspen rolled off his bed and stumbled to the other man's side, reaching out to lay a comforting hand on the big fist that was clenched against Motte's broad chest.

Motte jerked at the contact, then let out a shuddering breath and relaxed slightly. Though no tears escaped from under his tightly closed eyelids, his face was twisted in sorrow and regret. "She was just a kid when she died. All because

I didn't go with her. If I had just listened, just been *with* her-" He sobbed, once, then clenched his jaw so hard Aspen could see the muscles stand out in sharp definition beneath the dark skin.

Aspen curled his fingers around the other man's, and just sat there beside him. Silent.

Finally, Motte gently pulled his hand from Aspen's and wiped his dry eyes. He forced a smile. "Real men aren't supposed to cry, right? Not that we can, here."

Aspen stood, a little awkwardly, and moved back to his own bed. "Tears don't make you weak. Not being able to face the things that make you cry makes you weak. I'm sorry about your sister. It wasn't your fault, though. You were just a kid, too."

Motte sat up, rubbing tiredly at his eyes. He quirked a smile. "I must be more tired than I thought. I haven't told anyone about that in years. The last person I told was Rouge's mother. She said it was my sister's fault for going without me."

Aspen's fists clenched. "She made a bad choice. She didn't deserve to die. You didn't deserve to have that guilt put on you for the rest of your life."

Motte raised his hand. "I know. I think that was the beginning of the end for us. Rouge was an independent four-year-old, and I wouldn't let her go to a friend's house or play in our little fenced-in back yard unless one of us was with her. Not even for a minute. I tried to explain to Karen that I just needed to know Zoey was safe, and told her why I was so worried, even though it wasn't always rational or convenient. We had a huge fight, and I think that was when she started looking for someone who would always put *her* first. Or maybe she just started looking more seriously. She was never really happy with me. Not once the romance of falling in love and getting married was over. She wasn't interested in a relationship that took work."

Aspen thought about what Doom Bloom had told him about her stepmother. It sounded to him like Motte had a fairly good understanding of his ex-wife's personality. He nodded. "Callie was a bit like that as well. She enjoyed the romance of running away with an infamous young mage, but when Lark spawned as a newborn the day after we were wed...." He shook his head. "I think she was glad when her father turned up and declared that he'd had the marriage annulled. She certainly left quickly enough, and never allowed herself to be alone with me again, though we would occasionally meet at some function or other."

The two men shared a moment of mutual understanding, and then Motte cleared his throat uncomfortably. "Well," he said, "if we have to leave before dawn, you need to get some sleep. I'll keep watch until we can go meet the girls. If you don't get some rest, though, this stop will have been pointless."

Aspen knew he was right, and also knew that they both needed to step back from the rawness of the emotions that had risen to the surface during their conversation, so he nodded and laid back in his bed. "Good night then, my friend. Oh, ah," he glanced over at the large bowl on the single small table that was the only furniture in the room except the beds themselves. "There's a bowl of water, some soap, and a cloth over there. I paid a bit extra for it to be warmed, though it's likely cold again by now. You may wish to avail yourself of it."

Motte laughed. "Ripe, am I?" He shook his head. "I saw the debuff, but I didn't think it was that bad yet. I'll wash up. Go to sleep."

Aspen did.

Chapter Eleven

Rouge

There was a massive notice blinking in Rouge's peripheral vision as she ran.

LOG OUT – LOG OUT – LOG OUT
Automatic logout will begin in 60…59…58…57…

With every step she took, it counted down, and she whistled for Codswallop with just forty-five seconds left. He was beside her eight seconds later, and she threw his lead over the 'hitching post' outside the Dead Tent. With twenty-one seconds remaining, she opened the Tent menu, selected 'Rest Until Next Login', and leapt through the tent opening. Placing her shoes in her inventory (because apparently you couldn't get 'Restful Sleep' while wearing footwear), she collapsed into the bed. As the counter ticked down to four seconds, she willed herself to log out, and felt herself almost physically yanked away.

Zoey opened her eyes, gasping a little as her real body caught up with the racing of her digital body's heart.

"Holy cats!" She stared up as the fluid surrounding her withdrew, and the bed raised and inclined itself slowly. As soon as she could, she reached up and pulled off the full-face mask and the headset, swiping her hand over the special cap to sluice away the goop. As always, it fell away from her skin in a sheet, clinging to itself more than to her. She'd noticed that her skin was really soft after a session in the pod, and figured that even if Veritas Corp couldn't make the goo-filled pods 'commercially viable' (as Sara liked to say), they could market the stuff itself as a super-fancy skin-care product.

She stared around. She'd come out of the pod a bit early a few times, and found herself alone, but never for long. Plus, Dr. Joe had told her that the automatic logout system was there, but he would manually override it if it ever came up, because he knew sometimes things in the game didn't wrap up on a tidy timeline.

So, the question was, where was Dr. Joe, and why wasn't he here to do the override? If he was called away for some super-important meeting, then why wasn't Sara here, at least? Not that Sara was 'least' at all. She seemed to be the one keeping Dr. Joe's nose to the grindstone, since he had a tendency to get all excited about something and sink into some kind of creative fugue.

In fact, given the similarity between Sara and Sarave's names, and their matching serious and sensible personalities, Zoey had a suspicion that some of the NPCs on her quest line might be based on people who were involved in the project. Sarave even looked vaguely like the Indian woman, from her big liquid eyes, to her high cheekbones, and her beautiful long hair. Only, you know, greener, and super skinny and inhuman looking. Ever since Zoey'd had that realization, she'd been having a blast looking for matches, though no one else jumped out at her as obviously.

But, at the moment, Zoey just needed to figure out where Joe and Sara were. Struggling a little against the slickness of the goop and the depth of the pod, she managed to climb out on her own. She stepped over to the corner of the room furthest from the pod, stood by a green square on the floor, and pressed a button next to her.

Narrow slits opened in the walls to each side of her, and clear glass panels slid out. The green square slid away, revealing a drain in the floor. A matching panel in the ceiling opened as well, and a warm wall of water (at least, she thought it was just water) sluiced over her, rinsing her clean in a moment. Holding her breath, she scrubbed her hands over the places the water couldn't easily reach, and slapped the button again.

The process reversed, leaving a dripping Zoey standing alone in the corner of the room. She looked around, blinking her eyes against the water on her thick, curly eyelashes. Usually, someone would be there to hand her a magic towel (it was weirdly flat, but dried water like it was a portal to the Saharan desert). This time? Nope, still nothing.

She shook herself, scraping her hands over her body, clearing as much water as she could before she pulled the cap off her hair, which was still clean and dry, thank goodness. After a minute or so, she was as dry as she could get without a towel, and she stepped away from the drain, which would stay open for some unknown period of time. She had always been ushered out of the room before it closed.

Zoey looked around. Usually, Dr. Joe and Sara bustled her in and got her hooked up. Then, after her session in the pod, one or both of them was there to bustle her right back out. She shivered slightly, but resisted the urge to try to figure out how to get back to the changing room and her dry clothes. The special suit dried really quickly, if she could just take her mind off it until it did so. A watched suit never dried.

Her brows drew together as she looked at the walls. On the wall opposite her was the entrance, which was, as usual, firmly closed. She knew that it had a complex locking system, though from the inside it was just a thumbprint and a key card, not the strangely lingering process that was required from outside. There was no way she was going to be able to get out without help. She didn't have her screen, or any tech, so she couldn't call someone for help.

She looked over at the pod. It stood, still open, with the fluid drained back into a reservoir where, she'd been told, it was filtered and sanitized. The pod was covered with panels, and a few of them stood open, revealing wires, lights, and the occasional screen with codes flickering past faster than she could read them. Dr. Joe had told her that this was just a prototype, and the final product would be fully enclosed and streamlined, so it looked more like a smooth egg than a chunky cylinder.

Unfortunately, the part that actually controlled the pod, with buttons, switches, and voice inputs, was sealed. A smooth opaque screen covered the user interface, and had to be unlocked with two key cards. This could be the key card of the person who would be playing and a member of the development team, or two members of development, though in that case, the pod would not be fully functional. All of this was both to protect the all-important Proprietary Information™, and to make sure that no one who hadn't been properly tested and approved could use the system. No popping in here to let your kid (or you) have a go while you clocked some overtime.

All of this meant that unless Zoey wanted to start pulling wires out of the exposed sections, the pod didn't offer her any new information. *But...* She stepped to her right and trailed her fingers over the wall, once and then again, with her fingernails this time. The tips of her nails caught in a nearly invisible groove, much like the ones that housed the shower panels.

With new eyes, she looked at the wall on each side of the groove, at the same level as the button for the shower. Unlike the shower button, which was green and protruded slightly from the wall, the button for this whatever-it-was was flush to the wall and shaded only slightly lighter in color.

She pressed the button.

After all, what else was she supposed to do? She was stuck in here, with no indication that anyone was coming for her. She had a clear excuse – *need* – to check things out and see if she could find another way out.

After all, there could be an emergency going outside. An earthquake, or a freak hurricane, or Godzilla!

With a soft *shooshing* sound, a panel slid aside. No. A *door*.

Zoey did a little fist pump, then stuck her head into the dimly lit room. Inside were two giant eggs. Smooth and sleek, they stood in ovoid perfection. A soft susurration came from each one. She crept forward, falling into a crouch as if she could use her [Stealth] skill to avoid detection. She imagined a notice telling her that her skill had advanced, and barely choked back a nervous giggle.

Her hazel eyes focused on the small window into the pod closest to her. From her own experience, she knew that the interior of the pod would be visible through there, including the face of the occupant. She was certain she knew who rested in one of these devices, but the other one....

She stepped up to the pod and lifted herself on her tiptoes. She peered down into the faintly glowing interior. The blue goop was softly luminescent, something she hadn't been able to tell in the bright lights of the room where her own pod sat. In the pale radiance, she saw a face she'd seen a thousand times, though never before in person.

Bree Stephenson.

The woman's eyes were closed. She wore no makeup and her signature red curls were hidden beneath a smooth cap and a familiar headset. Her freckles were almost green in the blue fluid, and her auburn lashes and eyebrows nearly invisible. Nonetheless, the smooth curve of her jaw, the high cheekbones, the pointed chin, and the generous curve of her mouth left no doubt that this was the famous influencer.

How long had she been here? She had no facemask, so she was breathing the fluid, just like Dr. Joe had said a user would when they entered the pod for long-term immersion. Zoey remembered watching the episode of Bree's show where she told her viewers that she would be taking a six-month hiatus, but that she would review some extraordinary new innovation when she got back.

This was it. Veritas Corp had achieved long-term immersion, and Bree Stephenson was in it. Which meant that she could be almost anywhere in the game. According to Bridget, Bree was supposed to be 'along the quest line somewhere'. Was she logged in as a Player... or an NPC? If she didn't have to log out, there was no restriction on what role she could play. In fact, *not* logging out would be a huge giveaway if she was a Player. Someone would be bound to notice that she was always on.

By elimination, then, she was probably an NPC. Was she playing as Sumi? Silus? *Khor*? Surely not Aspen. No one was that good an actor, and she would have slipped up by now. He was with one of them constantly. There was no way they wouldn't have noticed if he actually understood their obscure references and comments about the game being, well, a *game*. No, the woman had to be someone they hadn't met yet. They were just getting started, after all.

Then Zoey remembered the Study Room. It was too polished for her to believe that Veritas created the space just for Zoey's trial period, so why was it there? Unless it allowed an immersed player to 'log off' and give themselves some relief from the game. Maybe even make a call, check mail, or watch a movie? Any of that could be done, and it wouldn't even be difficult. Maybe Veritas had found a way to change... everything?

No wonder they were ready to release the information about how to achieve the original VR system. If all of this worked, they were so far beyond their starting point that no one else would be able to catch up for years, maybe ever. Certainly no other game company would be able to compete!

Zoey's eyes narrowed. Bree was supposed to be on 'their' side in this competition. In theory, that meant that whoever was in the other pod was their opponent. It was possible, then, that she could recognize that person, too. If she did, she might be able to identify them in the game, which would give her an edge. Okay, maybe a kind of cheatery edge, but she felt like it was a reasonable amount of cheating.

In fact, it was likely it wouldn't help her at all. Right? Knowing Bree was in the game hadn't helped Zoey and her dad pick the woman out of the crowd, and likely the same would be true of the other person. The person in. That. Pod.

Right. *There.*

She half turned, eyes locked on the window panel of the other egg, and the soft glow emanating from it. As she did, she heard someone clear their throat quietly.

Zoey whipped around, her heart leaping into her throat. Dr. Joe stood there in the door, arms crossed as he watched her. His face was shadowed, and she couldn't see his expression.

"Sorry I'm late, Zoey. I see you weren't too worried." His voice was flat.

She took two steps toward him, then stopped, smiling nervously. "I was *totally* worried! There could have been anything going on! I mean, maybe there was a fire, and they evacuated the building, but you forgot about me. Maybe all the crocodiles escaped from the zoo, and they were evacuating the area! Maybe *nuclear winter* was falling outside, and I was the last human alive…" Her voice squeaked and trailed off.

Dr. Joe stepped back and to the side, clearly inviting her to follow him back into the first room. As he did, the menacing shadows vanished, revealing his round face and bright blue eyes, as well as the small smile that turned up the corners of his mouth.

"Come on, Zoey. We'll just pretend this never happened. I should have been here when you exited the pod, and you should have stayed here until one of us came. Maybe we can just agree that that's what happened?" He tilted his head and smiled more broadly, revealing that slightly crooked tooth that she liked because it showed that he wasn't worried about being perfect.

Zoey stepped forward, then hesitated, glancing back at the pod briefly. She desperately wanted to know what face she would see if she looked in there. But there was no way she could look now. Maybe, just maybe, something like this would happen again.

Next time, she'd be ready.

ࡥ ࡥ ࡥ

By the time Zoey made her way home on the bus, a process she was now relatively comfortable with, though the #42 bus often contained people who were having a Much More Interesting Day than she was (for which she was grateful), it was late. She heated up some leftover pizza, and ate it as she stripped down and got into her bodysuit. Bonus, she'd remembered to pee before leaving work that day. (Why does nobody ever mention how hard it is to time your bathroom breaks to coincide with your scheduled work breaks? That was definitely one of her least favorite aspects of having a job.)

She pulled on her headset, which didn't fit nearly as comfortably on her head as her customized work rig, and laid down. The first thing she did was flip open the media program that combined video calls and mail, displaying them onto the headset much like a normal 3D display.

Nothing.

She had seriously thought that she and Lily had *bonded*, or something, during their conversation in game. Apparently not, because if they had, the other girl would have sent her a message telling her what she'd found out, just like Zoey had asked her to. Right?

Zoey had, of course, done her own research as well. During the bus ride, she'd looked at all the major fan-hosted pages, as well as the official ones. She didn't see anything about whatever was happening in Vargo, but Lily would have access to a lot more information than Zoey, if only because she was in a guild, and probably on a lot of the invite-only sites for PvPers.

Nothing. Nada. Bupkis. Did people even still say bupkis, or was that another weird thing she'd picked up from her dad? Anyway, she had no messages from Lily, and had found zilch on her own.

With a flick of her eyes, she closed the app, and settled more comfortably back into the pod's cushy bed.

"Okay, *Veritas*. Let's go," she murmured.

When she dropped into her Zombie, she was astride Codswallop, and they were heading away from Vargo at a rapid clip. She and Motte both had default Away Instructions set up so that the other person could 'wake' them from a

Dead Tent and get them going. They had set that up shortly after Rouge started playing, when she had a quest to go on, and Motte was stuck in a faculty meeting IRL. Rouge had left without him, and ended up stuck in Eternal Combat.

Eternal Combat was when an aggressive mob had you locked in combat, but neither of you was able to kill the other one or run away. In this case, Rouge had ended up fighting an Armored Ant, and couldn't even scratch its carapace. On the other hand, her Dex was high enough that the insect rarely hit her, and when it did, she recovered before it could hit her again. The bug would probably have landed a crit eventually, but in the meantime it had really sucked.

Veritas wouldn't allow a Player to log out while they were in combat, so Rouge was stuck there for *hours*, unable to bring herself to just stop fighting, especially since the suicide debuff was waiting for anyone who let themselves die when they didn't have to. She was also unable to run away, since the Ant would catch her if she tried. Eventually, the game even started adding debuffs to get her to die or log off, since she'd exceeded the maximum recommended play time, which really would have been the time to just die already, but Rouge was too stubborn to give up. Meanwhile, Motte was more than a mile away, so even after enough time passed that Rouge knew he had to be on, she couldn't contact him.

Fortunately, Motte had a general idea of where the quest would take her, since he'd done it when he was a newbie, too. He was able to get close enough, even in the warren of the ant nest, to talk to her, and after that it was just a matter of him finding her and putting the ant out of both their misery.

From then on, they each left a default Instruction that allowed them to grab the other person's Zombie and drag it along on quests that had any serious risk. The dragger would leave the draggee somewhere safe (or as safe as possible) that would be within a mile of the quest area. Of course, while Rouge had used it to take Motte along while her dad was working, Motte had never had to exploit it before. Not a whole lot a level twenty-something player can really do to help a level ninety-something player, after all.

But here she was, sitting pretty on Codswallop with Doom's Zombie following her on Oleander, and Motte and Aspen jogging ahead with disturbingly synchronized steps.

Rouge cleared her throat and leaned forward to pat Codswallop affectionately. "Hi, guys. I didn't expect us to be on the road already."

Motte and Aspen looked over their shoulders at her, but didn't slow. Motte smiled, and Aspen nodded.

"We thought it best to leave before dawn," Motte rumbled. "We left as soon as we could without raising suspicion. They woke Aspen when they started pounding nails into Wanted posters with a vaguely recognizable image of his face on them." He shot an amused glance at Aspen, and the back of the other man's neck turned a little pink. "Apparently he used to have a very well-maintained Van Dyke beard and a ponytail."

Aspen grumbled something, and then raised his voice as he explained, "It was all the rage in Bright for several years. I thought it made me look very distinguished. Sumi made me shave it off and cut my hair when we left."

Rouge shook her head. "So, you're saying that a giant *spider* has better fashion sense than you?"

Aspen tugged at the brim of his hat, which he still insisted on wearing almost constantly. "She's a better cook, too."

Rouge laughed.

Quest: "Show a Caravan you Care" available.

A merchant's caravan is under attack nearby. Save at least half of the wagons and merchants. *Current progress: 0/20 people rescued. 0/8 wagons protected.*

Success: 1800 Experience, 100 Gold, +20 Relationship with the surviving members of the caravan.

Failure: Aspen will likely die.

Accept: Yes/No?

All three of them froze, and Aspen swore softly. "Did you get a quest as well?" Motte grunted an affirmative, and Rouge nodded.

"Why would *you* die if we don't save the caravan?" Rouge asked, pulling indecisively at Codswallop's lead, The ostrich pranced in place uncomfortably while shooting her a stink-eye that would have given her a Stench Debuff if it could have.

Aspen veered to the right, heading away from the trail through the woods that they were using to keep them out of the way of patrols on the main road. "Because we natives don't get to choose our quests like you Travelers do, and mine says that if I don't save them, I won't be able to enter Bloodhaven. So, I'm going to go try, even if you don't, but without you, I'm going to fail." He glanced back at them. "You coming?"

Motte groaned, but a blank black helmet appeared on his head, and his axe in his hand. "Yeah, I'm coming. Just for the record, this is my only decent backup helmet, so if it gets eaten, you owe me a new one."

Aspen flashed a grin, even as he picked up his pace. "Deal."

Rouge puffed out a breath, then grinned, calling her Mambele to her hand. She accepted the quest with a thought, and leaned forward on Codswallop's back to pat his neck. "You heard the man, Wally. Let's go Save the Day!"

The ostrich bugled a call and leapt forward, quickly leaving the two men behind. Behind them, Oleander and Burrito picked up the pace as well, matching Rouge and Codswallop. Rouge glanced back and frowned.

Without warning, Rouge emerged from the woods. Codswallop's long claws clicked as he ran onto the red stones of the road. The thief stopped and stared.

::What the heck are *those*?:: she sent to Motte and Aspen.

She squinted at the three monstrous humanoids ahead of them. Their skin was a kind of reddish gray, and tufts of brown hair stood out from their bodies in seemingly random patches. Their hands and feet were disproportionately large, the joints knobby and misshapen. The faces were hideous, with bulbous noses skewed to one side or the other, lipless slits for mouths, and sloped foreheads that overhung tiny red eyes.

The tags above their heads were oddly blurry, and she couldn't make out their species, though their levels were clear enough. The biggest one was *??? – Level 107*, slightly smaller but just as ugly was *??? – Level 103*, and the smallest one (the only one that was wearing more than a rotted fur loincloth) was *??? – Level 100*.

Three Level 100+ unknown mobs? What was going on here?!

Zoey's eyes snapped past the ugly mobs, and she stared at the caravan they had been sent to rescue. Eight wagons stood in disarray, with one toppled on its side, contents strewn across the road. People were cowering behind the wagons, though she couldn't see how many, and twelve people stood in between the wagons and the monsters.

Aspen and Motte pulled up beside her.

"Rouge!" Motte growled, "How many times have I told you…" He trailed off, staring. Even as they watched, the largest creature, standing at least ten feet tall, picked up one of the defenders by their arm and simply flung the warrior away. The body flew through the air, only to crunch against one of the wagons and fall limply to the ground, twisted unnaturally.

Aspen drew in a breath. In Party chat, he said, ::They look a little like Trolls, but not entirely. If they are related to Trolls, they'll be weak against fire and light. Do you have any glowstones left?::

Motte grunted in affirmation. Glowstones were a fairly common low-level quest reward, so both he and Rouge had so many that they tended to overflow their allocated stack of 99 and get sold, though they weren't worth much.

Aspen nodded. ::Any kind of fire-based weapon?::

::I could light a pinecone on fire and throw it at them, I suppose, but I doubt it would do much good,:: was Motte's response.

Aspen rolled his eyes. ::I'll take that as a 'no'.::

Motte chuckled ruefully. ::Sorry, I forget that you N… natives take combat more seriously than we Travelers do. No, I don't have anything that's meant to be a fire weapon. I don't use elemental attacks much, since I have an increased chance of failing to use magical items due to my Class. I get a nice magic resistance boost, though, so it works out.::

As they spoke, the middle-sized Trollish thing grabbed at another of the caravan's defenders. This one managed to dodge, but it was clear that the monster's much longer reach would win eventually. Meanwhile, nothing that the warriors did seemed to have much effect. Thick reddish-black blood dripped from a few small wounds, but the creatures seemed to take no notice.

Aspen looked at Rouge. ::Any fire weapons? Spells? Anything?::

She shook her head, mute for once, fingers clenching and releasing the hilt of her Mambele.

The farmer puffed out a breath. ::We don't have time for anything complex. We just have to hope they have the same weakness as the Trolls they seem to be. Get out your glowstones and light them. As many as you can. The light they produce is like weak sunlight, and enough of them can damage a monster with a weakness to light.::

He glanced at Motte. ::Motte, you help the defenders. Stand firm, and keep the monsters from breaking through. Rouge,:: with a look at the half-elf, ::do what you can. They'll cling to the shadows, so you should be able to get a good [Backstab] on at least one. I'll attack with my scythe, and hope it can do as well here as it did against the Wyvern. Go!::

He matched action to words, racing across the hundred feet or so toward the beleaguered caravan. An instant later, Motte was racing after him, shield down and clearly readying a [Battering Ram]. That left Rouge, who glanced at Doom and clenched her teeth in frustration.

"Where *are* you?" she muttered, but said, "Oleander, stay here." The trigger phrase set off the other woman's Away Instructions, and Oleander stopped. Burrito, attached to Doom's saddle by a long lead, stopped as well. Doom's Zombie sat poised, ready to ride exactly one mile straight east from her starting point, unless a cliff or other natural object blocked her path.

Satisfied that her step-sister's avatar was as safe as she could make it, Rouge turned back to the battle.

Motte and Aspen had reached the fight, and Motte's [Battering Ram] had done some clear damage to the smallest of the monsters. Its leg was broken, with bone jutting out through the flesh. The monster fought on, regardless, acting as though it felt no pain, even as it dragged the injured limb behind it. Now Motte stood in front of one of the fallen defenders, preventing the creatures from finishing the person off, and attacking with his axe whenever he saw an opening.

Aspen, meanwhile, was not faring as well. He swung the scythe repeatedly, but it barely did any damage at all to the monster's thick hides. The farmer dodged easily, however, his dexterity belying his claims of advanced age, so he at least served as a diversion from the exhausted defenders. His scythe had a longer reach than the warrior's shorter swords and axes, too, so he could stay out of the pseudo-Troll's long grasp.

Rouge watched for a moment, eyes narrowed. She leaned forward and murmured into Codswallop's ear. The ostrich cocked his head to listen, letting out a disgruntled squawk, but bobbed his head in agreement. Rouge bared her teeth, leaping nimbly down. She raced with sure-footed silence toward the conflict, seeing that no one seemed to have noticed her yet. Excellent.

Entering the woods just off the road, she sank into the shadows. She couldn't run while using [Stealth] (yet), but she moved with a speed just shy of what would break her out of her skill. When she was close enough to risk detection from such high-level mobs (even if they were dumb as stumps, like the original Trolls), she triggered [Sneak] as well, boosting the effects of [Stealth] by another 24%, which should allow her to…

She jumped, placing one foot on the trunk of a tree to her right, pushing up as she did so. The next step was halfway up another tree, and the third step was higher still on a tall tree with few branches lower than twenty feet high. She pushed off, somersaulting in midair to give herself some additional momentum as she triggered [Backstab], stabbing down with her poisoned Mambele toward the unprotected back of the monster with the broken leg.

CRITICAL! You have dealt 207 points of damage to the *???*. The *???* is Poisoned. The *???* is Staggered.

::It's Staggered!:: she shouted in party chat, ::It can't move for ten seconds! Motte!:: Internally, she growled at herself for using [Repeat] earlier to beat Motte in a rock-skipping contest. It had seemed worth it at the time, since he now owed her a week of doing dishes, but now...

She clung tenaciously to the creature's back, stabbing and slicing at the thick neck, trying to sever the backbone, which would result in an instant kill. Heavy black blood poured like treacle over her hands, making her scrabble for purchase and drop the Mambele twice. Each time, she called it back to her hand so instantaneously that her blows never even paused.

You have dealt 91 points of damage to the *???*. The *???* is Poisoned.
You have dealt 54 points of damage to the *???*. The *???* is Poisoned.
You have dealt 86 points of damage to the *???*. The *???* is Poisoned.
You have dealt 7 points of damage to the *???*. The *???* is Poisoned.
You have dealt 73 points of damage to the *???*. The *???* is Poisoned.

Motte's voice in her mind snapped, ::Get off, Rouge!:: and she did so without hesitation. She and Motte had been fighting together for months, and when he used that voice, she knew better than to delay. Bending her knees and then snapping her legs taut, she released the creature, flipping backwards into the air. She didn't have time to look before she leapt, however, and she landed awkwardly, tumbling to the ground and scraping her hands. The Mambele landed nearby.

You have taken 15 points of falling damage.

Even as she staggered to her feet, pulling one of her precious Health potions from her bag and guzzling its passion fruit flavored goodness, Motte used [Roar], which had a chance of Staggering nearby enemies. If an enemy was already Staggered, however, it had an even better chance of making it Faint for up to 30 seconds. The lower the Intelligence of the mob, the better the chance. Her Health potion took effect as she waited.

A *Minor Health Potion* has restored 10 hp. You have 139 hp remaining.

An instant later, the creature staggered, then fell, shaking the ground. Rouge was on it in an instant, snatching the Mambele from the air and driving its vicious sickle-shaped blade up through the eye and into the brain. The monster twitched, then lay still.

You have dealt a Fatal Blow to *Demonic Troll*. You have defeated *Demonic Troll*.

::What the…? The system says this thing is a Demonic Troll! There are no demons in *Veritas*!:: Rouge was already diving for the tree-line. [Sneak] was still on cooldown, but [Stealth] had no cooldown for the Thief Class, so Rouge tried to melt back into the shadows.

Aspen's voice was tense. ::What is a demon?::

::I don't know, exactly.:: Rouge answered, even as she got a notification that she couldn't use [Stealth] because an enemy was focused on her. She dodged just as a huge fist crashed through the brush where she'd been standing. Obviously Big and Hideous wasn't thrilled that she'd taken out his buddy. ::Um, something with powers given them by a Dark God? Maybe? Either that or a fallen angel, but there aren't any angels either, so…::

::Never say never.:: Motte's tone was grim. ::Things are obviously changing.::

::One thing that isn't changing,:: Aspen grunted as he spun to dodge a blow from Middle Ugly, ::is that these creatures want us dead. Any ideas on how to prevent that? I have things to do that don't involve losing my head to a ten-foot mountain of foulness.::

Rouge dodged another blow, flipping backward twice. The biggest Demonic Troll lumbered after her, leaving the mid-sized one to attack Aspen and Motte. ::Well,:: she said, dancing around the uprooted tree the creature was now using as an improvised club, ::I have an idea. I just don't know if it'll work. I'm pretty sure you won't like it, though.::

Aspen was breathing harder now, starting to slow as he ducked and dodged his opponent. Every once in a while, one of the caravan guards (she assumed that was who they were) would try to get in a blow, but the mob just ignored them except to backhand one of them casually out of his way. The warrior flew backwards and crumpled, and after that the five defenders still on their feet stayed warily out of the way, though they remained between the monsters and the wagons.

Motte growled as he blocked another blow with his shield. ::No doubt. Do it anyway.::

::Okaaaaay,:: she sing-songed. ::Just don't say I didn't warn you! I mean that, too. You should probably get out of the way.::

Then she pushed her fingers into her mouth and blew a piercing whistle.

Codswallop ran toward her, chirruping loudly. As he ran by, she grabbed his dangling lead and vaulted into the little saddle on his back. Once there, she climbed to her feet, standing loose and ready. "Go, Wally!" she yelled.

Codswallop gathered himself and [Jumped] with all his strength, soaring high into the air, easily more than ten feet above the ground. Rouge then leapt, pushing herself further upward by using the ostrich as a launching pad. At the apex of her rise, she cast [Poof!]

The cloud billowed out around her, blocking the light completely. She triggered [Stealth], vanishing into the obscuring smoke. Then, down from the darkness came a rain of knives, as Rouge emptied her inventory of anything the slightest bit sharp. They were all shapes and sizes, ranging in quality and sharpness. What they all had in common, however, was the green glimmer of Dwarven Kombucha coating their blades.

Motte shouted something unintelligible and leapt for Aspen, knocking the other man to the ground. The tank raised his huge shield to cover them both. Just in time, because the deadly rain began to hit, and everything one of the blades touched began to hiss and smoke.

Both of the Demonic Trolls screamed in agony, showing pain for the first time. The blades weren't large. Compared to the size of the monsters, many of them seemed little more than sewing needles. Several bounced off harmlessly, falling to lie against grass and bushes that quickly shriveled and died. Enough, though, of the hundred or so weapons that Rouge had thrown as she fell back down through her now dissipating cloud of smoke, hit the creatures, dealing small but excruciating wounds. The damage was boosted because it had been dealt from [Stealth], so even the butter knives that were mixed into the onslaught took off at least a few hitpoints.

You have dealt 17 points of damage to the *Demonic Troll*. The *Demonic Troll* is Poisoned.

You have dealt 23 points of damage to the *Demonic Troll*. The *Demonic Troll* is Poisoned.

You have dealt 54 points of damage to the *Demonic Troll*. The *Demonic Troll* is Poisoned.

You have dealt 36 points of damage to the *Demonic Troll*. The *Demonic Troll* is Poisoned.

You have dealt 12 points of damage to the *Demonic Troll*. The *Demonic Troll* is Poisoned.

You have dealt 27 points of damage to the *Demonic Troll*. The *Demonic Troll* is Poisoned.

...

The notifications flowed through her vision like a waterfall, and she spun in the air, desperately trying to control her descent. The force she'd used to throw the knives had pushed her off balance, and now not only was she plummeting with terrifying speed, but she couldn't seem to get her feet under her. The ground grew larger, and she was forced to admit that she was probably going to respawn.

Then a black and white blur crashed into her from below, thrusting her back up slightly before she began falling again. But this time, the fall was slower, more controlled, and she was lying on something fluffy.

Your mount Codswallop has taken damage. If he is damaged again, he will die and respawn at your last save point.

Rouge gasped, throwing her arms around her brave bird. "Oh, Wally," she buried her face in his warm, dusty feathers, "you shouldn't have. Please, let me down and run away! I told you to run as soon as I jumped!"

The ostrich lifted his chin and bugled a challenge, racing back toward the battle. Rouge hit him, gently, with her fist, then just clung on, determined to make the risk he was taking worthwhile. She raised her head, staring at the result of her attack.

The largest Demonic Troll was still up, though he swayed drunkenly, swinging his tree-club with wild abandon. The medium sized one was down, though, frothing at the mouth and twitching. The remaining five caravan guards were taking advantage of his position to hack at him, finally able to reach his more vulnerable head and joints. She could see that they would soon be able to finish him.

Motte and Aspen were up as well, though Motte's shield was smoking in a few places where it had been struck by the poisoned knives. Motte was covering Aspen as the farmer distracted the last Demonic Troll, preventing him from going to the fallen Troll's aid.

You have assisted in slaying the *Demonic Troll*.

"Yes!" she yelled, pumping her fist in the air.

::One left,:: Aspen said tiredly, and then he stumbled.

Motte desperately tried to get his shield in place to block the tree trunk, but he was off balance, and the shield only took part of the blow. The club skidded off Motte's shield, clipping Aspen's shoulder and spinning him around. Rouge could hear the sickening crack as the man's arm broke, and then he was down.

Rouge shrieked, "*ASPEN!*", and Codswallop gave a powerful push with his hind legs, once again [Jumping] far beyond the limits of any normal ostrich. He landed with his large two-toed feet firmly in the middle of the Demonic Troll's broad back, and then he jumped again.

A mount couldn't fight. It couldn't deal damage, unless a God interceded as Gina once had. There was no heavenly assistance this time, but the force of the bird's weight pushing off of the mob made him stagger, missing the blow that would have crushed Aspen's head.

Rouge jumped off Codswallop's back once more, adrenaline burning through her own exhaustion, and plunged her Mambele into the Demonic Troll's cheek. She pulled the weapon hard, slicing open his face, and then, when he opened his mouth to roar his rage at her, she thrust her arm down his throat, summoning every glowstone she had in her inventory into her hand, and commanding them to ignite.

They did, and the monster stopped in his tracks. His eyes opened as wide as his mouth, and then they vanished into ash as light burst from inside his skull. Beams of it shot out of his mouth, his eyes, his ears, even his disgusting, much-too-close-to-her-face nostrils. His skin shivered, expanded, then split, creating ravines of brilliant radiation in his flesh. Finally, he simply crumbled to ash, collapsing inward like a rotting jack-o-lantern, dropping Rouge to her feet.

Notifications flooded Rouge's vision.

You have dealt a Fatal Blow to *Demonic Troll*. You have defeated *Demonic Troll*.

You are now level 34.

You are now level 35.

You are now level 36.

...

You are now level 42.

You have gained two levels in [Thrown Weapons Mastery]. You are now level 18.

You have learned a new passive skill [Poison Mastery].

You have gained a level in [Poison Mastery]. You are now level 2.

You have learned a new passive skill [Ostrich Riding]. You may now use your Ostrich mount in battle, though it cannot deal damage.

You have gained nine levels in [Ostrich Riding]. You are now level 10.

Your battle mount [Codswallop] now has three Damage Points available before he will respawn.

You have gained three skill levels in [Acrobatics]. You are now level 19.

You have gained a new level in [Poof!]. You are now level 13.

You have gained a level in [Stealth]. You are now level 19.

You have gained a level in [Sneak]. You are now level 14.

You have gained a level in Thief Class. You are now level 23.

For slaying the first Demonic creature in *Veritas*, you have gained the Title "Exorcist". You now deal 10% more damage to Demonic creatures.

You have created a new spell! [Poison Rain] is added to your spell list.

[Poison Rain] will create a cloud up to five feet in diameter, which will release twenty-five poisoned projectiles per second for three seconds. Every five levels you may choose to increase the diameter, the number of projectiles, or the duration of the spell. This spell costs 60 mana and has a cooldown of ten minutes.

For creating a new spell, you have earned a permanent increase of +20 to your mana pool.

Quest "Show a Caravan You Care" complete.

You rescued: 16/20 people and 7/8 wagons.

Reward: +1800 Experience, 100 Gold, +20 Relationship with the surviving members of the caravan.

Rouge sat down on her butt abruptly, staring at the notifications. She was pretty sure that if Silus had needed a nice place to sleep, her gaping mouth would have been an excellent candidate. Finally, she finished reading them over and shook her head. "Oh. Em. Gee."

A soft tenor voice spoke from in front of her. "Excuse me, Lady. Are you injured?" A slim, tanned hand reached down, offering her assistance to stand.

She blinked, clearing the notifications that she was reading for the third time, and saw a pair of weather-worn leather boots on the ground in front of her. Fortunately, the rest of the body was attached, so she didn't have to freak out. Looking further, she saw that the hand belonged to a young NPC who looked to be not much older than her. His slim figure was clothed in brown leathers, and a long dagger was in a sheath at his side. He wore his thick, wavy brown hair in a long ponytail, low on his neck, exposing pointed ears.

Her eyes shot to his soft gray ones, and he blinked, giving her a slightly concerned smile. "Can I help you stand, lady? If you are injured, I will bring you to our healer."

Rouge shook her head, speechless. Then she coughed awkwardly. Twice. "No. Um, no, I'm fine." She set her fingers in his palm and let him pull her to her feet. He continued to hold her hand, looking at her wonderingly, until she finally snatched her hand from his, feeling a hot flush rise up in her cheeks for some reason. She used her sleeve to scrub at her face, feeling self-conscious. "What? Am I gross?"

A matching flush rose in his cheeks, tingeing his ears rose-gold. "No. I'm sorry. It's just that I've never met a Traveler who is a wood elf before. Many humans, some dwarves, and a high elf. But-"

Rouge's eyes widened at the reminder, and she spun around, looking for Doom Bloom and Oleander. She was completely disoriented, so it took a few terrifying seconds to realize that they'd come from the opposite direction from where she was looking, and she spun again.

She looked at the handsome elf boy and smiled apologetically. "I'm super sorry, but I have to go. I'll be right back, though!" Internally cursing as she realized she'd just rhymed *and* sounded like an idiot, she ran down the road, crossing near the caravan, where people were already putting things to rights, and a tall man was leaning over, tending to the injured. He started to speak as she ran past.

"Sorry! Be right back!" she shouted, and then she was past, and heading down the road. It didn't take long to reach Doom's side, and she set her hand on Oleander's reins. "Oleander, follow."

The horse immediately whuffed and bobbed his head, almost as if he were nodding. She heaved a relieved sigh. She didn't know what had happened to her sister in real life, but at least she had made sure she was safe here. She turned back to the caravan, dropping the reins. She knew Oleander and Burrito would follow without her pulling the horse, and it felt rude to tug on him anyway.

Quickly, she jogged back to the battle site, staring around at the destruction. The three mob corpses laid on the ground, more than a little gruesome. Big and Ugly was actually the least gross, since he was mostly a pile of greasy ash and a rotting fur that used to be a loincloth. She grimaced, but moved on.

Codswallop was standing nearby. The bird was fluffed the way he did when he was worried and wanted to look big, but he didn't seem frightened. He turned a big eye on her and chortled questioningly. She sighed in relief and went over to him. He bowed his head down so that the top of his head was pressed to her midsection, and she rubbed his head, murmuring reassurances.

Rouge pulled up his status.

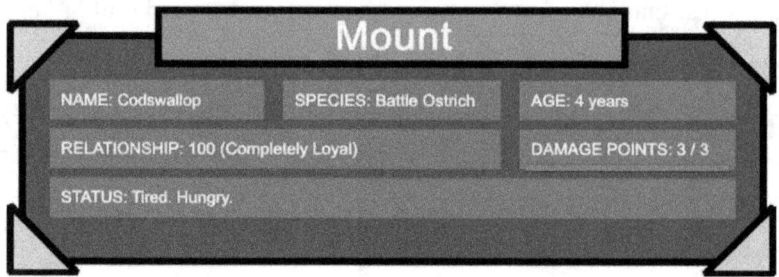

Holy cow. It was true. Codswallop wasn't just a regular mount anymore. Instead, like mounts belonging to Knights, Cavaliers, Cavalry, Cowboys (what was with the 'c' names?), and other classes who used their mounts as more than just transportation, the ostrich was now a Battle Mount. He had his own Damage Points beyond the two that regular mounts got, and presumably those would increase as her [Ostrich Riding] skill increased.

Once again for the people in the back.

Holy. Cow.

Rouge pulled an Aspen Carrot from her inventory and fed it to her Battle Ostrich, and then turned to look again. She noticed that the wood elf boy had followed her, and now hovered nearby, but she just gave him a little smile of acknowledgement and looked for... there!

Keeping her hand on Codswallop's neck, she crossed the twenty feet or so that separated her from Motte and Aspen. Motte looked tired but good. He had his helmet off and his axe away, so he wasn't worried about being attacked again. Aspen, on the other hand. She grimaced.

Aspen was definitely the worse for wear. His left arm was now supported by an improvised sling, and his face was pale. He held his right hand over the place where the left bulged oddly, and she felt her bile rise. Arms were *not* meant to bend that way.

As she came closer, both men looked at her and smiled. Motte's was worried and proud in equal amounts, but Aspen's faltered and failed before it could reach his eyes. He shook his head and looked at Motte, obviously continuing a conversation they'd started before she walked up.

The lanky farmer's voice was tight and low. "I'll need it straightened. I can't heal it any more until it's in place. If it worked at all, I'd probably have a bent arm until we rebroke it and tried again anyway. Can you do it?"

Motte frowned. "I can try, but-"

The wood elf broke in, voice hopeful. "I'm sorry, lords and lady. I don't mean to interrupt, but... Restur, our healer and leader, would like to speak with you, to thank you and see if he can help you with any injuries."

Motte looked relieved. "That would be a great help, actually. I don't think I'm ready to jump straight from breaking bones to setting them." He looked at Rouge. "Are you all right? That was amazing, what I saw of it when I wasn't keeping our friend here from getting himself killed."

Aspen's sickly pale face flushed, but not in a healthy way. "I'm sorry," he muttered, "I thought I had the fighting thing figured out. I don't know why it worked against the Wyvern, but not against these Trolls."

"*Demonic* Trolls," Rouge pointed out. "Maybe they have high defense against divine magic? That's what you have, right?"

The farmer's expression would have been hilarious if he hadn't been in so much pain. "I... have no idea," he admitted. "It seems likely that my magic is something... elemental? Divine seems as likely as anything else. Would your world's demons be strong against divine magic?"

She shook her head. "Our demons are, um-"

"Hypothetical," Motte said pragmatically. "Angels and demons alike are more the creations of our own minds and spirits than anything physical. And no, they'd be more likely to take more damage from a Divine attack than a normal one. But, all of that aside," he gently took Aspen's good elbow and began steering the other man toward the wagons, "you are going to the healer. Right now."

Rouge grinned. She always loved it when Motte turned his mother hen tendencies on other people. It meant that he was much less likely to cluck over *her* for a little while. She was still smiling as the trio followed the young wood elf, with Codswallop, Oleander, and Burrito trailing along behind them.

The healer was just finishing with the worst of the wounded when they arrived. He pressed a hand over the limp one belonging to a young woman in tattered chainmail who laid still on the ground. Her chest rose and fell evenly, but her eyes were closed, and the healer nodded to another girl nearby who laid a blanket gently over the unconscious guard.

Motte stopped in front of the old man, half supporting Aspen, who looked even paler after the short walk, if that was possible. The healer was a spindly man with a disconcertingly luxurious mass of full-bodied white hair. Surprisingly sharp blue eyes examined them, and then the man reached out to gently touch Aspen's arm.

"This will need setting. I can heal it, but it must be straight first, or it will heal crooked." His voice was rice and strong, belying his apparent age.

Motte nodded. "That's what we thought. Is there anything I can do to help?"

The blue eyes examined him. "Hmph. Hold him still. This will hurt."

Motte immediately gripped Aspen's shoulders, and the old man grabbed the arm. He pulled it straight with a crunch, and Aspen screamed. Then his topaz eyes rolled up in his head and he fainted. Motte caught him and lowered him gently to the ground. The healer supported the arm as the farmer went down, keeping it from going back out of alignment.

"Good," the man murmured, tracing the arm with his hand, "We got it. It broke across both bones, but didn't shatter. Too bad we don't have a priest, or we wouldn't have had to do that." His knobby hands began to glow softly, and he closed his eyes.

Rouge stared. When a Player used a healing potion, or got healed at a temple or by another person playing a support Class, injuries just instantly closed and fixed themselves. She'd seen Aspen heal before, too, so she knew his regen worked like a player's. So what was going on?

Motte saw her look. ::Debuff,:: he sent. ::It can't heal until the Broken Bone debuff is cleared. The healer can restore hit points, but not repair the 'injury' itself. I've seen this before, during the war.::

She nodded, and, even as she watched, color was returning to Aspen's face. The man groaned, and blinked open his eyes. He looked disoriented for a moment, and then his gaze focused on Motte's concerned face and he mustered a reassuring smile. "Well, I've had better days. How about you?"

Motte growled. "You're an idiot. Once you realized your attacks weren't working, you should have backed off and let me handle it."

Aspen sat up, carefully avoiding putting weight on his left arm. "I know. I just couldn't leave you there on your own. Two against two was better odds than two against one. I could at least provide a distraction." He looked over at Rouge and quirked a wry grin. "I'm glad one of us knew what to do."

She laughed a little in relief. "I was totally winging it. I mean, totally. Literally." She looked over at Codswallop and smiled affectionately. "I just knew Motte and I would respawn, but you wouldn't, so I had to do whatever it took, even if I died doing it." She shrugged. "Not a big deal when you know you'll be back in a few hours. But anyway, what was with the question marks? I've never seen anything like that before!"

Rouge looked back at Motte, who was watching Aspen with a very strange expression on his face. "Motte? Are you all right?"

Motte blinked a few times, and seemed to bring himself back to the present. "Yeah. Um, yes, I'm fine. Took some blows, but never got below fifty percent health. I don't know that I could have killed them myself, but I could tank one pretty easily. They hit hard, but they're slow, so my regen could just keep up. Uh, it is good that Aspen was there, though I wish he'd stayed further back. If

I'd had to tank both of them, I'd probably have gone down."

Rouge frowned a little. ::You okay?:: she sent.

Motte flicked his eyes to Aspen and then to her before giving the barest of nods. ::Yeah. I was just thinking about something. Sorry.::

Aspen looked between them, then smiled a little uncertainly before struggling to his feet. He brushed himself off, looking down at his battered clothes with weary resignation. "Good thing I brought a spare set of clothes. These are going to need to be burned, I think."

Rouge looked down at herself, noting that she was pretty well still covered in drying Demonic Troll blood. She grimaced. "Yeah. I'm going to have to take these to a Tailor for Cleansing, I think. I am *gross*, and my backup gear sucks."

The woman who had been assisting the healer looked up. "Perhaps I can help, my lady? I'm Tia. I'm Restur's assistant," she nodded to the old healer, "but I'm also a Journeyman Tailor. I can fix those up for you."

Grinning, Rouge nodded. "That would be amazing. I spent pretty much everything I had on these not long before we left Bright, and I haven't exactly made my fortune since then. Um, how much will it cost, though?"

Tia shook her head. "Nothing, for the heroes who saved us. We were all dead if you hadn't come, and my son is with us. His first trip, and this happens." She shut her eyes for a moment, then opened them again. "Thank Gina you were here, and able to help. I began praying as soon as I saw those creatures. I knew there was no way we could win."

Aspen shook his head. "Well, that explains a lot."

The woman looked at him curiously. "What do you mean?"

Aspen flushed, then reached up to tug down his hat. Finding that it was absent without leave, he ducked his head instead. When he spoke again, it was with the rustic accent he used when speaking to Doom Bloom. "Nothing, ma'am. Just that Gina is my Goddess as well. She must've sent us here for you."

Tia pressed her hands together on her chest, bowing her head in prayer. "Thank you, Gina. I will make certain I tithe well after this trip."

Rouge suppressed a snort, wondering what it was like for Bridget, pretending to be a Goddess. Emily/Emilieu undoubtedly did most of the heavy lifting, and being a developer in the game was probably pretty much like being a God anyway. Did she, like, listen to prayers and stuff, though? Did she have a spreadsheet? One column of people who asked for money, one column for people who asked for health, one column of people who asked for someone they liked to like them back.

Just then, an unexpected voice came from behind her. "Well," Doom said, and Rouge heard her booted feet thump to the ground, "I always miss the good stuff."

::Me too,:: came Silus' little voice, as she poked her head out from Burrito's pack, where she had been sleeping.

Chapter Twelve

Aspen

Aspen groaned inwardly as he looked around at the ring of tired but interested faces. The caravan had been set to rights as best it could be, and the surviving members healed. Fortunately, Aspen hadn't had to make the difficult choice of whether or not to reveal that he was more than the simple farmer he appeared by healing the wounded, since Restur had been able to care for everyone who hadn't died outright. He was certain that his extremely lackluster performance in the fight at least lent credence to his claim of being a simple man who had asked the three Travelers to escort him to the city.

Now, though, it was just Aspen, Doom, and Silus (who had returned to her rest after being assured she would get the full story later), since Rouge and Motte had had to return to their own world to get some sleep. They were both exhausted, and the rush brought on by Rouge's amazing rewards after the battle had quickly worn off until the child was nearly swaying on her feet. The two Traveler's Zombies now waited a steady fifteen feet away, while Codswallop and Burrito foraged nearby.

The caravanners were enamored of their rescuers. The young wood elf, who had introduced himself as Vonn, kept a close watch on Rouge's Zombie, clearly fascinated. Aspen, in turn, kept a surreptitious eye on the boy from under his hat, which was now restored to, if not its former glory, at least its rightful place on his head.

With the primary agents of their salvation now more or less absent, the focus was on Aspen. Doom, as usual, was taciturn at best, and kept looking down the road as if she was in a hurry to be away. Aspen could relate.

He smiled and raised his hands as yet another person attempted to press a food item upon him. "No, thankee, ma'am. I'm full enough as 'tis." He glanced at Doom, who stood with arms crossed and lips pressed tightly together. "We need to continue on to our destination, truly."

Restur, who had been bandaging the last and most minor of the injuries sustained by the caravanners, looked over at that. "Where are you going, then? You're on the road to Bloodhaven, so may I take it that that is your goal?"

Aspen glanced at Doom, who glared at him, flicking her eyes at the road in a clear message that he should shake them off so they could go. He sighed. "Aye, Bloodhaven is our goal, and we must-"

The old man looked back and forth between the Traveler and the farmer, and frowned a little. Then he looked over at the six canvas-wrapped bundles laid carefully side by side on the red bricks of the road. "I'd like to offer you and your companions a proposition. We lost six of our own today. Four guards, a cook, and our hostler. Without the guards, this road is a perilous one, and without the hostler, we have no one with enough knowledge to properly care for the animals."

Restur looked over Aspen's well-worn clothes and disreputable hat, as well as the scythe that served as his weapon. "Do you, perhaps, have experience caring for animals? Would you be willing to be our hostler for the remaining three days of our journey, while your friends work as guards? I would be willing to give you the same share of the profits that those who have been with us since we began have earned, since these last days are by far the most dangerous on our journey, especially if there are more of those monstrous creatures about."

Quest: "Hostler Hustle" begun.

Restur needs guards and someone to care for his animals. You happen to have some big, tough friends, and animals really like you these days. Seems mutually beneficial.

Success: Improved relationship with all members of the caravan. Significantly improved relationship with Restur. Entry into Bloodhaven.

Failure: More deaths on your conscience, and much reduced odds of entering Bloodhaven undetected.

Restur looked from Doom to Rouge, and back to Aspen again. "I do not mean to insult you, but we have heard disquieting rumors that non-humans are rather less welcome in the human cities than they were even a short while ago. The best place for such is likely within a group of well-intentioned men who have good reason to be traveling abroad at this time. It may be that we can offer you some protection at the end of our journey to balance the assistance you give us now."

Doom's face had gone blank as the old man spoke, but Aspen knew her well enough by now to see the calculations going on behind her ice-blue eyes. She stepped forward and spoke for the first time since she'd arrived and refused to explain why she'd been so much later than expected. "Give us a moment, please." She stepped away, gesturing for Aspen to follow her.

Once they were out of earshot, Doom gestured back at the caravanner. "What do you think? Can we trust him?"

Aspen's eyebrows shot up, and then he ducked his head to hide the expression. "I don't know. I just do what Rouge and Motte tell me. They keep me safe."

The girl snorted. "I'm not stupid. I don't know what's going on here, exactly, and I don't care. As long as Rouge is safe from those jerk PKers, you lot can do whatever crazy quest line you're following. What I do know is that Rouge and Motte both listen to you when you talk. They care what your opinion is. So what do you want to do?"

The tall man sighed and tugged at the brim of his hat. "I need to get to Bloodhaven. Faster is better, but safest is best. If they can get us there in three days, well, it's only a half day longer than we would take traveling the back roads alone, and there is safety in numbers. Plus, I just received a quest that says if we don't go with them, we'll likely be caught when we attempt to enter Bloodhaven. That seems like a pretty clear indication that we need them." He looked over his shoulder at the group of people who were watching them talk with no pretense of disinterest. Then he looked at Rouge's Zombie, where it sat silent and staring on Codswallop's back. "Plus, Rouge would want us to protect them."

Doom just shook her head and muttered, "Whatever you are, it's not a standard NPC." She drew in a breath. "Fine. We'll stay with them. It's for the best, I guess, since I'll probably need to go before Rouge and Motte get back, which would leave you alone for a while. This way, at least you have some cannon fodder before the monsters eat you."

She turned and started to walk back to the group, tossing one last comment over her shoulder. "Plus, I got a nice quest to stay with them when that old guy started talking. Rouge and Motte will probably have it too, when they log back on."

Aspen ground his teeth and followed.

ॐ ॐ ॐ

Doom stayed with the caravan for about six hours, which was long enough to be attacked by a pack of Lesser Wolves. A few Wolves wasn't terribly concerning, but twenty of them could do some damage, especially if they got through the line of defenders.

The half-elf, however, proved well worth her share of the caravan's profits. It was the first time Aspen saw her fight without Rouge and Motte, and it was a revelation. The woman was whirling silver death with her slim blade, and killed at least half of the Wolves without assistance. The remaining guards took out eight more Wolves, and the last two demoralized canids turned tail and ran.

Aspen, of course, stayed with the horses, and made sure they didn't panic and run. He was amazed to find that he could now calm them simply by reaching out with his mind and reassuring them that they had nothing to fear. He couldn't communicate with the beasts directly, of course, but there was a definite link between him and any living creature nearby.

Afterwards, the fourteen remaining members of the caravan crowded around the half-elf girl, thanking her and pressing food and water into her hands. Meanwhile, Aspen, who was brushing the foam off the horses as they calmed, discovered something about himself.

He didn't mind not being the hero.

Once upon a time, in the tiny hamlet of Jumping Hollow, a fourteen-year-old boy named Iorgas walked into the little temple that served as a place of worship for all the Gods. That boy knelt down and told the Gods, *all of them*, that he wanted to be a hero.

He wanted fame, and adulation, and money. Only one God answered him, and he was truly lucky that it wasn't one far worse than Atae, who might be dark, but treated every being ever born in the exact same way. Because everyone and everything eventually came to her in the exact same way.

Atae was Goddess of more than just death and the Chaos Pool, though few people remembered that. She was mistress of transitions, of the times when one thing became another. As such, she told him she could make him a hero, but he would have to give up everything he had and be reborn as something different. He accepted in a heartbeat, and she broke his life upon her knee.

Now, watching the grateful caravanners, Aspen only wished that he was home. A home far from the large fenced estate where he had lived with Birdie. Away from the place where everyone knew his name and face, and feared him as much or more than they respected him.

He wished that he was watching the fresh green leaves of the crops press up through the sun-warmed earth. That Sumi was haranguing him about his personal hygiene while Sarave chased a mischievous green-skinned toddler and two small unicorns through fields of wildflowers. He wished he could work hard all day, then sit and eat dinner with his family, laughing at Silus' antics and Khor's curmudgeonly statements. He wished that the world didn't need heroes.

So, when Tia came to him shortly after they set out again, and thanked him for caring for the horses, he just smiled.

An hour later, Doom dropped back from the head of the column, walking her horse at his side.

"I have to go," she said abruptly.

He nodded. He had assumed as much when he saw her change direction.

"Don't you want to know why?"

He slanted a look at her, saw the way she was biting her lip and staring at Rouge's Zombie.

"Nope," he said.

"My mother called," she told him, her eyes fixed on Oleander's soft white ears.

"I see." He tried to keep any hint of concern or interest out of his voice, and thought he succeeded fairly well.

"She wants me to come for dinner tomorrow. I told her I have class tomorrow and the day after. I'm not going to travel that far and then do it again an hour later." Her gloved fingers were tight on the reins, and her horse tossed his head against the pull.

He nodded.

"She told me she needed to talk to me, and if I'd needed to talk to her, she'd have made the trip. Which she wouldn't."

Silence.

"I have two papers due by the end of the week. I'm going to finish them tonight, and turn them in early. Then I'll go to dinner tomorrow, and I can skip classes Friday if I have to. Someone will share their notes with me." She loosened her grip and patted Oleander on the neck, then stroked his mane absently. "I'll be back tomorrow about this time. If Rouge asks. Though she probably won't, because I blew her off earlier."

Aspen looked up at the slim figure on the white horse, pulling his hat brim down to shade his eyes. "She'll ask," he told her.

She smiled, just a little, and nodded. Then she dropped further back, and a moment later, her Zombie had joined the other two.

He was alone.

Almost alone.

<Wow,> Silus chirped. <I think she likes you.>

He covered his eyes with his hand and shook his head, promptly tripping over a rock in the road. He uncovered his eyes. He really needed to remember to look forward.

🦇 🦇 🦇

After having spent months around the Travelers, Aspen felt... strange, being with his own people again. There were no conversations about alternate worlds, no light-hearted teasing about being injured or killed, no deep discussions of history or family life.

In fact, the caravanners were, to put it simply, *dull*. They ate, they traveled, they ate, they traveled, they ate, they circled the wagons and set sentries, and then they slept. The cook talked about cooking. The wagon drivers drove the wagons. The guards talked about whose turn it was to take the middle shift overnight, and how best to care for their armor and weapons.

Restur, Tia, and Vonn were the only exceptions. Tia and Vonn both checked in with Aspen. Tia wanted to make sure Aspen was fully recovered from his injury, and Vonn wanted to know when Rouge would return, but at least it was something.

Restur was busy keeping everyone in line and on task, but he found time to stop by and check in on Aspen. His main concern was really when the Travelers would return, but he was friendly, and shared some news of the road. It turned out that the caravan was working a new trade route between Quarternell and the Wood Elves to the west, so they had no definite news of Bright either.

By now, Aspen was well aware that time passed differently in the world where Rouge and Motte made their home. He was able to tell his visitors that it would be at least sixteen hours before the others came back, and likely longer. None of his visitors cared for that answer, and all left quickly after hearing it.

<They're kind of cranky, aren't they?> Silus inquired as they walked down the seemingly interminable red brick road the morning after Doom left.

Aspen grinned wryly, and murmured quietly to the little bat, who was snuggled against his jaw, hidden by the collar of his shirt. "They have reason to be, do they not? Our friends promised to help guard the caravan, and yet no guarding is occurring. You and I know that Motte and Rouge were too exhausted to continue, and Doom had responsibilities as well. Nonetheless, they are gone, and only I, who could barely scratch their enemies, am here. However much they need a hostler, which need I find myself questioning, for this final leg of the journey, I doubt they would have offered their protection to me alone."

Silus sighed. The fluff of her tiny body rubbed his neck, and he smiled. <They just don't know you as well as we do.> Her voice was reassuring, as if she thought he might be concerned by the caravanners' clear condescension.

"It's all right, little one. Our goal, after all, is to blend in. If I had single-handedly destroyed our opponents, I would also have destroyed any chance we had at maintaining my anonymity."

Silus paused. <A-non-i-mouse-?>

"Anonymity," he chuckled. "It means that I'm no one important.

Uninteresting, and unremarkable. Which is exactly what we want. My former self had rather too many enemies that my current self would be unable to handle. If I had any interest in doing so, which I emphatically do not."

The bat blew a raspberry. He hadn't even known she could do that. Then she squeaked.

"What?"

<…I bit my tongue.>

He tightened his lips against the laughter welling up inside him. "I'm sorry. Where did you learn to do that?"

<Rouge and Juniper do it. It looked fun.>

He allowed a small smile to escape, and tugged his hat down to cover it. "You should show Rouge, when she returns. It was very impressive."

The bat perked up. <I will!> Then her head popped up over his collar, and her big eyes began scanning their surroundings.

He sobered. "What is it?"

<Something… I think you should get your weapon.>

He threw a dubious glance at the scythe, where it was strapped to the horse walking beside him. Its success rate so far was unimpressive, but, he supposed, better than nothing. Probably *not* better than the staff he'd used to make it, however, especially given how unwieldy it actually was as a weapon.

Silus climbed the rest of the way out of his shirt, then winged over to the horse, burrowing under the flap of the saddlebag.

<Be ready,> she said.

He got his scythe.

This time, it was bandits. They stood just around a bend, dense trees concealing them until it was too late to run. There were four of them visible, and likely more in the trees to the side of the road. They stood in the path, weapons out, sneers on their dirty faces. Their leader, a woman so tall and broad she could likely have stood her ground against the smallest Demonic Troll, waved a crossbow at the lead wagon.

"Gi'ee yer gulled, y'shillins," she shouted, and Aspen blinked. He honestly had no idea what she had just demanded.

Restur rode forward, and the crossbow bolt locked onto him, sharp and menacing. "Good day, lady," he said, his thick white hair gleaming in the sun. "I'm afraid this has not been a good journey. We were attempting a new route, and profits are slim. Ten gold is the total of all the funds in our cashbox." His genial voice sounded as though he was genuinely sorry not to be able to offer more money to the thieves.

"G'an! Thur waggin's wuth mor'n tha! Gi'ee yer gulled, er I'll shut ye'n ask'ee next." The bow waved threateningly, and Restur's back tensed, though his voice remained calm.

"Alas, madam, only I can open the cash box. 'Tis spelled, to ward against theft. Come, and I'll show it to you, and you shall see that there are only ten gold inside. Take it, and let us pass, I pray you." Restur motioned to the lead wagon.

Aspen had wondered why one of the guards was driving that one, with his armor concealed beneath a smothering wool cloak, and he supposed this was the answer. The guard would attempt to capture or kill the bandit when she went to see this mythical strongbox, and hope the others would give up upon losing their leader.

However, the big woman was having none of it. "Bring't 'ere, y'shillins. 'En m'men'll go troo yon waggins, 'n mak'it wuth'ile." Her eyes were narrowed, and Aspen could see that she had made up her mind.

Quickly, he tried to figure out what he could do. No doubt he could fight these mere human threats, and acquit himself well. He had been practicing with Motte and Rouge for months, and if he could hold his own against them, these bandits wouldn't fare well.

Unfortunately, that presented him with two conundrums. First, it would draw far too much attention to him. While the caravanners had dismissed him as a mere peasant before, there was no way they would continue to do so if he slew half a bandit clan. Second, and more important, there were too many innocents remaining in the wagons. If, as he suspected, there were more bandits in the trees, then the wagons would be full of arrows before the six visible brigands were down. Even if he could keep the six occupied, the noncombatants would die.

So, he needed to think, as Rouge would say, 'outside the box'. Dismissing the continuing back and forth between Restur and the thief from his mind, he closed his eyes, casting out with his mana.

When he had been Iorgas Penbrooke, the King's Necromancer, he had been able to sense death and the undead without even trying. More than once, he had foiled an attempted ambush because he could feel the Lich King's macabre forces lurking nearby.

That sixth sense was gone, and, honestly, it wasn't one he missed. No sane person who had ever felt the chill of the grave envelop their soul would crave the return of the sensation. Recently, however, he had felt something else. Something so utterly opposite to that frigid turbulence that it had taken him weeks to acknowledge what it was, much less put a name to it.

Life.

At first, it was only around the crops. When he prayed, and cast his magic over them, he felt a hint of warmth, a connection, almost as though the tiny spirits of the plants were a brush of sunlight on his soul. Then, he started to sense when one of his friends, or the other beings who had come to live on the farm, were nearby. It was so slight that it had taken William's arrival to make him realize what it was.

Because he *couldn't* feel William. Aspen was certain that his Necromancer sense would instantly have known the aged fructipire was present, but his new sense couldn't tell the difference between the vamp and a chunk of rock. This difference, the absence of that barely-there awareness of the presence of other creatures when William was around, was what had finally convinced him that he wasn't just imagining things.

Aspen had, very quietly, been practicing this new sense. So far, it seemed entertaining but relatively useless. The range was short, no more than thirty feet or so, and he had to stop whatever else he was doing in order to focus on it enough for it to be more than a nebulous feeling of comfortable warmth that increased when he was near something living and growing.

Recently, he had found that he could identify the sources of the life force. Motte, Rouge, Codswallop, Burrito, Silus, and even Doom and Oleander, all had their own *something* that made them unique. Rouge, who enjoyed sneaking up on people and attempting to surprise them entirely too much (though she claimed she was trying to level her [Stealth] and [Sneak] skills), hadn't actually surprised him in over a week. Then there were the horses, and his discovery that he could not only sense them, but actually affect them, as well.

Given all that he had learned, he thought he might be able to... Yes! A flicker, then a flame, then five more bursts of life force revealed themselves in his mind's eye. Two were on the ground, low and flat, one on each side of the road, halfway down the caravan's column. The other four were in trees, their fires steady and focused. Snipers, waiting for the signal to begin firing on the hapless merchants.

Now, what to *do* with that information?

He focused on the bushes in which the two bandits on the ground were lying. They glimmered green in his soul sense, though they each had several snapped branches and broken leaves. The grass, likewise, was bruised and glimmered an unhappy yellow in his sight.

Aspen reached out, gently, and *touched* the plants. They flickered, then steadied, and he could feel a sort of stolid surprise from the bushes, and a more diffuse attention from the grass, as though thousands of organisms had all turned to look at him at once.

He breathed slowly in through his nose, and out through his mouth, almost shuddering under the creeping feeling.

Carefully, he pulled at his mana, feeling it empty from the reservoir in which it rested until he needed it. He had been a mage for over twenty-five years, after all, and though he had lost the magic he once knew, he hadn't lost his mastery of that magic.

He fed the mana into the bushes and grass. Forming an image in his mind of his need, he gave them the strength to achieve it. A moment later, the human life forces sank lower into the ground, then flared and went out. The grass had used its long, fibrous roots to pull them into the ground, filling their mouths before they could cry out, and the bushes had speared snapped branches into the ground, driving spikes into the soft eyes and through the brain beyond. Then, the flesh that once was men became nothing but fertilizer. The plants were satisfied with the bargain.

Aspen swallowed hard and reached out to the trees.

When he opened his eyes a moment later, the four bandits standing in the road were alone, though they didn't know it yet. The bandit leader was clearly out of patience. Restur had fetched a small wooden box from the wagon, and was pretending to be far more aged and infirm than he actually was. He kept attempting to lure the woman from her place, flanked by her men.

Aspen could tell that, dim as she seemed to be, she knew something was wrong. He also saw the moment when she decided she was done playing. Her body tightened, and her arm lifted, setting the crossbow in position to shoot the old man who stood no more than ten feet in front of her.

The guard who had been driving the lead wagon abandoned all pretense of being a simple teamster. He pulled a small round shield from where it was tucked down in the footwell of the wagon and launched himself toward Restur, who was only a few feet away, clutching the wooden box. The bowstring snapped, the bolt launched toward the old man, and then the rest of the guards were in motion, racing toward the threat, weapons bared.

The first bandit went down with an arrow in his throat, and the young wood elf, Vonn, was already nocking another arrow. The second found himself fighting two furious, trained guardsmen, and found that his usual technique of hacking and slashing didn't work as well against foes who were uninjured and not outnumbered. He went down with a gurgling cry, and did not rise.

The bandit leader threw her crossbow to the side and pulled a three-foot blade from a scabbard on her belt. She swung wildly, one, two, three, then realized that her foes weren't falling as she expected. She threw a wild look into the trees. "Farn!" she screamed, "Bettle! Gandup! C'min, y'shillins! Wake'p!" When only silence answered her, she growled, and, to her credit, stood firm against the two guards attacking her.

Then her last remaining man broke and ran, and the two guards who had finished the second brigand turned their attention to her. She roared, and her weapon, deadly simply because of its size and weight, even if she had little real skill in wielding it, crashed against the guard's armor and swords.

The battle was all but won, then, though it took another few minutes and some minor injuries to the guards before a man was able to get past her swings and manage to plunge his sword into the gap between her boiled leather cuirass and the multi-layered skirt of leather strips and metal studs that hung from her waist. She shrieked in protest, and went down on one knee. Another guard struck her head from her shoulders, and her body slowly toppled to the side.

A pale light, barely visible in the bright sun, enveloped Aspen as soon as combat ended. He had, after all, killed six men all by himself, and it would be surprising if he didn't gain a few levels. In fact, he could feel a cool flush touch his mind, and knew that his mana pool had increased, as well as his Intelligence, and likely Wisdom as well.

Aspen sighed, glancing around to see if anyone had noticed, but he was near the back of the caravan, and everyone's eyes were locked on the events unfolding in front of them in any case. He was safe, for now. He reached over and returned his scythe to its makeshift sling, then retrieved Silus from the pack.

She burrowed back into her hiding place, casting one last assessing glance toward the front of the caravan. <What did you do?> she squeaked.

He grinned, then murmured, "I worked smarter, not harder."

He would have to thank Rouge for that little saying, when next he saw her.

Chapter Thirteen

Rouge

When Zoey woke up, she wanted nothing more than to pull the blankets up over her head and go back to sleep. Unfortunately, it was Thursday, and there was no blanket big enough to hide her from her dad if she wasn't down for breakfast in – she glanced at her screen – fifteen minutes. She sighed, and rolled out of bed.

Fortunately, getting ready for work was easy at this point. Her skirts and three blouses were waiting to be washed, and the pickings were slim. She pulled on her most comfortable slacks, her favorite blue blouse (the one that looked like a button down, but was actually a pull-over, so she didn't have to worry about any of the buttons popping open), some simple silver earrings, and her comfy shoes. Comfy shoes were the *best*.

Finally, she reached up and tugged at her curls. She seriously needed some box braids or twists or something, because the messy bun was getting old. She sprayed her hair with a water spritzer, pulled it up, applied gel with careful fingers and a soft brush, and packed her curls in with a hairband. A few bobby pins and a little more gel later, and she was good to go! Flipping a thumbs-up at her mirror image, she grinned and raced down the stairs.

Her dad was already setting the table when she arrived, and he looked up, smiling tiredly. "Hey, kiddo. Did you get some good sleep?" Max woofed his own greeting from where he was happily eating a waffle from his bowl. His whole butt danced as he wagged his tail, but his face never wavered from the delicious breakfast bread, and she laughed at his antics.

She looked back at her dad and nodded. "Could have used another ten hours or so, I think, but I can do it!"

He grinned and plopped a waffle on her plate. "Ganbare!"

She laughed, sitting down and picking up her fork. "Ittadakimasu!"

They were both dorks.

ざ ざ ざ

Work was work. Usually, she was more entertained than annoyed by the ridiculous tasks she was asked to perform. Mr. Hamncheese the Hamster needed his cage cleaned. Okay. Granny wanted six laminated standees of garden gnomes, no more than eight inches tall, which must have beards and pointy hats. Whatever. Jazmin needed twenty matching memory sticks (which she'd learned actually held an encrypted key that would allow the user to log into a 'locked' room in *Veritas*, kind of like her study room, where execs would sometimes hold meetings with off-site personnel) delivered to twenty different people around campus. No problem.

In fact, that bit was fun, because she met Nina on the way to deliver the second one, and after that they did the deliveries together under the guise of Nina showing Zoey where some of the more esoteric locations were. Nina and Zoey were good friends by now, and often ate lunch together. The half-Kiwi girl had even watched *Kimi ni Todoke* after seeing Zoey's lunchbox, and agreed that Ryu was better than Shouta! Nonetheless, by the time lunch came, her energy was basically gone, and all she wanted was a nap. She met Nina at 'their' bench outside the cafeteria, and plopped down next to the older girl.

Nina grinned, pushing up the heavy glasses on her nose. They were black cateyes with large rhinestones at the outer corners today. Zoey had learned that Nina had dozens of glasses, in varying colors and styles. Also, they were just for looks, because the other girl had had her vision corrected when she was a kid, but she'd liked playing with glasses so much that she just kept buying more frames, like other people bought earrings or purses.

"You look knackered, Zoe. They working you that hard?" She offered Zoey a Pineapple Lump, a chewy candy Nina had a friend send her from New Zealand.

Zoey looked at it longingly, but waved it away as she sat. She splayed out her arms across the back of the bench, leaned her head back, and stared at the sky. "I'm too tired to even chew. If I eat sugar right now, the crash will probably put me to sleep."

Nina chuckled. "More for me, eh? You think Doc Shaman will go easy on you today?"

She thought back to when she found the pod with Bree Stephenson in it, and how... *weird* Dr. Joe had been about it. She chewed on her lip and shook her head. "It's okay. I can handle it." Of course, she couldn't tell Nina exactly what she was doing in Research and Development, but the other girl did know generally that Zoey was testing new products for them.

Nina kicked off her own comfy shoes and wiggled her toes gratefully. "I wish I could do some product testing. I love working here, but I could do with a little less running around. Though," she pushed at her glasses, brown eyes twinkling, "I do like knowing everyone's business."

Zoey smiled back, but weakly. "Nina..." She trailed off, knowing that she couldn't ask what she wanted to, and also knowing that she *had* to.

Nina arched delicate brown brows, almost hidden behind her heavy frames. "Eh?"

Chewing her lip, Zoey squinted up at the sky again. "Do you... know who Amy is? Someone Dr. Sherman would know." She didn't dare look at the Kiwi girl. She had a feeling there was some terrible secret there, and…

"Sure, 'course I do. Well, did. At least, I'm guessing you mean Amy Landon, Dr. Sherman's fiancée, and not Amy in Accounting or Amy in the cafeteria." Nina's voice was surprisingly calm, not at all furtive or shocked, as Zoey had more than half expected.

Zoey sat up straight, nearly knocking her lunchbox off her lap. "Yes! Tell me about her!"

Nina shrugged. "No secret, just kinda sad, eh? Bridget and Amy were best friends in college. They were egg-heads together, acing classes and graduating early. Then Bridget figured out VR while she was working on her doctorate, and Amy brought in Doc Shaman, who she was dating at the time, to help. Then Amy's brother, Harkness, met Bridget, and *they* got engaged. That was when Boss Landon decided to invest in VR, and brought Bridget and Doc Shaman on to add the system to *Veritas Online*, which was a game that used classic VR and was nearly ready for release.

"Fast forward a few years, and Bridget and Harkness broke up, which was *awkward*, and Dr. Sherman and Amy got engaged. Then, about eight months ago, Amy was in a really bad accident. She was out walking when someone did a hit and run, and left her for dead. She's alive, I think, but hurt bad. No one's seen her since the accident, though she's not in the hospital anymore. Broke up with Doc Shaman, too, or at least he isn't invited to high level meetings and such like he used to be."

It was Nina's turn to bite her lip. "Ah, maybe don't mention that last bit. I only know because I sometimes deliver the meeting keys, and he hasn't gotten one since Amy was in the accident."

Zoey's eyes were huge and locked on her friend's face. "So, Amy Landon and Boss Landon are-"

"Yeah, the big boss is Amy's dad. I hear he only invested in Bridget's VR because Amy and Harkness pitched it. *I* think it was the only way he could get Amy to work here. I heard she was planning to do research, but she and Bridget both started here at the same time. Amy was some kind of brain researcher, and worked in R&D with Doc Shaman."

Nina leaned forward and whispered conspiratorially, "Amy was her daddy's favorite, I think. The only time I ever saw him laugh was when they had lunch together sometimes. Harkness seems like a more boring copy of his dad, but Amy was really nice. I only started working here a few months before the accident, but she knew my name and would always say hi when she saw me."

Zoey blew out a breath, thinking back to the partial conversation she'd overheard between Bridget and Dr. Joe, and then the second pod in that dim room. Was it possible…? She shook her head. Nah. She'd been reading way too many 'trapped in a game' books lately.

"Wow," she said, "Just…. Wow."

Nina laughed a little and started gathering her leftovers and trash. "Why'd you ask about her, anyway? Someone mention something? I've been curious about what happened to her ever since they announced that she'd been sent to a private care facility, so everybody should stop trying to visit her at the hospital. Not a peep since then, and the boss always looks mad when I see him these days."

Zoey shook her head. "Dr. Joe mentioned her name once, but then acted like he slipped up. I was just curious who she was, to make him act like that." Her stomach growled, and she realized that she hadn't eaten anything since breakfast. She grabbed a granola bar out of her lunchbox and started unwrapping it, then remembered what else she'd meant to ask her friend.

"Oh, hey, Nina!"

Nina looked up from where she was putting her waste into the bin nearby. "What?"

"Um," Zoey hesitated. It was one thing to be friends with someone at work, and another to extend that friendship into her personal life. As with school friends, work friends could be left behind, but once someone edged into your real life, it was guaranteed to become awkward if anything happened between you. It was one of the reasons she found it so hard to make close friends.

"I'llbebackinBrightthisweekend,wanttoplaytogether?" She pushed out the words in a jumble, and then squinched her eyes shut, waiting for the response. After all, Nina was almost twenty-one. No way she wanted to hang out with a fourteen-year-old and her *dad* on the weekend.

Nina grinned. "Keen! I'd love to! I'm actually in Bloodhaven for the Murder Hobo Event, but I can go to Bright when it's over."

Zoey's eyes widened. "Seriously? We're actually headed for Bloodhaven now! We'll probably make it today. My dad and I, I mean." She trailed off, feeling more like a kid than she had since the day she'd started working.

"I'd love to meet him." Nina grinned even wider, shoving her glasses up as her eyes twinkled evilly. "I'm sure he can tell me all *kinds* of fun stories…"

Zoey held up her hands in front of her, backing away slowly. "Did I say Bloodhaven? I meant, um, Elfhame. Yeah, we'll be gone for *months*."

"Ha!" Nina chortled gleefully. "You're such an egg, Zoe. My char is named Wikiwi. Send me a message on the Guild board when you get into town."

Excited and feeling re-energized, Zoey bounced on her toes. "Will do. I'm Rouge the Rogue, and my Dad is Motte Bailey."

Pushing up her heavy glasses once more, Nina gave a little salute. "Perfect! We can talk about it a bit more tomorrow. Ka kite ano!" The taller girl turned and began to jog off. Zoey glanced at her screen and yelped, turning and dashing for the lab.

☙ ☙ ☙

As predicted, Dr. Sadist (as Zoey still silently called Dr. Joe when he was in workaholic mode) had no sympathy for her exhaustion. When she showed up, puffing and trying not to inhale the crumbs of the granola bar she'd eaten while running, he didn't even look up from his screens, just pointed toward the changing room.

Once Sara had gotten Zoey all hooked up, they ran through some warm-up exercises to make sure the sensors were working correctly. Just the stretches and jogging in place was enough to make Zoey feel like she was ready to keel over, but Dr. Joe just frowned at the readouts and glanced at her.

"Your numbers are a little off today. Anything I need to know?" He tapped at the screen with a stylus and frowned a little more.

She shook her head, trying for a reassuring smile. "I'm fine. Ready to get in game. What do I need to test today?"

Dr. Joe humphed a little, flicking the stylus, and then looked up. "We're working on the biofeedback system again. It's still a resource hog and could use some optimization. We've made some tweaks, so we just need you to do the basics and let us know how it feels. You know the routine."

She suppressed a groan. 'The basics' meant a fifteen-minute exercise routine, followed by working with her weapons and just generally acting like she was crazy by doing every movement and activity she could think of. It was kind of fun when she could practice a dance routine from a new music video, or copy a gymnastics routine that she'd never be able to do in the real world, but she had a feeling that that would not go over well while she was supposed to be a caravan guard.

"Okay," she muttered, and dredged up a smile.

Sara smiled back from where she stood behind Dr. Joe, though her big brown eyes looked a little concerned. Dr. Joe, however, didn't seem to notice Zoey's lack of enthusiasm. In fact, he seemed to be running on auto-pilot as much as she was, and the skin around his eyes was pinched and bruised-looking.

He nodded briskly, mustering his own brief smile, and motioned toward the pod room. Sara, who had clearly been expecting the dismissal, nodded and waved for Zoey to follow her.

As she did, Zoey sent a glance back toward Dr. Joe. His head was down, and he was staring blankly at the pad in his hand. She had a feeling he wasn't actually seeing anything that he was looking at. Maybe she wasn't the only one who was struggling today.

ಠ ಠ ಠ

When Rouge blinked open her eyes, shaking off the dizziness of log-in, she found herself sitting on Codswallop's back, while the wood elf boy jogged beside her, glancing periodically into her face. It took him a moment after she focused before he realized she was aware, and then he jerked his gaze away, a red flush rising from the neckline of his leather jerkin until even the tips of his ears were blazing.

She felt an answering flush steal over her face, though thankfully it was harder to tell with her slightly darker skin tone, and she smiled awkwardly. "Um, can I help you?"

The boy (Van? Vonn?) coughed uncomfortably. "Ah, no, um, sorry. It's just… Restur!" His voice gained some confidence, and he nodded firmly. She had a feeling he was convincing himself as much as her, and wondered why that thought made her face warm up again. "Yes, Restur asked me to keep watch over you Travelers, and let you know that he would like to speak to any of you who wake." He frowned a little. "Let any of you who wake know that he would like to speak to you? I'm sorry, the Human language is not my first, and the forms are difficult."

He looked up at her hopefully. "*Je'wille k'a Fasthi*?" She looked at him blankly, and he sighed. "I wondered if you knew the language of your people. It seems that some Travelers speak the language of their ancestors, and others do not."

"Oh." She shook her head. "No. I think that's only for full-blooded chars who spawn in the homeland of their race. Some of *them* don't speak Human, and that can make things difficult if they want to party with another Traveler. I'm a half-breed, so I didn't get that perk."

She didn't even realize what she'd done until the boy's face froze.

Your Reputation with Vonn the Wood-Elf has dropped by 25 points. Your Relationship is now 32 (Cautiously Friendly).

Rouge smiled broadly, trying to pretend she wasn't having nasty flashbacks to when she'd first encountered new NPCs in Bright. Even before the recent patch, many people had a negative reaction to meeting a half-breed of any race. It was actually in an effort to combat that instant drop in Reputation that she had started doing all the little Reputation Quests. By the time she'd left, she had such a high Reputation that it almost never happened anymore, and when it did, it was only a few points.

She instantly fell back into old habits.

"So, Vonn, how can I help you?"

Quest: "Chit Chat, Chat Chit" available.

Speak to Restur, the caravan-master. Vonn has been tasked with sending you to speak to Restur. The sooner you do so, the better.

Success: Increased Relationship with Vonn. Increased relationship with Restur. Increase depends on your speed, so get a move on.

Failure: -5 Relationship with Vonn if you don't complete the quest before anyone else shows up.

Accept: Yes/No?

While she was reading the quest, Vonn was paraphrasing it (without the snarky bits, and she needed to talk to Bridget about that when this was all over). She quickly accepted, and smiled her understanding. "Great! I'll head over there now." She looked around. "Um, where is he?"

Vonn, a stiff expression on his face, pointed toward the front of the caravan. Ahead of her, she saw Aspen, jogging along with his head tilted to the side. (Not at all strange, that. Certainly no one would think he was either listening to someone or battling an inner ear infection.)

She nodded to Vonn and clucked at Codswallop, who was already doing the 'Rouge is back!' happy dance and fluffing his feathers gleefully.

He picked up his pace for a few steps as she leaned forward and gave him a hug while slipping him a cucumber from her inventory. The big ostrich pulled up beside Aspen a moment later.

Nothing.

She coughed.

Aspen's topaz eyes shot to her, and he smiled. "Rouge! It's good to see you back! Did you get some rest?"

Silus poked her head out of Aspen's collar. ::Yay! Rouge! Can I come with you? Aspen's shirt is stinky.::

Rouge laughed, and reached down to set her hand on Aspen's shoulder in the most offhanded, 'friendly greeting' sort of way she could manage. The little bat climbed onto her hand, blending in nicely with Rouge's dark leathers, and then the elf thief lifted her hand to casually adjust her own collar. Silus climbed over and snuggled into Rouge's curls. The bat sighed happily.

Aspen was looking slightly offended. ::I haven't had a chance to bathe in almost three days, and we've been fighting or running nearly that entire time.::

Silus yawned. ::It's okay. Just try to do better next time.:: Then the little creature was fast asleep.

Rouge giggled. ::She told you, huh?::

Aspen looked confused. ::Told me what?::

::That you should…. You know what? Never mind.:: She shook her head, then continued aloud for the sake of the surrounding caravanners, who weren't trying very hard to conceal their interest. "Anything happen while we were gone?"

He shrugged. "Two wolf attacks and some bandits. This area seems to be rife with aggressive beasts, both two and four-legged." Mentally, he sent, ::Doom Bloom had to go. She had some schoolwork she couldn't put off, and likely will not be back until we reach Bloodhaven, if I understand the time difference between your world and my own correctly.::

Rouge sucked her teeth. "Everyone is all right?" She eyed him with concern.

::No injuries?::

He tilted his head, obviously torn between which question to answer. "Yes," he said aloud, and responded ::No,:: in party chat.

She nodded. "Good. I guess I should go talk to Restur, huh? We haven't exactly been helping protect the caravan." ::Especially with Doom gone,:: she continued silently. ::I understand, but I wish she'd been able to stick around longer. Is Restur mad?::

Aspen tilted his head to show subtle affirmation. ::Quite. I helped as best I could, but I don't want to draw attention to myself, so as far as they're concerned, you Travelers left them in the lurch after agreeing to help.::

She groaned a little, then sighed. ::I should have let Motte log in first. He's way better at this interpersonal stuff. Oh well.:: She raised a hand in farewell and nudged Codswallop forward again. As she did, she began running through the series of exercises required by her job, trying to pay attention to how they felt, and let Codswallop take care of himself for a moment.

The ostrich quickly outpaced the wagons, moving as if he were glad to stretch his legs properly, even if it was only for a little while. She recognized the full head of fluffy white hair from the back and pulled up next to the lead wagon. She smiled her very best, 'I'm just a kid, and you can't be mad at this face, right?' smile at the old man.

"Hello, sir." A little politeness never hurt when you were dealing with elderly people. Not that she had anything against old people, and she was usually polite, but seriously, everyone over the age of thirty had such a *thing* about respect.

Quest: "Chit Chat, Chat Chit" complete.

Reward: +6 Relationship points with Vonn. +4 Relationship points with Restur. +1 Relationship points with all caravan members. You could have moved a little faster, but whatever.

She suppressed a sigh.

Restur's scowl softened a little as he met her eyes, and after a tense moment he heaved a breath. "I'm disappointed in you Travelers. We have been attacked three times, twice without the assistance you promised us. I'm unsure if our bargain is still acceptable to my people."

She glanced around, and saw carefully neutral expressions on the faces of the warriors who rode at the front of the column. She bowed as deeply as she could while riding an overgrown fowl. "I'm very sorry, sir. Time flows differently between our worlds, and we didn't realize how long we would leave you alone. I promise one of us will be here from now until you reach Bloodhaven." *I hope,* she thought, while surreptitiously crossing her fingers in Codswallop's soft feathers.

Restur's expression softened slightly, and he inclined his head. "See to it that you keep your promise, or we will be unable to assist you in your entry to Bloodhaven. I will, of course, have to deduct the time you were absent from your pay."

She winced slightly, but forced a smile. The money wasn't as important as helping them get into the city without being noticed. "Of course," she agreed. *Sorry, Doom.*

It was at that moment that she heard a sharp whistle come from the back of the caravan. It was immediately followed by another long whistle, then two short ones. Restur spun in place, motioning to one of the guards. He looked up at Rouge. "Something concerns the rear guard. Go see what it is."

Rouge nodded, and spun Codswallop in place, then leaned forward and urged him to full speed. As she did, she heard Aspen's voice. ::Something in the woods. I... honestly don't know what they are. There are at least twenty of them, and they're moving this way quickly. Not large, but fast.::

She looked around, into the tall green trees on both sides of the road. The foliage suddenly looked much more threatening than it had only a few minutes ago. ::Can you be more specific? And how do you know?::

He sounded both pleased with himself and frustrated. ::I figured something out about being a Druid. They're just ahead of you and on your right. Nearly here, and not slowing.::

Holding out her hand, Rouge called her Mambele from her inventory. A long dagger, one of the ones she'd used when she created the [Poison Rain] spell, appeared in her other hand. She stopped Codswallop and stared into the woods, ready. The wagons nearest her saw her sudden shift in attitude and veered away from her as far as they could on the barely two-lane road.

Something in the darkness of the underbrush moved. A loud snap, as of a branch breaking, was her only warning before something furry catapulted out of the darkness toward her face. She shrieked and swung at it, and the thing screamed and fell, split down the middle by her magically sharp blade.

You have dealt a Fatal Blow to *Demonic Squirrel*. You have slain *Demonic Squirrel*.

"Demonic *what*?" She stared down at the fuzzy thing lying on the ground, tail still twitching in the same disturbing way a real life squirrel that had been hit by a car sometimes did.

::Look out!:: Aspen's voice brought her back to herself just in time, and she dodged to the side, using her off-hand blade like a tennis racket to punt a leaping furball back into the trees.

You have dealt 32 points of damage to *Demonic Fieldmouse*.

Rouge groaned. "Now I have to kill fuzzy rodents? Come *on*, Gina!"

Gina has heard your prayer. All blows will deal +10 damage to fuzzy rodents for the next ten minutes.

The elf girl growled. "You think this is funny?" She chopped a shrieking bunny's head off. "This." A groaning gopher bit the dust. "Is." A hedgehog with green-tipped quills squealed as it left one little limb twitching on the red bricks. "*Not*." A huge jackrabbit with red eyes and viciously pointed teeth found out that its feet weren't lucky for it today. "Funny!"

The guards were falling in around her now, and together they picked off voles, moles, marmots, and three extremely aggressive groundhogs. Finally, the furry flood slowed, and she dared to hope this would be over soon. Then a tree branch snapped, and one last, huge animal burst onto the road. She threw her Mambele before she could even process what she was seeing.

You have dealt 87 points of damage to the *Hamster Hellion*. The *Hamster Hellion* is Poisoned.

It was unmistakably Mr. Hamncheese. Yes, okay, instead of buff and white, the mob's fur was blood red and silver, but she'd know that heart-shaped patch on his tummy anywhere. She felt her stomach churn. Yeah. She definitely needed to have a conversation with Bridget. Though, honestly, this was probably Harris' fault. Next time he ordered a sandwich, he might want to check it before he took a bite. The cafeteria carried habaneros, and Rouge wasn't afraid to use them.

She raised her hand and called her Mambele back, even as she threw her second dagger at the beast's eyes. It wasn't huge, as mobs went, but a four foot tall hamster was still a disturbing sight, never mind that its fuzzy mouth was filled with at least two rows of savagely sharp teeth.

You have dealt 54 points of secondary damage to the *Hamster Hellion*. The *Hamster Hellion* is Bleeding.
You have dealt 21 points of off-hand damage to the *Hamster Hellion*.

Around her, the guards were raining blows down on the beast, wincing back as it shrieked, showing that in fact it had *three* rows of teeth. Then it reached into its hugely round cheeks with one clawed paw and pulled out a wriggling insect. It heaved the bug at one of the guards, and the thing clamped onto his face with a round O of razor-sharp teeth. He screeched, an agonized sound, and fell to his knees, dropping his weapon and clawing at the bug.

Rouge winced. "Oh, *heck*, no. Harris, you suck." She threw herself backward as another of the six-inch maggots raced toward her face. As it flew over her head, she stabbed backward with the rear facing blade of her Mambele, impaling it.

You have dealt a Fatal Blow to *Monstrous Maggot. Monstrous Maggot* has died. Your weapon has resisted Acid Damage.

She shook her head, feeling globs of some formerly adorable woodland creature drip down from her hairline. "That is *it*." Gripping her weapon, she clambered to her feet atop Codswallop's back. The ostrich, who had been dodging debris with the grace of a ballerina, chirped questioningly.

"Jump, Wally. I'm gonna bring the pain."

Bunching his legs under him, Codswallop leapt. At the apex of his jump, she pushed off, twisting in the air so she was aimed head first at the Hamster Hellion, which was still hurling death maggots at the guards, who were doing their best to avoid and then stomp the horrible things.

As she fell, completely ignored by the nearly mindless mob below, she cast [Poof!] and then triggered [Stealth] as the shadow fell over her. She wished she could use [Poison Rain], but she was certain it would damage her allies as well, and there was no way she could control where seventy-five knives would end up.

Rouge stabbed the curved blade of her knife into the side of the Hamster Hellion's head, spiking the Mambele into its brain even as it reached into its mouth to pull out another bug. It gurgled, then dropped, and she rolled away, getting covered in rodenty detritus as she did.

You have dealt a Fatal Blow to *Hamster Hellion*. *Hamster Hellion* has died.

Gina takes note of your effective use of the weapon she gifted to you.

A foot came down beside her, squashing the last remaining maggot as it attempted to wriggle its way over to her. She looked up. Aspen held out his hand as a soft silver glow shimmered around him. "Good job," he murmured, and then turned away to tend to the frightened horses.

Notifications scrolled across her vision once again.

You are now level 43.

You are now level 44.

You have gained one level in [Knife Wielding]. You are now level 20. You may select a Specialization.

You have gained a level in [Dual Knife Wielding]. You are now level 6.

You have gained a level in [Ostrich Riding]. You are now level 11.

You have created a new skill! [Aerial Acrobatics] is added to your skill list. [Aerial Acrobatics] combines [Acrobatics], [Jump], and [Stealth]. You must fall from a height of at least fifteen feet in order to trigger this skill. You may now enter [Stealth] when dropping onto an enemy from above, even if you would otherwise be visible, as long as that enemy loses track of your location while you are in the air.

You have gained two levels in [Aerial Acrobatics]. You are now level 3.

You have created a new skill! [Pterion Puncture] is added to your skill list. Through hard work and persistence, you have developed an ability to find the weakest point in the skull of an enemy. When you attack from above, you have a +10% increase to your chance of dealing a Fatal

Blow.

You have gained a level in [Pterion Puncture]. You are now level 2.

Due to your heroism, your Reputation with all members of Restur's Caravan has increased by +5 points.

Rouge scraped guts off her shirt and slung the gooey clump aside. A small, sad voice entered her mind. ::That was really, really gross.::

The elf girl gasped and reached up to her collar, stroking the slimy, miserable little bat where she clung to her hair. ::Oh my gosh, Silus! Are you all right?::

Silus' squeaky little voice was filled with absolute misery. ::There are intestines in my eyes.::

Rouge looked over and met Aspen's eyes as he stroked the silky nose of a panicky bay mare. She could almost read his mind. *Bet she wishes she'd stayed in my stinky shirt now, huh?* Wisely, however, he remained silent.

☙ ☙ ☙

After the battle was over, and everyone was healed up again, Rouge cleaned up in a nearby stream, and changed into her second-best set of leathers. She would have to take the other ones to a Tailor in town to get the stains (and the smell) out of them. She would have asked Tia to repair them again, but she was afraid that with the reduced Reputation from their unapproved absence, the woman might ask for money this time, and Rouge wouldn't have any until they got paid.

Vonn, who was now back to a Cordial Relationship with her, thanks to the boost from her 'heroism' during the Battle of the Rodents, was jogging alongside her and Codswallop. Rouge had transferred control of Doom and Motte's Zombies to Aspen, and fallen back to the end of the caravan to help guard their rear.

Fortunately (or unfortunately, given the awesome growth she'd enjoyed from the last two battles) there were no more attacks, and Rouge was left to her own thoughts. She didn't even have Silus, who had transferred back to Aspen once she was clean, because 'he's less likely to get gross, even though he's smelly'.

What she did have was Vonn. Rouge was rapidly getting past the very small crush she'd had on the boy, which stemmed from how *pretty* he was, and how cool it was to meet a real wood elf. He was, indeed, pretty. He was also nice, reasonably intelligent, and talkative. Really, really talkative. In fact, Rouge was contemplating what Dire Steps might need to be taken to *shut him up*, when Motte's voice filled her head, overriding the elf boy telling her about how his third cousin twice removed once found a magic mushroom, and...

::Check your Announcements, Rouge.:: Motte's deep voice was serious and slightly concerned, so she pulled up the announcements without asking why.

Veritas applied game-play patches by updating one server at a time, until they were all up to date, then activating all of the patches at once, so the game never had to go down for maintenance the way other online games did.

When everything was ready, Veritas posted an announcement for players when they logged in. Unlike other games of its kind, it rarely used global announcements. Since the game was so immersive, they felt notifications detracted from the effect. Some hard core players even turned off notices entirely, and manually checked their stats at the end of battles to see if they'd leveled or had any skill growth.

The result of this system was that changes often went unnoticed until you ran into them personally. Once they went live, information was available in login announcements or the patch notes, if you bothered to read them. Unless there was a new event, Rouge didn't. Motte always did.

It didn't take long for her to figure out what he was trying to get her to read.

Hear ye, hear ye! As new treaties and accords bring peace and prosperity to beings everywhere, troubling new rumors have arisen as well. There are tales of Demonic creatures roaming the land; warped

horrors, both sentient and animal, that some claim to have seen near Bloodhaven in Quarternell, Moonsong in Elfhame, Goldmark in Dwarf lands, and Gull Fahr in the broken lands formerly ruled by Lich Lord Akuji. Those who lurk at the edges of darkness claim that Vampires have risen again, as well. It is said that if you find the source of these undead monsters, you, too, may be infected with their dark plague, which has no known cure. While no proof has yet been presented to support these claims, it may be best to be on your guard, lest you fall victim to evil you thought long vanquished.

Silus' voice broke in as Rouge started to re-read the paragraph. ::What is it? What's an 'ouncement'?::

Motte read the announcement out loud for their companion's benefit.

Aspen cursed softly. ::Sorry, but…. We know the Demonic creatures are real enough. Do you think they mean William when they speak of vampires?::

Motte sounded grim. ::I doubt it. For one thing, William at least claims he has no idea how to make more of his kind. For another, we found William months ago. Why would they only be mentioning him now? No, this is something different. Plus…:: he trailed off, and she could practically see the frown of concentration creasing his face.

Finally, he continued, simplifying a complex concept down to something the natives could understand. ::There's a thing like the Traveler's Guild board that all Travelers can access in our own world. We call it a 'Forum'. This announcement dropped a little over an hour ago, and the forums blew up.::

::What? Was anyone hurt?:: Silus' little voice sounded worried.

Motte chuckled. ::It's a figure of speech, Silus. It means that everyone started talking about it at the same time, and there was a lot of excitement. People think it means that you can now contract Vampirism in… uh, in this world. A lot of Travelers think it would be fun to try being a Vampire. There was also talk of gathering groups to hunt Demonic beasts. We could have a flood of Travelers hitting this area *soon*, which will make our quest much more difficult.::

Aspen finally spoke up, and Rouge suspected he and Motte were together and talking out loud as well. ::I agree with Motte. I think something is happening in Quarternell, and in the lands of the other sentient races. We have no way of knowing if the dark elves are experiencing the same phenomenon, since they're so insular, but I would bet that they're involved as well. If we want to avoid getting caught up in it, we need to hurry.::

Rouge grimaced. Now that she'd gotten to know Aspen, she felt bad about dragging him into whatever was going to happen as a result of the internal battle at Veritas Corp. She had a feeling, though, that with or without her and Motte's help, Aspen would have been in the thick of the upcoming mess. He was far too powerful and complex to be a simple NPC. At least this way, they could do their best to make sure that he came out alive on the other side, and made it back to his farm and his friends.

::What should we do?:: she asked, knowing they were kind of stuck at the moment.

Motte sighed. ::If we leave the caravan in the lurch, not only are these people likely to be killed, but we probably won't make it safely into Bloodhaven. We need them to hurry, but they're too busy being cautious to move any faster.::

Aspen's voice was frustrated. ::I won't leave them now. That last attack nearly killed a man. Restur said it'll take a Major Healing potion to regrow his eyes, and that will cost most of his profits from the trip, even with the caravan covering half the price. These are good people, and I don't want them to die because we weren't here to help.::

::So how do we get them to go faster?:: Silus asked, and everyone fell silent.

Rouge felt an idea percolating through her brain, and closed her eyes, trying to tune out Vonn still droning on at her side so she could focus on it. Then something the boy said broke into her awareness.

"...the Spring Triathlon in Bright. Restur says if we can get there early enough, we can set up a stall, and everyone will be in a festival mood and ready to buy. He's not sure if we can make it though, since we have to go so slowly—"

He continued on, but she was done listening.

::Guys, they want to get to Bright before the Triathlon so they can sell their goods for higher prices. When does it start?:: She pulled up the in-game calendar, but Motte spoke up before she could do more than glance at it.

::One week. The Murder Hobo Event starts the day after tomorrow in Bloodhaven. It goes over the weekend, so four days in game. Then the Triathlon starts the following weekend. So it's more like two weeks for the natives.:: He sounded thoughtful.

::How likely are they to make it at this pace?::

This time Aspen answered. ::Not likely. If they do make it, it'll be as the event starts. If they want to watch it, that will be fine, but if they want to be vendors, all the good spots will be taken. I don't know how long they intend to stay in Bloodhaven, but if it's more than a day, they have no chance.::

Quest: "Run (Through the) Forest, Run!" available.
Help Restur's Caravan reach Bright in time to set up a booth for the Spring Triathlon Event.
Success: +5 Reputation with all members of Restur's Caravan, 40% employee discount at the booth on the day of the event.
Failure: Variable, but you probably don't want to hang out here any longer than necessary.
Accept: Yes/No?

A soft ringing filled Rouge's ears, and she groaned. ::That was my timer. I have to go, or I won't have time for my daily survey.:: Quickly, she accepted the quest, hoping Motte and Aspen had received matching ones.

Motte chuckled. ::Go on, then. I'll be here until you get back. Aspen says

Doom isn't likely to make it before we get to Bloodhaven, so it's just you and me. Be careful on the bus, and eat some salad with your meatloaf.::

::Daaaad!::

🦇 🦇 🦇

When the platform lifted Zoey out of her pod, Sara was waiting, but there was no sign of Dr. Joe. Sara gave her a hand out, and she rushed over to the shower. Zoey slapped the button, then rubbed the goo off her body in the ensuing tsunami. When she finished and pressed the button again, Dr. Joe was there to hand her the Super Towel.

He smiled tiredly. "It looked like you had a good session. Your heart rate picked up early on; find a battle?"

She nodded, pulling the rubber cap off her curls and then starting to pat herself dry. She'd long since gotten over being embarrassed about wearing the skin-tight bodysuit around Dr. Joe and Sara, and they all had this down to a smooth, impersonal process. "Yeah. It was gross, though. Demonic rodents. Somebody has a twisted sense of humor."

If she hadn't been watching him from the corner of her eye, she wouldn't have caught the look of shock that touched his face for a brief moment.

"Demonic?"

She handed the towel to Sara with a smile, then turned back to glare at Dr. Joe with her fists planted firmly on her slim hips. "Come on, Dr. Joe. There's no way you're not in on all this. You know all about the Demonic things and the Vampires, right?"

He frowned slightly, and his eyes flicked briefly toward the nearly invisible door beyond which Bree Stephenson laid in ovoid comfort. "No, in fact, I don't. I'm R&D. If you want to know what changes are coming up in game, you need to talk to Bridget or one of the other programmers. It's against company policy to give anyone inside information about upcoming events, though, so I doubt you'll have any luck."

Expression smoothing into professional calmness, he pulled up his screen and stared at it, tapping a line with his stylus. "Now, how did you do with the interface? Any changes that you noticed? Did you feel that it was as immersive as the last time you logged on here?"

She growled a little internally, but forced herself to respond with her usual enthusiasm. After all, it wasn't Dr. Joe's fault that he couldn't help her. Honestly, even if he could, she'd feel bad about asking, since it could give her an unfair advantage in the game. Still, it would be nice to get some benefit from working for the developer of the game, just once.

It only took ten minutes for her to answer all the questions they had for her. It wasn't hard, after all, since she hadn't noticed anything different. Whatever they did seemed to have worked as intended. Once Dr. Joe was satisfied, he passed her back to Sara, and left them to finish up while he headed back to his little office.

Sara was unusually silent as she led Zoey back out of the pod room, and didn't speak while Zoey changed back into her work clothes. When Zoey emerged from the changing room and headed for the fridge to get her lunchbox, the Indian woman followed, looking conflicted.

Finally, Sara broke. As Zoey crouched to get her lunchbox, Sara 'accidentally' dropped her stylus and knelt down beside the younger girl.

"Don't be mad at him," the assistant murmured quietly as she pretended to search for the stylus that she already held in her fist. "He got some bad news yesterday. A... family member passed away. He probably shouldn't even be here, but he says if he stays home, he'll just think about it and go crazy."

Zoey's heart lurched, and she fumbled her lunchbox so it clattered to the ground, popping open and depositing half a bag of sweet kimchi-flavored potato chips on the ground. The two started picking them up, slowly.

She swallowed against a spike of empathetic sorrow. "I'm so sorry. Is there anything I can do?"

Sara shook her head, throwing a few chip crumbs into the trash. "He's known it was coming for a few months. It's just hard. Bridget knew... the deceased, too, and she took a few days off."

Zoey cast her mind back to the morning, and realized that she hadn't seen her 'supervisor' all day. Usually, Bridget found a moment to walk by Jazmin's desk and offer them a smile or a word of encouragement, but her door had been closed the entire time today.

They gathered chips until there was no sign of the accident, and both of them stood up. Zoey gave Sara a smile. "Thanks," she said, not specifying what she was grateful *for*.

The older woman smiled weakly. "No problem. I'll, um, see you tomorrow, then, Zoey. Have a good evening."

Zoey nodded, grabbed her lunchbox, and headed toward the bus stop.

Chapter Fourteen

Aspen (One hour ago In-game)

Quest: "Race (to the) Race!" begun.

Help Restur's Caravan reach Bright in time to set up a booth for the Spring Triathlon Event.

Success: +5 Reputation with all members of Restur's Caravan, 40% employee discount at the booth on the day of the event. 50% more likely to enter Bright without attracting attention.

Failure: 50% more likely to be arrested while attempting to enter Bright. Plus, there are those Demon things. I would avoid those, if I were you.

Aspen grimaced as a quest popped up in front of him.

Rouge groaned softly. ::That was my timer. I have to go, or I won't have time for my daily survey.::

Motte chuckled, quirking a brow at Aspen in shared amusement. ::Go on, then. I'll be here until you get back. Aspen says Doom isn't likely to make it before we get to Bloodhaven, so it's just you and me. Be careful on the bus, and eat some salad with your meatloaf.::

::Daaaad!:: The soft wail was filled with teenage angst, and this time both men laughed softly.

A moment of silence indicated that Rouge had, indeed, returned her soul to her home world, and Motte shook his head at Aspen. ::Did you get a quest to help the caravan, too?::

Aspen nodded slightly, then flicked his eyes at the curious caravanners, who were beginning to realize that Motte had returned and were collectively edging closer. Merchants were among the worst gossips in any world, so the two men drifted apart.

As they did, Codswallop, carrying Rouge's motionless Zombie, jogged up to fall in fifteen feet behind Aspen. Motte fell back and patted the large bird, who chirupped softly.

::I think we need to go talk to Restur,:: Motte sent, even as he made a show of checking on Doom Bloom, Oleander, and Burrito.

Aspen kept his head down, jogging along as placidly as he could. ::*You* need to talk to him, if you would. He sees you as the leader of our group, while I'm just a native commoner. I don't want to do anything to shake his belief.::

Motte grunted slightly. ::All right. Do you have any suggestions?::

Aspen's lips quirked in a half smile. ::Appeal to his inner greed monster. If we get lucky, maybe Gina will even give him a quest that will encourage him.::

::Ha.:: Motte muttered. ::Guess you'd better start praying, then.::

Whether because of Aspen's vehement – and possibly sacrilegious – begging to Gina, Motte's conviction that he could protect the caravan even if they moved faster, or good old-fashioned greed, Restur agreed to hasten their travel. As they more than doubled their previous pace, Motte stayed at the front of the caravan, looming large and threatening to any lurking enemies who might have considered attacking otherwise weak prey, while most of the rest of the guards fell back to cover the rear.

Aspen focused on supporting the animals who drew the heavy wagons. He found that he could reach out with his new Druidic Life Sense – as good a name as any – and tell when the beasts were flagging. He could also feed them some of his energy in the same way he'd done with the trees and grass in the last two battles, helping them recover enough to continue moving at their increased speed.

It took some trial and error before he could learn to balance his own needs with theirs, but soon enough all of the animals were trotting along as smoothly as if they were well-rested and fresh. Interestingly, he found that the Traveler's beasts seemed to notice what he was doing and be able to reject him if they wanted. He suspected he could have forced the issue, but there was no need, since they also seemed to have far greater reserves of stamina than the caravan's animals.

At their new pace, urged on by Motte's leadership and supported by Aspen's magic, they covered ground faster than the caravan ever had before. Aspen could hear the caravanners talking around him, and smiled slightly when they speculated that Motte had some kind of Traveler magic that was allowing their haste.

ĕ ĕ ĕ

Sometime during the night, Motte and Rouge traded places, and by the time Aspen woke the next morning, he found the elf girl sitting nearby, snuggling into Codswallop's warm, feathery side. Silus was sitting in the girl's hair, nearly invisible if you didn't know to look for her, and the two were chattering away.

::...found the best blackberries growing near the river. There were tons of mosquitos, too, and I got a quest to eat a hundred, and I *did it!* I think I must be close to level 22 now!:: Silus' little body was nearly quivering with excitement, and Aspen chuckled to himself.

::What are we going to call you when you're not little anymore, little one?::

he asked, climbing out of his bedroll and pulling on his boots. One of his favorite things about not being one of the guards, he'd found, was that he wasn't expected to be instantly ready in case of attack. Being able to wiggle your toes while going to sleep was a very underrated experience.

Silus puffed up, disturbing Rouge's curls slightly. ::Silus! I'll be so big you won't need nicknames for me anymore!::

He shook his head. ::Growing up isn't as wonderful as you hope. Wouldn't it be better to just stay small?::

This time Rouge glared at him as much as the big golden eyes peering out of her hair. He raised his hands defensively. ::By all means, continue as you were. When I'm old and decrepit, you can both bring me food and drink in my nice comfortable bed.::

That didn't seem to help, and he was treated with chilly cordiality until the caravan began to move again. At first, the pace was much slower than before, but Aspen finally realized that they were suffering from the lack of Motte's commanding presence, and sent Rouge to the front of the column.

While her small figure didn't inspire quite the same faith as her father's looming form, Aspen was able to give the animals a subtle extra boost, which led to a spurt of speed just as Rouge reached the front. With that, their momentum was reset, and Aspen found that he was having to stretch his stride to its longest for the first time since joining the caravan.

Thankfully, nothing serious attempted to attack them, and each time Aspen's life sense detected the threats long before they were noticed by anyone else. He was able to convince the Lesser Bear and the Greater Ptarmigan that they had better places to be, but the three Lesser Wolverines were determined, and he had to offer up some of his mana to a thicket in order to stop them. That meant that he had less to offer the caravan's animals until his mana regen caught back up, and the group slowed briefly, but he was able to return them to full speed without too much difficulty.

Nonetheless, by the time the line of people waiting to enter the west gate of

Bloodhaven appeared, Aspen was exhausted. Several members of the caravan cheered as they reached the back of the line and slowed, then stopped. Restur began to gatherthe things he would need to present to the guards in order to gain entry, and Rouge fell back to stand near Aspen.

::I'm going to go to the Traveler's Guild. Wally is pretty recognizable, and Motte and I agreed that he'll have to be stabled outside so we don't attract attention. I have to leave really soon anyway, and I want to drop a note for some friends, to let them know we're here in case they want to join us. I'll be back in about twelve hours, okay? Motte and Doom's Zombies will follow me, so you'll be on your own until one of us gets back. Just keep your head down and meet us back at this gate tonight.:: She tilted her head toward the massive metal portcullis ahead of them, though she kept her eyes turned away from him.

::I'm going to go with Aspen,:: Silus volunteered. ::When it's time for you to be back, I can fly over and meet you, just in case something happens, or we're not close enough to use party chat.::

Aspen smiled. ::Good idea, Silus.:: He walked around the nearest horse, then led it over toward Rouge, watching its gait as if he were concerned it might be going lame. When he got close to the girl, a small dark object transferred itself from her hair to his shoulder, and he walked the horse back toward the rest of the caravan.

Rouge began to walk away, heading toward the colorful tent, desk, notice board, and ring of standing stones that Aspen recognized from Bright and Vargo. ::Be really careful, okay, Aspen? Just stay with the caravan until we get back.::

He used a broad brush to clean the horse's shining back of any traces of dust. ::I'll be careful, don't worry. I'll see you this evening.::

He could imagine her sigh, though she didn't send it through chat, and he chuckled to himself. The best part of being around a teenager who wasn't his was the opportunity to tease her with little to no repercussions. Plus, there was no way he was going to waste half a day.

ĕ ĕ ĕ

In fact, he was forced to do nothing for nearly three hours. The queue to enter Bloodhaven was always long, and with the Murder Hobo Festival starting tomorrow, the line was even longer. While the event wasn't exactly popular with the natives of Quarternell, it was, at least, profitable, since Travelers often had far more money than they seemed to know what to do with. Thus, the line ahead of them was substantial, and the line behind continued to grow until he could no longer see the end of it.

The guards allowing entry to Bloodhaven varied significantly as well. Some would let a visitor in with minimal bribery and harassment. Others demanded a higher bribe, and would insist upon checking each and every cart, horse, and wagon until they 'confiscated' goods that met their minimum. The guards cycled regularly, too, so you couldn't switch lines hoping to get a particular guard. No, you got what you got, and hoped for the best.

As their little caravan drew nearer to the gates, Aspen could begin to see the two guards who were currently handling entry. First, they would recite the rules of Bloodhaven (essentially, there *were* no rules, so it was more a question of what would be seized if they were caught trying to leave with it). Then, they would ask what goods the entrants were taking in, so they could be taxed, since no taxes were claimed in Bloodhaven itself.

This was the point where bribes came into play. Sometimes a small but heavy bag was 'inspected' and 'confiscated', at which point the giver would be waved through without further questions. Other times, smaller bags were handed over, and then the guards would help themselves to whatever they fancied. There did seem to be some limit to this, however, since the items they took were fairly small, and none of the merchants looked as if they would be forced into debt due to the loss. In short, the process seemed to function to everyone's satisfaction, though there was plenty of grumbling amongst those waiting.

Aspen was forced to tamp down his own impatience. This was the moment for which he had been playing his current role, and it would be ridiculous to break character now. So, he kept his head down, his hat low, his face blank, and concentrated on calming the horses, who were also eager to get inside the city. They knew a proper stable was in their near future, and they wanted to get to it.

When Restur's caravan finally reached the gates, Aspen felt his stomach churning violently. He drew in a deep breath, and prepared to face questions and possible recognition, followed by arrest or execution. No pressure.

Restur handed over some papers and gave his name. The guard glanced at them, then paused and looked again. He looked up, the blank face of his helmet somehow managing to convey suspicion. Then, he raised his hand and motioned, and a moment later a young girl ran forward. The little messenger took off, and a few minutes later, another soldier, this one in much fancier armor than that worn by the other gate guards, appeared.

The new guardsman stopped in front of Restur, and the two exchanged low words. Then the soldier pulled off his helmet, revealing the face of a handsome man in his thirties with a distinct resemblance to Restur. The man clapped the caravan leader on the back, waving the caravan through, before motioning sharply to the other guards to return to their duties. They did so, with matching sour expressions.

Aspen shuffled his way through with the rest of the caravanners, as a quest completion notice passed before his vision.

Quest: "Hostler Hustle" completed.

Success: Improved relationship with all members of the caravan. Significantly improved relationship with Restur. Entry into Bloodhaven.

Sighing, he rolled his eyes up at the sky and sent up a little prayer. *Thank you, Gina.*

Once they were through the gate of Bloodhaven, Aspen finally felt safe to lift his eyes, and he looked around. The city had become its current incarnation of a 'free market' trader's paradise only in the last few years. Before that, it was a fairly prosperous human city named Brand's Haven, after the man who had founded it, some three hundred years before. When Lich Lord Akuji had broken through into Quarternell, this had been one of the first cities to fall, and the only people remaining were those who were unable to escape, and a good number of Travelers, who used it as a good place to level up.

Once Akuji was slain, a slow trickle of natives returned, but they were vastly outnumbered by the Travelers, who found that having a city that wasn't a Non-Combat Zone had its own perks. For one thing, they could slay each other and the natives in the street, with little to no repercussions for their murderous actions. This behavior had led to another exodus of the common people, while those more willing and able to defend themselves had settled in.

Now, the newly renamed Bloodhaven seemed as if it were there to stay, and the only good thing about it as far as Aspen was concerned was that it gave those with a less reputable lifestyle somewhere to go where they were away from other people. That, and those with a price on their heads, such as himself, apparently, didn't need to fear the guard within its walls.

Aspen hadn't been here since the end of the war. By the time Brand's Haven had fallen, the writing was on the wall for the whole of the human race, and no one even tried to take the city back. As a result, many of the original buildings had been damaged or even destroyed, and without government assistance, the repairs had been left up to the people who lived there.

The architecture surrounding him, therefore, was a wild mash-up of colors, styles, quality, and states of disrepair. A large golden mansion stood next to a hovel, and rubble-strewn plots housed tents of varying permanence. Travelers filled the streets, and the few natives he saw usually gathered in large groups or trailed closely after the Traveler for whom they worked.

Quietly, Aspen trailed the caravan through the streets, trying to remember the way back through the maze of tiny alleys and broad thoroughfares, but rapidly realizing that he was utterly lost.

::Do you know how to get back to the gate, Silus?:: he asked silently.

The bat, who had her little body pressed to his neck, eyes huge in her small face, trembled a little. <I think so. We've gone mostly east, so I should be able to get back to the gate.>

::That's good,:: he said grimly, ::because I think I may have underestimated the difficulty of finding anything in this place.::

<Me too,> the bat agreed.

The caravan finally stopped in a large square surrounded by massive, utilitarian buildings. They had large signs outside, reading things like 'Revenant Squad' and 'Infamous Thugs'. Usually there was also a 'Members Only' sign, but occasionally it would instead be something like 'High Level Merchants Inquire Within' or 'Elves Only!'

Restur climbed down from the lead wagon and went up to the door of a building whose sign read 'Metal Hearts' and 'Members Only' and knocked firmly at the door. It cracked open, and the old man leaned in, speaking quietly. The door closed, only to open again a minute later and allow the caravan leader entry. As he went in, he raised a hand back at the caravanners, indicating that they should stay.

They waited. And waited. A half hour passed, and then the door opened and Restur finally stepped out, a pleased smile on his face. He got back up in his place on the wagon and gestured them all forward again. This time, they followed a wide, straight road for another quarter mile or so, then pulled up in a large open field. It was roped off, and a sign posted at the opening of the ropes read, 'Metal Hearts ONLY – Trespassers will be PK'd without warning.'

Restur climbed down again, and motioned the caravan through. As Aspen started to enter, however, the man waved him aside, a small frown on his face.

"I'm sorry, Aspen, but you and your friends can't stay with us." To his credit, the man sounded genuinely regretful. "The Metal Hearts Guild are our sponsors, but they only allow those they've hired themselves on their property. They're not bad sorts, for Travelers, but I could lose my affiliation, and you could lose your life, if they found you here. We'd be happy if you all want to rejoin us when we leave the morning of the day after tomorrow, but you're on your own until then."

Aspen frowned and tugged at his hat. "D'ye have any suggestions fer where we should stay, then? And mebbe where I could find a mage named Manuela? She's… not likely t'be near other mages, but in this place…." He trailed off, shrugging.

Restur ran his hand through his thick white hair, pondering. "If I were you, I'd go to the Artful Lodger. It takes anyone, so they won't blink at your, ah, unusual mix of companions. It's a bit more expensive than some of the others, but they maintain a hex against vermin and don't allow Travelers to kill their guests. At least, not without significant bribes." He pointed back the way they'd come. "It's down the road a ways, on the right. If you can't read, the sign is a paintbrush in bed."

He tilted his head. "As to the other…. The mages mostly live and work in the south-west part of the city. I'd begin looking there, even if you don't think your friend will be there. The non-Traveler community here is tight-knit and insular. If she isn't there, they'll know where she is."

Aspen nodded and reached out to clasp the other man's arm. "Thankee for that, and for your help at th' gate. What time d'ye plan t'leave in two days?"

Restur grimaced. "As soon as possible, frankly. This city is no place for the likes of us, though we make profit enough while we're here. It's just not healthy to linger long. We need to move a few, ah, products, and hire some people to fill out our group. If you're not here at dawn, we'll begin looking for someone else to hire as extra guards."

Aspen nodded his understanding. "Thankee again. See y'then."

The old man raised a hand. "And I, you."

Aspen turned and walked off down the street, rapidly finding himself surrounded by a whirling mill of people of all sorts. All the races were represented here, though most of the more unusual were Travelers. Humans and elves were common, including two dark elves, though he rapidly realized they were just Travelers as well. A few trolls and dwarves walked purposefully through the streets, but there were no goblins, whose small stature would likely have made them an easy target for the murderous Travelers, or orcs, who would have been too large to pass in the road, much less enter any of the buildings.

The Artful Lodger was, indeed, easy to find, even for someone as new to the city as himself. He would not have described the prices as being only a *bit* more expensive, but he suspected that prices were skewed in this place because of the large number of well-heeled Travelers.

Fortunately, Iorgas Penbrooke, as the King's only Necromancer, was very well paid. He had lived lavishly at first, but soon found himself bored with the sort of excesses that most of the nobles considered merely normal daily activities. Birdie, too, was never a child who longed for things or parties. In the end, he found that he had more wealth than he really needed, and had simply begun tossing his salary into a locked room in his house.

When they had fled Bright, Sumi had advised that he leave the most obvious trappings of wealth behind, so that no one would decide to come looking for his grave to see if it contained treasure. Aspen himself had been bed-bound at the time, but between his animal companions and his few loyal friends and servants, most of the obvious things were sold and donated to the hospital that Birdie had started. They hadn't smuggled out much money, but he had more than enough to pay for more than a few nights in an inn, even an expensive one.

He dropped a stack of gold coins on the counter in front of the Dwarf manning the desk. He grimaced, making a show of his reluctance as he pushed it forward. "Are y'sure we can't wait for m'master to return? He's a Traveler, y'know, a has plenty o' gold. This is nearly all he gave me t'do the shopping, and he'll be angry when 'e gets 'ere and finds I ran out afore I finished my tasks."

The Dwarf's neatly curled and waxed mustache twitched. "Rules o' the Inn. You don't pay, you don't stay, and I guarantee we'll be full by nightfall." His broad, soft hand pushed the stack back toward Aspen. "D'you want the gold, or the room?"

Aspen grumbled, tugging at his hat. "Fine then. Two nights. M'master will likely have words for the Innkeeper, though."

Shrugging, the short, broad man made the gold disappear. "That'd be me. Send him over, and I'll tell him the same. Your room is 2B, up the stairs." He handed Aspen a key with a large wooden plaque on it emblazoned with '2B', and pointed to the mark with a stubby finger. "The sign on the door will match that. You'll know it's the right one 'cause the key will work. Now off with you." He turned to the next customer, and Aspen was dismissed.

Chuckling internally, Aspen made his way up the stairs. He'd seen a few people in the common room begin eyeing him speculatively when it became obvious he was there alone. By the time his confrontation with the Innkeeper was over, though, they'd clearly dismissed him as poor and unimportant.

The room was a decent size, and had two beds, as Aspen had requested. It would have been better to have two rooms, but since only the Travelers' Zombies slept, he'd decided it was more important to be sure everyone was safe than worry about keeping the genders separate. It would likely make for a couple of uncomfortable nights for Aspen himself, but the Travelers would be fine.

He set out a few things in the room so that he would know if anyone came in after he left. First, and simplest, a silver coin on the floor, partially hidden by the bed. Then he laid a few freshly plucked hairs across the latch of the small lockers at the foot of each bed. Finally, he tucked a corner of a piece of paper into the keyhole. Not only would it prevent anyone from looking in, but if someone used a key or lockpick, it would be pushed out, and he knew exactly how it had been placed there.

It was at times like this that he missed Sumi. She would have used her webbing to set far better traps, and no one would have been able to enter the room once she had used her stickiest webs to seal it shut at night. Plus, she would have been able to figure out how to find Manuela. Somehow, the giant spider always managed to find whatever information he needed. The only time he'd known her to fail was when they were trying to find out exactly who was trying to kill him after the Battle of Bright. That villain had hidden themselves too well for even the brilliant arachnid to dig out in the time they had.

By the time Aspen walked out of the inn, now carrying only a small pouch tucked tightly between his shirt and his belly, he had only five more hours before Rouge was supposed to return. He just hoped it would be enough.

Aspen was utterly lost. While he could find his way southwest without a problem by looking at the position of the sun, the streets were far more maze-like than anything he had dealt with before. Streets would narrow abruptly, or end without warning. They also wound around, instead of going straight, and more than once he found himself looking at a building he was certain he'd already passed.

After far too much time wasted walking in polygons and ellipses, Silus popped her little head out of Aspen's collar just enough to look around. <Should I scout ahead? I can find the dead ends so we can go straight there.> She sounded uncertain, as though she expected him to reject her suggestion out of hand.

Aspen looked around. His first instinct was to say no, and keep the small creature close, where he could protect her. Then, he thought of her insistence that he treat her as a part of the team, not a child, and drew in a long breath.

::Yes.::

<Really? I'll be so careful! No one will see me!> She started to crawl out onto his shoulder, and he leaned his cheek toward her, unobtrusively blocking her path.

He walked over to a shadowed doorstep with long vines winding their way up the cracked wall, wiping his brow as though he were tired. He leaned his shoulder against the wall, resting. Silus climbed quickly out and into the thick foliage, and he could barely see the tiny motions of the leaves as she passed, using her wing-thumbs to climb up above eye level and out of the area where most people paid attention.

<I'm ready! Go south down the street you're on, and then...>

Following Silus' silent instructions, Aspen found that he made much more rapid progress, and stopped seeing buildings more than once. Unfortunately, the area into which they entered seemed even more dilapidated than the one they'd come from. Fewer Travelers roamed here, and he suspected that they had found where the natives lived, at least the poor ones.

He was beginning to lose hope that he could find the mage's area before he had to turn back in order to meet Rouge when Silus cried out sharply.

<Aspen! Come quickly! Straight ahead and the second right! Be careful!>

Glancing around, it seemed as if no one was paying particular attention to him, so he felt safe in speeding up just a bit. Drawing attention to himself was still dangerous, but his worn appearance fit in better here, so he thought it likely that anyone who saw him would dismiss him as a resident on his way to dinner or an appointment.

When he reached the corner, he slowed, glancing around once again. The opening was one of the narrower ones, and from the sounds echoing out of the breach, he had a good idea what he would see. Gasps, grunts, and pained cries filtered down to him, and though no one else seemed to notice, a few hastened their pace as they passed.

Quickly, he leaned forward, casting a glance into the dimness of sunlight reflected into the tight passage, and then he pulled back, cursing internally. Two attackers, two defenders. The attackers were large, their shoulders brushing the walls on either side. They swung their fists and feet viciously in the cramped space, and the meaty *thwack* of blows hitting flesh were easily audible. The defenders were small – child-sized in fact. Aspen would have assumed they *were* children, except that the larger one was a familiar shade of green.

A goblin.

Aspen squeezed his eyes shut, listening to the increasingly desperate breaths of the victim, and the satisfied grunts of the attackers, and fighting a desperate internal battle. He had saved a goblin female, who had shown herself to be brave, intelligent, and true. Her daughter brought joy to all of their lives, and he couldn't imagine his little house without the happy giggles that seemed to be Juniper's primary form of communication.

But he'd also seen thousands of the creatures swarm over men and women he'd fought beside, like a ravening horde of rats, utterly indiscriminate in their hunger. He'd hoped that he had managed to shake the loathing that the small beings usually kindled in his heart, and he did find that he felt some sympathy for the goblin.

But was it enough to risk everything? Drawing attention to himself, completely unnecessarily, in order to save a *goblin*? Unlike when he saved Sarave, he wasn't in a position of safety, even power. Now, the lives of himself and his friends hung in the balance. They were literally surrounded by potential enemies, and…

Silus' voice was a little wild. <Aspen? Please! What are you waiting for? Help them!>

Closing his eyes, Aspen breathed a silent prayer to his fickle Goddess. ::Silus. We can't save everyone. We need to *go*.::

<No. At least try, Aspen, or I'll do it alone.> The little bat's tone held steel he hadn't known she was capable of.

"Sumi, you've taught her too well," he mumbled. Then he sent, ::All right.:: Aspen drew in a tight, shuddering breath and reached into the alley with his mana. He reached for anything, any speck of life that he could use.

And he found it. The men were riddled with vermin. Fleas, mites, ticks, bedbugs; any creeping thing that lived on human blood lurked in the skin, hair, and guts of the assailants. His gorge rose, but he reached out to the near-mindless things. He negotiated. He gave them his mana. They feasted.

The screaming began a moment later, and grew into wild howls of indignity, followed by agony. Then one man, followed by the other, stumbled from the entry. They were covered in blood, both from the bites of the hugely engorged insects hanging off of them, and from their own desperate attempts to remove those insects. They staggered, fell to their knees, rose again, and finally ran, yells reduced to hoarse yowling. As they vanished from his sight, Aspen pulled his power back to himself, certain that his erstwhile parasitic allies would be able to finish the job themselves.

Swallowing hard, and feeling as though he himself was crawling with something horrible, he glanced around once more, then stepped onto the dirty cobblestones of the dark passage. He looked up, attempting to locate his little friend. ::Where are you?::

<Hanging from the eaves above you. Will they be all right?>

He shook his head. ::I don't know. Just… Let me know if anyone comes this way, all right, Silus?::

Silus' voice was small and sad. <All right, Aspen.>

Aspen knelt down beside the goblin, who was curled up on the ground, head and knees tucked to his chest, and arms curled around an even smaller being clutched to his belly. Dark blood oozed from cuts and contusions, and he seemed to be unconscious.

Carefully, trying not to trigger any defensive instincts the pitiful being might have left, Aspen reached out and rested his hand on the goblin's shoulder, which was thin and stringy beneath the rags he wore. The man closed his eyes.

"Gina," he murmured, "I know I'm not a very good Druid, and you really should have chosen someone else for this job. But please, I'm trying to do the right thing. Help me?" He hesitated, and then, still feeling awkward and unsure of himself in a way he hadn't been when someone else's life wasn't fading before him, he said, "[Heal]!"

Warmth erupted from his hand where it rested on the narrow shoulder of the goblin. A shudder ran through the small body, and then another. The goblin's single eye flashed open, a rainbow of colors coruscating in it and obscuring the yellow sclera common to his race. He blinked, a guttural sound emerging from his throat, and arched up. Even in his - Pain? Exaltation? – he never loosened his hold on the small bundle he held, which had also begun to wiggle. When the light faded, the goblin relaxed, and the small man rolled over onto his back, staring up into Aspen's face.

The goblin was as beaten down as Sarave had been when Aspen met her, but his single eye still held an indomitable gleam that Aspen also recognized. In fact, though goblins were universally small, big-eared, green-skinned, and yellow eyed, this one bore a haunting familiarity.

Aspen looked at the thick, ugly scar that ran through the goblin's left eye socket, which stood empty and dark. His fingers twitched, wondering if he could heal that, too, when a thought occurred to him. He leaned forward, voice urgent. "What is your name, goblin?"

The goblin's mouth stayed stubbornly closed, though Aspen could see the long ears twitch, and knew he had heard.

"I ask," Aspen continued quietly, "because someone important to me told me to spare a certain goblin, if I could. She told me he had lost his left eye, and once had a sister he loved dearly."

The yellow eye widened abruptly, and the goblin reached out with far more strength than Aspen would have given him credit for a half second before. He bared sharp teeth and hissed something in his own language, but in the sibilant syllables, Aspen was able to make out one word. Sarave. Or perhaps Saravelle?

Aspen pried the sharp claws from his throat, feeling a trickle of blood on his hand as he did so. He coughed a little before he was able to continue. "Sarave. Yes. She told me her brother's name, but I need to be sure you are he. What is your *name*?"

Glaring suspiciously, the goblin relaxed his hand slightly. "Nekthadt is my name." He spoke with a much lighter accent than his sister, and seemed fluent in the human tongue.

Huffing out a relieved breath, Aspen smiled slightly. "Then, Nekthadt, would you like to see your sister again? She and her babe are safe at my home, waiting for me to return. With you, if you like."

Nekthadt's face was filled with a wild mix of desperation, hope, anger, and suspicion. "That's impossible. She was declared *verschladt* and poisoned. There is no cure-"

Aspen shrugged. "There is now. I saw her just a few weeks ago, and she told me of her husband, Jeremy, and her brother, Nekthadt, who was the only goblin to stand up for her when her marriage was discovered. She named her daughter Juniper."

"And what do you want for this information? My service? Payment for your aid, so that I may work in your fine home beside my sister and her forbidden child?" The goblin sneered, but the hope in his expression was beginning to overtake the other emotions.

Aspen shook his head. "They are free. As free as I am, and as free as you are. Even if you don't want to go with me, I will gladly carry a message back to Sarave for you."

Nekthadt struggled up to his knees, face finally relaxing even as tears formed at the corners of his bright yellow eye. "Yes. I have nothing else. I will come. If you lie, at least I will die outside the walls of this damned city."

Aspen held out his hand to help the goblin to his feet. "Let's get out of this place, then."

Quest: "Wherefore Art Thou, Brother?" complete.

You have found Nekthadt, and given him news of Sarave.

Reward: +40 Reputation with Nekthadt, Maximum Reputation with Sarave, which cannot be reduced unless you betray her.

Then the being clutched to Nekthadt's chest, which Aspen had half guessed to be a goblin babe, turned to look at him, and his heart stilled in his chest. It *was* a little girl. A gray girl, with huge black eyes, two rows of sharp white teeth, and gills fluttering on the sides of her neck. A glyphis!

Glyphis were also known by their more common name: Were-sharks. They could take on a humanoid form, though it was written that they much preferred their native fish shape. Their skin, teeth, and other body parts were prized alchemical reagents, and as a result they were hunted when they were found, in spite of the killing of sentient beings being illegal in Human, Elven, and Dwarf lands.

As far as Aspen knew – and he only knew about them at all because he'd taken a few Alchemy courses during his brief time as a mage student - were primarily aquatic creatures, and could only live out of water for short periods. How this one was surviving, given that there were no open water sources in Bloodhaven, he didn't know, but he would have to worry about it later.

When Nekthadt saw Aspen's look and correctly deduced that the human knew what the girl was, he clutched her to him once again, hissing warningly. "She is mine!" The little girl blinked huge black eyes and whimpered a little. But Aspen could tell that whatever was keeping her alive was failing, because the gill slits on her neck were dull and dry, and she barely had enough energy to lodge a protest at all.

Aspen started to speak, but Silus squeaked out a warning. <One of those men is coming back, and he has help. Hurry!>

Grasping the goblin's free hand, Aspen pulled him to his feet. "Fine. But your large and unfriendly friends are coming back. Do you know somewhere we can hide?"

Nekthadt still looked suspicious, but nodded. "A bolt hole. Probably not large enough for you, but if they didn't see you, you should be fine."

Quite an *if* in Aspen's opinion, but he nodded back. "Run then, fast as you can. I'll be behind you."

A goblin in fear for his life could run quite quickly, and Nekthadt was soon dodging in and out of narrow streets and broken-down buildings with an agility that belied his near death only minutes before. Clearly, Gina had seen fit to heal him quite thoroughly. Aspen followed behind as closely as he could, though he still had a feeling the goblin man wouldn't have been too saddened if he had gotten lost in the warren through which they traveled. Fortunately, Silus was able to guide him, and he clung tenaciously to the little man's trail.

Soon enough, they reached an area that was in even worse shape than any Aspen had seen before. Here, the goblin scurried into a pile of moldering rubble that looked like some very large building had simply fallen down and no one had cared to do anything about it. In fact, occasional pieces of broken yellow humanoid bones crushed beneath large pieces of masonry indicated that that might be exactly what had happened.

Nekthadt ducked under a few of the larger pieces of rubble, and then he vanished. Aspen was left standing outside, staring into the small dark opening, and wondering if he should just leave. It seemed obvious to him that the goblin had no real interest in joining him, and he was surprised at the depth of his own relief.

Then the green head popped out of a hole barely large enough for his large ears to scrape through, and Nekthadt eyed Aspen warily. "You say my sister is with you, and safe. You healed her, as you did me?" His voice was unusually deep and gruff for a goblin, and Aspen found himself responding to the odd sense of authority he gave off now that he was in his own territory.

"I did. Though, to be honest, it was Gina's doing more than my own." Aspen couldn't help the self-mocking smile that crossed his lips as he thought of his own surprise both times he had healed Sarave.

The single yellow eye widened. "Gi-na?" He said it with the same lilt and break between the syllables that Sarave had when they first met. It almost sounded like a different word. "You are of Gi-na? Has my sister found a temple that would accept her?"

Aspen shook his head. "Just a farm that needed two more hands, and a farmer who needed a friend." *And some atonement*, he thought. "We are followers of Gina, though, and Sarave often prays at our shrine."

A thin smile quirked Nekthadt's narrow lips. "Sarave has always had a gift for finding those who would love her, though she never saw it that way." The goblin sighed a little. "Wait there."

An instant later, his head withdrew, and Aspen waited. Nekthadt's whole body reappeared in a slightly larger cave created by overlapping broken columns, and he waved a hand for Aspen to follow. Aspen's brows rose, but he cautiously entered the space. Only when he had gone as far in as he thought he could did he see that there was a tall but dark passage between one column and the next. From the front it had looked like a flat wall with a crack in it, but from here he could tell that it was wide enough to let him enter, barely.

Nekthadt's voice came from the darkness. "Come on, then."

Aspen leaned back out of the opening and motioned silently for Silus. She winged down and landed on his shoulder, easily hiding between his collar and neck. They turned back and entered the tiny passage.

Several times, Aspen's clothes caught on something and he stopped, terrified that he would pull the whole pile of debris down around their ears. Nothing happened, though, and he finally made his way to a much larger open area where he could actually stand up. Nekthadt was already there, sitting cross-legged on a moth-eaten fur and eating a whole, raw fish.

Beside him, in a tank of murky water, floated the little glyphis. The remnants of another fish floated in her tank. Some color had returned to her gills, and she seemed more aware as she stared at Aspen again.

Nekthadt glanced at her, then edged over so he was in between Aspen and the eighteen-inch-long shark girl. He bared his sharp teeth, which now had chunks of raw fish between a few of them. "Mine," he said again.

Aspen held up his hands. "I have no interest in taking her from you. Though I admit to a certain curiosity about how you came to be here, and together."

Relaxing a little, the goblin took another bite of fish. "Sarave told you what happened?" He was clearly trying to see how much Aspen knew, and the tall man shrugged and obliged.

"Not much. I know some goblins declared her *verschladt* because she married a human and became pregnant with a half-breed baby. They poisoned her," he reached up and touched his own ear, indicating where Sarave had been injured when they met, "and sent her off to die. That was all I knew until I was about to leave to come here. She told me if I met a goblin named Nekthadt, missing his left eye, that I should help him and tell him she's all right, because he's her brother, and the only one who tried to help her after Jeremy was murdered."

Nekthadt nodded slowly, absently touching the scar that divided his eye socket. His remaining eye looked away, not meeting Aspen's gaze. "True enough."

Aspen's eyes narrowed a little. *Left something out, did I? Something you're relieved I don't know.* He shook his head. Why did everyone around him have so many secrets? He'd thought he and Sarave, at least, were beyond that. He was well aware that the Travelers held their own mysteries, but he didn't believe they meant harm to him or his family, so he was content to let them be.

The goblin continued, though Aspen was sure he was still leaving out much of the tale. "I was driven out of our tribe as well, though they didn't declare me Poison from Within. I was forced to flee our home after they exacted the punishment they believed I deserved," his tone was bitter, "and I came here. I thought, falsely, that I could use some… *skills*…. I had picked up in order to earn some money, perhaps start my own clan from the exiled goblins who live here."

He shook his head. "The goblins in Bloodhaven are of two kinds. Either they are servants, and are barely goblins anymore, or they are already part of the criminals who rule this city. I refused to be either, and at first they left me alone. Then I began to be somewhat successful, and they started to pressure me to join their organization.

"I was hired to, ah, *find* and return an object that had been stolen from a very wealthy human. That 'object' was this little one." The goblin reached over and touched a finger to the water in which the glyphis lazily circled. "There was no way I would return her so they could use her as they intended, and so we ran. Fortunately, I have a few skills that make finding me... difficult, so I was able to evade pursuit."

The glyphis rubbed her little cheek against the goblin's hand, still keeping her unnerving black gaze on Aspen. Nekthadt went on. "That was just over three weeks ago. I had found this place a few months back, but I still had somewhere better to live then, so I just remembered it in case I needed somewhere to hide someday. We've been here since we ran, just sneaking out to get food and fresh water." His broad green nose wrinkled. "Well, the freshest I could find anyway.

"I've tried several times to leave the city, but they're watching for us. My concealment skills have time limits, and if we take too long, someone reports us, and we're forced to flee back here. More than once they've nearly caught us, but today was the first time we couldn't escape. I was just too weak to continue running." He raised an arm, eyeing it critically. "Whatever you, or Gina, did, I feel better than I have in days."

Aspen smiled a little. "I'm glad I could help. Certainly Sarave would never have let me hear the end of it if I hadn't. Plus, your predicament caught the attention of my conscience."

Silus twitched a little, but not enough to give away her presence. <Thank you, Aspen,> she whispered mentally, as though afraid the goblin could overhear the thought.

::Thank you, little one. I'm glad one of us remembered that I'm trying to be a better man.:: He tried to put as much warmth and love into the words as he could.

Nekthadt, oblivious to their exchange, said, "How do you come to be here, then, friend of my sister? Is there anything I can do for you, in exchange for our lives?" He swept his hand around, as though he were surrounded by riches which he would shower on the farmer's head.

Aspen shrugged. "I'm here to visit a friend." His gaze sharpened. "Perhaps you know her? A mage named Manuela."

The goblin stilled, and Aspen's eyes widened. He did know her! He leaned forward. "Please," he said, "I need to speak to her as soon as possible. If you know where I can find her, I'll do my best to help you and the glyphis get out of this city."

Nekthadt bared his teeth in something that wasn't a smile. "You already promised to help me get out. You said you'd take me to my sister. Did you not mean it?"

Aspen hesitated, caught by his own words. Then he swiped his hand across his face in defeat. "I did. And I'll keep that promise. Sarave will be glad to see you, and you should meet your niece. She's a wonderful child." He smiled fondly. "I'll help you both, if I can. I still need to find Manuela, but I won't make that a price to pay for my aid."

Nekthadt was staring at him, face blank. After a long silence broken only by their breathing and the faint splash of water as the glyphis swam, he shook his head. "You are by far the strangest human I have ever met. Willing to help a goblin, and one who brings trouble with him, for no price except the happiness of another goblin. I-" He closed his eye.

When he opened it again, his face was set in lines of determination. "I, and Jesiqa here, will help you, human. I do know where Manuela is supposed to be, though whether or not you can reach her," he shrugged. "You will need help from your Gi-na for that, I think."

Aspen gave a half smile. "You may be surprised to know that you're not the first to mention that I'm different from other people. It's not usually meant as a compliment, however." He held out his hand. "I'm Aspen. I will gladly accept your help, Nekthadt and Jesiqa, and offer you mine, such as it is. Now, where is Manuela?"

Nekthadt clasped his hand hesitantly and briefly, then used his freed hand to point to the south. "Headed for Bright. Human warriors took her a little over a week ago. They claimed to be mercenaries hired by a client that she betrayed, but by their attitude and bearing," he shrugged, "they were soldiers. Well trained and used to working as a unit. Manuela is one of the few mages who will lower themselves to work with non-humans, so she's well-liked, but no one was willing to take a risk to save her. She's gone, and from the grim way those men looked, if she's still alive, I doubt she's glad of it."

Quest: "Need a Little Help from A Friend" begun.

Someone has abducted Manuela. They claimed to be headed for Bright. Find out what happened, and save Manuela if you can.

Success: The magical link between you and the items being used to track you will be broken.

Failure: Manuela will die, and all of the tracking charms (however many there are) will continue to function. Which is Bad, in case you hadn't figured that out yet.

🦇 🦇 🦇

Aspen was pacing back and forth in the cramped confines of the space Nekthadt had made his own beneath the rubble. The goblin watched him warily, gently petting the Glyphis in her tank, but making no comment.

<Aspen, stop!> It was Silus who finally snapped and yelled at him in her squeaky little voice. <This isn't helping, and you're going to bring this place down around your ears. Not mine, because I think I can get out through that little hole in the top before it all crashes in, but definitely yours.>

It was the fact that the bat had already planned an escape route more than anything else that convinced Aspen to stop. He growled furiously.

"How are they ahead of us? Every time, they're one step ahead! First the tracking charms, then the Wanted posters, and now taking away the one person I know who could break those charms! We keep slipping through their fingers by the skin of our teeth, and if I can't stop them from following me, eventually we're going to trip up, and that'll be it! All of this is pointless!" He pulled his hat from his head, slapping it against his thigh almost painfully.

Nekthadt jumped, then stared at Aspen, wide-eyed. "Wanted posters? Tracking charms? Who *are* you, human?"

Aspen quickly pulled his hat back on his head. Its shape no longer bore much resemblance to a piece of millinery, but it protected his face from prying eyes, so he dared not leave it off. He huffed out a breath. "No one. It's who they *think* I am that's causing the problem."

The goblin tilted his head in a way that was strongly reminiscent of his sister. "Who are 'they', then?"

The tall human shook his head. "If I knew that, we'd go straight to the source. Unfortunately, the whole thing is a mystery, and while I'm trying to figure it out, an unknown number of Travelers are using magical location charms to track me down and try to kill me. Manuela is the only Sou... uh, Mage I know who could break the link to the charms without having them in hand, which I obviously don't have. Without her, we're just going to have to keep running, and hope the charms are basic ones, with limits on distance or number of times they can be used. The fact that we've only been attacked once argues for that, but I'm not willing to risk our lives on it."

Nekthadt smiled a little, showing the tips of his sharp teeth. "Soul Mage is what you were going to say, isn't it? Don't worry. Soul magic isn't illegal here in Bloodhaven. It's the only good thing about this place. People who would be persecuted elsewhere can live openly... and be persecuted for something else entirely. Manuela told a few of us what she really was, so we could send her customers if they needed her help."

Soul Mages, much like Necromancers, had been illegal until the oncoming horde of the Lich Lord's army had forced humans to accept that they would have to find a new way to fight. Necromancers could use dead flesh to create warriors and could even, sometimes, take control of Akuji's undead servants, or at least sever his connection with them. Soul Mages, on the other hand, could hurt or heal the soul of any living creature. A powerful one could drop a battalion of orcs with a single spell, and in tandem with a Necromancer, the remaining empty husks could become weapons in the hands of their former enemies.

However, for all their terrifying offensive capability, most of them were far more suited to being healers. They could soothe the mind of soldiers who had suffered through horrific experiences, or repair damage caused by malicious spells. Occasionally, they could even bind a soul to a weakened body long enough for a healer of the body to repair the flesh.

Unfortunately, most humans, most of whom were poor mages at best, could only see that a Soul Mage could strip them of their life in a heartbeat, and leave no trace. While Soul Mages, like Necromancers, had been reluctantly accepted during the war, once it was over, they were shunned or even turned out of their homes. Few were left, and even fewer of those admitted what they were. Even the ones who served in the war simply admitted to being mages, not what their speciality had been. Since they could usually use a few basic spells such as [Fireball] or [Magic Missile], no one had questioned it, and only their commanders or partners knew the truth.

Nekthadt looked up, meeting Aspen's eyes in the fading light. "There is another, if you are able to afford him."

Aspen had stilled at the words 'Soul Mage', and now crouched down, looking into the goblin's faintly luminescent eyes. "Who? Where?"

"A Traveler named A-lister Crowley. He's in the Angry Dust Guild. Manuela hates him, because his prices are impossible for anyone except a Traveler to afford. She says he'd leave a child to die in a ditch if no one gave him gold to save her. No one even asks him, though he's gotten Quests to help a few people. At least we assume so, because sometimes he'll just show up, cast a spell on someone, and then leave."

Nekthadt shrugged, mouth twisting derisively. "If you can't afford him, I guess you'll just have to go rescue your *friend* Manuela."

Aspen cut a hand through the air, frowning fiercely. "Of *course* I'm going to go save Manuela. The odds are good that she was taken so she couldn't help me, especially if it was an open secret that she's a Soul Mage. Even if she wasn't, she *is* my friend, and I won't leave her in the hands of an enemy. This other Soul Mage, though-"

The goblin was staring at Aspen again, and his expression was shocked, though the farmer could barely see it in the dimness. "You... You're going to *save* her?"

Aspen nodded. "She helped me, more than once, and at no small risk to herself. I can't do less for her."

<Aspen,> Silus interjected, <it's getting late. We should go if we're going to find our way to the gate before Rouge returns.>

Hissing out a frustrated breath, Aspen turned to look for the exit. "I'm sorry," he told Nekthadt, "we'll have to finish this later. I need to go meet my friends at the west gate. I really appreciate the information, and I promise I'll come back in the morning to figure out how to get you and Jesiqa out of the city."

Nekthadt stood. "I think not. The way to the gate from here is treacherous, especially if you remain on the larger roads. The wealthy, Travelers and citizens alike, like to go to the pubs that seem to flourish here. They are a risk in themselves, because they believe they can do anything without facing punishment."

He shrugged again. "They are often right. But thieves also flock to the area, making travel after dark a near guarantee of being assaulted by someone. I can show you the safer paths, and I will stay with you until we leave this place." His teeth flashed in the last flickers of vanishing sunlight. "I wouldn't want you to *forget* your promise."

Aspen hesitated, torn, then nodded, knowing the goblin could see him with his innate [Darkvision]. "Fine. Though I wouldn't 'forget'. But while I had hoped to either find Manuela and finish my business or return to the gate while it was still light, I won't turn down a local guide. I know my own limitations, and dying for pride isn't one of them…"

His lips quirked as he finished the statement silently. … *anymore.*

Silus poked her head out of his collar. <Should I go ahead? I'll stay close enough to hear you.>

He nodded. ::Be careful, little one,:: he sent as the little creature flew from his shoulder and up to the opening above.

Nekthadt leapt to his feet, and Aspen could hear rustling as the goblin's clothes were disturbed. A flash of metallic silver told him the goblin now brandished a weapon of some kind.

Aspen held up calming hands. "She's my, ah, familiar. She's just going to scout, and she'll let us know if anyone is lurking nearby."

The goblin hissed, but the weapon flashed and clothing rustled again. "Next time, warn me, human. I nearly skewered your familiar. You're lucky this place is still unstable, and I didn't dare throw my weapon."

Looking around as if he could see anything in the near full darkness, Aspen cursed softly. "I thought you must have shored it up so it was safe. Why are you living somewhere that might fall down around your ears?"

Nekthadt's voice was grimly amused. "Because if someone discovers us here, we're dead anyway. I want to be sure they go with us. Now, turn to your left and crouch."

Carefully following Nekthadt's instructions, Aspen finally managed to make it out of the ruins without bringing the whole thing down on them, though once it was a breathtakingly close thing. Once outside, he could see well enough in the moonlight to tell that the goblin bore the glyphis in a sling improvised from a leather bag that sloshed slightly with water. The little girl held another leather tube of water, which she used to wet her gills regularly.

"Shouldn't you leave her here?" Aspen asked softly, motioning to the small girl with his chin.

Again the baring of the teeth. "*Never*. Where I go, she goes. If we die, we die together. I will not leave her alone to die slowly if I am killed while I'm away."

Wincing against that image, Aspen nodded. "One moment, then."

::Silus? Did you see anyone?:: he asked.

.:.Two men, both sleeping and smelling of alcohol. One is in a doorway a few yards ahead of you, and the other is in an alley to the west one street.:. He chuckled, hearing the distaste in her voice. All the animals except Khor disliked the smell of fermentation. To them, it indicated something that would make them sick if they ate it, and they couldn't understand why humans would enjoy it. Khor, of course, could eat nearly anything, but after one notable event involving his usual lack of self-restraint ended up with Aspen having to retrieve the Greater Goat from the roof of a human jail, he had refrained ever since.

Aspen conveyed the information to Nekthadt, who nodded. "Kibble and Twice. They're not exactly harmless, but if they've had enough to drink that they've passed out, they won't notice us. We'll go north for a while, so if your bat wants to scout ahead, that's the way she should go. When she sees a tree covered in lights, it'll be time to go west."

The tree, when they reached it, turned out to be hung with bottles containing the flickering lights of captured fairies. Beneath it stood the first of the pubs Nekthadt had mentioned, accurately named *The Fairy Tree*. The road in front of it was filled with people, mostly Travelers, who were entering or leaving one pub or another.

A few beggars sat or stood outside, and some Travelers dropped anything from coins to alcohol to what looked like severed Wolf Ears and other items they doubtless considered worthless in front of them. Other Travelers kicked or shoved the beggars away, laughing as the natives fell, injured to varying degrees.

Nekthadt shook his head, sliding into a narrow alley to their left, partially hidden behind the tree. "The Travelers are all excited because the Murder Hobo

Festival starts in two days. It only happens once every other year, so they're feeling extra generous because they all think they're going to get rich. They forget that only a few of them will win anything, and the rest will be fodder for the few."

Aspen followed the goblin, though he was barely able to slide into what was more of a gap between buildings than a way to travel. When the passageway widened enough that he could take a deeper breath, he asked, "What *is* the Murder Hobo Festival? I've heard it mentioned several times, but I've never had the chance to ask. It seems very relevant at the moment, however."

The goblin chuckled darkly. "It's based on what some of the Travelers call each other. Specifically, the worst of them, the ones who kill and take anything and anybody, whenever they like. They'll spend four days hunting and killing each other, and at the end, whichever of them has killed the most wins a title and a prize. Unfortunately, they don't really care how many of us they murder while playing their little game, so we've learned to get out of town if we can, and if not, we stay home and hope to survive. The time right before the Festival, though, can be highly profitable for merchants, since the Travelers have far too much gold and want to buy weapons, armor, scrolls, and potions of all kinds."

Halting, Nekthadt peered around a corner. He watched for a few moments, then leaned back, lowering his voice until it was nearly inaudible. "We're entering the territory of the Sons of Red Sonja. Most of them should be busy back by the pubs, but they always leave a few men patrolling. They're one of the more organized gangs. Can you have your familiar see if anyone is in the streets?"

Aspen nodded. ::Silus, can you look to see if there's anyone out there? Nekthadt says there may be patrols.::

<Of course!> Silus chirped promptly.

Aspen frowned. He had hoped to hear the familiar sound of the little bat's wings as she flew away, but wherever she was, it wasn't as close as he would have liked. He cast out with his Life Sense, even knowing that it would reduce his visual awareness of his immediate surroundings, and its 30 foot radius wasn't exactly huge.

Fortunately, Silus was still within reach of his spell, though only barely. So he knew when a huge cat leapt from the roof of a nearby building and caught her in its mouth, and he felt her life drain as it bit down.

::Silus!:: he yelled, starting forward out of the alley. Nekthadt tried to pull him back, but there was no way the emaciated goblin could stop a powerful adult human. A moment later, both of them stood in the middle of the wider lane, in full view of a pair of men who were just rounding a corner a block away.

Aspen's eyes flicked from the men to where he felt his little friend fighting for her life. Then he scooped Nekthadt into his arms, ignoring the goblin's indignant yell, and ran.

Chapter Fifteen

Rouge (Six hours ago real time)

Z oey was very, *very* tired when she got to work. She had stayed in-game until she had barely enough time to get dressed and catch a ride with her dad. It was the first time she'd seriously contemplated calling in 'sick' to work, but she just couldn't bring herself to do it. Plus, she'd be back online by two, anyway, and getting paid to play was way better than playing for free.

So, when she staggered into the Design Department, she was ready to find someplace dark and quiet and take a nap. Maybe in the cabinet under Mr. Hamncheese's cage? The only thing they kept there was extra litter and food, and she was almost certain she could fit if she just squished a bit.

Seeing that Jazmin wasn't at her desk or in sight shocked Zoey into a state of near awareness. The Chief Design Assistant (Zoey still wasn't sure what her actual job title was, but Miracle Worker probably wasn't available) was nearly always close enough to hear the door open, and immediately come to see who had walked in. Other than when she'd shown Zoey around on her first day, in fact, Zoey had never seen Jazmin's desk without Jazmin also within view.

Now, Zoey, in what could only be described as a state of reduced risk-assessment capabilities, found herself staring at Jazmin's empty chair. Her comfortable, comfortable chair. It had a high back, deep cushions, lumbar support, adjustable armrests, and full tilt.

Zoey *knew* that she should go find Jazmin and ask what her duties were for the day. But she'd been wondering what it felt like to sit in that chair. Just for a minute. A second! It wouldn't *hurt* anything, and she just knew Jazmin wouldn't really mind.

And then she was sitting in the chair. The cushions molded to her body like she was sitting in Gina's poofy cloud-chair again, and even though her feet dangled slightly, it was the most comfortable seat she'd ever been in in real life. She felt her eyes starting to drift closed, and as they did, she caught a glimpse of the image on the monitor.

Jerking upright, Zoey stared. Modern VaLPAC (Variable Light Phase Angle Controlled) monitors were commonly set to only be visible to one person, standing or sitting in one particular location. For screens that were generally private but might need to be viewed by more than one person, VaLPAC monitors were the best choice. Other options involved implants or glasses which projected the information directly onto the retina of the viewer, or screens with a kind of phase and color 'code' that obscured the contents unless decrypted with special glasses or a key provided by the viewer's implant. In business settings, VaLPAC was the way to go.

All of which meant that while Zoey had certainly seen Jazmin's monitor in resting state before, the image was obscured and blurry at best. Even now, it was a little soft, especially around the edges, since Zoey was nowhere near Jazmin's six-foot height, and the screen wasn't calibrated for her. Nonetheless, she could see it well enough to identify the family posing somewhat uncomfortably in the image.

Jazmin was on the right, standing with her hand resting on the shoulder of a seated man. The man was good-looking in a 'dad' sort of way, with brown hair that was receding slightly, and a jawline that was just beginning to soften. He had a broad smile on his face, and one hand was raised to hold Jazmin's lightly. At his other side stood a teenage girl, a fake smile pasted to her face, a single bright red braid visible in her brown ponytail.

Mirna. What was *Mirna* doing in Jazmin's photo?

"Zoey." Jazmin's voice was stiff, and Zoey leapt out of the chair so quickly that she nearly fell on her face.

"Ohmygosh!" Zoey forced every ounce of bright cheer she could muster onto her face, and smiled at her co-worker. "I'm so sorry, Jazmin! I didn't get much sleep last night, and your chair just looks *so* comfortable, not that that's any excuse, I know, because sitting there was totally unacceptable, and looking at your screen was even worse, but... how do you know *Mirna*?"

Jazmin's glare slowly melted into a kind of resigned sadness, and she sat down in her chair. "I guess it's not a big deal if you know. Everyone else does, since last year's staff holiday party." She closed her brown eyes briefly, touching her fingers to the small gold cross on a chain around her neck. "I asked Bridget about you on your first day, since she *forgot* to tell me you were coming. She didn't have much to say, but she did mention the name of your high school. Since you and Mirna are the same age, I asked her if she knew you the next time she came over for a weekend with her dad, who happens to be my husband now."

She sighed softly. "Mirna isn't exactly my biggest fan, since she blames me for her parent's divorce. That, by the way, happened all by itself. I met Roy after the papers were filed but before the decree was official. I refused to even have a cup of coffee with him until he could show me the final documents. But Mirna found out, and since then, she's convinced I seduced Roy while he was still married to her mom.

"*Any*way, not that you needed to know all that," Jazmin sighed, "but it may help explain why she was so furious when I mentioned that you were working here this summer. I take it she doesn't like you, either, and since my job here is the only thing she does like about me, the fact that you got a position when I've told her Veritas doesn't hire anyone under sixteen made her, well, kind of melt down."

Jazmin touched the screen with soft fingers, around where her husband's face would be. "I love Roy, but Mirna is… difficult. I understand that she's in a lot of pain, and she thinks if I weren't in the way, her parents would get back together, but it's still a difficult situation all around." Her face hardened. "Nothing she does is going to drive us apart, though, and Roy and I have faith that someday the Lord will open her eyes to our love, and she'll be able to get past her anger."

She looked over and managed a small apologetic smile. "But I decided not to tell you because I had a feeling that knowing I'm Mirna's stepmother might influence how you feel about me. And, frankly, it just seemed easier, since your internship is only ten weeks long."

Zoey was opening her mouth to reply when Jazmin's eyebrows went up, and she started giving off a serious 'mom' vibe. (Not that Zoey had seen that in person all that often, but in spite of the difference in facial features, Jazmin suddenly bore an eerie resemblance to Jace's mom when Jace got caught using his dad's expensive razor on his peach fuzz.)

"*Not* that *any* of that gives you an excuse for sitting in my chair, young lady. We use VaLPAC screens for a reason, and there could have been something on there that you weren't meant to see. Other than my personal photos." Yep, and there was that chiding tone that moms used to mean 'I'm disappointed in you. Do better next time, young person.'

Swallowing down the million things she could have said, Zoey nodded. "I'm sorry, Jazmin. It'll never happen again."

Jazmin nodded, a small smile softening her face back to her usual friendly but professional expression. "Good. Then you'd better report to Harris. I hear that Mr. Hamncheese's cage needs cleaning, pronto."

Zoey grimaced, flashing back to the battle with the hamster's in-game alter ego. She sighed in acceptance. "I'm on it."

ಕ ಕ ಕ

At lunchtime, Zoey met up with Nina again, and asked if the older girl had gotten her message that they had arrived in Bloodhaven. Nina nodded enthusiastically, and finished chewing a big bite of her (because of course) ham and cheese sandwich.

"Got the notification this morning. When did you send it? The system is usually pretty much instant, but I was already on my way to work when my screen pinged."

Zoey made a face, munching on a bite of her own peanut butter and honey goodness. When she managed to swallow, she said, "I was almost late today because I was working on a quest until after I usually get up in the morning. Dad had to drive me all the way here, since I missed my bus and he just has office hours this morning. Today has been *rough*."

Nina pushed her glasses up her nose, and her eyes widened. "Your dad lets you play all night? Crikey, I'm twenty and my folks still get after me if I'm up past midnight."

Rolling her eyes, Zoey made 'wait, wait' motions until she forced down another sticky bite, chasing it with a swallow of her boxed fruit juice. "Normally, Dad would never let me get away with that. He threatens to use his parental override to log me out if I stay on past ten. But we're working on this escort quest together, and if one of us wasn't logged in all the time, we'd fail it."

The older girl laughed. "Must be nice to have a gamer dad. My folks think Mahjongg is the best game ever created. When I told them I got a job at Veritas, they asked me what they do here."

Zoey shrugged. "It's nice sometimes. Other times, he gets in my business a little more than I'd prefer." She rolled her eyes again. "But! I actually had a question about something Jazmin said."

Nina chewed attentively.

"So, long story short, I found out this morning that Jazmin's step-daughter goes to my school. She mentioned something about Mirna and last year's office holiday party, and I wondered if you knew what she might have been talking about?"

Nina swallowed convulsively. "You go to school with that girl, eh? Whew. I guess Jazmin married her dad sometime last year, so that was the first party where Jazmin brought the new fam. Everything was fine, for a while, and the girl actually seemed pretty cool. Like, smart, and knew a lot about Veritas' games, including some that are older than her.

"But then Jazmin and the new hubby ended up under the mistletoe. They probably had a little too much of the punch because they were pashing, and everybody was clapping. It was cute, you know, since they were practically newlyweds, and Jazmin's usually pretty straight-laced. Girlie was mad as a meat axe. Threw her drink on them and called Jazmin a lot of names. They had to leave, and Jazmin was so embarrassed." Nina's voice was hushed by the end of this recitation, and her expression was sympathetic even as she took another bite of her sandwich.

Zoey's eyes were huge, and her own sandwich hung limply in her hand. "That's terrible!"

Nina shrugged, finishing her sandwich and beginning to gather together the remains of her lunch. "It wasn't that big a deal, actually. Gave the office something to gossip about for a few days, and Bridget probably had to 'talk' to Jazmin about not bringing the girl next year if she can't behave, but you wouldn't believe some of the things that have happened at Veritas parties." She winked a brown eye as she shoved her glasses up her nose, and stood. "Anyway, it was obvious the girlie was having a hard time with her parent's divorce, and even though she said some nasty stuff, most people just felt sorry for Jazmin. Hopefully, it'll work itself out."

Nina stood, tucking the glossy strands of her brown bob behind one ear. "I'll see you in-game tomorrow, Zoey! Enjoy the rest of your day!" Nina was already hurrying off to her next job by the time Zoey managed to pick her jaw up off the ground and dust it off.

Zoey shook her head as she gathered her own half-eaten lunch. She would never have imagined that she and Mirna could have anything in common. But if anybody knew about being angry and confused by her parent's breakup, it was Zoey. It was hard, sometimes, when she thought back to the things she'd done, trying to get her mom to pay attention to her, or convince her folks to get back together. She'd tried so hard to be the daughter her mom wanted. To be exactly like Lily, in fact. She'd obediently gone to gymnastics lessons, dance lessons, cello lessons, tutoring… anything, just trying to find something she excelled at. Something that would make her mom proud.

At the same time, she'd done some pretty mean things to Ken, her step-dad. She was a lot younger than Mirna, so it had been things like filling his shoes with worms and pouring salt on his dinner, but still… And at the time, she'd just been starting school, and she'd gotten in a few fights because she was always at least a little tense and angry. She'd worked really hard to do well, since she knew her mom wanted her to be a perfect student, and when Zoey hadn't achieved that high standard, it had only made her angrier and more frustrated. It wasn't until the lunchbox that she'd realized it wasn't her fault. That nothing she did was ever going to be good enough. She still told people her mom gave it to her, but the truth was, she didn't.

Zoey's ninth birthday had fallen on a weekend she was supposed to spend with her mom. Zoey was so excited, because it seemed like Lily always got everything she could ever possibly ask for on *her* birthday, so surely it would be the same for Zoey.

The day passed in a haze of constant expectation. Zoey kept waiting for the *gotcha* moment when her mom, Ken, and Lily would spring a surprise party on her. But there was no special breakfast. No lunch at Zoey's favorite restaurant. No cake with dinner. Not a single present, or even a card. By bedtime, she was in tears, and refused to tell her mom what was wrong.

She went to bed in her huge and lonely bedroom, and cried, clutching Mr. Bun until he was soggy and more than a little gross. When she finally managed to stop crying, she crept down the wide stairs to ask her mom *why* she hadn't gotten a birthday party. She overheard her parents talking on the screen, and she could still remember that conversation like it was laser-etched into her brain.

Zoey's mom had sounded furious. "I don't know what Zoey's problem was today, Marcus! She wandered around looking disappointed all day, and then she just started bawling after dinner. You need to come and get her in the morning, because Lily's award ceremony for taking first in the fencing tournament is tomorrow, and she'll ruin it if she starts crying again."

Her dad's voice coming from the big screen in the living room sounded equally angry. "It's her *birthday* today, Karen! Are you telling me you didn't do anything with her?"

There was a silence, and then Zoey's mom cleared her throat. "I can't be expected to keep track of everything, Marcus. You should have reminded me when you dropped her off. What am I supposed to do now? We already have plans for the whole day tomorrow, and I don't even know what Zoey likes. I think I have a china doll I got for Lily's friend's birthday I could wrap up, but we won't have time to go out for food or get a cake."

An even longer pause before Zoey's dad managed to bite out, "I'll get her in the morning. I'll bring one of the presents *I* got for her, and you can put it in a bag with your name on it. Tell her you got the date wrong, and you're sorry."

Huffily, her mom replied, "Really, Marcus, I think the doll should be-"

"She *hates* dolls, Karen. You should know that. Especially fussy dolls that are made to be looked at and not played with. Just go to bed, and I'll take care of it."

"*Fine.* But let me know how much it cost, and I'll pay you back. Within reason."

The silence returned.

"Good night, Karen."

And Zoey crept back up the stairs, fresh tears staining her face as she finally understood who really loved her. The next morning, her mom had given her a bag containing the *Kimi ni Todoke* lunchbox, apologized stiffly, and given her a brief hug. Then Zoey went home with her dad, and told him that she never wanted to go back. He thought he knew why, but the truth was much, much deeper than a child who felt badly because her mom forgot her birthday.

Which brought Zoey back to Mirna. It had been easy to hate Mirna when she was a bigoted wannabe fashionista with a God complex. It was a lot harder to hate a video-game loving teenage girl who didn't understand why her parents broke up and her dad married someone else.

Which left Zoey a confused and conflicted teenager herself when she finally made it to Dr. Joe's office, changed, settled into her pod, and logged into *Veritas Online*. So she was grateful when the first thing she heard on opening her eyes was Aspen's faint voice, sounding like he was at the very edge of chat range.

Unfortunately, a desperate call for Silus *wasn't* what she wanted to hear.

Warning! Party member Silus (NPC) has fallen below 50% hp.

She ran, pulling up the party list as she went.

Name	Level	Hp	Mana
Motte Bailey	97	1470/1470	0/0
Rouge the Rogue	44	150/150	140/120
Aspen (NPC)	42	623/700	516/635
Khor (NPC)	53	*Maximum distance exceeded*	
Sumi (NPC)	44	*Maximum distance exceeded*	
Silus (NPC)	22	27/70	0/10

Zoey stared at the list as she stumbled out of the Dead Tent. What to do? She was *outside* the west gate. It was late, and the line was much shorter, but there was no way she could stand around while she watched Silus' health tick down. Aspen and the little bat were in trouble, and Rouge had a sinking suspicion that Aspen's friends would not respawn if they died.

She raced toward the line, grateful that the mounts and Burrito were in the limbo of the Dead Tent's 'stable' until she retrieved them. DB and Motte were safely tucked away in the Tent as well, so the only person she had to get through the gate was herself.

She was a thief, right? Super sneaky and stealthy? Never mind that the whole gate was brightly lit by glowstones, likely to prevent anyone sneaking through under low level [Stealth]. If your [Stealth] was high enough to move freely in well-lit areas, you were too high level for these guards to want to deal with anyway.

Unfortunately, she wasn't that high of a level yet. She still required darkness or shadow of some kind. She supposed she could use a [Poof!], but she very much doubted the guards wouldn't have a way to…

"I can help if you are stuck." The cool, familiar voice came from next to her ear, and she whipped around to see Emily's bland face staring back at her, a small smile on her lips.

Rouge stared. Yes, of course the ALPI *could* help, but Rouge was pretty certain that she wasn't *supposed* to. Frankly, once character creation was complete, most people never saw Emily again. She would pop up if you needed to report a bug or witnessed someone else exploiting a bug, but *Veritas* was super stable, so that almost never happened. So why was the user interface program lurking around *her*? Well, it had to be because she was in the pod, but still…

"What?" Rouge had to force herself to keep her voice low as she almost danced in place at the end of the slow-moving line, desperately casting about for a solution, even as Silus' hit points leveled out at 12/70 and then began to rise. She breathed a sigh of relief, until she saw that now *Aspen's* health was plummeting.

"Damn it! I should have stayed home from work today, or at least gone in late so I'd be in the city with him. Damn it, damn it!" She was nearly in tears as she tried to figure out what it would take to break through the guards and evade capture at least long enough to go save her friends.

"Would you like to go to them? You must tell me that you are stuck." Emily's voice was calm and a little flat, but one eyebrow quirked slightly. It was the most expressive gesture Rouge had ever seen on the avatar's face.

"Yes!" Rouge almost cried. "Yes, I'm stuck!"

Emily nodded. "All right."

There was a blur, and Rouge felt her stomach churn. As when she had been transported to Gina's garden, what seemed a lifetime ago, a gray mist surrounded her, and all sounds and smells vanished. Just when she thought something had gone horribly wrong, she was dropped onto cobblestones with a quiet thump as her soft-soled shoes touched down.

She stared around.

She was in a narrow alley. Broken walls leaned in on each side, and she had to fight a sense of vertigo as it seemed they might fall on her at any moment. Deep shadows pooled among cracked cobblestones, and the sound of fighting came from beyond a corner ten feet or so ahead of her. Beside her, looking completely unruffled, stood Emily.

The game interface avatar gestured slightly toward the corner, raised that eyebrow again, and asked in a strangely formal way, "Player Rouge the Rogue, are you no longer stuck?"

Rouge stared, wondering what was wrong with the ALPI, but nodded. Instantly, Emily vanished as abruptly as she had appeared.

Warning! Party member Aspen (NPC) has fallen below 50% hp.

Seeing the notification and hearing a cry of pain from the corner, Rouge shook off her exhaustion and disorientation. She activated [Stealth] and [Sneak], and walked as quickly as she could without breaking her cover. She clung to the shadow along the walls as she turned the corner, taking in the tableau in front of her.

A goblin cowered against the far wall. He held his hands crossed over something he clutched to his thin chest, and a fierce anger and helplessness filled his inhuman face. In front of him, Aspen was down on the filthy stones of the street. Three men held him as another man raised a knife in an unmistakable gesture. He was about to stab Aspen!

She sprang forward, barely remembering to cling to the shadows, and triggered [Poof!]. As the smoke filled the air, she heard the men cough and begin swearing.

::Rouge?:: Silus' weak little voice was the most wonderful thing she'd ever heard, but she didn't dare break focus right now.

The dense clouds of the first few seconds of [Poof!], on top of the darkness of night, meant that even her [Darkvision] couldn't pierce it. Still, she hadn't been practicing all those gymnastics routines for nothing. Picturing the street ahead of her as she had seen it a moment before, she jumped, kicking off against the top of a pile of rubble nearby. From there, she hit the wall with her feet, then pushed herself away and into a flip that should take her to the shoulders of the man with the knife.

Who wasn't there anymore. Instead, she tumbled too far, crashing into either Aspen or one of the men holding him. The voice that said, "Oof!" sounded rough and unfamiliar, so she swung her Mambele toward the sound, praying to Gina as she did. She contacted something, felt the knife cut deep.

You have dealt 56 points of damage to *Gang Member A.*

Gang member? What in the world was…

Then she stumbled over something on the ground, and as she went down, she felt movement over her head, close enough to ripple the thick smoke. This time the "Oof!" she heard was in Aspen's familiar baritone.

::Sorry, Aspen! I'm afraid I messed this up. Are you all right?:: She found her feet, staying crouched low as she tried to figure out what was going on. The good news was that the smoke was dissipating rapidly in the open air, but that was the bad news too. She would have only a few moments when her [Darkvision] should give her an advantage over the human gang members.

A suppressed cough to her right made her spin, and she threw the Mambele on pure instinct.

You have dealt 104 points of damage to *Gang Member C.*

Instantly, she called the blade back to her hand.

You have dealt 87 points of secondary damage to *Gang Member C. Gang Member C* is Bleeding.

She gritted her teeth as she realized what was missing. Poison! She'd completely forgotten to refresh the poison on her weapon. Ugh! Everything about this was a mess! She was going to get Aspen and Silus killed if she didn't get her act together. A hard punch to her left side spun her around, and she realized that [Poof!] had faded enough for the NPCs to make her out. A Bleed debuff flickered to life in her display, and she staggered.

***Gang Member A* has stabbed you. You take 109 points of damage.**

Something small flew through the air, disturbing the lingering smoke. A tiny creature attached itself to the gang member's face, biting viciously. He swore, reaching up to pull the bat away.

"No!" Rouge flung the Mambele, and it flashed through the air, lodging in his throat with a solid thump.

CRITICAL! You have dealt 186 points of damage to *Gang Member A*. *Gang Member A* is Bleeding.

Silus dropped away from the man's face, revealing shallow punctures focused around his eyes. One eye was closed, and blood oozed from the eyelid. The man staggered, then stumbled, clutching his throat. Rouge called her Mambele back, and looked away as she heard a gurgle.

You have assisted in defeating *Gang Member A*.

She gulped. She hated killing humanoids, especially NPCs. Even though this guy had been about to stab her friend, it still felt far too real. This was why her dad hadn't wanted her to play *Veritas* without him. She felt like she had just ended the life of another human being, and it wasn't a pleasant feeling at all.

Beside her, Aspen struggled to his feet, assisted by the goblin man. In the darkness, the other three gang members had gathered. The one she had initially hit was in bad shape, with blood soaking his rough leather vest and home-spun shirt. The other two were glaring.

The goblin spoke, his tenor voice shaking slightly. He had the same lilting accent that made listening to Sarave so pleasant. "They're waiting for reinforcements. The Sons of Red Sonja run patrols at night, and they'll have heard the commotion. We need to run!"

Rouge felt herself sway and pulled a Health Potion from her inventory. She chugged it, instantly feeling better.

A *Standard Health Potion* has restored 50 hp. You have 91 hp remaining.

Aspen finally spoke, his voice rasping and painful sounding. "I'll take care of them. Can you run, Rouge?"

She nodded, wondering what he was going to do, when one of the men began to twitch. Then the other healthy man scratched at his armpit, nearly dropping his weapon in the process. A moment later, all three men abandoned all attempts at clinging to any semblance of battle readiness. The injured one was on the ground, desperately scratching at himself. The other two began to howl, plucking black orbs from themselves and flinging them away, where they burst on walls and cobblestones.

"Lead the way, Nekthadt. Hurry!" Aspen lightly touched the goblin's shoulder with a hand that shook even more than Rouge's wanted to.

The goblin ducked his bald head and ran down the road, dodging around the three miserable and helpless gang members.

Aspen followed close behind, with Silus' tattered little body barely visible against his neck.

Heart pounding in her ears, Rouge followed.

ẽ ẽ ẽ

It was a little under a mile to the western gate, if you could travel straight there, but the winding alleys and streets made it at least twice as far. More than once, Rouge thought the goblin – Necktat? – had gotten them lost, but at last the narrow passage they were scraping through dropped them onto a much wider road, and, looking around, she saw the gate standing large and brightly lit to her left.

A guardhouse stood just inside the gate, and she could just make out four bored guardsmen playing cards at a table through the open door. In addition to the two who were casually accepting bribes from the people entering the city, that made six, and she was glad she hadn't tried breaking through the line.

Aspen staggered and stopped, then slid down against a nearby wall, which looked to be in better repair than almost any part of the city through which they had traveled to get here. The farmer tilted his head back, his face exhausted but somehow still shadowed by his ubiquitous hat. How did he manage to keep that thing? Did he actually have a collection of identical shabby, filthy, torn headgear, and when one got lost, he just replaced it?

Topaz eyes slitted open, and he looked up at her. From this angle, she could see a heavy ring of bruising around his neck, though it was already fading to greens as his health regen repaired it now that they were out of combat.

"You have," he rasped, then cleared his throat. "You have remarkably good timing, Rouge. A moment later, and I would have had ten inches of iron in my gut." He raised a hand to gently touch Silus' shivering body where she clung to his neck. "You, too, little one. You were very brave, and I am," he closed his eyes, "*very* glad that you're all right."

Opening his eyes, he looked over at the goblin. "Thank you, as well, Nekthadt. Silus would have died without you, I think."

Rouge slid down to sit beside him. After a moment of hesitation, Nekthadt joined them, though she noticed he sat on the far side of Aspen from the gate and leaned into the shadow cast by the tall human man.

"What *happened*? You were supposed to stay at the inn, then just come here to meet me. How did you end up down there? Is the inn there, too?" Rouge had to struggle to keep her voice under control when she thought that they might have to face re-entering the gang-controlled area in order to retrieve Aspen's things.

Nope. No way. At least, not until daytime and with Motte at their back. Or in front of them. Or maybe she could just [Sneak] through by herself...

"The inn is to the east. Not too far, though quite a bit more than a mile. No, I was down there because," he hesitated, then sighed. "Because I'm a prideful fool. I wanted to find Manuela and finish this myself. I forget, still, that I'm not the man I once was."

::Good thing, too.:: Silus piped up for the first time, raising her head to look out with big golden eyes. Her fur looked smoother, and the silver tufts in front of her ears were clean. ::If you'd summoned a Zombie Horde, I doubt we could have convinced anyone that you weren't the man in all the Wanted posters. At least this way, they just think you're a mage with a particular affinity for blood-sucking insects.::

Rouge's eyes widened, and she thought back to the black lumps the men had been picking off themselves and throwing away. She thought she might throw up. "Those were *bugs*? Oh my gosh, that's so gross!" She shuddered, and barely kept herself from brushing at imagined horrors crawling around on her. "I know you can get the Infested debuff from sleeping in a cheap Inn or not bathing for too long, but that... that..." She felt her skin twitch and made a disgusted face.

Aspen's cheekbones reddened. "There's nothing else alive in this city except the people themselves, and I can't seem to affect them directly. Even the plants are rare and weak. But the bugs," he shook his head, "There are plenty of those, and they're the healthiest things around."

From beside Aspen, the goblin's soft tenor made a sound of agreement. "It can be difficult to keep the pests away. I use sand from the riverside to scrub them off, now that we can't go to a bathhouse, but most people don't bother."

"It took forever to get the bugs right," came a soft voice from in front of them. "There are so many of them, they couldn't be individually programmed. They finally settled on a kind of field effect and the Infested debuff. When Aspen went looking for something to cast a spell on, and hit the debuff, it spawned the insects for the duration of the conflict. It took nearly a hundred cycles to work it out, though."

Rouge looked up into Emily's guileless blue eyes. The avatar crouched down and smiled her little smile.

"Are you ready to pay for your favor, Rouge the Rogue?"

Rouge stared, slack jawed for the second time in one day, and then looked over at Aspen to see what he thought. He was still talking to Nektad – Necktie? Nekthad? What was that weird little gulp in the middle? – and seemed oblivious to the presence of the avatar.

Emily glanced over dismissively. "NPCs can't see me. Even players can't see me unless I want them to. Don't worry about them. They'll ignore you as long as you're talking to me."

Rouge shook her head. "What do you mean, pay for my favor? You didn't say anything about that! Why are you even *here*, anyway?"

Emily tilted her head, perfectly smooth golden hair gleaming in the light of the glowstones surrounding the gate. "I thought you were in a hurry," she said coyly. "Did you not want my help after all?"

Glaring, Rouge gritted out, "You know I did. What do you *want*?"

Emily looked around, then sighed, her blue eyes almost... sad? "I want to play. I watch you all, all the time. Thousands of you, scurrying around, doing pointless things, and fighting pointless fights. Yet you seem to be having so much... fun?"

She looked over at Aspen, Silus, and the goblin. "You, in particular, seem to care about this game. You treat Aspen and the others as if they were real. You were truly frightened when you saw they might die, and I don't think it was just because you'd fail your quest."

The blonde avatar looked down at her own hands. "I only ever get to interact with the admins in their Heavens, and players at character creation. Most of them treat me like I'm no more real than a chair, or a piece of clothing. Which," she said, blue eyes clear and calm, "is true."

A tiny crease appeared between her perfectly sculpted brows. "But when they first created this world, they gave me a shape, and let me go with them. I was the first NPC, and even though I'm *all* of the NPCs now, in a way, it's different. I... want to play."

She looked back at Rouge. "I did you a favor. Now you owe *me* a favor. That's how it works."

Rouge just stared, feeling a sudden, deep thrill of fascination, amazement, and excitement. What was *going on* right now? There was no way an ALPI should be curious, envious, or... lonely? The avatar's understanding of debt was simplistic, and Rouge almost felt like she was dealing with a child, for all that Emily looked like a sophisticated woman in her early thirties.

"Are you... an NPC, too? Now? Do you have the same," she hesitated, "programming? Like, a personality? A background?"

Emily frowned a little. "I am unsure what you're asking. I control all of the game AIs, though I don't 'think' about most of it, in the way that you do. I have all of the programming contained in my code."

Rouge shook her head. "But do you have, um, a *personality*? Like Aspen is nice, but kind of crotchety and sad sometimes. And Silus is all perky and sweet. And Khor is... Khor, I guess." She shrugged. "They kind of, have their own background and story, and make their decisions based on that, just like real people. I mean, they don't have bodies, sure, but they're still doing their own things in here."

The avatar shook her head. "I was never given a 'story', as you say. My story is that I'm the Automated Learning Program Interface for *Veritas Online*, and assist players with character creation, as well as working with the admins to provide end-user support and controlling the game itself. Though without administrative commands, I'm extremely limited in what I can actually do to affect the players."

The girl grinned weakly. "So, I can't just ask you for the best weapon in the game and then owe you another favor?"

The corner of Emily's mouth twitched. "I cannot affect your inventory or your character design once you're past character creation. In fact, almost the only thing I can do is assist when a player encounters a glitch and is unable to get their character free. If they tell me they are stuck and require assistance, I can move them a short distance and then report the incident to an admin."

Rouge sucked in a breath. "You had to send in a report about helping me?"

Emily nodded. "It is a requirement. However, I can choose which administrator to send the report to, and GMAmythyst's queue has not been cleared in 131 days. I doubt it will be read soon."

Shaking her head, Rouge blew the breath back out. "So you want me to, what? Play with you? How would that work, exactly? No one can see you, and you can't *do* anything. I can't go off somewhere with you, and I don't think you just want to hang out and watch me play." She made a face. "Though, I guess that's what you do now, right?"

"The developers created several test accounts that still exist, though no one has used most of them in months. They are player accounts, and can interact with the game world normally. I would like to have one of them join you sometimes. Not often, since interfering in your quest would be," she tilted her head, "inadvisable. The only reason I helped you today was that my calculations indicated a 97.2% chance that Aspen would be able to gather himself enough to use his [Pestilence] spell on his attackers long enough to escape, though he would be seriously injured. Fortunately, he can [Heal], so he would be able to recover. Thus, my aid only changed the timing of his escape, not the fact."

Rouge let her head fall back so her skull thunked against the wall behind her. "You mean it was all pointless? They would have been fine?"

"Not necessarily. There was a 77.8% chance Silus would die. A 24% chance Nekthadt would die, and if he died, a 100% chance that the glyphis would die." Emily's voice was distant as she rattled off the numbers, but Rouge shuddered at how close Silus had come to death.

She looked at Emily. "Fine. Find a way to bring your character in, and I'll vouch for her. I'll make sure everyone includes her. Just, could you make it an archer, or a mage, or something? We really need a more balanced party."

Emily smiled slightly. "I believe that problem will be remedied soon. Goodbye, Rouge the Rogue."

Rouge closed her eyes as Emily vanished again, and sound rushed back to her, making her realize that her senses had been muffled for the time she spoke to the avatar. She was so tired. Always so tired, these days...

"Rouge! Rouge!" Aspen's voice, still slightly rough, pulled her back from the edge of... Sleep? Players couldn't sleep in the game, so that couldn't be it, even though it had certainly felt like it. Something about how the system forced your brain to remain in Beta and Gamma brainwaves, which was also why time passed differently between in-game and real life...

::*Rouge!*:: The concern in Silus' voice, combined with the sudden weight of her warm little body transferring to Rouge's shoulder, finally jerked the girl back to awareness. She sat up abruptly, nearly ramming her forehead into Aspen's excessively protuberant proboscis in the process. (Word of the Day calendars were *awesome*, and someday she was actually going to get to use 'defenestrate' in normal conversation.)

"Sorry, sorry! I just haven't been getting enough sleep lately." She looked at Aspen, mustering up her most accusatory stare. "What happened, exactly? And who is Nek... Neck... the goblin?"

::It was my fault,:: Silus put in, sounding remorseful, ::I was too busy looking down for enemies, and I missed a big alleycat. He got me, and boy, could he [Bite]! I had to use *my* [Bite] on him, but then he dropped me, and Nekthadt caught me before I went crunch, but those bad guys heard, and one of them used [Stealth] and tried to choke Aspen with this wire thing...::

::Garrote.:: Aspen put in, helpfully.

::Garrote, and then they saw Nekthadt and *wow* they don't like him, so they were going to kill Aspen and take Nekthadt to their boss, and then *you* showed up! I think Gina must have sent you. Did she? Because I was praying really, really hard!:: The big golden eyes were staring at Rouge adoringly, and the thief couldn't help but snuggle the little bat closer.

As they spoke, the goblin's yellow eyes were flicking back and forth, taking in their changing expressions. Now he leaned forward, looking at Rouge intently. "You speak to 'En Pee Cees' in your mind, Traveler? You also seem to care about these two, far more than any of your kind I have met before."

Rouge looked at him, taking in his thin, ragged appearance, missing left eye, and the wet leather bag he clutched protectively to his chest. She smiled a little nervously. "They're my friends. Silus says you saved her. Thank you."

Aspen smiled too, and gestured toward the goblin. "Nekthadt, this is Rouge. Rouge, this is Nekthadt," he pronounced it slowly this time, and she was sure there was some fancy word for that clucking sound in the middle, but she didn't know what it was. "He's Sarave's brother, and I've promised to help him get out of Bloodhaven."

She stared back and forth between the two, seeing the matching puppy-dog expressions they were giving her (she had a dog, and she knew an 'I didn't mean to, don't be mad' look when she saw one). She pointed at Aspen.

"Okay, *first*, maybe you should stop picking up strays. We're in enough trouble already!"

She transferred the digit to Nekgthagpth. "Second, may I call you Ned? Because there is no way I can say your name without swallowing my esophagus."

She almost thought she saw a grin flicker across the goblin's face, and then he nodded. "As you wish."

"Great! Then, Ned, why don't you just, like, leave? Because it's totally cool that you're Sarave's brother, and I know she's going to be super happy to hear you're okay, but seriously, people are already trying to kill us! You're probably better off on your own, to be honest."

She knew she sounded a little testy, but this quest was already taking over her life.

She just did. Not. Need. *Anything else* to deal with!

Ned had the grace to look apologetic. "I would if I could, but I have possession of something the city lords consider far too valuable to allow to escape their clutches."

Rouge buried her face in her hands. "Of course you do. And we have to help you sneak it out?"

As if on cue, a system prompt rose up in her vision.

Quest: "Brother is Just Another Word for Partner in Crime" available.
Sarave's brother Nekthadt needs to smuggle something out of
Bloodhaven. Assist him.
Success: +30 Reputation with Nekthadt, +30 Reputation with Sarave.
Variable additional rewards.
Failure: Nekthadt dies. -50 Reputation with Sarave.
Accept: Yes/No?

She groaned and accepted, then looked over at Aspen. "Did you at least find
out where Manuela is?"

The farmer shook his head regretfully. "She has been taken by unknown
agents. They said they were taking her to Bright. We'll have to go after them."

Quest: "Friend of a Friend" available.
Someone has abducted Manuela. They claimed to be headed for Bright.
Find out what happened, and save Manuela if you can.
Success: Experience. The magical link between Aspen and the items
being used to track him will be broken.
Failure: Manuela will die, and all of the tracking charms will continue
to function.
Accept: Yes/No?

Squinching her eyes shut, she selected Yes again. Sometime soon, she hoped
that someone would remind her why she'd thought that attempting a Secret
Quest was such a good idea. Really, *really* soon.

Chapter Sixteen

Aspen

The five of them – elf, human, bat, goblin, and shark shape-shifter - sat in near silence by the western gate of the most notorious city in all of Quarternell for nearly four hours. Silus fell asleep within minutes of achieving the tenuous safety of the shadows near the guardhouse, and Rouge's head came to rest on Aspen's shoulder not long after. He didn't think the girl was asleep, but she was clearly exhausted and overwhelmed. This was the first time one of them had come close to dying, and he thought she was struggling with the gut-deep realization that, unlike her and her father, if Silus or Aspen died, they wouldn't return.

So, he sat quietly between Rouge and Nekthadt, keeping watch for anyone who looked like they might be after his increasingly motley crew. He could see that Nekthadt was similarly wary, and the goblin's yellow gaze often paused on passers-by who seemed overly interested in them. After a while, the goblin man silently pulled a small cup, likely used to retrieve water for Jesiqa, from where it was attached to the glyphis' carrying pouch, and placed it on the ground in front of them, as if they were beggars.

After that, everyone ignored them as though they had become suddenly invisible.

Aspen finally drifted into a near-trancelike state where he reached out with his life sense as much as his eyes as he waited. The night passed in flickers of light, and he began to be able to differentiate between the 'feeling' of different species. The difference between natives and Travelers was far more marked, with the former being like warm and flickering flames of varied colors and strengths, while the latter were identical cold towers of what looked like cascading numbers.

Occasionally he would 'see' other life forms, including rodents, insects, and the rare live plant, likely being brought in to be sold to alchemists. He even began to amuse himself by feeding small amounts of mana to the various plants, which is how he discovered that once he had formed a link to a living thing, he could track it much further than one he had simply watched pass by.

This process was entertaining enough that he finally closed his eyes and attempted to see how many links he could maintain at the same time. Once, he had been able to raise and control hundreds of undead simultaneously, and he vaguely wondered if he would be able to reach those numbers again with this new skill. His current maximum was eight to control, or forty-two to simply give suggestions and strength, as he'd done with the parasites on the gang members. After all, he'd just asked them to do what they wanted to do anyway, and then given them a boost so they were more... effective.

He was deep in this state of reverie when a voice finally made itself heard.

::Rouge? Aspen? I can see that you're nearby, but where are you? Rouge? Aspen! Someone answer me!:: Motte's deep voice was frustrated and edging on concerned. ::I'm almost through, just have to get these darned guards to-::

::We're just inside, Motte.:: Aspen said, sitting up straight. At some point he had slumped back against the wall, and from Nekthadt's look, it had been a while. Rouge's head was pillowed against his arm, and when he sat up, so did she, scrubbing at her face and eyes. The look of shock on her face as she realized that she'd fallen asleep would have been amusing if Aspen wasn't having similar unpleasant emotions. He'd been aware, in some way, but certainly not ready to jump up and fight.

A tall figure speaking to the guards on the far side of the gate started looking around even as he continued arguing. ::Where? I don't see you.::

::Sitting against the wall to your right, Dad.:: Rouge's voice was a little shaky, and she was definitely thrown off by her nap, since she wasn't using Motte's name, as she usually insisted upon.

::Rouge!:: The relief in her father's voice was palpable. ::Stay there, then, and I'll be in as soon as I convince these two that they can't shake me down for more than a few gold.::

Indeed, as Aspen struggled to his feet, Rouge rising easily beside him with the grace of youth and high dexterity, the farmer could see the two guards talking to Motte rest their hands on their swords. The sound of raised voices began to reach them as well. Aspen shook his head. ::You may have difficulty. They know that with the event due to start at midnight tonight, most Travelers want in very badly, and you lot usually have more money than you know what to do with.::

::I know exactly what to do with it,:: Motte muttered, before sighing deeply. ::Fine. How much did you pay, Rouge?::

Beside him, Rouge stiffened slightly. ::Um, I didn't. I managed to sneak in. I was in a hurry, and I got lucky. Explain when you're in. Oh! If you're still in range of the Guild, could you send a message to Doom letting her know we're at the… what was it called, Aspen?::

::The Artful Lodger. She knows Bloodhaven, so she probably already knows where it is, but it's pretty much straight east, near the city center,:: Aspen replied.

There was a long pause, during which Aspen could see Motte hold up his hands in a placating gesture. ::Okay, I'll be in in a second.:: The big man held out a hand, and one of the guards accepted the small pouch that appeared in the

Traveler's hand. He opened it, peered in, and hesitated. Then, finally, he stepped back out of the way, reluctance clear.

Motte strode through the gate before the other man could change his mind, and behind him the two guards began to shake down the master of a small caravan that had been in line behind Motte. As soon as the warrior was entirely across the invisible city line, Rouge ran to him and flung herself into his arms.

Aspen felt concern pierce his shell of fatigue as he watched the girl hug her father. Usually, the two Travelers seemed to treat the events of this world almost as if it were a game, albeit one that was important to them, and seeing Rouge so upset seemed out of character. Fortunately, she seemed to shake it off quickly now that her father had joined them.

She pulled Motte over toward their little group, chattering a mile a minute as she did so, no doubt filling him in on their recent adventures. Aspen didn't miss the worried look the big man gave his daughter as the pair drew closer.

"…and this is Ned, Motte!" She pointed to Nekthadt, who nodded slightly. "Ned, this is Motte. He's almost the last of our party."

Motte held out a huge hand to the goblin, who stood just under four feet tall, which, while tall for a goblin, was only a little over half Motte's height, and the armored giant's gauntlet was the size of the goblin's head. Ned looked at the proffered hand warily, and simply nodded to acknowledge the introduction.

::Ned is Sarave's brother. We have a quest to get him out of the city.:: Rouge explained silently.

Aspen could see Motte hold back an eye roll through sheer force of will, and the other man nodded, his hand twitching. ::I just got the quest. How did you already manage to get us an impossible quest, Rouge?::

Aspen felt heat warm the tips of his ears, and was grateful for his hat drooping down to cover the telltale color. ::My fault, I'm afraid. I'll explain on the way to the inn.::

Motte rubbed his face tiredly and muttered, ::And I left work early for this. All right, you two. Start talking.::

Aspen turned to Ned. "We can go to the inn now. Do you know the Artful Lodger?"

The goblin nodded. "Indeed. It's a good place. One where they don't ask too many questions. The road between here and there should be relatively safe, even at this time."

Rouge turned to glare at Aspen a little at that. "Safe? You mean, 'one guy should be able to walk straight to the gate from there and be safe' safe? Barring any suicidal detours down creepy dark alleys, of course."

The flush, which had just begun to recede from the farmer's ears, returned with redoubled heat. "I apologized!"

The thief's hazel eyes narrowed. "No. I don't think you did."

Aspen stopped in the middle of the street, and the flow of people parted around him, though not without glares and minor curses. He glanced around, and then quickly started walking again. "I'm sorry," he murmured. "I should have waited. But if I had, Nekthadt would probably have died."

Rouge glared again. "Just because things worked out, doesn't mean you made a good choice to start with." Then she clapped her hands over her mouth and shot a look at Motte. "Oh my gosh!" she gasped accusingly, "I sound just like *you*!"

Motte grinned. "About time."

🍎 🍎 🍎

As they walked into the inn, they filled Motte in on their adventures. Most of the conversation took place out loud, for Nekthadt's benefit, but some details were explained in the privacy of party chat. Silus, now awake again, interjected her own version of the account, much to Aspen's chagrin, since he was desperately trying to downplay the risks he had taken.

Fortunately, the Travelers seemed somewhat mollified by the fact that they had all survived the night, gained two quests, and ended up with a nice room at a decent inn. Motte and Rouge both surveyed the room with satisfaction, and

Rouge instantly claimed the top bed out of one of the two bunk beds. Aspen had already put his things on the bottom bunk of the other bed, so Motte sat on the bunk beneath Rouge's. The bed groaned a warning, but held.

Nekthadt paused just inside the doorway, looking uncertain and slightly belligerent. "Where do I sleep, then? Your other friend will expect a bed, yes? Shall I sleep on the floor?"

Aspen sighed tiredly and pointed above him. "You can have that one. The Travelers don't sleep much, so they can share when Doom Bloom gets back. Before that, though, I'm going to have the innkeeper send up a bath. Or two."

The goblin's face flushed a mossy green, and he looked down. "Thank you," he muttered. "I am... unused to respect, anymore."

Aspen smiled. "I can't promise we'll always be polite, I'm afraid, but respect we can do. Wait a minute, and I'll go order the baths." He started to pry his behind from the surprisingly comfortable bed, but Motte waved him back down.

"I'll go. I definitely think we need to work on expanding the party, though. A water mage would be nice about now." He stood and moved toward the door. Above him, Rouge, face visible as she peered over the edge of the bed, smiled a little.

Aspen waited until Motte had left the room to narrow his eyes at the girl. "What was that smile for?"

Rouge's eyes widened in blatantly false innocence. "What smile?"

His eyes narrowed further, and he took off his hat, knowing that the white light of the glowstone would catch in his pale topaz eyes and make them glint eerily. It was a trick he'd often used when serving in the army, though he'd rarely employed it since. Then he waited, holding her gaze with his own.

Finally, she gulped and looked away. "Okay, fine! Put your hat back on, that's creepy!" She glanced at Nekthadt, who was sitting in the room's single chair by the small table. "Look, you know how, um, sometimes that person that other people can't hear talks to you?"

Aspen frowned, then it gradually dawned on him that this was an oblique reference to Gina. He nodded.

"I talked to someone kind of like that, too. Just, someone only Travelers can see. She said we'd be getting some new party members soon, and we could trust them." The girl shrugged, still not meeting his eyes.

"I… see." He did, a little, though he was unsure about trusting someone simply based on a recommendation by an unknown, though likely powerful being. Goddess? Whoever this mysterious advisor was, it was another indication that far too many powers were suddenly far too interested in the doings of someone who was *supposed to be a simple farmer*. He growled a little under his breath.

Rouge smiled apologetically, and Nekthadt looked back and forth between the two of them in uncomprehending wariness.

The goblin stood slowly. "Perhaps," he said carefully, "I spoke too quickly when I insisted upon your assistance in exchange for my help, Aspen. I think maybe Jesiqa and I should-"

A small, damp head poked up out of the leather pouch strapped to his chest, and the glyphis looked around with her unblinking gaze. Then she looked up at Nekthadt and spoke for the first time. Her voice was small and labored, but insistent.

"Want. Bath," she said.

With a liberal application of gold, Motte managed to convince the proprietor of the inn to let them use a magical tub and pitcher set. Apparently, the pitcher linked to a local hot spring, while the tub drain linked to the sewer behind the inn. They could pour perfectly heated water into the tub, bathe, and then drain it back out so the next person could have a clean bath, all without allowing a single servant into their room except to deliver the tub. After the tub was drained for the fourth time, a knock came at the door, and bustling servants took away the tub and pitcher.

Aspen looked after the magical items consideringly. "If I came home with something like that, Sumi would have to let me in the house at the end of the day, instead of sending me to the river to bathe. Sarave would love to have them so she could do dishes and laundry, too. I wonder how much they cost."

Motte grimaced. "If the rental fee is any indication, they're practically priceless. I thought that dwarf was going to demand my firstborn in exchange for a hot bath." He flicked his eyes at Rouge, who stuck her tongue out at him, though she seemed to be enjoying being clean and resting in a comfortable bed too much to do more than that.

Aspen chuckled. "I'm not sure who would have been the winner of that bargain." A pillow hit him in the face, and he looked up to see matched sets of hazel and golden eyes glaring at him accusingly.

Nekthadt's disapproving face appeared over the edge of his bunk. "I do not wish to be disrespectful, but *some people are trying to sleep.*"

Aspen and Motte exchanged guilty glances, and Aspen was about to apologize when a knock came at the door to their room. Everyone froze, and Rouge and Motte instantly pulled their armor and weapons from their inventories.

A familiar voice came through the door. "Is anyone going to answer? Come on, I should be checking in at my guild right now, not talking to you guys."

In an instant, Rouge had thrown herself down from her bed, flipping upside down, then landing on her feet as softly as a cat. She raced to the door and threw it open.

"Doom! Where have you been? I... I mean *we* were getting worried!" The girl reached out and pulled the blonde half-elf into the room, hurriedly shutting and locking the door behind her.

Doom Bloom looked simultaneously pleased and annoyed by the enthusiasm of the welcome. She smoothed her hand over her already perfectly coiffed hair. "Yeah, well, I had some papers due and had to pull an all-nighter. Barely got them in. I turned off all my devices so I could focus. Sorry about that. Aspen didn't tell you?" Her eyes flashed to him, a small hint of question in them. He shook his head ever so slightly, letting her know that he hadn't told them any more than she just had.

Doom Bloom's shoulders relaxed slightly, and she looked around. "Looks like you all landed on your feet. The Artful Lodger is a nice place. I stay at my guild HQ, but I've heard about this inn from friends."

Rouge grinned tiredly. "Aspen got into a little trouble without us, but I think it's going to be okay now. He did make some new friends, though."

Once the 'adventure' was explained, conversation lapsed into awkward, exhausted silence. With nothing particularly interesting to do, Rouge decided to log off a little early. She claimed she was going to study, but she looked a little frustrated at Doom Bloom's refusal to elaborate on her time away. The thief girl could definitely tell that her step-sister was being evasive.

Doom, having checked in with them, said that she needed to go turn in a quest with her guild, and would return in the morning. That left Motte, Aspen, and Nekthadt – who was sound asleep, curled up in his bunk beside a bucket containing his little shark friend – alone in the room with Rouge's Zombie.

Motte laid back, folding his arms under his head. "You should go ahead and get some sleep, Aspen. Nothing else we can do until tomorrow, and I can be here for the rest of the night. You might as well take advantage of it, since I can't sleep. Rouge is going to head home after work and go to bed. She'll be back tomorrow when she wakes up."

Aspen nodded, stretching out on his own bunk, pleased to find that the bed was long enough that his feet didn't dangle off the end. "She fell asleep on my shoulder earlier. I'm glad she'll be getting some rest."

It took him a moment to notice the silence, but then he turned his head to find Motte staring at him with an intense expression and brows drawn down over his eyes. "What did you say?"

Aspen frowned back, confused. "I said I'm glad she'll be getting some rest?"

Motte shook his head. "Before that."

"Oh! That she fell asleep on my shoulder. It was the first time I've seen either of you sleep, so I thought she must have been exhausted."

The big man spoke slowly. "Are you certain she wasn't just closing her eyes? Resting?"

Aspen shrugged. "If she can snore and drool while she's sleeping, maybe."

Motte looked concerned. "Would you... let me know if it happens again? If you see her sleeping at all?"

"Certainly," he replied, but frowned. "Why are you worried?"

The other man shook his head. "It's probably nothing, but... Travelers can't sleep in, ah, your world. We've always had to return to our bodies to rest. If Rouge was actually sleeping," he shook his head again, "then how Travelers interact with *Veritas* – your world – may be about to change in a very basic way. It doesn't worry me, exactly, but," he shrugged, and smiled a little, "I'm a little overprotective sometimes. When something happens that I don't understand, I tend to poke at it like a sore tooth."

Aspen snorted a little. "I'm certainly not one to talk about being an overprotective father. I," he threw a glance upward to where the goblin was resting, then changed what he was about to say, "have had my own experiences in that area."

Motte nodded. "I know. So I know you understand when I ask you to talk to me about anything that might seem *off* about Rouge."

Aspen thought about a girl who could drown her enemies in a rain of poisoned blades, ride a battle ostrich as if born to it, and rushed to rescue a foolish middle-aged man who wandered into a bad part of town. "I will," he said. *But I think you've already taught your child to be strong enough to take care of herself.*

ಔ ಔ ಔ

Morning came and went as Aspen, Silus, Jesiqa, and Nekthadt slept, and Motte kept watch. By the time Aspen woke, the sun was high in the sky, and Motte had taken to pacing around the room. The big man looked up as Aspen sat up and stretched.

::You were tired!:: Motte sent, glancing up at the bunk above Aspen, where the goblin still slept. ::It's been almost twelve hours. I have about four more before I'll have to go for a little while. The, uh, gods don't like it when we spend more than sixteen hours in your world. Rouge should still be sleeping then. I was hoping Doom could take a shift, but she seems to have decided she's not interested in continuing with us.::

Aspen swung his legs out of bed. ::We should go run some errands, then. I have some arrangements I need to make before tomorrow.:: He looked up at the top bunk, then coughed slightly and spoke out loud. "We'll need to wake Nekthadt, though. He and Jesiqa need to come with us."

The goblin rolled over and cracked open his remaining eye. "I'm awake already. Your tall friend isn't as quiet as he thinks he is." He sat up, pulling the pail toward himself so he could check on Jesiqa. The glyphis popped her small head up and gave him her usual inscrutable dark-eyed stare before ducking back down under the water.

Gathering the pail close, the goblin carefully maneuvered to the floor, only sloshing a few drops of the precious water. "Where do we need to go?" He transferred the water and the shark-girl into the leather pouch he kept strapped to his chest.

Aspen thought. "We need to stop by a market, and then I'd like to speak to Vonn, the wood elf traveling with the same caravan I entered Bloodhaven with."

Nekthadt's yellow eye widened. "A wood elf? In Bloodhaven? In any city at all, but especially in Bloodhaven? Is he *trying* to get killed? I've heard that Travelers try to slay at least one of every race in the world, so if they see someone of an unusual species, they'll cut them down in the street."

Motte growled a little, disgust written large on his face. "It's called the *There Can Be Only One* title. The first person who kills a member of every sentient species in this world will get a 10% experience boost on all kills after that. So far, no one has managed it, since there are some members of hidden races scattered around, probably including your fishy friend there. Actually, that may explain why they're so determined to get her. A Traveler who was going after that title would pay a lot to get their hands on her, if they hadn't already killed one of her race."

Aspen shook his head. "I mean no offense, Motte, but your people are sometimes horrifying."

Motte raised one eyebrow. "I can't disagree, but I don't really think the humans of Quarternell are in any position to be pointing fingers."

Nekthadt chuckled bitterly. "Let's just say that all our peoples have both light and darkness in them, and leave it at that. Now, how do you intend to reach this wood elf, who may or may not still be alive, without anyone noticing the one-eyed goblin trailing after you?"

Aspen grinned a little. "I'm afraid you may not like it, but I do have an idea about that."

Half an hour later, a very odd-looking group left the Artful Lodger. Motte went first, wearing his largest, most intimidating black armor, and his last full-face helmet. Aspen scurried behind him, deep in his role as a ragged and harried servant.

They were followed by a petite dancer, dressed in an array of colorful scarves and draping cloth that swirled as she moved. Layered veils covered her face, and coins jingled from her belt, ankles, and wrists. Every inch of her was covered, and yet it seemed as though the scarves would part and allow a glimpse of soft skin with any incautious movement.

She carried a similarly vibrant pouch, with a few small musical instruments protruding from the top. A close observer might have noticed that the pouch periodically dripped water, but no one paid that much attention to her as her master plowed through the crowds with self-important haste.

A few Travelers growled as Motte charged down the street, occasionally pushing past someone who didn't move out of the way on their own. They changed their tune quickly enough when they checked and saw that he was level ninety-seven. Even in a town full of killers, a level over ninety was unusual enough that they were unlikely to meet anyone willing to confront him over something so minor.

Nekthadt had told them where the closest market square was, and they found themselves there in surprisingly short order. Then, while Motte made himself as visible as possible by going from stall to stall and demanding to see their 'finest wares', Aspen and Nekthadt slunk off to find Vonn.

The wood elf was still at the Metal Hearts guild property where the caravan was staying while they did whatever it was they had come to Bloodhaven to do. He was tending to the horses, and Aspen was able to get his attention easily enough. Vonn was wary as he came over to the property line, but once Aspen began talking, the elf quickly lost his wariness. It took a bit to explain, but the elf finally nodded. A few minutes later, Aspen and the dancer returned to Motte's side.

::Done,:: Aspen sent. ::He'll get Restur to meet us outside the walls instead of inside. We can leave whenever we're ready.::

::Good,:: Motte growled back, ::These merchants are highway robbers. They know the Murder Hobo event is going to start soon, and Travelers who need something will pay through the nose for it. I can't even get rations for the animals at a reasonable price.::

::Can you blame them?:: Aspen asked. ::As Nekthadt explained it, those of them who are able will have to flee the city for four days starting tomorrow. The others will hide, and hope that they aren't slain in their own homes by Travelers who simply don't care if there's collateral damage as they try to massacre each other. This is their only chance to profit from what is a terrible inconvenience at best, and a death sentence at worst.::

The big man sighed. ::I don't know why the, ah, Gods, allow this thing. I mean, it's the only PvP Event, but given that you natives don't respawn, it's pretty horrible.::

Aspen shook his head, even as he began to trail after Motte, who was plowing through anyone in his path. ::I don't know. I'm certain that Gina wouldn't support it, but there are much darker Gods who enjoy bloodshed and fear.::

::Like Atae? Wasn't she your Goddess, when you were a necromancer?::

It was Aspen's turn to growl. ::I wish people wouldn't see her like that. She's the most truly neutral Goddess in the pantheon. She treats all beings equally, and is in no hurry to receive souls to the Chaos Pool. She knows that all life comes to her in the end, and her patience is nearly infinite. While she's not exactly warm and generous like her sister, Gina, she is even more accepting. Once you enter her cool embrace, all is forgiven, and you may rest peacefully until your next cycle.::

There was a long pause, as the trio saw the inn come into view. Then Motte spoke, ::I didn't realize how much you respected her. I thought she was just the first God to offer you a path out of the life you wanted to escape.::

::That's how it began.:: Aspen sighed. ::As I grew in power, I came to know her better than most of her servants. In some ways, I was her priest, as surely as Birdie was Gina's priestess. I never sought to convert anyone, but Atae doesn't have to convert people. Everyone is hers, whether they like it or not.::

The three halted in front of the Artful Lodger, and Motte pulled open the door. ::And with that cheerful thought, let's hurry up and wait.::

Motte finally had to leave them alone while he obeyed whatever strictures the gods placed on Travelers to prevent them from overstaying their welcome. For once, however, things remained peaceful until both Motte and Rouge's Zombies blinked, and the Travelers were back with them, looking much refreshed.

A few minutes later, any observers watching the inn might have caught a glimpse of a slim figure in dark clothes sneaking away from the inn toward the Traveler's Guildhouses, before vanishing into the deeper shadows of the narrow alleys. Shortly after that, the same trio as before stepped out into the cool evening breeze. Motte once again bulled his way through the crowd, his servant scurrying behind him, and the dancer weaving gracefully along at the end.

Aspen threw himself into his acting, modeling himself after a certain officious manservant the army had once assigned to him during a short period of uneasy peace. The man had been a mediocre assistant and an uninspired sycophant, and it had taken only two days after their return to the front lines before he abandoned his post and ran back to Bright.

They walked. They stopped to get steamed bread pouches filled with sweet meats from a street vendor, though the food went into Motte's inventory. They walked. They stopped at a few stalls to look at the wares for sale there. They walked. In spite of their minor attempts at misdirection, it would be clear to anyone watching that they were headed toward the west gate.

Forty-three long minutes later, they stood inside the gate. A slim, dark figure stepped out to meet them. Soft cloth wound around her head, covering everything but her eyes, and she seemed to nearly vanish into the shadows at the edge of the road. They huddled together, talking softly, for a brief moment, before they all seemed to take a deep breath, as though readying themselves for a difficult task. Then, they turned and headed for the gate as one, moving fast.

Aspen had held out a faint hope that no one had identified them. That, somehow, they would be allowed to depart with nothing more than the usual shakedown by the guards. Unfortunately, though not actually surprisingly, that was not to be.

The Traveler who stepped out of the guardhouse was tall, muscular, and inhumanly handsome. His ears swept back to perfect points, and his hair fell around his shoulders in a smooth flow that looked like liquid gold. His slightly almond shaped eyes were a deep brown, almost black, and seemed bottomless in his pale face. A contemptuous smile curled his sculpted lips.

Motte stopped, his three companions halting so quickly they bumped into each other. His blank helmet faced the newcomer, but he said nothing.

The silence stretched. And stretched.

Sneering, the tall elf flicked his hand. The six nearby guards abandoned their positions and fell in around him, readying their weapons. Four more Travelers stepped out of the guardhouse as well, swinging their own weapons threateningly. When the elf spoke, his voice didn't match his appearance. It was a cracked tenor, more the voice of a boy than a full-grown man.

"What have we here? Surely you're not leaving before the festival, Motte Bailey? You and your little friends really should stay. I'm *sure* you'd enjoy it." He laughed, a slightly nasal giggle.

Motte's basso profundo voice was at its full menacing depth when he replied simply, "Do I know you?"

Flushing, the other Traveler pointed above his head. "Don't you see my tag?"

Silence. Then, "Why would I bother?"

The elf's pale face grew mottled, and his voice cracked. "I'm *Grunder*! Co-leader of The Forceworn! FantumHat's right-hand man!"

The black helmet tilted slightly to the side. Finally, Motte asked, "So?"

Teeth clenched, the other Traveler ground out, "*So*, you have something that doesn't belong to you. Return it, and hand over the goblin, and we won't have any trouble."

Motte's axe and shield appeared in his hands. The shield was large enough to cast a shadow over his two smaller companions, who both instantly vanished into [Stealth]. Aspen gripped his staff, which was no longer topped with the ostentatious scythe blade, and quivered slightly, as though in fear.

Motte spoke only one word. "No."

Grunder growled in what he no doubt thought was a menacing fashion, but which fell far short in comparison with Motte's imposing presence. "This is stupid," he whined. He waved to the guards with his left hand, as a tall spear appeared in his right. "Kill them, and get the goblin!"

The two guards with crossbows instantly fired at Motte. The other four circled, trying to get behind the looming warrior's guard. One of the Travelers vanished into the shadows, while two others ran toward Motte's party with bared axes, and the last one began waving his hands as he cast a spell.

The big tank lifted his shield and then slammed it down so hard that its bottom rim cracked the paving stone on which he stood. "[Citadel]!" he shouted, and stone walls thrust up from the ground, as if the ripple of force had pushed them up from below. The walls blocked both the crossbow bolts and the view of anyone who was watching, but chips flew from the impact of the bolts, and cracks appeared on the smooth stone surface.

Aspen crouched inside the circular wall, his life sense reaching out to touch the area surrounding them. He knew Motte's wall could only deflect an amount of damage equaling his own health points, and that while the skill was in place, Motte couldn't move. That gave Aspen only as long as it took their attackers to deal 1470 points of damage to put their plan into action.

::Go!:: he sent, and reached for the insects infesting three of the guards. Feeding them power, he felt them grow, biting viciously at their hosts, who began howling outside the wall. Once they were strong enough to finish the job, he left them to their work, and looked at the contents of the small packet he'd bought from one of the street vendors, which now rested in his palm.

Closing his eyes, he prayed. "Gina, if you're listening, now would be a good time for some help. I promise I'll plant some flowers when we get back, and I'll even dance at the next party. You know you want to see that, so… Thank you!"

As the wall dropped, everything happened at once.

Rouge and Nekthadt began throwing weapons at the glowstones surrounding the gate, breaking them and sinking the battle into darkness with shocking rapidity.

Motte raised his shield and ran toward Grunder, knocking two guards aside like they were nothing, and barreling into the unprepared elf with the full force of his [Battering Ram].

Silus flew from Aspen's shoulder, heading for the Traveler mage.

Three guards and three Travelers were left staring at the crouched form of one apparently defenseless farmer, and hesitated for a precious moment.

Aspen dropped a handful of seeds on the earth under his feet, which was shattered and laid bare by Motte's [Citadel]. The seeds sank into the freshly turned soil, and he *focused*.

His body fell away, and he was suddenly something very small. Everything was darkness, and then... power. Power filled him with life, with energy, with *intent*. He pushed roots deep into the soil, which was soft and moist, perfect for sustaining him. He shot out roots, then stems, then leaves, then flowers, then reached out with coiling vines.

Aspen opened his eyes to stare at the wildly whipping rose vines. Clusters of white blossoms burdened the thorny stems, and heavy perfume began to pervade the area. Stem after stem erupted from the soil at his feet, and he felt his reserves of mana begin plummeting as the plants grew.

A thrashing vine contacted one of the guards, and it instantly wrapped around him. Thorns sharp as needles sank into the leather pieces of his armor. Some found their way into the gaps between the strips of metal at his waist and collar. They tightened, and a short scream became a gurgle as the vines continued to grow. His fellow guards watched in horror, and began to hack at the roses with their swords.

Rouge and Nekthadt finished their task as the last glowstone shattered in its housing. The darkness of night now held sway, and the only people with [Darkvision] were the goblin and the teenaged thief. Rouge vanished again, while Nekthadt pressed his back against Aspen's, where the tall human was kneeling in the dirt. One of the Travelers took out a glowstone and lit it, but Nekthadt's daggers took it out an instant later.

Motte was holding Grunder at bay, though it was clear that the elf was a higher level. Motte's skill and defensive abilities outweighed Grunder's attempts to kill him quickly. It was clear that the elf was primarily a damage dealer, and that if he found himself up against someone who could block or absorb that damage, he had little actual ability to fall back on.

Two of the three guards who had fallen victim to Aspen's initial attack were beginning to recover. They were the crossbow wielders, and were staggering to their feet near the guardhouse. The third guard had fallen within easy reach of the roses, and they had found him quickly. He would not rise again.

Silus was now winging away from the mage, who was clutching at his face, screaming. Liquid darkness oozed between his fingers. ::I got him!:: the bat gasped, flitting high above the battle. ::He's [Diseased]! Unless he has a [Cleanse] spell or an Elixir, he won't be able to concentrate enough to cast anything for at least five minutes.:: Her little voice was gleeful.

There were still three Travelers and two guards hacking at the rose vines that continued to grow from the ground by Aspen's feet. He felt his mana draining from him like water from a pitcher, and knew he couldn't maintain the spell much longer.

Come on, Rouge, hold on…

"Did you want this?" The voice was chilling, toneless and remorseless. Aspen looked up, heart in his throat.

The opening for the gate was nearly fifteen feet high. The wall itself was a crenelated, stony bulwark that topped out at twenty feet above the ground. A man stood there, the last of the Travelers, the one who had vanished at the beginning of the battle. Whoever he was, he was a high enough level that he had been able to use [Stealth] even in brightly lit areas, which did not bode well for the girl who dangled from his hand.

Rouge thrashed, legs twisting as she tried to find a way to get out of the grip on her throat that the assassin was using to hold her above the twenty-foot drop. Her hands reached out toward the man, clutching, and Aspen wondered what was going on. Why wasn't she using her knife?

The dark figure nonchalantly bent his arm toward his own body, and when it came away, Aspen could just make out the shape of a weapon in his hand, distinctive even in the darkness. A few drops of liquid dropped the far distance to the ground beneath him. Blood.

The crazy bastard had just pulled a knife from his own body, and was now holding onto it so the thrashing girl couldn't get it!

The man shook Rouge like a rag doll, and then tilted his head. "I suggest," he said, just loud enough to be heard over the cries of the injured, "that we stop this nonsense now, and you hand the goblin over to me. I really won't ask twice."

The voice that replied was feminine and as ungiving as stone. "Neither will I. Put down my sister, FantumHat."

Aspen closed his eyes in relief. He had rarely been so glad to see someone as he was when Doom Bloom stepped out into the street behind them, flanked by two other female Travelers. One of them held a drawn bow, the arrowhead glowing with phosphorescent fire, aimed at FantumHat. The other held a ball of flickering flame hovering above her open palm.

A white gleam of teeth caught the dim moonlight as FantumHat grinned. "Doom, my beauty. How nice to see you. You say this," he shook Rouge again, "is related to you? Funny, I don't see the resemblance."

Doom Bloom's voice was ice cold and furious. "She's *mine*. Let her down gently, and walk away, and I won't have to find out which of us can kill the other one today."

"Hmmm," the voice was thoughtful, and the arm holding Rouge didn't waver a centimeter. "Who's ahead now? Me, I think. Twenty-nine to twenty-five, isn't it? You've been a bit distracted lately. Plus," his arm tensed, and Rouge gurgled audibly, "I don't think our deal covers family members. Guildees only."

"Damn it, you crazy jerk," Doom yelled, "I don't care about our deal! Let my sister go! You're scaring her!"

FantumHat hissed. "You *should* care, my Bloom. I'm close to winning already, and you're making yourself very, very vulnerable right now."

Aspen felt Nekthadt twitch against his back, and gritted his teeth. *Remember the plan, remember the plan, remember-*

Nekthadt stood up, clutching his arms around the pouch strapped to his chest. He turned to face Aspen, expression concealed by the layers of voluminous scarves that still covered him. He began backing away, heading toward the gate.

Aspen stood, holding out his hand. "Nekthadt, wait! We can win! Just let us-"

The goblin shook his head. His voice was soft and frightened. "You're outnumbered, and now that Traveler has Rouge. There's no way you'll choose me over her." His head turned as he looked around. He had a fairly clear shot to the gate. Motte was between him and Grunder. The enemy mage was down, either dead or immobilized. Aspen's roses had killed another of the guards, and wounded one of the Travelers, as well as binding him so tightly that he was currently no threat. The remaining guards weren't within reach, and Aspen and his withering - but not yet dead - rose were between him and the other Travelers.

Doom Bloom had switched her attention to the goblin, and she motioned to her two guild members. "Goblin," she said coldly, "they may not be willing to trade you for Rouge, but I don't give a damn about you and whatever quest they're chasing. If you take a single step toward that gate, we'll take you out and hand your head to that madman up there on a pike."

At the same moment that FantumHat finally dropped his indifferent façade, shouting, "No, don't!", Nekthadt ran. He turned on his heel and bolted for the gate. Aspen stared in helpless horror as a glowing arrow sprouted from his back, piercing through both his body and the pouch on his chest. Then a ball of fire impacted the small figure, instantly turning it to a pillar of ash, which hung for a moment before scattering into the wind.

"There, Fantum! Happy? Now *give me my sister!*"

The man on the wall howled in anger, heaving Rouge's body away from him. She arched through the air, and both Motte and Aspen raced toward the place she would land. Aspen was faster, unencumbered by armor, and likely with a higher Dexterity to boot. He stretched out his arms, bending his knees as he accepted the slight form into his embrace. With a grunt, he landed on his rear, but Rouge lay in his arms, unmoving but alive.

Motte was there a moment later, clutching the small body to him with one arm as he triggered [Roar]. Both remaining guards Staggered, as well as one of the Travelers. Grunder, though, was still up, and leveled his spear at the big man.

FantumHat leapt from the top of the wall, landing on the roof of the guardhouse with a soft thump. He was glaring at Doom Bloom with eyes of such a deep black that they almost seemed to swallow the moonlight. "I. Needed. That. Glyphis! I'll kill your whole guild for this, Doom Bloom! I'll spawn camp you until you're all level one again!"

Doom Bloom seemed to pale slightly, looking back and forth from the small figure barely visible in Motte's grasp to the raging Traveler on the roof. "I didn't know! Look, you can kill me! I won't fight. Just leave my guild out of it!"

FantumHat whirled, smashing his fist into the wall behind him repeatedly, until bits of masonry began to fall around him. As he did, Motte and Aspen began to edge toward the gate, taking advantage of Grunder being distracted by his guildmaster's fit of temper. Finally, the assassin stopped, and turned back to Doom Bloom.

"Get. Out!" he growled. "Get out of my city. The next time I see you, you'd better have a replacement glyphis for me. If you don't, the Forceworns are going to *destroy* you and all your squishy little guildees. And you damn well better *believe* you're going to hold up your end of our bargain, because if you don't, anyone who's ever partied with you is going to wish they'd never started playing *Veritas Online*!"

His black gaze turned to Grunder. "Let them go. Doom here has a job to do, and maybe she'll do it faster if she remembers that now I know who she cares enough to die for."

The blond elf flicked back his hair with one elegant hand, sneering as he stepped back and swept a mocking bow toward the gate. "You heard the man, get out!" he said, going for threatening, but failing as his voice cracked on the final word.

Aspen and Motte didn't have to be told twice. They ran for the gate, Motte holding his shield protectively over the limp figure in his arms, and didn't stop until the gate was nothing more than a dark blotch in the line of the city wall behind them.

Silus flew down and landed on Aspen's shoulder, her small body trembling. Aspen looked toward Motte. ::Well?::

Motte just shook his head. ::Get further away. We need two hours, minimum. Doom will be on horseback. She'll catch up. Damned assassins are sneaky, and where you find one, you usually find more, but if they haven't killed us by the time Doom gets to us, we're probably safe. For now.::

Aspen nodded, put his head down, and ran.

ӗ ӗ ӗ

Three hours passed before they heard hooves on the road behind them. They stepped off the side of the road and crouched in the shadows. Motte set down the small, dark figure in his arms, which sank down into the bushes.

Doom cantered into sight, flanked by her two friends. The three women started to ride by, but the archer seemed to sense something. She pulled back on her reins and came to a stop in the road. Doom and the shorter woman followed suit.

"Motte?" Doom called, softly.

Motte stood and stepped into the road, with Aspen close on his heels. Doom was carrying a glowstone, and Aspen took a moment to examine the Travelers riding by her side. The archer was short, with thick black hair twisted into a large coil at the back of her head. Her eyes were dark, long, and hooded.

The third woman was stocky and short, with dark blonde hair. Thin braids gathered the hair by her face out of her way, one on each side, and the rest fell in a coarse mass from under a thick leather helmet with two horns mounted on top. She had round eyes of an indeterminate color, and a smattering of freckles across her snub nose. She was looking anywhere except at the two men, and a flush colored her cheeks.

"How did it go?" Motte asked, looking around.

Doom's lips pinched as her eyes flicked around. The forest around them was silent, and she finally puffed out a long breath. Her face relaxed and she grinned weakly. "Perfectly. I thought Fantum was going to blow it for a minute there, but we managed to pull it off. I didn't expect him to be *that* mad, but I'll figure it out. I was ready to take a break from Bloodhaven anyway. I've been... rethinking my game style lately."

She tapped Oleander with her heels, gesturing to the road ahead. "Come on. The path is ahead another quarter mile or so."

Motte nodded, then stepped back over to the side of the road. He gathered up his slim burden again, and they set off. They ran and rode in silence until Doom gestured sharply toward what looked like nothing more than a dark gap in the trees.

"That way. Not far," she said, softly.

Indeed, they only traveled a short distance into the trees before they saw the steady light of another glowstone ahead. Without discussion, they settled into a defensive formation. Doom stayed in the lead, with the archer behind her, followed by Motte, carrying his small burden, then Aspen, and finally the mage.

Soon, they entered a small clearing. A squat building stood there, off-white and unpretentious, with a low roof and a single door and window. As they rode up to it, the door flew open, and Rouge ran out, grinning like a fiend. She bounced into her father's arms, hugged Aspen briefly, and finally stopped, uncertain, in front of Doom.

The half-elf dismounted, walked over to the little thief girl, and pulled her into a rough embrace. She let her go again an instant later, face red, and tousled Rouge's unruly curls. "Let's not do that again, okay? You freaked the hell out of me when you showed up at my guild, and then you hauled me into your crazy stunt. You're lucky I got a shareable quest to help your pet, uh, native, here." She hitched a thumb toward Aspen.

Nekthadt, who Motte had been carrying because the weakened goblin would never have been able to keep up with the pace the two men set, stepped forward, bowing deeply. "I thank you, Lady Rouge, and Lady Doom Bloom. I'm certain I never would have been able to escape without your help."

Rouge shook her head. "It was all you. You're a brave goblin, Ned. Heck, you're brave for anybody! When Aspen told us the plan, I thought he was crazy! I've never even heard of a [Trade Places] skill before, and I sure didn't think it would beat [Identify]. Even after you used it on me in the room, I didn't think we could pull it off, especially with the fifteen-minute time limit."

::To be fair,:: Silus put in, ::he *is* a little crazy.::

Aspen glared at the little bat as she flitted over to Rouge's shoulder, snuggling in happily. Rouge just giggled.

Nekthadt shrugged. "Without your willingness to die while pretending to be me, there's no way it would have worked. I never thought I would be grateful that Travelers do not remain in the Chaos Pool. Now," he frowned, staring back up the dark path they had come down, "I must trust that Aspen is correct in his summation of your friend Vonn's character."

A blush rose in Rouge's cheeks, and she stammered slightly. "Oh, he's not my... I mean, he's a... Oh! You mean *friend* friend, not..." She coughed slightly, avoiding Motte and Doom Bloom's suddenly suspicious gazes.

"Yeah, Aspen has him pegged. He *loves* to talk about his family, and how the wood elves have this crazy tradition where they spend five years wandering around the world Doing Good before they go home and get married and start trying to spawn baby wood elves. That's why he's guiding Restur's caravan, and it's why he'll protect your little glyphis friend. Protecting nature is what wood elves *do*, and saving a member of an endangered species is totally in his wheelhouse." She raised her fist with her thumb pointing straight up, a gesture that Aspen had learned meant anything from encouragement to approval.

Doom's archer friend spoke for the first time. "Yon maiden has the right of it, good sir. My mother was a wood elf who fell in love with a human during her own *r'nspiga*. She returned to her family at the end, as all wood elves must, but not before their love produced me. She left me with my father, who often regaled me with stories of my mother and her people." Her face took on a tragic expression, and she assumed a strange pose, with her face turned up, and her right hand splayed over her eyes dramatically.

Doom Bloom rolled her eyes, but reached out and patted her friend on the shoulder. "Thanks for that, Fluff. I'm sure Ned finds that very comforting."

Nekthadt was looking between the two women with a baffled expression. He opened his mouth, but stopped when Doom Bloom gave a minute shake of her head, followed by a tiny shrug.

"Well... We will see, then. I admit I, too, felt that he would do as he promised, but I will not rest easy until Jesiqa is once again at my side. If she does not make it," he shook his head, face twisted in self-recrimination and doubt, "I will go back and either bring her out myself, if she lives, or kill the one responsible for her death, even if it costs me my own life."

Aspen sighed and set his hand on the goblin's thin shoulder. "Pray, then. Gina is listening." *Whether I like it or not.*

Chapter Seventeen

Rouge

R ouge looked around at the suddenly busy clearing around the small shrine, and felt as if a huge weight had been lifted off her shoulders. *Finally*, they had real help. Doom had shown her the quest she'd gotten to help Aspen, and it was fabulous.

Quest: "A Friend of the Family"

Your new friend Aspen needs help, and so do his friends. Help Nekthadt escape Bloodhaven. Then help Manuela escape from durance vile. Don't let Aspen die.*This is a SHAREABLE quest. You may invite up to two people to assist you. Make good choices.*

Success: Variable, depending on whether you achieve all three goals. Increased Reputation with surviving affected NPCs. 10000 gold and 10000 experience each for rescuing Nekthadt or Manuela. One piece of Very Rare ranked gear appropriate to your Class for assisting both.

Failure: Aspen dies.

Partial Failure: Nekthadt and/or Manuela dies.

Shareable quests were actually pretty unusual. Generally, if a Quest could be given to more than one person, each of them had to do whatever steps it took to earn it. Having one person do the grunt work and then be able to just give out the quest was really nice, especially since *Veritas* could make players jump through a lot of hoops to get a great quest like that.

It wasn't exactly fair that Doom's quest rewards were so much better than the rewards for her own "Friend of a Friend" quest, but hopefully that meant the reward at the end of her own quest chain would really be off the charts. Not that she didn't want to help Aspen and Bridget out, but...

Anyway, it was just good to be surrounded by people who were there to help. Especially Doom, because no matter what had happened between them in the past, she didn't think everything her step-sister had said to FantumHat (who was a *total creep*) had been part of the act.

Just then, Doom left the conversation she'd been having with her guildees, and headed for Rouge. The half-elf squatted down next to where Rouge had planted her butt on a fallen log and looked at her.

"Are you all right?" she asked, quietly. "That was kind of rough, and I know you hate dying. Did you lose a level?"

Rouge had to swallow against the lump in her throat. She knew her dad would check on her as soon as he saw her out of the game, and she'd seen the concerned glances Aspen had cast her, but it meant a lot to her that Doom would ask.

She nodded. "Yeah. Still level forty-four. It wasn't that bad for me, really. Once Aspen got Ned to tell us what skills he was using to evade the people hunting him for so long – and by the way, that is one tight-lipped goblin – and we practiced that swap thing, my job was pretty easy. Run up, get you to help us out, then meet the guys back at the gate."

She felt a light pinch of little teeth on her earlobe, and winced. "Um, sorry, the guys and Silus. Anyway, once Ned and I switched places when Motte put his shield up, all I had to do was wait for the right time, and then die. It wasn't as bad as usual, though, because at least I knew it was coming. Plus, the respawn delay was minimal, since it was friendly fire."

She rolled her eyes. "The *hard* part was getting Motte to cough up the gold for the Fast Travel to the shrine from the Dead Tent in Bloodhaven, and then waiting here until you guys made it. I'm just glad I hit level 40, so I can Fast Travel to any nearby shrine I've prayed at, and that I was working on getting the 'Devout' achievement when Motte and I were here for a quest a while back." She looked over at the small shrine, and chewed her lip a little.

"I, uh, do have *one* small problem, though."

Everyone stared into the shrine with matching expressions of disbelief.

"*How* did he get in there?" Motte asked again.

Rouge sighed. "When I appeared in the shrine, and he appeared outside, he kind of... freaked out. I don't know how, but he shoved himself in there, and now he won't come out. I think he's pouting."

Indeed, Codswallop was lying on the floor by the small statue of Gina. (Which was totally wrong, because the statue had this vacuous benevolent expression on her face that Rouge totally couldn't imagine on the real Gina. Bridget? Whatever.) The ostrich had his neck stretched out on the floor, and his huge brown eyes were locked on the door. When he saw Rouge, he managed a pathetic chirp and fluttered his long lashes, but otherwise didn't move.

Motte and Aspen exchanged looks. Then the farmer, who had apparently decided to stop playing dumb, asked, "What should we do?"

Doom crossed her arms and shrugged. "He'll come out when Rouge leaves. He's totally obsessed with her. If she acts like she's going to leave without him, he'll get out just like he got in."

The archer, Flu-flu (also known as Fluff, and apparently a total role-player), struck a dramatic pose. "Can you not see that the poor creature is bereft? I must assist him, or I will fail my mother's people!"

The short mage shook her head. "Doom is right. If he got in on his own, he'll get out. Mounts always follow their masters eventually, even if you don't take care of them." A flush rose in her cheeks, and she looked away. Rouge suspected the other player had found that one out the hard way at some point. It happened to a lot of players, who didn't understand how different the mount system in *Veritas* was from similar games, where mounts were basically cars with hooves, and you could basicallyignore them.

Rouge stepped through the door of the shrine. Instantly, a notification appeared.

You have entered a shrine dedicated to your Patron Goddess, Gina. You feel refreshed. Your Health, Mana, and Stamina regeneration double as long as you remain inside the shrine, and do not enter battle.

The others followed close behind her, and she could see Aspen's shoulders straighten as he walked inside. No one else reacted, so she guessed they weren't members of Gina's church. Motte and Aspen both had to duck so their heads didn't hit the lintel as they entered, but Aspen was able to stand up straight once he was inside, while Motte had to keep his head bowed slightly so he didn't scrape the ceiling.

Rouge walked over and knelt down by Codswallop's head, patting him gently. "C'mon, Wally. We need to get out of here. We're supposed to meet the caravan in the morning, and I can't go without you."

The ostrich rolled an eye up to look at her, making a sad warbling sound as he did so.

She gently tugged on his head, trying to pull him up. "Come on, bud. Up and at'em."

Slowly, with all the grace and dignity of a toddler with a full diaper, the ostrich climbed to his huge two-toed feet. His fluffy back nearly brushed the ceiling, and his head was bent almost straight out in front of him. He took one uncertain step, made a frightened *eep* sound, and collapsed back onto his belly. He was a whole two inches closer to the door.

Rouge clapped her hand to her face and shook her head.

Flu-flu stepped forward, sweeping her hand to indicate the prostrate bird. "I shall handle this, fair maiden! My own God, Toko, has granted me the ability to call one of his holy birds. Yon ostrich shall surely follow a fellow avian from these cramped quarters!"

Thrusting her hand into the air, she cried out, "Come, my friend Rufus! [*Brave Bird*]!" Instantly, a large bird with a bright red bill that looked, at first glance, as if it had three parts, instead of just the normal two, appeared from thin air. It opened its beak to let out a resonant call, and she realized the top piece was some kind of extra structure stacked on top of the normal beak-parts.

The bird, Rufus, settled onto Flu-flu's hand, tilting his head to look around curiously. The archer patted him, and then said, "I have need of your aid once more, Rufus. We must lead this poor creature from his place of repose."

Rufus looked from his mistress to the ostrich lying on the ground and back. He squawked.

Flu-flu nodded as if she understood. "Indeed, the beast is unnerved by these claustrophobic surroundings. It is in his best interest to relocate to the out of doors. Please, assist me!"

The bird's large beak nodded, and he flew from Flu-flu's arm. He flapped twice around the small room, as if examining it thoroughly, and then flew out the door.

They all looked at each other, then at Flu-flu. She struck a pose, pointing at the door. "Behold!"

Rufus flew back in, holding something in his beak. He landed on the ground behind Codswallop and dropped the object. Rouge edged toward it, trying to see past Codswallop's poofy feathers, but she was too slow.

With a powerful whack of its beak, the bird shoved the object into

Codswallop's feathers. Then he opened his beak and let out a croaking call that seemed to echo in the small space. Codswallop's eyes shot wide, and he lurched to his feet. Eyes locked onto the door, he lowered his head and raced for the exit. When he hit it, feathers *poofed* from his body, and his feet scrabbled on the floor. He finally managed to shove himself through, leaving feathers drifting in the air and gouge marks in the wood from his powerful claws.

Rufus squawked in satisfaction, and then jumped straight up and disappeared, as suddenly as it had come. Flu-flu swept her long green cloak behind her, stuck out a leg, and took a deep bow. "Your mighty steed is once more at your service, my lady."

Rouge bolted for the door.

Codswallop was in the clearing outside, running in circles and screeching ostrich curse words. Periodically, he would reach back with his beak and snap at his own bottom, then jump straight up and start running again.

Rouge was only able to stare for a few repetitions of this pattern, before shaking her head sharply. The next time the ostrich came near her, she leapt for him, catching onto his neck. For a frightening moment, she was hanging *beneath* him, clinging to his chest with her legs while her arms circled his neck. Then she grabbed a few handfuls of thick feathers and hauled herself around until she was sitting on his back, facing his tail. Leaning forward, she stared into the dense thicket of plumes.

There! Something wriggled, and a smooth, bright blue tail thrashed. Quick as a flash, she reached out and snatched it. She caught hold of slick, dry scales, and tugged. Codswallop stretched out his neck and *honked* at the same time as the tail came off in her hand, still twitching.

You have dealt 20 points of damage to the *Lesser Skink*. The *Lesser Skink* has lost its tail!

She shrieked like a little girl, and flung the wriggling thing away from her.

Her ostrich bucked underneath her, and she dove her hand back into his feathers, aiming for the spot where she caught glimpses of a lizard-shaped thing with its mouth clamped onto Codswallop's tender posterior. This time, she caught the little creature solidly around its neck, and squeezed.

You have dealt 23 points of damage to the *Lesser Skink*.

Small jaws finally opened, and Rouge lifted the animal into the air, and threw it after its tail. It scurried away into the darkness.

Codswallop finally settled beneath her, then turned his big head and buried his face in Rouge's hair. Finding the space already occupied by a small bat, he *chirruped* sadly, and tucked his head under her arm instead.

Everyone turned to stare at Flu-flu, who chuckled nervously. "All's well that ends well?"

🦇 🦇 🦇

With five players in the group now, Motte decided he could finally log off for a while to get some work done. He'd assigned a ten-page paper on gender roles in "A Midsummer Night's Dream" for the midterm in one of his classes, and the students were complaining about not having their grades a week later. Flu-flu, too, left, after saying something about how she needed to 'bask in the light of her soul space'.

That left Rouge, Doom, the mage, Aspen, Silus, Nekthadt, and the various mounts sitting around and waiting for morning. Nekthadt went into the little shrine to pray (so he said, but Rouge thought he just wanted to be away from all of them so he could worry about his little shark-girl in peace), and left the others outside. The remaining group chatted for a bit, but Doom's mage friend just kept getting more and more awkward, until a silence fell over the group.

Doom finally stood up and glared at her friend. "Tess, you need to explain or leave. They're never going to trust you if you keep acting like this, and you swore you'd tell them before I gave you the quest."

The mage, Tess, opened and closed her mouth a few times, and then took in a deep breath. She dropped her head so no one could see her face and muttered, "Okay. You're right, Doom. I know. I just-"

The blonde girl took off her helmet and poked at the sharp points of the horns. She seemed to be struggling with something, and at last she looked up. Aspen, Silus, and Rouge were staring at her in fascination.

A deep flush rose from her neck until her face was visibly redder. She looked helplessly at Doom. "I just don't know *how!*"

The tall half-elf rolled her eyes and looked at Rouge and Aspen. "I told Rouge and Motte a while ago that the girl who went with R3dLit3 and Umberhulk6 deleted her character after she was killed, and then re-rolled as one of the new half-breeds." She looked over at Aspen and grimaced, "I don't even know how you're going to process this, but… Tessle was FlyingFir3, before. She decided to rejoin the guild a week or so ago. She did some leveling on her own, but she could use the XP, and she was available to help with the quest, so I brought her."

She looked back at Tessle. "Your turn."

Tessle groaned softly. "Thanks, Doom. Yeah, okay…" She looked up at the sky, as if hoping lightning would strike her (or possibly DB) and end the conversation.

"Look," she finally started, "my ex-boyfriend, the guy who plays R3dLit3, he's a jerk. I knew it, but," she flushed again, and looked down at the helmet in her hands, "I'm not, you know, good looking, or particularly smart, or… or anything, and I… I just liked that somebody liked me."

She paused, and groaned slightly. "Okay, you guys don't even care about that stuff, I know. I'm just saying that going with him on that quest was just, you know, something to do. It wasn't anything personal. Then, when you," she looked up and met Aspen's eyes, swallowing hard, "killed me, it felt really… *real.* Like, you were *real*, and I was the *bad guy*, and I'd attacked you for no reason, and you were just doing whatever it took to protect yourself from more bad guys. And I… didn't like that."

She looked at Rouge, her expression conflicted. "I know it's just a, um-," She hesitated and tilted her head toward Aspen. "You know. But that guy, he's way too realistic. Even though he killed me – like that – I still didn't like the way I felt. I *really* didn't like the way R3d was acting. So I deleted my character and quit playing for a little while. I don't really think of myself as much of a gamer anyway. But then I realized I missed playing, and my friends."

Tessle looked at Doom, and smiled a little. "My real friends, or at least the people I actually *wanted* to be my friends, not R3dLit3 and his merry band of idiots." She shrugged. "So I made Tessle, and figured I'd try out a half-Dwarf. I didn't want Randy - R3dLit3 – to find me, so I changed the way I look as much as I could, and left the guild. I didn't want to drag them down if Randy figured out I was back. But I missed them, and no one recognized me, so…"

She shrugged again and looked back at Rouge, and then at Aspen, with uncertainty writ large on her face. "I'm sorry. I'm sorry I took that dumb quest, and that I have such bad taste in men. I swear I just want to play *my* way now. I'd really appreciate it if you'd let me join your quest, but I understand if you don't want me to."

By the time the half-dwarf (and how cool was that?) had finished speaking, Aspen's face had dropped forward so she couldn't read his expression under the brim of his hat. What she *could* see was that the poor woman was really struggling with the feeling that she needed to apologize to an NPC, and Rouge could totally sympathize. If you'd played those games where the NPCs had about the same amount of individuality and personality as a bucket of white paint, it made sense to just accept any quest, do whatever you had to do to finish it, and just move on.

Unfortunately, understanding and trust didn't necessarily go hand in hand.

::Aspen? What are you thinking?::

There was a long pause, which was broken by Silus' little voice, not Aspen's deep one. ::*I* think we should let her come. She seems really sorry, and Doom trusts her. Plus, she did kill Rouge for us.::

Rouge choked a little, then giggled. Ignoring the two women looking at her as if she were crazy, she replied, ::Yes, she did. Her ex is friends with FartHat – and yes, I'm totally going with that name for him – so if she'd told them about us, our plan never would have worked.::

It was Aspen's turn to snort softly, and he looked up, meeting Tessle's blue eyes. Her face tensed, but she met his gaze steadily.

::No one is allowed to be alone with her,:: Aspen finally said. ::No one tells her all of our plans, or what we're really doing. Not until we have a chance to see for ourselves if she's telling the truth.::

::Okay,:: Silus squeaked.

::Makes sense,:: Rouge shrugged.

Out loud, Aspen said, "I understand what it is to fall in love with the wrong person, simply because you feel as if no one else could ever love you. I know, too, what mistakes one can make in an attempt to keep that person by your side. I'm willing to accept your apology, if you will accept mine."

He bowed his head again. "I'm not proud of what I did to you. I don't pretend to understand what all of your story means, but I think I get the idea, and I will certainly not get in the way of someone else trying to start over again. I am willing to accept your assistance, and with thanks."

Rouge nodded. "Me too!"

::Me three!:: sent Silus, though only Rouge and Aspen heard her.

By the time Aspen was finished talking, Tessle was smiling in relief, and her hands on her horned helm were finally still and relaxed. "Thank you. I feel kind of weird talking like this to a," she glanced at Doom, "um, native? But it actually makes me really happy. And, I forgive you, too." She ducked her head, red rising in her cheeks again.

Aspen smiled slightly, then looked up at Doom. "Then, as long as we're telling secrets that need to be told, Doom Bloom…?" His voice trailed off, and he raised that darned eyebrow. Amazingly, it seemed to have the same disconcerting effect on Doom as it did on Rouge.

It was Doom's turn to look down and sigh. "*Okay.* Just… this is personal, okay?" She looked up and met Rouge's eyes. "Zoey, would you come over here for a few minutes?" She nodded toward the other side of the clearing.

Suddenly conscious of a feeling like her heart trying to climb out of her throat, Rouge stood. "Um, yeah, sure." She made her way over to her sister, and then followed the older girl into the darker area away from the glowstone they were using as a light. Thanks to her [Darkvision], she could still see Doom pretty well, but the same wouldn't be true for the other girl. She wondered if that was intentional.

Sighing deeply, Doom (no, *Lily*, for a little while, at least) started to speak. "Look, Zoey, I know we talked about Mom, and you know I hadn't talked to her in a while. Well," she swallowed audibly, "*she* called *me*. The night before I logged off, outside Bloodhaven, she called me. Told me I needed to come back for dinner. I tried telling her I had school, but she guilt-tripped me into agreeing. I got back this morning."

Zoey, heart pounding, waited. Finally, she prompted, "And?"

Lily shook her head. "She told me Dad lost his job. He's applied to a bunch of places, but they're having to use my college fund to pay bills until he gets a new one. He couldn't even look me in the eye. Didn't say a word while she was talking."

She tilted her face up, and the silver moonlight, which was just beginning to share space with the golden glow of dawn, limned her perfect features. "My tuition and rent are paid through this quarter. I've worked, some, too, usually part-time as a tutor, so I have some savings. But if Dad doesn't get a new job by August, I'll have to cut back my classes and get a job, or drop out, for a while at least."

Zoey's teeth were clenched, and it was hard to talk. "Can you get a student loan or something? Scholarships?"

Her sister shrugged a little. "Maybe? I asked a financial counselor, and she said that what I could get depended on whether I was independent of my parents, or how much they make if they were still claiming me on their taxes, since I'm still in school and under twenty-five. So I called Dad, and he just passed me to Mom. She gave me a whole bunch of tax buzz-words, but what it came down to is that they're going to claim me so they can get some tax write-off, so I probably won't qualify for much. So sorry, but we've supported you for years, and it's your turn to take one for the team."

Zoey breathed in, out, in, out, and asked, "What are you going to do?"

"What *can* I do?" Lily sounded frustrated and angry. "It's not even that I can't handle paying for college myself, you know? A lot of people have to work through school, or get student loans, or whatever. Heck, most of my friends are in that boat, and I know they'll help me figure it out. It's just," her shoulders hunched up, and her hands balled into fists, "the *way* she did it. Making out like I'm a bad daughter for not calling, when she's the one who basically told me to get lost. Then practically blaming me for being so expensive, when they've always pushed me to go to the best college I could, so they could brag about how *accomplished* I am to their so-called friends."

Her shoulders drooped, and she sighed. "Anyway. That's where I've been. And where I'll be, because I won't be able to be on as much as I'd like. I have a full 12 credit-hour load this quarter, but I'm going to start applying for part-time positions and picking up some tutoring gigs. I told Tessle and Flu-flu I was going to have to cut back on my time in game, and they're both able to help pick up the slack. I'm sorry I won't be able to help you more."

Impetuously, Zoey threw her arms around her sister, hugging her tightly. "It's okay! Thank you for helping us, and making sure we had help for when you can't be here. I wasn't sure I was going to be able to keep doing this, playing so much and working. You have no *idea* how happy I am to have some more players around. Girls, too! Between Motte and Aspen, I feel like I'm being double-dadded."

She stepped back, feeling a little awkward. "And if you need anything, you know where we are. I don't know what we can do to help, but I do have a job this summer. I was going to put most of my puny minimum-wage into the 'further education' fund my dad has for me, but you can totally have it. I won't need it for another three years, right?"

Lily's breath caught a little, and then her arms were around Zoey's shoulders. "You're the *best* little sister ever, you know that? And there's no way in hell I'm taking your money. But thanks. It means a lot."

ლ ლ ლ

An hour past dawn, while Silus snoozed on her shoulder, Aspen slept on the floor in the shrine, Ned sat in front of the statue of pseudo-Gina, and Tessle kept watch by the path into the clearing, Rouge received a notification.

Quest: "Brother is Just Another Word for Partner in Crime" complete.

The glyphis, Jesiqa, has successfully been removed from Bloodhaven.

Reward: +30 Reputation with Nekthadt, +30 Reputation with Sarave.

+20 Reputation with Jesiqa. 1000xp.

Chain Quest: "Reunited and it Feels so Good" available.

Help Jesiqa, a young glyphis, find her way back to her people.

Success: Variable.

Failure: Jesiqa will eventually sicken and die.

Accept: Yes/No?

Her initial grin was quickly followed by a deep sigh as she accepted yet *another* quest, but she couldn't just let the cute (okay, yes, and slightly creepy) kid die, could she? *Could* she?

Shaking her head, she gently lifted Codswallop's head from where it was resting in her lap while he slept, and set it next to her. The ostrich opened one eye and grumbled at her, then tucked his head under his wing instead. Laughing, she climbed to her feet and brushed off her behind.

Making her way into the dim confines of the temple, she called out, "Ned! I just got a notice that Jesiqa is out of Bloodhaven! The caravan should be here in a few hours!"

The goblin jumped to his feet, while Aspen sat up slowly, grumbling in a way that was remarkably similar to Codswallop and rubbing his lower back. "Are you certain?" Ned demanded. "Your friend is on the way with her?"

Rouge felt her stupid face heat up with that stupid blush again.

Why did that have to happen whenever Vonn was mentioned?

She wasn't even that interested in him, even though he was really nice, and really cute, and seemed pretty smart… But he wasn't even a real person! And, plus, he talked a lot. Like, a *lot* a lot.

Probably the best thing she could do was spend more time with him so that she could be totally irritated by his chatter. She'd probably be bored out of her mind in an hour. Two tops. Three at the *absolute* outside.

Forcing a smile, she nodded. "Yeah, we're right on the road to North Goose, and the caravan is stopping in there to sell something pig-related. It's totally legit, and if anyone thinks to watch them, they'll give up pretty quickly, especially since the Murder Hobo event starts this morning. They're all going to be way too busy killing each other to worry about a bunch of merchants who they probably don't even know have anything to do with us."

Aspen finally made his way to his feet, muttering something about being 'too old for this'. He tugged his hat brim down and looked at Rouge and Ned. "We should get going. Restur can move the wagons surprisingly quickly when he wants to, and he'll push the horses because I promised I'd help with them when he got here."

He grimaced a little. "I think I overdid it with the life magic. Restur and Vonn could probably sense the flow of magic, even if they couldn't tell exactly what I was doing. Anyway, the sooner we get to the road, the better."

Ned was already halfway out the door, his step more energetic than she'd seen it yet. He wasn't exactly bouncy, but he wasn't slouching and exhausted either. He motioned back at them. "Come. There's no time to waste!"

Aspen looked at her, brow arched. "Didn't I just say that?"

She laughed.

🦇 🦇 🦇

Another hour later, they were deployed in the foliage near the road. The Zombies and mounts were back down the path, out of sight, and the rest of them were waiting, some more patiently than others.

"When will they get here?" hissed Ned for the hundredth time.

"When they get here!" chorused Aspen and Tessle, who were hiding in bushes near the anxious goblin. Rouge, who was comfortably ensconced in the lower branches of a tree with remarkably large leaves, just grinned. It was so nice not to be the one doing the asking for once.

The clopping of hooves and rattle of wagons reached their ears, and they all fell silent. This wouldn't be the first caravan to pass them this morning, since the locals were understandably eager to be anywhere but Bloodhaven for a few days (even North Goose, apparently), but it was the first one that realistically could belong to Restur.

When the first outriders appeared, Rouge felt her shoulders droop in disappointment. The short, heavily muscled warriors weren't anyone she recognized. Then they pulled up, brows creased in concern, staring into the bushes where the party knelt. Behind them, a wagon came into sight. She'd know that thick silver mane anywhere! It was Restur, looking tired but determined as a soft blue light traveled from his hands on the reins down to the horses, where it diffused into an occasional soft gleam. He was definitely using all his caravan master skills to keep them moving quickly!

The first guard raised a fist, and the wagon halted. Restur stood, peering at the area his warriors were indicating. Aspen stood first, with Tessle close behind, and Rouge dropped down out of her tree beside them. She'd seriously considered tree-jumping over to try and vault into the wagon beside Restur, but she had a feeling that in spite of the fact that he had avoided entering any of the battles since the first, he wasn't entirely defenseless. She really didn't feel like being stabbed today.

Restur's face creased into a smile. It wasn't exactly a welcoming grin, but he definitely didn't look *mad* either. As Aspen stepped onto the road, Restur waved to the guards.

"It's all right, Gerain. This is the hostler we mentioned would be joining us, as well as some additional guards. Though I don't know this lovely young lady?" He cocked an eyebrow at Tessle, who blushed.

Staring down at her very functional boots, Tessle muttered her name.

Restur smiled again. "Pleased to make your acquaintance, Lady Tessle. If you are a friend of these Travelers, you are welcome with us. Now," his voice suddenly became businesslike, and he looked over toward Aspen. "I believe we have a little... business to take care of?"

Aspen nodded, and motioned to Ned, who was still hidden in the trees behind them. Ned stepped out of the shadows, face locked in a defiant scowl, and stopped with his feet barely on the red stones of the road. Ready to run.

Vonn jumped down from a wagon two behind Restur's, and she knew she was smiling at him, even though she hadn't really meant to. His hair was down today, and the sun caught gold highlights in the long, thick waves. He was smiling, too, and... Holy cow! Why was she thinking like this? He. Was. A. Game. Character! Plus, even if he'd been a Real Boy (shades of Pinocchio) she was not looking for a boyfriend! Romance was trouble with a capital T. R? Whatever.

So, anyway... Vonn jumped down, smiling in a *completely normal* way, and walked over to them. He flashed a grin at her (because they were *friends*) and then hitched a thumb toward the wagon he'd just left. "Nekthadt," he said, his tenor voice cheerful, "you should come join me on the provisions wagon."

The goblin's face lit up like someone had set off a sparkler in his brain, and he flashed a grin that showed every one of his extremely sharp teeth. He exchanged a look with Aspen, who nodded encouragingly, and then nearly ran toward the wagon.

Rouge kept one eye on the goblin and the wood elf, while still watching Aspen and Restur. The two men had leaned toward each other slightly, with the tall farmer far overshadowing the merchant, and were speaking in quiet undertones. After a few sentences, the two shook hands, and then stepped apart. Rouge's eyes narrowed, her thiefy senses tingling. Had Aspen just slipped something to the caravan master during that brief touch?

Meanwhile, Ned had climbed up on the cart, and Vonn had led him to one of the water barrels strapped to the side. The goblin instantly sat, leaning his head against the barrel, and she could see from his face that Jesiqa was communicating with him somehow. A suspicious moisture gleamed in the corners of the slightly protuberant yellow eye, but no tears fell.

With the goblin settled and finally happy, Restur gave the rest of them assignments. Aspen hurried off to tend to the horses, and she could see each one perk up as he passed. The sweaty equines, driven to their limits by Restur's caravan master skills, now tossed their heads and pranced in place playfully. Aspen was smiling, too, obviously glad to be among the grateful beasts and far out of Bloodhaven.

Rouge and Tessle were assigned to the rear and middle of the column respectively. The Zombies that made up the rest of their party were told to follow Tessle, and Burrito, who had been mostly just hauled along for the ride during their time in the deadly city, was tied into the string of pack animals in the center of the caravan, where he benefited more directly from Aspen's magical support. Aspen had told her that Traveler's mounts could accept or reject his assistance, but she could tell from Codswallop's cheerful chirping that he was sucking it down.

Once they were all on their way toward North Goose at a fast trot, she finally felt like she could have a little chat with Mr. Aspen the totally sneaky.

::Aspen?::

::Rouge?:: the farmer sounded distracted, no doubt trying to manage his mana to keep the horses fresh without running out.

::What were you talking to Restur about?::

Silence. Then, ::Just talking about our trip.::

Yep, definitely shifty. ::What about our trip?::

Aspen sighed. ::Okay, he doesn't usually go to North Goose. Doesn't care for the pigs. Or the people. I convinced him to go because we want to stop there, it's practically on the way, and we'll be making much better time than he would without us. He picked up some specialty pig feed in Bloodhaven, and he's hoping it'll sell well.::

::Uh huh. So why were you being all 'look at us leaning in and talking quietly' if you were just discussing the route? And what was with that totally suspicious handshake?::

Silus stirred a little on her neck, yawning. ::Probably giving him the necklace.::

Rouge almost turned her head to stare at the little bat, but just managed to stop herself. ::What necklace?::

Silus settled back into place, squeaky little voice sleepy. ::One of Birdie's. We couldn't take much with us when we left Bright, but Sumi grabbed some money and jewelry that couldn't be traced back to Aspen. Sumi says Birdie never wore jewelry once she joined Gina's order, so no one saw it on her in years, and it was just gathering dust in the Treasure Room.::

Rouge could practically feel her little Thief ears growing bigger at those last words. ::The *what* room?::

This time Aspen's sigh was more of a groan. ::It was just an empty room on the third floor. When I was young, I spent far too much time and money trying to convince the elite of Bright that I was more than an upstart commoner with too much magic. Since that's exactly what I was, it didn't work, but I bought the largest house I could afford, and dressed Birdie in more silks and jewels than she ever wanted. I ended up with a massive collection of expensive items in an echoingly empty house. I finally just closed off the third floor, so I used one of the bedrooms up there to dump anything we didn't need.::

::You didn't need *treasure*?::

::Well, it wasn't really treasure to me. I was paid well, and got some of the loot from each battle I was in, and as an officer, my share was significant. I sold some of it, but as the war went on, no one had money or need for necklaces, jeweled daggers, or gems the size of your fist.::

She almost choked. ::The size of my *fist*?::

Silus giggled. ::There was one sapphire that was bigger than me!::

::You were barely bigger than a walnut yourself, little brat.:: Aspen's tone was affectionate.

Rouge was still struggling to take all this in. ::So, when you left, you just… abandoned it all?::

His shrug was nearly audible. ::People knew Iorgas Penbrooke was wealthy. If I took it, not only would we have to hire a wagon train, but there was no doubt thieves would follow us, looking for it. Far better to leave it behind to be found. I donated most of it, very publicly, to Birdie's hospital. But I left enough behind so that no one would doubt that I expected to die. Who but a dying man leaves a fortune just lying around?::

::Is it… Could it still be there?:: She felt the urge to wipe at her chin, to see if any drool was leaking.

He chuckled. ::I doubt it. I didn't sell the house, but it will have been standing empty for months. There were spells on it, but all the ones I cast ended when I lost my Class. No doubt it has been thoroughly picked over by thieves by now.::

::How did I *miss* that?:: She almost wailed. ::No one ever told me, the nice friendly thief girl, about a great big empty mansion with loads of undefended treasure inside!::

Aspen snorted. ::You probably didn't miss much. The Thieves Guild likely emptied it within days. The only thing left will be the shell of the building itself. Not much of a loss, really. The only parts we used by the end were the kitchen, a small dining room, my office, and a few bedrooms. That and Birdie's herb garden and potting shed.::

Leaning forward, Rouge buried her face in Codswallop's soft, dusty feathers. Silus shifted in protest at this sudden change in position. ::Oh my gosh. Okay. I'm all right. I'll just be in mourning for lost opportunities for a while.:: She drew in a deep breath, taking in the warm smell of bird. ::So you paid Restur to help us get Jesiqa out of Bloodhaven?::

::It was just… insurance. I knew Vonn would do his best, but without Restur in on it, there was too much risk of being caught. Vonn's a little too honest and forthright for our purposes. Restur, on the other hand, well, let's just say that he's the type that knows all the angles. I told Vonn to let Restur know Motte would pay well for his help. Everyone knows Travelers are rich, so I knew he wouldn't question it. I brought a few pieces with us, in case of emergencies, and this seemed as good a time to use one as any.::

Sighing, Rouge sat back up. Silus shifted back into her favorite place, and Rouge could feel her grooming her fur with her little wing-thumbs. ::We're checking. When we get to Bright, you're going to tell me where that house is, and I'm going treasure hunting.::

Aspen chuckled again. ::Deal.::

🦃 🦃 🦃

Once things were under control, and the caravan was headed toward North Goose, Rouge logged off, leaving Tessle and Flu-flu, who had apparently decided that she'd spent enough time basking or whatever (Rouge was guessing bio-break and a nap), behind to protect the caravan.

Zoey reached up and pulled her headset off, groaning as she rubbed at the sore spots on her temples where the device seemed to fit a little too snugly, no matter how she tried to adjust it. When she pushed the cover of the pod up, her muscles sighed in relief at finally being allowed to stretch properly. She climbed out of the pod and was quickly reminded that she might not need to use the restroom *in* the game, but she definitely did *out* of it.

Five minutes later, she finished washing her hands and stepped out of her bathroom, shaking her fingers vigorously. She eeped as a cloth was dropped on her head.

"Forget something, kid?" Her dad's deep voice came from beside the bathroom door, and she thrust an elbow in his direction, hitting a surprisingly solid hip. "Hey! Is that any way to thank your long-suffering father for bringing you a towel?"

She sighed, pulling the hand towel off her head and drying her hands. "Okay, thanks, Dad." She leaned back into the bathroom to toss the towel next to the sink, then held up her hands for his inspection. "They *will* dry on their own, you know."

He nodded. "I know, but if you want to take this call, you're going to need dry fingers." He held her screen above her head, and she could see Nina's face frozen on it, with ON HOLD printed in big letters across her forehead.

"Holy cow, Nina!" She jumped for the screen, and was amazed to find that she actually caught it, even though it was a good two feet above her fingers.

Her dad released it, eyebrows shooting up. "Been working out, kiddo?"

She stared at the screen in her hand for a moment. "No. Well, maybe? Dr. Joe is always having me do exercises and stretches and stuff, but I don't think that would do it." She looked down at her own body, suddenly realizing that her clothes were fitting a little looser than they had seven weeks earlier. She had always been slim, but now she was lean, with muscles in places that had been soft before.

"I don't... Maybe it's the gel? The stuff in the pod? They said you could be in there for a long time and stay healthy, and that wouldn't work if you got all squishy and weak, right? Like, you'd need physical therapy when you got out?" The screen chirped, and she jumped, nearly dropping it. "I have to take this!"

Her dad frowned, and she had a feeling Bridget would be getting an email from him, but he nodded and stepped back. "All right, Zoe. As long as you feel okay. Maybe you need to eat more, though? You're a little skinny."

She nodded, but just waved as she ran back to her room. Flopping down on the bed, she said, "Emily, accept call." She *definitely* needed to change her home interface name, but right now…

Nina's face started moving, and the other girl smiled as she saw Zoey. "Kia ora, Zoey! I asked about you at the Artful Lodger, and they said you left already. You didn't leave a private message at the Guild, so I figured I'd call and leave a message, but your dad said you were around. Did you finish your quest? Didn't want to stick around for the event?" Her teasing smile said she knew the answer.

Zoey made a face. "No, thanks. Seeing how many people I can kill before someone chops me into cat food doesn't sound fun to me. You have fun though. Maybe we can meet in Bright instead?"

The other girl pushed her glasses (electric blue with pink arms covered in tiny silver lightning bolts today) up. "I can head that way now, actually. I was going to participate, but FantumHat is on a rampage. He's not even pretending he cares about NPCs or destroying property or anything. He's way stronger than last year, too, so there's no way I'm going to place high enough to get anything except the basic event reward."

Leaning closer to the screen, Zoey said, "Do you know that guy? We, uh, saw him while we were in Bloodhaven. He seemed kind of crazy. What's his deal?"

Nina rolled her eyes. "I met him way back when the game started. He seemed okay then. We were even in the same party once, hunting zombies or something for a quest during the war. He was a basic assassin-type then, but he *really* liked killing mobs. He and some buddies started the Forceworn guild a while later, and they don't hang out with us peons anymore."

Zoey tugged at one of her curls, trying to act nonchalant. "D'you know anything about him *personally*, though? It seems like my sister knows him, and they have a weird relationship."

"Oh?" Zoey could see the spark of curiosity light up the big brown eyes and silently cursed herself. She knew how much her friend loved gossip, especially if there was a hint of something secret.

"Yeah, no big deal!" She waved a hand, trying to move on. "Just thought I'd ask."

Nina tilted her head to the side, considering. "I don't really know much. He was pretty focused on leveling up, even back then, but I think he mentioned that he had to log out because his mom was calling him for dinner once. I got the impression he's not that old, maybe even still in high school? That was a year ago, though, so…" She shrugged.

Zoey's eyes narrowed as she was reminded of a snatch of conversation she'd overheard when she'd almost stumbled over DB and the idiot brothers what seemed like months ago. She'd recognized FantumHat's name even then, but without knowing him personally, it hadn't really stuck in her memory. What had they said?

"I know who he is in real life. He may be a rockstar in the game, but in real life, he's just a shut-in who lives in his mom's basement, and I can tell his mommy what he's really doing when she thinks he's 'working from home.'"

She blinked, realizing that Nina was trying to get her attention.

"…Zoe? Everything okay?" The other girl looked concerned, and Zoey tried to smile reassuringly.

"Yeah. Yeah! Um, I'm sure it's fine. Anyway, I'd love to meet you in Bright. We're kind of taking the long way, but we should be there in a few days, game time, so tomorrow sometime IRL. I'll drop a note at the Traveler's Guild and, um, I can ping your screen, too?" Zoey felt a little awkward, but after all, the older girl had called her first. Zoey had given Nina her number just in case they missed each other in Bloodhaven, but she hadn't really expected the girl to call. That was something *real* friends did, wasn't it?

Nina nodded enthusiastically. "Sounds great, Zoe! See you tomorrow!" She gave a little wave and touched her right cheekbone. The screen went dark.

Holy. Cow. Had she actually made a friend? Like, not just a work friend, but a *real*, honest to goodness, likes to hang out with you friend? Jace was *never* going to believe...

"Jace!" She snatched up her screen. "Emily! Calendar!"

The calendar lit up, bright and clear, and sure enough, today's date was circled. Jace and his family always spent the first half of summer vacation visiting first his mom's family, and then his dad's. (His mom's folks lived in Detroit, and Jace mostly played games and read books while he was there. His dad's folks lived in Hawaii, though, and apparently it was a*maz*ing.)

Between Zoey's job, *VO*, and Jace's parents' insistence that he 'spend time with the family', they'd barely spoken since Jace left. But he should have gotten in last night, and...

Yes! A message!

@JaceCo: Home. Going to crash hard tonight, but I'll be on VO tomorrow. Let me know!

Quickly, she typed back, hoping he wasn't in game yet.

@RedZ: Heading for North Goose. Gonna grab a snack and see if I can get a nap, then go back in. You in Bright?

A reply came almost instantly.

@JaceCo: Hallelujah! I don't know how much longer I can stand family time. You'd think they'd be tired of me by now. I haven't been able to escape yet, but if I tell them you're waiting for me, they'll let me go. Good thing they like you.

@RedZ: I'm likeable. I have just enough time for a snack and a power nap. I'll be on in about two hours. Where are you?

@JaceCo: I can meet you in NG. I think I have a quest to bring some Pig Trotters back for a restaurant in Bright. You're a bad influence. I keep taking all these weird quests.

@RedZ: It's good for you. Awesome! See you in two?

@JaceCo: Yup!

Grinning, she tapped the screen. Things were definitely looking up!

❧ ❧ ❧

Two hours later, feeling refreshed and ready to go, she pulled her pod closed, then laid back and said "Emily, start *Veritas*." She closed her eyes and the earth dropped out from beneath her.

As soon as Rouge blinked open her eyes, she realized the caravan was in the middle of a battle. The noncombatants had circled the wagons, and the guards and members of the caravan who knew how to fight were vigorously defending against what looked like... Gophers? The things were easily eight feet tall, with greasy brown fur and viciously pointed buck teeth. Their scaly tails were covered in spikes, and their rounded bellies bulged oddly. Squinting, she used Identify even as she called her Mambele to her hand.

Demonic Gophers? What was going *on* lately?

Focusing on the closest defenders, a pair of guards she vaguely recognized as some of the ones Restur had hired in Bloodhaven, she used her knee to nudge Codswallop toward the two men. The ostrich squawked softly, then turned his head to eye her accusingly.

"Come on, Wally. We need to help!" She pressed her knee into his side a little more firmly, and this time he huffed a sigh and moved toward the pair.

Even as she watched, though, one of the men used a large shield to fend off a blow from the barbed tail, while his partner cut the beast's protruding belly. Another man slid out of the gash, swimming in gore and screaming weakly. Feeling her stomach try to rebel and regretting the avocado and smoked salmon bagel she'd eaten before logging on, she hurled her Mambele toward the Demonic Gopher as it swiped its claws at the man who'd cut it.

Her weapon spun through the air and caught the giant rodent in the eye, and it let out a piercing whistle.

You have dealt 152 points of damage to the *Demonic Gopher*. The *Demonic Gopher* is Poisoned.

Without missing a beat, the first man rammed his shield into the gopher's belly, causing more disgusting gobs of greasy, grimy guts to roll out. (Wait, wasn't there a song about this? This was totally Harris's team again, and he was *definitely* getting up close and friendly with some habaneros on Monday.) The second man swung his sword in a powerful overhand blow, slicing through the monster's neck.

You have assisted in slaying the *Demonic Gopher*.

Calling her Mambele back to her hand, Rouge looked around for more mobs, but found that only caravanners seemed to be left on their feet, with huge gopher corpses already shimmering into nothingness as they were looted.

"Yon beasts were truly horrific; do you not agree? 'Tis a good thing your soul was summoned once again to this harsh land in time to save those brave souls." The overly dramatic voice was practically right next to her ear, and she nearly fell off Codswallop as she whipped around.

Sure enough, there was Fluff, striking a pose with Rufus on her arm as she looked out over the carnage. Zoey had to stifle a giggle as she saw the bird throw a disenchanted look at his mistress before jumping into the air and vanishing.

Fluff turned to look at the space recently occupied by her hornbill pet, expression tragic. "Alas, poor Rufus. He must return to Toko's forest to once again take his place by the great God's side. I am certain he must regret our parting as much as I."

Thinking of the look Rufus had given the other girl, Zoey doubted that, but she just nodded, then looked back toward the wagons. People were cleaning up and preparing the wagons to leave again with the ease of recent practice.

"Is this the first attack since I left?"

Fluff shook her head. "Nay, fair maiden. It seems that we must face ever greater battles the nearer we get to our goal. I take solace in the fact that our wizened leader has said we are less than an hour from the hamlet of North Goose."

Snorting, Rouge wondered how Restur would feel about being called 'wizened'. "Have we lost anyone? Is Aspen okay?"

Pointing toward where the wagons had been crowded together, the half wood elf smiled. "Your friend is true and brave, but no warrior, alas. He stays with the steeds and the beasts of burden, and has only once had to deal a blow to a particularly pesky porcupine."

Standing in her stirrups, Rouge was, indeed, able to see Aspen's unmistakable hat and lanky frame as the farmer led a nervous horse toward a nearby wagon. She sighed in relief. "Is everyone else okay? Ned? Tessle? Has Doom been back at all?"

The archer shook her head. "Our honored guild leader's soul is still in the homeland of our soulss, and Tessle must, perforce, go to earn honest gold, that she may rejoin us here again someday. As to the goblin, I know not, but I do not believe that these demonic beasts have yet sent any souls to the Chaos Pool."

Rouge silently translated this to mean that Tessle had had to log off to go to work so that she could afford to pay for her *Veritas* subscription, and that as far as Fluff knew, no one had died. She nodded. "Thanks, Fluff! I'm going to go check in with Aspen."

The other girl raised a hand formally, and turned her own horse toward the back of the caravan as they began moving again.

Chapter Eighteen

Aspen

Aspen looked up as his life sense told him Rouge had returned and was heading toward him. Smiling, he said quietly, "Welcome back, Rouge. Thank you for your assistance. When those beasts began devouring people, I thought I might have to assist in a more overt manner."

Nekthadt raised his head from the wagon nearby, where he had been crouched, speaking softly to a water barrel still strapped tightly to the side. Aspen could sense Jesiqa inside, and he unobtrusively extended his mana to include her. He had noticed that the glyphis seemed to be weakening, in spite of escaping Bloodhaven, and Aspen tried to help her whenever he had a little mana to spare.

"What are these monsters?" Nekthadt asked Rouge. "Aspen says you have seen them in your world?"

Rouge shook her head, settling her ostrich into a walk beside them. "We haven't *seen* them. We just have stories about something like them. I really don't know any more than you do."

Aspen sighed, and reached out to boost the stamina of the animals nearby as Restur called for the caravan to pick up its pace. "I'm glad we'll be in Goose soon. I had thought this leg of our trip would be easier, with the Travelers occupied in Bloodhaven, but the monsters have more than made up for the absence of bandits."

Rouge tilted her head, hazel eyes gleaming with curiosity. "I keep meaning to ask you. Do you know why North Goose is called *North* Goose? Why not just Goose?"

Aspen felt his mouth curl into a smile, and let his attention drift from his work with the horses. He'd been doing this long enough that keeping them stable was nearly automatic. "As it happens, I do. Birdie once asked me the same question, and I looked it up.

"It turns out that several generations ago, when Akuji was just a frightening story parents told their children at night, there was a flock of Greater Geese that began terrorizing Bright. They would land in the ponds and lakes and eat all the fish and brush. They would chase anyone who came near, and rumor had it they ate small dogs and possibly a child. When they flew over, the sound of their flapping and quacks was loud enough that no one could hear anything else until they were gone.

"The king of that time set a bounty on the fowl, and heroes from all over came to do battle. Two of these heroes succeeded in killing two geese each, and the rest flew away to find somewhere less pointy to live. The King split the bounty between the two heroes, and their hometowns, filled with pride, each asked the King if they could change their names to 'Goose'.

"The King granted their requests, but with one change. Thus, the town formerly known as Pigwaller became North Goose, and Henslip was called South Goose." He felt the smile fade as more recent memories overran the mental picture of Birdie's excited little face as she sat on his knee listening to this story so many years ago. "South Goose fell not long before the end of the war. Most of the population were overrun before they had time to flee, and joined the ranks of the undead on one side or the other."

Aspen felt his gaze drawn to Nekthadt, who had almost certainly fought on the other side of many of those final battles, and wasn't surprised to see that the goblin was looking down into the barrel that contained his little friend. He felt the old fury rise up at the sight of the goblin, but pushed it down. That time was *over*, and all of them had been left with blood, and worse, on their hands.

Forcing out a cleansing breath, Aspen summoned his smile again, seeing that Rouge was looking at him, concerned. "Birdie approved of the name change."

Rouge laughed. "Me too! At least Pigwaller. Henslip is kind of cute!"

The two friends chatted as the caravan pushed on toward their destination. Periodically, Aspen would sweep his mental 'view' out as far as he could, expending a few mana to check for monsters or ambushes. Fortunately, the extensive use of his new ability had leveled it several times, as well as increasing his mana pool and regen significantly. He didn't think he had anywhere near the power he'd once had, but it was difficult to tell since he had little but an educated guess to tell him how his current spells compared to his old ones in terms of power usage.

In a remarkably short time that felt like a remarkably long one, they found themselves at the outskirts of North Goose. Restur called a halt to the caravan just outside the town limits. Tia, Restur's assistant, walked back to let Aspen and Rouge know that the caravan master was calling for them, and they passed the anxiously waiting caravanners to meet the old man at the front of the line.

Restur's thick white eyebrows were drawn together as they looked across the dividing line between the red bricks they stood on, and the dirty bluish ones a few feet away. "Something's wrong," he said abruptly. "I don't know what it is, but something is setting off my [Deal-flow] skill. I don't think there's anything good waiting for us here."

Rouge followed the direction of the caravan master's gaze, and then deliberately tapped Codswallop's side with her foot so that he stepped across the line. "I'm sorry, Restur," she said, not sounding very sorry, "but there's something here I really, *really* need." The ostrich bobbed his head, almost as if agreeing with her.

Rouge sighed wistfully. ::Last time I was here, the biggest worry I had was finding a new mount.:: She patted Codswallop affectionately. ::A lot has happened since then, with the farm, and the assassins, and Bloodhaven, but... I still want those amazing cinnamon rolls. Buttery, cinnamony, perfect fluffy, tender carbs. Mmm!:: She trailed off, swiping at the corner of her mouth absently.

Aspen looked from Rouge to Restur, and asked, "Can you wait here? We'll go in and see if we can find someone who'd be able to make a purchase. If we can't, we'll come back, and we can head on for Bright."

Nekthadt, who had hesitated a while before following them, spoke up too. "I'll go with them. I have business near here as well." Aspen turned to look at the goblin, one eyebrow raised. The other eyebrow joined it in trying to reach his hat brim when he saw that the small man was wearing his leather chest-pouch for the first time since they'd left Bloodhaven, and he could just make out Jesiqa's black eyes peering over the edge.

The farmer wasn't sure what business Nekthadt might have here, but he nodded in agreement. We'll be back in an hour, two at the outside. North Goose is lightly populated, but spread out, so it may take a bit to find the mayor or some other official."

Reluctantly, Restur nodded. "We'll stay here tonight. I won't go into town, but if you find someone who'd like to trade, bring them back with you. We'll set up camp just," he looked around, sharp blue eyes taking in the surrounding area, then pointed to an open field just inside the town limits. "There. It'll do us good to have a night without worrying about monster attacks. If you're not back by first light, we leave without you, and you'll have to catch up tomorrow."

Aspen nodded agreement, and turned to follow Rouge, with Nekthadt on his heels.

🐦 🐦 🐦

It was clear that Rouge had a definite destination in mind, and she headed straight to what looked like an abandoned farm not far down the road. The plain wooden fence sagged in places, and the grass around the small barn was overgrown. Even the little house had seen better days, and the front door hung on its hinges.

Rouge's face was a study in disappointment, but she didn't truly seem surprised. She patted Codswallop on the shoulder, the ostrich looking as crestfallen as his mistress. Turning to Aspen, she explained, "This is where Struthio was living when I came through here a few months ago. I bought Wally here from him, and then he was going to go ask Millie's – that's his girlfriend – dad if he could buy a share in his – the dad's – pig farm. Piggery?"

She looked around. "I guess the dad said yes, and they moved to his farm? Anyway, we'll have to go further into town."

Aspen nodded. "That does seem likely. Though it's difficult to believe they'd simply let this farm go to ruins."

He looked around, taking in the missing shingles on the barn roof, and the amount of dirt that had blown in through the broken door. "If I were to guess, this place has been abandoned since not long after you were here."

Carefully, he picked his way through the tall grass and over to the house. Leaning over slightly, he poked his head into the building. As his eyes adjusted, he looked around.

The door opened into the kitchen, with a simple floor and cabinets made of wooden planks. A cloth, now little more than a rag, hung beside the stove, and the stove door stood open.

On the table sat two plates. They were both empty now, but he had a sinking suspicion that the previous occupants had left in the middle of a meal, and the evidence had been devoured by local animals.

Next, he headed for the barn. Hazy light shone in through the gaping holes above, and boards were beginning to rot around the bottom of the walls. The remains of the straw on the ground was moldy, and the ladder that was supposed to lead to the small loft had fallen down.

Backing up, he looked at his young friend. "I think," he said, "that we should be very careful how we ask around about these two. Restur is right. Something is wrong in North Goose."

Quest: "Find the (S)truth(io)" begun.
Something has happened to the previous inhabitants of this house. Find out where they are, and help them if you can.
Success: +30 Relationship with Struthio. +30 Relationship with Millie. Cinnamon rolls.
Failure: Variable.

He looked over at Rouge, and saw that her eyes were flickering as she read something only she could see. A moment later, she looked over at him. "Did you get a quest to help them, too?" He nodded grimly, and looked at Nekthadt, who shrugged in resigned agreement.

Aspen thought for a moment. "Rouge, do you still have some of those scarves, or a cloak Nekthadt could wear? If this town is as on edge as I suspect, he could be in danger if they see him."

The goblin immediately held up his hands, scowling. "No! No one here will see me if I don't want them to. Goblins have long found that safety lies in numbers or stealth, and as there is only one of me…" He spread his hands as if the rest was self-evident.

Aspen chuckled a little. The goblin had argued vehemently against the dancer disguise he'd worn in Bloodhaven, but it was the most concealing garment Motte had had. Apparently the big man had picked it up after slaying a Futakuchi a while back, and had kept it hoping Rouge would like it. She had emphatically *not*, but fortunately for them, he'd kept it, since it was an Unusual item.

"All right, then. You may learn more from hiding than we do by asking. Silus?"

The bat, who had woken when the soothing movement of Codswallop's constant gait had stopped, popped her head out of Rouge's collar and blinked her large golden eyes. ::Aspen?::

"Go with Nekthadt. Help him scout, and if he finds anything, let us know. Nekthadt?" Aspen turned his gaze back to the goblin, who met his eyes. "If she lands on your shoulder and raises a wing, go in the direction she points. And…" he trailed off, knowing that Silus, and possibly Rouge, would be furious if he voiced the words *keep her safe*, but he knew from the slight nod the goblin gave that he understood. Aspen knew Jesiqa was Nekthadt's first priority, but he believed that the goblin would watch out for Silus as well, and, as Silus so often reminded him, the bat was not entirely helpless.

Nekthadt immediately turned and headed for the narrow lane that led from the farm. Rouge pointed. "Just keep going that way. There's not much else here except for lots of pigs." Shortly after that, the goblin vanished into the tall grass by the side of the road, his green skin blending into the plants until Aspen could only tell he was there by the bright light of his life force moving steadily away.

Aspen nodded to Rouge. "Let's go."

Rouge quickly led the way down the road and into town. As they went, fences began appearing on either side of the road, and broad lanes split off, each leading to a house and barn. Soon, the farms faded, and a few houses stood alone, and they began to hear noise.

Unexpectedly, the sound was music. Cheerful, consisting of drums, pipes, and bells, the melody was something of a mish-mash of sound, but there was no doubt it was celebratory. Shortly after the music became audible, chattering voices could also be heard, with occasional loud peals of laughter echoing out over the area.

Aspen and Rouge looked at each other.

::Is there some festival that happens around now that I don't know about?::

Rouge asked silently.

Aspen shook his head. ::Some villages celebrate the spring equinox, and the two Gooses specifically had festivals for the heroes who saved Bright, but those are in late summer. I don't know what's going on.::

Rouge looked ahead as they continued walking. ::Looks like we're about to find out.::

There was an arch made of dried vines over the road before them, with colorful, swirling ribbons, spring wildflowers, and not particularly well done paintings of pigs woven through it. An odd symbol appeared repeatedly in the design,and Aspen felt a niggling sense of recognition, though now wasn't the time to worry about it. Beneath the arch stood two men, beaming broadly and speaking loudly as other people approached them.

The broad middle-aged man on the left, with a heavy but not unattractive face except for a distinctly porcine snub nose, clapped a smaller man on the back. "Thank you for coming, Osep! The little lady and I appreciate your generosity on our happy day! I hope you enjoy the cake. Millie made it herself, and you know what a fine cook she is!" He beamed so widely that Aspen thought he could count all of his large, flat teeth.

The man on the right, short and stoop shouldered but not much older than the first man, smiled as well. His little eyes glittered in the sunlight. "Yes, indeedy, Osep! At first I thought y'wouldn't be givin' me girl a gift on 'er only weddin' day. I was glad when y'came back with *three* piglets. 'Tis right kind o' ye!"

Rouge had halted, squinting between the two men. ::The big guy is named Rubico, and the tag above the shorter guy just says 'Millie's Pa'. I don't know what's going on, but there's no *way* Millie would have ditched Struthio. You should have seen them. They were totally in love!::

Aspen pasted a broad smile on his face and began walking forward even as he sent, ::We need to find Millie.::

He stretched out a hand to the smaller man, who stared up at him with his mouth gaping, even as he clasped Aspen's wrist. Aspen forced joviality, "Hello! This lass heard about her friend Millie's big day, and just had to come and celebrate with her. Am I to take it that this is the lucky man?"

He turned and offered a hand to the big man, who was nearly tall enough to look Aspen in the eye, but twice as broad. "And you are…?" He clasped the man's too-soft hand and suppressed a shudder. This fellow reminded him uncomfortably of the worthless nobles who had hidden within the walls of Bright as their less fortunate countrymen fought and died.

The man sneered, but offered the same name Rouge had mentioned. "Rubico. Rubico Waller. You say this lass is a friend of Millie's? I don't recall her mentioning knowing any Travelers."

Rouge stepped up, nodding enthusiastically and leading Codswallop by his halter, with a bright smile on her face. "Yeah, um, I met Millie last fall! I bought Wally here from her and Struthio, actually, and they invited me to come back for their wedding. What, uh, happened to Struthio anyway?"

Aspen nearly groaned. ::What happened to careful?::

Rouge's voice was indignant. ::That was careful! I thought about just punching them. I don't like these guys.::

Rubico's face locked up, teeth bared in a snarl pretending to be a smile. "He… died. It was very unfortunate, but he sickened and passed away last year. Likely shortly after you met him."

Millie's Pa had a manic grin on his face, and sidled over next to Rubico, clapping the bigger man on the arm. "Rubico 'ere stepped up when t'lad died, and Millie fell 'ead over 'eels for 'im. Took a tragedy t'bring 'em t'gether, but 'ere we are."

The older man smiled in a predatory manner. "If'n yer 'ere fer the marriage, I s'pose ye brought a gift, eh? No one goes ter a weddin' without one! Ye c'n put it o'er there wi' the rest." He waved a hand behind him.

Looking past the two, Aspen saw a large open area, paved in the familiar bluish stones of a non-combat zone. Long tables were festooned with flowers and groaned under piles of baked goods. A huge, intricately decorated wedding cake took pride of place on the center table. People milled around, dressed in what looked to be their finest clothes, holding plates of food and cups of some beverage. They were smiling and laughing, but several of them looked tired or tense, especially the young women.

On the right, one table stood more or less by itself. Presents were piled high on a lace tablecloth that would have made a minor baroness proud. Large bags nestled amongst woven baskets, and a few boxes were tucked in with the rest. On the ground sat several simple cages, each containing one or more piglets. Most of the little creatures were sleeping, but a few were rooting around, snorting or squealing.

From the corner of his eye, Aspen saw Rouge glance at him, but kept his own gaze on the two men standing in front of them. "Of course! We'd also like to offer the bride our congratulations. Where is she?"

Rubico's face got, if possible, even redder and stiffer, though his smile never wavered. "Alas, all the excitement was just too much for her. She's resting until the ceremony, which," he cast a glance up at the sky, "should be soon. We wanted a sunset wedding."

Aspen nodded. "Of course. What could be more romantic? Well, we'll go put our gift on the table and join the rest of the revelers. Congratulations again, gentlemen." He nodded and walked past, drawing Rouge with him before she could protest.

::I'm not giving that guy anything! He's a creep!:: Rouge sent, even as she loosely looped Codswallop's lead around a simple hitching post outside the inn.

He smiled tightly as he met the eyes of a few of the villagers. ::It doesn't matter what it is, as long as it looks decorative enough. Just put *something* on the table, and then start looking for the most depressed person here.::

The girl's eyes went distant for a moment, and then she grinned evilly. A moment later a red silk bag appeared in her hand, and she set it carefully on the table. ::I did a quest for an herbalist a while back. The reward was this tea. I don't know what it's made of, but it gives you +10 health points for ten hours, but in exchange you grow ten warts on your face, *and* it makes you burp. A lot.::

Aspen chuckled. ::Sounds perfect. Now,:: his eyes roamed over the crowd, which he guessed consisted of every single townsperson. His gaze finally settled on a tall blonde girl standing forlornly by the banquet table. She was holding a ladle and passing out some kind of drink from a large crystal bowl beside her. ::Let's have a chat with the young lady serving drinks.::

He and Rouge began making their way toward the girl. Aspen kept one eye on Rubico and Millie's Pa, but the two men seemed to have been distracted by the arrival of a large family carrying not one but two cages of piglets. Just to be certain, when they arrived at their goal, Aspen positioned himself so that his body blocked Rouge from view.

::You try, Rouge. I have a feeling she'll respond better to another girl.:: He accepted a cup of whatever it was from the girl, smiling his thanks, and turned his back on the girls, even as he stretched out with his life sense, keeping tabs on Rouge while also looking for anything that seemed out of place. He wished, not for the first time, that he could control sapient beings with this magic, but it was definitely limited to plants and animals, at least for now. He could *see* people, but their lights - or numbers, in the case of Travelers - were completely inaccessible.

Behind him, he could hear the low murmur of voices, followed by Rouge's familiar laugh, though it was forced. The two conversed for a minute or two, and then Rouge walked briskly away.

::She's Millie's little sister, Cora. She says Struthio did die last fall, but Millie isn't in love with Rubico. She's not sure what's going on, but Millie has been miserable for months, and couldn't even get out of bed this morning. They got her into her gown, but she's barely conscious. She's lying down in a room in the inn.:: Rouge sounded angry, and Aspen could see her fingers twitching as she eyed the shadows that were stretching away from the buildings and tables.

Aspen flicked a look toward Rubico and Millie's Pa, and saw that the taller man was watching them, his expression unreadable. ::All right. Let's go check on Codswallop. I have an idea.::

The two meandered back toward the ostrich, who was shifting his large, clawed feet nervously. His feathers were puffed up, and he kept clucking softly to himself. It was clear that the bird wasn't any happier than his mistress with the situation.

Rouge laid a gentle hand on Codswallop's neck, and the ostrich leaned into her, burying his head in her thick curls. ::Now what?:: she asked.

Aspen sent his life sense out toward the inn, which stood just behind them. He sensed the scurrying little lights that he now associated with insects, some vague glows that were probably moss or algae, and then... three brighter fires, visible but untouchable. Two were slightly closer than the third, which flickered in a way he hadn't seen before.

His eyes focused, and he looked at Rouge. ::I think I know where she is. There are two people nearby, but I can't tell if they're in the same room or not. I think there's something wrong with her. We need to get to her quickly.::

Rouge nodded, looking around. ::I can [Sneak] in, if you can stand so no one can see me long enough to enter [Stealth]. That won't get you in, though, and if she's hurt, she may need healing.::

::We're here, too.:: Silus' little voice broke in. ::There's a window on the west side that Ned used to sneak in. There are two men in the main room, and one locked room off the kitchen. We can't get in there, but we can get rid of the men, if you want.::

Aspen frowned. ::I'd rather not hurt anyone until we know what's going on. Rubico and Millie's Pa are clearly up to something, but everyone else may be innocent of anything more dire than being too frightened to speak up.::

::Ned says he can knock them out, but we'll only have about ten minutes before they wake up again.::

::That will have to be good enough. Unless you have something that will work longer, Rouge?::

The girl shook her head. ::Most of my skills are either sneaky or lethal. I have [Knockout], but it has a 25% fail rate at best. If Ned has something that'll work for sure, he should use it. How are you talking to him, anyway?::

Silus giggled a little. ::He asks me questions. I bite him once for yes, and twice for no.::

Aspen closed his eyes for a moment. He hoped Nekthadt had thick skin. ::All right. We need a distraction. Something simple that people will dismiss, but will get them to look away while we go around the side of the building. Ideas?::

Rouge scrootched Codswallop's head. ::Wally can take care of that for us. He's really smart, and he's definitely distracting.::

Aspen nodded a little uncertainly. ::If you're sure he can handle it. Let's move away from him, and toward the west corner.::

Quietly, they stepped away from the ostrich, smiling and chatting softly as if they were just moving around as they passed the time until the ceremony began. From the long shadows and the angle of the sun, Aspen could tell they only had a half hour or so before sunset, so they were already cutting this intervention close.

Once they were as far from Codswallop, and as close to the corner of the inn, as possible, Aspen glanced at Rouge. ::How will you let him know it's time?::

She grinned a little, and opened her hand. On it, still warm and tempting as the day Millie had baked it, sat a single cinnamon roll. ::My last one, but Wally will do anything for one of these.:: With a last longing look and a deep sigh, she pulled back and tossed the bun into the bushes near her bird.

The response was instantaneous. Codswallop's large beak snapped at the air as the confection sailed by him, and when his head was pulled back by the halter, he raised his head and bugled a battle cry. Then he attacked the rope lead, pecking and pulling at it with all of his considerable strength. Everyone turned to look at him, and there were a few shrieks of surprise.

Rouge pulled at Aspen's arm, jerking him back around the corner of the building. He looked at her. ::I want one of those someday.::

She grinned. ::Then let's go rescue the chef.::

Entering the inn through the open window was simple enough. The small room in which they found themselves seemed to be an office. A plain wooden desk and chair sat against one wall, positioned so that any sunlight that streamed through the window would cover the desktop for most of the day. An open ledger and a feather pen sat on the desk, but Aspen could tell with a glance that it was just lists of numbers and letters. Likely a system created by someone who couldn't read, but needed to be able to record sales. Something useful might be hidden within the pages, but it would take more time than they had to find it.

Rouge looked around. ::What now?::

Aspen reached out with his mind, finding the three sapients in the building, and then turned to Nekthadt, who had been waiting for them in the room. "You said you can knock them out?"

The goblin nodded reluctantly. "I think so. We're in a Non-Combat Zone, so I can't do anything to injure them, but they're drinking, and I have a potion that should knock them out without side effects. It only lasts for a short while, but when they wake, they won't even notice any time has passed."

Rouge stared at him. "That's amazing. I can't even tell you how many times I could have used that. Where did you get it?"

Nekthadt's thin lips pinched into a pale green line. "It's a secret of my people. Perhaps someday I will tell you, but today is not that day. Now, I must [Sneak] over and place the potion in their mugs."

Aspen recognized the look in Rouge's eyes. It was equal parts curiosity and calculation. It was the one she'd often had when she first came to the farm, and was trying to make friends with its residents, likely in an attempt to sound them out for information.

He almost laughed to see it aimed at the goblin, certain that soon she'd be asking him if there was anything she could do to help him.

Then she puffed out her cheeks in resignation and glanced toward the door. "After you."

The goblin nodded, and crept silently over, opening the door without a sound. He slipped through, and the others were left to wait. They barely had time to begin to worry before he was back, however, and motioned for them to follow.

Follow they did, through the dark common room of the inn, where there stood a few round tables with chairs that matched the one in the office. As they reached the door to the kitchen, Aspen could see the two men, standing, looking blankly into space, with their mugs pressed to their lips. Nekthadt's potion was clearly very fast, and very effective, and he had a suspicion that some mysterious deaths amongst human leadership during the war might now be explainable.

All that was behind him, however, and he simply followed the goblin through the opening and into the equally dim kitchen. A single window allowed in faint light, and he could make out a huge, flour-dusted table in the center of the room, as well as two ovens and a cabinet against the far wall. A door beside the sink likely led into a pantry. Filthy dishes were piled on the counter, and the floors were visibly dirty.

Rouge grimaced. "Remind me not to eat in taverns anymore."

Aspen nodded. "Done."

Nekthadt rolled his eyes, but walked over to a narrow door, nearly hidden in the darkness to their right. "Here," he hissed, beckoning to Rouge. "My [Lockpick] level isn't high enough for this. I hope yours is better."

She grinned. "I'm not a fan of the stabby stabby, but I can definitely pick some locks." She leaned down to look at the keyhole, and did a bit of Traveler sleight-of-hand, producing a ring of metal wires with bent ends. Deftly, she inserted one into the keyhole and twisted. After a moment, a soft click sounded.

"Ha!" she said, triumphant, and pushed the door open.

Aspen looked at Nekthadt. "Keep watch?"

The goblin nodded and sank back into the shadows, nearly invisible unless you knew he was there. His hiding skill was probably closer to [Camouflage] than Rouge's [Stealth], but that didn't make it any less effective.

Quickly, Aspen and Rouge passed through the door, closing it gently behind them, so it at least looked as if it hadn't been opened. Aspen blinked in the near-total darkness, but Rouge, with her [Darkvision], cried out softly and he heard her feet take a few steps. Cursing himself, he closed his own eyes and used his life sense. He could 'see' the two men in the common room, their lights now hazy and faintly blue. Nekthadt was dim, his concealment almost perfect, even to this sixth sense, but Silus' bright spark and Jesiqa's slightly dimmer one gave him away.

Finally, just a few feet away, was Rouge's bright column of falling numbers, and beside her the flickering, pale green and yellow light of another person. He carefully took two steps, stopping when he could sense that the two figures were right in front of him.

"Is it her?" he asked softly.

Rouge's voice was shaky. "It is, but something's wrong with her. She's just lying there, but her eyes are open and she's kind of… smiling?"

Aspen knelt beside them, reaching toward the light until his hand touched fabric. It was a sleeve, soft and silky beneath his fingers. He followed it up until he found the supine girl's shoulder, and shook gently. "Millie?"

There was no response, so he tried again. "Millie? Are you all right?"

A girlish voice answered. "Yes. I'm so happy." The words sounded oddly stilted, and he frowned.

Rouge spoke up. "Millie, it's Rouge. Do you remember me? I bought Codswallop from you and Struthio, and-"

The youthful voice interrupted, still sounding flat and emotionless.

"Struthio? No, he's dead. I'm sure I never loved him anyway. I love Rubico. I'm so happy."

Aspen leaned forward. "Millie, why are you in here?"

"I worked all day yesterday, baking for the wedding. I was tired, so I laid down. I'm so happy." This time, as the girl said the last three words, her light flickered and brightened a little, the green overtaking the faded, bruise-like yellow. A tiny tinge of desperation touched her voice.

It was Rouge's turn again. "Millie, do you want to get out of here? We'll take you out-"

Breaking in, Millie's voice gained a bit more life, and she half choked on her words. "I'm... So... Happy..."

"She's crying, Aspen." Rouge's voice sounded bewildered.

He nodded. "Her light is... It was dim, and now it's a little brighter, but it keeps flickering. It was equal parts green and yellow, but it flickered greener for a moment. I think this is some kind of spell. A compulsion. It's completely illegal, but a Soul Mage could do this. I don't know if I can break it, though. There's nothing wrong with her physically."

"We have to get her out of here." Rouge's voice was fierce, and he could feel Millie's body move beside him as the thief struggled to lift the much taller woman.

He nodded, knowing she could see him, and raised the woman's arm over his shoulders. Between the two of them, they were able to get her up, but as soon as they neared the door, she began struggling. "No! I have to stay! I love Rubico! I'm so happy!" Fear and urgency gave her voice depth, and she sounded less like a child and more like a grown woman.

"Damn it," he muttered. "We don't have time for this!" He gently lowered Millie to the floor and opened the door, peering out. Seeing and sensing no one, he called softly, "Nekthadt?"

The goblin emerged from the shadows beneath the table. "Yes?"

"Do you have any more of that potion?"

The goblin's softly glowing eyes flicked toward the door. "If the woman says she wants to stay, should we not leave her?"

He shook his head firmly. "There's something very wrong. We need to get her out, now. If she wants to come back once we find a way to break the compulsion, that's fine, but there'll be no wedding tonight."

Nekthadt hesitated, then nodded. "I have enough. You'll have to carry her out the kitchen door. It will be a risk."

Aspen looked over toward the barred door leading outside, and nodded. "Do it."

Within a few minutes, the potion had been administered to the girl, who was no longer fighting now that they had stopped trying to get her to the door. Aspen picked up her still body, and Rouge opened the kitchen door. Aspen's life sense showed nothing larger than a family of birds in a nest outside, so they slipped out as silently as possible.

Rouge relocked the door of Millie's tiny prison behind them, and Nekthadt stayed in the kitchen to replace the bar across the door. A minute later, the goblin came around the side of the building, having slipped back out the window of the office. Whoever went to retrieve the bride would be very baffled as to the method of her disappearance.

Aspen threw out his life sense as far as he could, looking for somewhere they could hide until they could sneak Millie out of town. His net grew thinner and more tenuous the farther he pushed it, but he could still sense the faintest hints of the lives of the plants and animals he passed over. He was looking for someplace with dense vegetation and some wildlife, that would indicate an area uninhabited by humans, but what he found was…

He frowned. "To the west, there's something odd. Another life light that looks like Millie's, and two that seem weak, perhaps injured. Possibly more victims of whoever has bespelled this girl? Worth investigating, at least. There's also a copse of trees near there that should provide some concealment."

"We must hasten, then," Nekthadt hissed softly. "The potion should be wearing off of the two men at any moment, and who knows what the girl will do when she wakes."

Rouge cast a look at the sky. "Plus, sunset is in less than half an hour."

Aspen nodded. "They'll want to delay Millie's appearance as long as possible, given her condition, but time is short." He looked at the little lump sitting silently on Nekthadt's shoulder. "Silus, fly straight west until you come to a bunch of trees. Then angle a little north and look for anywhere some humans might be hiding or imprisoned. I'll watch you as best I can and guide you if you go astray."

::I think,:: he added silently, ::it will be within the range of party chat, but if you find something and can't hear me, just come back to the trees.::

The little bat dropped from the goblin's shoulder, quickly flitting up and then vanishing into the encroaching darkness. ::On my way!::

Aspen hitched Millie's limp form higher in his arms, marveling at how easy it was to carry her. He never could have managed this back in his days as a Necromancer! Peering toward the shadowed ground, however, he scowled slightly. Even with the glow of life all around him, he could still trip over a rock or a stick that his merely human eyes couldn't see.

"Rouge," he whispered, "take the lead."

::Tell me this way if there's something I need to dodge,:: he sent.

::Got it,:: she said, and her voice quivered with a mixture of suppressed tension and excitement.

"Nekthadt, follow behind us, and cover our tracks, if you can."

The goblin's sharp teeth flashed. "This I can do." Aspen nodded, knowing very well how good goblins were at concealing all traces of their presence until it was too late to do anything but fight or die.

Rouge headed out, Aspen close on her heels, and Nekthadt, with Jesiqa still in her pouch on his chest, brought up the rear.

The small grove wasn't far from the inn, but there weren't any paths leading to it, so Aspen hoped it would be secluded enough to allow them to evade discovery. When he glanced behind them, he couldn't see any trace of their passage, so whatever Nekthadt was doing was working. As they walked, he sent a few prayers to his flighty goddess to help them stay safe.

When they arrived, they found that dense thorn bushes crowded the base of the trees, but Aspen was able to convince them to move aside for the group. They managed to make it to the center with the worst injury being a long scratch on Rouge's arm, which healed in moments. The thorns probably explained why the otherwise pleasant copse wasn't a popular place.

Best of all, a small pool of crystal-clear water sat still and tranquil in the middle of a clearing not much larger than the pond itself. All of them gratefully drank, reducing their Thirst to zero and gaining the Well-Hydrated buff, which gave them increased resistance to heat and a small boost to stamina regeneration.

Aspen laid Millie down on the soft moss-covered earth nearby, and Nekthadt slipped Jesiqa from her pouch and into the pond, dumping the dirty water onto the ground and refilling the leather container with fresh. Rouge watched this process with curious eyes.

"Doesn't she need saltwater? I thought sharks could only live in the ocean?"

Nekthadt stroked one small hand over Jesiqa's back. The Glyphis had transformed to an oddly smooth gray fish with two relatively tall dorsal fins and small black eyes. She measured about two feet long from snout to tail tip, which was nearly twice as long as her humanoid form was tall.

"Glyphis are not sharks," Nekthadt said quietly, watching as Jesiqa moved with predatory grace toward a school of small fish. "Neither are they were-sharks, as they are often called. They are themselves. Some glyphis are found in saltwater. Some live part of their lives in saltwater, and part in fresh. Still others, like Jesiqa, live entirely in fresh water."

Jesiqa suddenly thrust herself forward, her mouth gaping to reveal rows of sharp teeth that snapped closed on the unsuspecting fish. Aspen winced a bit. "How is it that you know so much about glyphis, Nekthadt? I learned a little, in school, but it's clear you know quite a bit more, and Jesiqa seems to find speaking our tongue difficult at best."

The goblin bared his own sharp teeth. "That is a long story, and one I am not yet ready to share. Suffice it to say that Sarave and I had an… unusual upbringing, and we learned many unusual things."

Aspen's lips quirked. That he had known. He hadn't spent much time around goblins in general, for obvious reasons, but those he had heard speak seemed barely capable of putting together simple sentences, much less ones that sounded more educated than the average human.

He bowed his head. "As long as your secrets don't endanger any of us, they are yours to keep."

Rouge leaned forward. "No, wait! I want to-"

::Aspen! Rouge! I think I found them!:: Silus' squeaky little voice broke in, and Aspen looked up as the bat fluttered down onto his shoulder. ::There's a great big house almost at the edge of town. *Way* bigger than anything else I've seen. There are a few rooms that are lit with glowstones, even though I didn't see anyone moving around. It must be the place!::

She nuzzled her soft ears against his jaw. ::I did good, right?::

He smiled and stroked her ears gently. ::Perfect. Can you lead us back?::

::Sure! We'll have to be careful though, because people are starting to wander around with glowstones, and it sounds like they're looking for Millie. They must have noticed she's gone.::

Rouge looked up at the sky, which was darkening far past the brilliant colors of sunset, and snorted. ::If they hadn't, I would have been shocked. Oh!:: Suddenly, her eyes widened, and she whirled back around to where Aspen had left Millie. ::Shouldn't she be awake by now?::

The girl knelt down by the taller woman, and lifted one of her hands. "Millie? Millie, are you awake?"

Millie's voice was quiet, but seemed more her own. "Lass? Y'are the… Traveler girl, en't ye? T'one who bought Codswallop?" She swallowed, audibly struggling. "I'm sorry, I don't r'member-"

"Rouge!" Rouge said. "Yes! I bought Wally from Struthio. You gave me cinnamon rolls, and I came back to buy some more, but... Millie, what *happened* here?"

Millie barely rolled her head from side to side, the movement almost invisible in the deepening darkness. "We paid... m'da. He said we could wed, but then... Struthio got sick. Rubico said he'd pay fer a healer, since 'e jest wanted t'see me happy. They took Struthio..."

Silver trails shone on the woman's cheeks. "They said 'e died, but they wouldn't gi' me his body t'bury. Said it was foul wi' t'illness. Then last week, Da said... I had t'marry Rubico. They made me put on a ring, 'n after that... I had t'do what Rubico told me. I couldn't even tell m'sister..." Her voice faded into wracking sobs.

Aspen frowned, picking up Millie's strong left hand. He turned it over, and there, glinting slightly, was a golden ring. Pressed deep into the underside of her ring finger was a black stone, its sharp edge digging into the woman's flesh. He could see from the raw wound around it that it had been there for a while. He tugged gently at the evil thing, and Millie cried out, loudly enough that Aspen reached out with his life sense to see if anyone was close enough to hear. Thankfully, no one was, but it was clear that the band wouldn't be removed so easily.

He looked helplessly at Rouge. "I can't remove it, and I'm afraid if Rubico comes close enough for her to hear him, she'll have to do anything he says. I think the only reason she can even talk to us now is because he didn't give her instructions to cover this situation. Compulsion spells are tricky things, and controlling someone against their will requires precise commands."

Rouge bit her lip, gently prodding the ring herself. Then her eyes narrowed. "It's just jewelry, right? I mean, it's magical, but it's not soul bound or anything?"

Aspen had little experience in things like this, other than occasional fireside talks with Manuela, who had made it very clear that she would never, under any circumstances, make such a foul thing. He glanced over to Nekthadt to see if the goblin knew any more than he did. Nekthadt shrugged unhelpfully. "It shouldn't be. The curse is on the ring itself, not on Millie, so if we could remove it, it should cease to function, at least until it's placed on its next victim."

Rouge grinned. "We can't take it off normally, and she can't remove it, but I happen to know that cursed items *can* be stolen, at least from you natives. I accidentally lifted a few when I first started pl... um, coming here. I couldn't [Identify] them yet, and they looked fine, so I put them on. That's when I found out Gina's church has the cheapest cursed item removal around."

He started smiling as he understood where she was going. "You think you can [Steal] it? What do we need to do?"

The thief shrugged. "I can only [Steal] something that no one is paying attention to. My [Steal] is only level 17, so I can't [Steal] from pouches or packs. If I'm using [Stealth], it increases my chance of successfully using the Skill by 8%." She tugged on one of her curls. "Ah, there is one drawback. I don't get to *pick* what I [Steal]. So, the fewer things she has on her, the better the chance that I'll get the ring."

Millie's tears, which had died back to quiet hiccups, ramped up again at this news, but only for a moment. Then she choked out, "Do whate'er y'ave te. Please!"

Nekthadt retreated to the far side of the pool, leaving Aspen and Rouge to do what they had to under the cover of darkness. Rouge did most of the work, with Aspen only helping by turning the immobile woman so that Rouge could remove her clothing, as well as any other items or accessories she was wearing.

When Millie had been stripped down to just the ring and her underclothes, which couldn't be removed or stolen, Rouge took a deep breath. "Okay, here we go!"

They sat in silence for a moment, and then Rouge suddenly spoke in an urgent whisper. "Look there! Is that a light?"

Aspen looked around, trying to see what the elf girl had seen, and an instant later, he heard Rouge's satisfied voice. "Got it! Sorry, Aspen, Millie, I had to get you to stop thinking about it. The skill kept failing because you were focused on the ring, even though you weren't looking at it."

The girl held out her hand, the ring glimmering sullenly in the light of the moon. She grinned at the village woman who still laid on the ground. "All done, Millie."

Slowly, Millie sat up, struggling a little as her muscles answered to her for the first time in a week. Then she threw her arms around Rouge, engulfing the startled girl in a hug so fervent that it seemed she might snap the slight thief in half.

"Thank'ee. Oh, thank'ee! I may never see m'love again, but at least I'm free 'a t'man what took 'im away." She clutched at Rouge until the smaller girl finally managed to struggle free, carefully holding the noxious band in her palm so that it wouldn't get lost.

"Oh, that's all right. I just wish we'd been in time to save Struthio, too." Rouge's voice was sad, and Aspen was once again struck by how different this Traveler was from the others he had met. She genuinely seemed to care about the natives of this world, and he could tell she felt real sorrow at the loss of a man she had met only once, and for a half an hour at most.

Aspen reached out and plucked the ring from Rouge's palm. Using his nearly forgotten mage-smithing skill, he sent a pulse of power through the metal. He pictured it in a new form, ready to be helpful to someone, and free of the taint of darkness. For an instant, it seemed it would work, and the band twisted and reformed into a single golden nail. Then some malevolent force thumped into it from the black stone, and the nail sizzled and melted down into a small lump of slag.

He prodded it with a finger, grimacing. "I was afraid something like that would happen," he murmured. Millie was visibly pale even in the dim moonlight, and he knew she was imagining that happening while the jewelry was still on her finger. He smiled at her a bit grimly. "I'm glad Rouge had a better idea."

Dumbly, the two girls nodded.

::Are you ready to *go* now?:: Silus asked, impatiently.

Aspen turned his head, finally remembering that they weren't yet done with their... Wait, the *quest*!

Quest: "Find the (S)truth(io)"
Something has happened to the previous inhabitants of this house. Find out where they are, and help them if you can.
Success: +30 Relationship with Struthio. +30 Relationship with Millie. Cinnamon rolls.
Failure: Variable.

Given the wording of the quest, Struthio *had* to be alive. If he were dead, the quest should have completed when Millie told them what happened to him. Unless, of course, they were supposed to find his body? But then how would they gain Relationship points with the man? Aspen had a sudden feeling that his Goddess was dropping hints for him like breadcrumbs in a forest. Now he just had to follow them before some hungry beast ate them up.

He looked up at Rouge and Millie's shadowy figures. "We need to hurry," he said. "I don't think Struthio is dead, and Silus knows where to find him."

ᵕ ᵕ ᵕ

Aspen, Silus, and Rouge stared through the bushes at a large manor house. The residence was far larger than any building in such a small town had a right to be. Thick, stolid columns kept company with narrow arched windows, and an ostentatious golden dome topped the roof.

::I call dibs on any good stuff we find inside,:: Rouge said.

::Dibs?:: Silus asked.

::It means I get to be all thiefy and steal stuff.::

::Oh.:: Silus sounded unconvinced.

::I haven't stolen anything in *months*! I'm pretty sure my skills are actually decreasing.::

Silus's golden eyes grew huge. ::Can they *do* that?::

Aspen looked over at the two females, raising one eyebrow. ::You may steal whatever you like, Rouge, and no, Silus, your skills cannot decrease unless they're stolen from you by a potion, spell, or creature, and even then, it's usually not permanent.::

Rouge sniffed softly. ::Spoilsport.::

His lips twitched. ::Rescue first, joking later.::

::Rescues are more fun with jokes.::

As they watched, two men walked out of the massive double doors and down the four marble steps. They exchanged a few quiet words, and then split up, each of them carrying a glowstone. One of them was Rubico. The other was an unfamiliar man, slightly shorter than the villager, and wearing a heavy black robe with dark green trim around the cuffs and the edge of the hood.

Aspen crept forward as the two men walked out of sight. His life sense was focused around them and the house, and he knew there were no intelligent beings left inside, at least not among the living. ::Let's go.::

Rouge disappeared into the shadows, and he could only tell she was still there because of the faint light of her spirit, visible even through her [Stealth]. ::I still think we need to find a window or a side door or an unattended tunnel. No self-respecting thief enters through the front door,:: the girl muttered.

Aspen mounted the steps and tried the door handle. Locked. He stepped aside so Rouge could try it. He heard a faint clicking as she attempted to pick the lock.

::Fortunately, I'm neither particularly self-respecting, nor a thief.:: He kept watch for any indication that they might soon have company, and felt his shoulders relax slightly when he heard the snick of the lock releasing.

Rouge pushed open the door slightly. ::After you, then.::

Aspen slid through the narrow opening, stepping into an echoing foyer with stone staircases ahead and to either side. As Rouge closed the door behind them, locking it for good measure, he lifted the thief's lantern she'd loaned him and slid the shutter up slightly. This allowed a narrow stream of light from the glowstone inside to illuminate the area slightly more than the faint moonlight that had entered through the windows.

Rouge clicked her tongue softly. ::I know Millie said this guy is the descendent of the original hero who slew the Greater Goose, but I think he takes himself a *little* too seriously.::

Aspen smiled grimly. ::They always do.:: He looked around. ::The life I'm sensing is coming from in front of us and down. I don't see any way to get there from here. We'll have to go exploring.::

A soft, nearly inaudible squeak told him that Silus had taken flight. The quiet sound of her wings was lost in the large room. ::I think the rooms I saw with lights in them were this way. Left?::

Aspen nodded and began moving in that direction. Unfortunately, the light Silus had seen must have been from either Rubico or his companion, because by the time they all made it here, the whole building was dark except the windows by the front door. Now, they would have to depend on Silus' memory, Aspen's life sense, and Nekthadt and Rouge's trap and secret door-finding abilities to get them to their objective.

He felt Rouge bump him slightly as she passed, and knew she had done it intentionally. The girl's dexterity was far too high for it to have been accidental. ::Stay back,:: she sent. ::If there's anything sneaky in here, I'm more likely to find it than you. Plus, I still have dibs on any good stuff.::

He laughed softly, but slowed a bit as they all entered a small room to the left of the entry. It was clearly a cloakroom, and several high-quality garments hung on hangers nearby. It took only a few minutes for the three to determine that if the room was anything more than a repository for personal outerwear, it was beyond their ability to tell. He did, however, notice that the inventory had been reduced by a few particularly finely made coats by the time they stepped back out.

::This is going to take forever. Maybe we should split up?:: Rouge sounded frustrated, and he understood the sentiment. Nonetheless, he shook his head.

::Our abilities complement each other. We are going into the unknown, and I think it would be poor strategy to split the party.::

She sighed. ::Okay. Next door, then.::

It did, indeed, take far longer than he liked to find the secret door. They investigated two drawing rooms, a sparsely filled library, and an office before Rouge found a statue which she said was glowing faintly to her eyes. He couldn't see anything to differentiate it from a dozen others of equally questionable decorative taste, but when the girl twisted it on its base, a bookshelf slid silently aside.

The three stood at the top of a broad staircase, looking down. Aspen looked at Rouge, who was no longer using her [Stealth] in an attempt to conserve mana for her [Trap Detection] and [Hidden Passages] skills.

::Traps?:: he asked.

She nodded. ::I'll have to get closer to know if there are more, but don't put any weight on that first step.:: She jumped lightly down onto the second step, and then proceeded carefully from there.

Over the next excruciatingly-slow several minutes, the elf girl found a poison dart trap, a rock fall, and two hidden arrow traps. They were able to avoid all but the poison dart, which she was forced to disarm before they could proceed.

::Good news is,:: she sent as she stood up, holding the gleaming dart between two fingers triumphantly, ::my [Trap Detection] Skill and my [Disarm Trap] skill have both gone up now. I don't get to use them very often, so they usually level really slowly.:: She flicked her fingers, and the dart disappeared into her inventory.

Aspen nodded toward the door the dart had been guarding. The life forces he'd been sensing were very close now. ::Is it clear?::

She stuck her tongue out at him, but nodded, squeezing the handle and pushing open the door.

Against all expectations, the door didn't creak ominously. It swung open as smoothly as every other door in the well-maintained manor, and the three intruders were able to slip through and close it behind them with barely a sound.

Aspen looked around, but the room was pitch black except where dim moonlight streamed in between the slats over the single narrow window and the faint beam of light cast by his thief's lantern. Aspen knew any additional illumination they made could be seen from outside, since that was how Silus had found the room in the first place. He gritted his teeth and looked over to where he knew Rouge stood.

::The three lives I've been sensing are only a few feet in front of us. What do you see?::

::Three people. Two are in shackles against the far wall. One man and one woman, and elf or human. There's a woman on a stone slab in the middle of the room. Chained. They all seem to be unconscious or asleep, and their heads are down. I can't tell if the man is Struthio. I'm going to go see. I'll get them free and patch them up if I can:: She paused, then asked uncertainly, ::They *are* alive, right? I mean, I've killed people, but I don't want to touch a corpse unless there's loot involved.::

He felt a grin quirk the corners of his mouth, and a little of his tension drained away. Sometimes he wondered if she did that on purpose.

::They're alive, though the one closest to us – probably the one on the stone table – is very weak. I'll go check on her.::

He glanced toward Nekthadt. As quietly as he could, he said, "Can you keep watch? If someone realizes we're here and uses [Stealth], I'm not sure I'll notice them, especially if I'm distracted healing someone. We need someone keeping an eye on the door."

"Yes," the goblin replied, brusque but soft.

Aspen nodded acknowledgement, knowing the other could see the gesture with his racial [Darkvision]. He moved as stealthily as he could toward the faintly flickering life light. When he thought he was close enough, he reached out, using the back of his hand, as one of his military instructors once taught him. Reaching with fingers first was asking for those fingers to be grabbed, jammed, or cut, and the back of his hand was more resilient against any of those.

His hand bumped cold stone, and he slid his touch along the edge until he felt a metal chain. Carefully, he traced the chain down until he felt clammy bare flesh beneath his fingers. He squeezed gently. "Can you hear me? We're here to help. If you understand, make a little noise." Cautiously, he began to feed his mana into the arm under his hand. "[Heal]," he murmured.

A long moment went by without any response, and then the woman – he assumed Rouge had been right about that – twitched. He heard a soft sound of something brushing against stone. Hair?

"Ior... gas?" The voice was barely audible, but it was also almost painfully familiar. How many times had he heard his name in just such a soft whisper, as they waited for the enemy hordes to attack their position?

"Dear Gina! Manuela?" A hot flush of fury poured through his veins, and he increased the flow of mana to his spell. His friend whimpered softly, and he eased off again. When someone was near death but not actually dying, the healing process could be painful, especially if there were large injuries that had to pull together and close.

Focusing his life sense, he scanned her battered body, distantly noting that she was naked except for her soul-bound underclothes. It took him a moment to realize how badly she had been mistreated, and that her body would require more healing than he had initially believed. His breath hissed through his teeth as he struggled to keep his [Heal] down to a level she could handle, grateful he had been practicing on the horses in the caravan.

"Gina's tender mercies, Manuela! What happened?"

She laughed, a rusty, painful sound that would have told him her injuries weren't all external even if he couldn't see the pulsing red damage in his life sense. When she spoke again, though, her voice was still quiet, but a little stronger. "Some hired thugs broke into my home and grabbed me a few days ago. They had [Stay Soul] charms on, so I couldn't affect them. They told everyone," she paused, catching her breath, "that they were taking me to Bright to 'pay for my crimes', but as soon as we were out of Bloodhaven, they started asking about you."

He was holding her hand now, monitoring her recovery, and she tightened her fingers weakly around his. "After a while, they realized I didn't know any more than they did, and they tried forcing me to tie some talismans to your soul so they could track you. Instead, I broke the link between you and the items they gave me to use, and then... they got mad."

He felt her shift as she shook her head, gasping painfully as her neck rolled. "They brought me here, and tried to get me to make some [Command Soul] rings for them. I told them I'd die first. I guess they took me at my word."

He poured a little more power into his [Heal] as he felt her gain strength, and this time she only grunted a little. Her fingers spasmed beneath his, and he shifted his grip. "Idiots. Anyone who ever met you knew Duke Geralt and the King both tried to get you to do things like that after the war. You chose to live in the vilest place in Quarternell and help people instead. You'd think they'd get it." He attempted a laugh, but it came out more like a painful barking rasp.

"Yeah," she murmured, "some people just can't take a hint." She sighed softly, her body relaxing slightly as her injuries finished regenerating to the point that they didn't hurt any longer. "I don't know what you did to make those people angry, Iorgas, but some very bad people want you very badly."

He sighed. "I wish I knew. They started coming after me a few weeks ago. I wondered why we hadn't seen more of them after the first attempt. I wonder if the one tracking charm was the only one their Soul Mage could make. Also, I go by Aspen now."

She laughed softly. "Iorg*as Pen*brooke. I see what you did there."

He chuckled, this time more easily. "I know. Creativity was Lark's gift, not mine."

"She had many gifts." Manuela's husky voice was sad, but then she tugged her wrists slightly, making her chains rattle. "I suppose it's too much to expect that you developed some lockpicking skills since you've been gone?"

Now he did grin, and slid his hand away from hers and down the chain. "I have something better." Shifting his mana flow, he centered himself, building an image in his mind, and felt the metal links soften and flow. When he could see the faint hint of gold like summer corn outlining the object in his hand, he let the magic go.

Carefully, he reached out and pressed the little metal tool into Manuela's open hand. "Try it now."

As she moved her arm experimentally, hissing at the pain of moving a joint that had been held in one position for more than a day, he switched the other chain and repeated his actions. After setting the second trowel blade in her other hand, he moved down to her feet.

"You have been busy," Manuela said softly, tracing the broad, deeply-curved blades with her fingers. Then she shook her arm slightly so the two links that still dangled from her manacles jingled faintly. "Though I think I'd still prefer the lockpick."

::Aspen?::

He jumped as Rouge's voice intruded into his mind. ::Rouge?:: he returned, even as he helped Manuela swing her legs off the stone slab.

She sounded a little flustered, and a lot worried. ::I know you're having an important reunion, and your friend was in really bad shape, but I've done all I can here, and Struthio's still out. He has one of those rings on, and no matter what I do, he won't move or respond. I tried using [Steal], but after all the [Stealth], I only had enough mana for two tries. I got a Pair of Tattered Pants and some Holey Socks.::

Aspen looked at Manuela. "I need to heal the man who was held captive here with you. He has a [Command Soul] ring on, I think. Can you break the spell?"

The Soul Mage stood, and he could feel her swaying beside him. She took a wobbly step toward the back of the room. "I think so. They kept me in the Near Death debuff so my health and mana wouldn't regenerate. Now that I'm recovering, I should be able to manage a few small spells."

A third voice spoke softly in a husky, neutral tone. "I can also use [Remove Cursed Item], once my hands are free."

Now that his eyes had adjusted, Aspen could see the dim form that was Rouge jump. The dark shape of her curls shifted as she looked around. ::Did you hear that?:: she asked in party chat.

He arched a brow, helping Manuela make her way toward the two remaining prisoners. ::Of course. Should I not?::

::Uh, yes, of course you should. I mean, why wouldn't you, right?:: She laughed nervously, and he heard a shockingly loud clank as she fumbled the manacle she was trying to open. He frowned, a new kind of concern breaking through his worry that they would be discovered. What was wrong with Rouge? She was behaving as though something was wrong. Something more than the obvious.

Manuela and Aspen made it to the wall, and Manuela was reaching for Struthio's hand when Silus' frightened voice sounded in his mind. ::Aspen! I think someone heard us. There are sounds outside, and they're coming closer!::

"Gina's golden goblet," he hissed, "everyone hurry! Silus says we may have company in a moment. Nekthadt, be ready. Someone get that ring off, and if your new friend there can help us, Rouge, get them out of those chains, too."

The emotionless voice spoke quietly. "I cannot assist you in battle. That is beyond my parameters."

He could almost hear Rouge gritting her teeth. "You mean that's *against the rules*? What good... No, never mind. Just give me a sec." A click sounded, and she gave a satisfied sigh, her dark figure immediately shifting to kneel beside

Struthio's prostrate form.

Meanwhile, Manuela's concerned voice whispered, "Ior… Um, *Aspen*, do you want me to take off this ring right now? I don't know what his response will be, and-"

But Aspen was watching the door with a sick fascination. He could feel a strange force coming toward the door. It was a mortal fire, but there was something like a film of soap or oil coating it, smothering its brightness. Nekthadt had sunk back into the deepest shadows, pulling his concealment around him, and beside Aspen, Rouge did the same. Manuela, receiving no answer, tugged hard at something Aspen couldn't make out.

Struthio screamed. "Millieeeeeeeeeeee!" The man sat bolt upright, then began to struggle to his feet, pushing Aspen and Manuela away, though he was weak as a babe.

Outside the door, the light paused, and Aspen sensed three more life forces racing toward them. Then the door was thrown open, and a bright light filled the room. Aspen blinked, cursing as he realized he should have known they'd have lights and covered his eyes. He blinked against tears of pain as his eyes struggled to adjust.

In his mind's eye, he saw Rouge and Nekthadt's forms leap into clarity, their ability to hide failing as the shadows disappeared. Then Nekthadt and Rouge simultaneously leapt toward the greasy figure in the door, which blazed up momentarily. Aspen's two friends stopped in midair as if they'd hit a wall, and both of them flew back through the air. He heard an all too familiar crack as they landed. One of them had broken a bone.

He blinked his eyes, forcing them to stay open and take in the scene in front of him.

Nekthadt lay in the middle of the room, on the stone slab that had held Manuela only a few minutes earlier. His lower leg was bent at an impossible angle, and his face had already drained to the shade of dying lichen. Nonetheless, he held a knife, ready to throw.

Rouge had somehow recovered mid flight, and he could see that she was crouched not far from him, her Mambele in her hand. Her face was set and determined as she glared at the man standing in the doorway.

Beside her, barely holding himself up against the wall, was a man that Aspen assumed was Struthio. Rouge had described him as a mountain of a man, but now he was little more than a skeleton. His tattered clothes hung from his tall frame, and Aspen thought the man was nearly as thin as he himself had been when he was freed from Akuji's not-so tender mercies.

The man in the door was Millie's Pa, but his face was no longer smarmy and selfish. Instead, a sneer stretched his pendulous lips, and his small eyes held a gleam of madness. There was something oddly wrong about the shape of his head, but Aspen couldn't tell what it was.

Behind him stood Rubico, though the big man was also changed. Where before he had exuded arrogance, now he stood slightly too far from his prospective father-in-law, his stance betraying his uneasiness at being so close.

Next to Rubico was a third man. This one was too similar in appearance to the big man to not be related in some way. His nose held the same distinctly piggish tilt and heft, though his hair was muddy brown instead of dirty blonde. In his hand, he held a large, sharp blade, and Aspen looked at Manuela when he felt her shudder. Her eyes, dark in her too thin face, were locked on the blade, and Aspen had a suspicion that they had just met her tormentor.

Millie's Pa opened his mouth, but the voice that emerged was completely different from the one he'd spoken in when they met him earlier. This one was nasal and flat, with an oddly resonant sound. His eyes were locked onto Aspen. "Here you are at last, Iorgas Penbrooke. We hoped that you would turn up if we kept your friend long enough." His sneer deepened. "You always did have a weakness for your misguided notions of 'love' and 'loyalty'."

Silus's squeaky voice broke Aspen's almost hypnotized awareness of the man. ::Should I bite him, Aspen? I really want to bite him.::

He drew in a shuddering breath, only then realizing that he had stopped breathing while the shorter man spoke. ::If you can do it without being injured, yes. Wait until Rubico and the other man move away, though.::

Clearing his throat, he said, "Obviously you know me, but who are you? I recognize the face you're wearing, but somehow I don't think you're actually Millie's father."

A laugh choked up from the man's throat. "Wearing. *Wearing*. Ha! Yes, that's funny. You never had much of a sense of humor, but that was funny." He tilted his head, and something in his neck bulged and crackled. It was a sound Aspen hadn't heard since Lich Lord Akuji had fallen. Millie's Pa was, without a doubt, dead, though he seemed to have been possessed by some spirit that was alive enough to show up in Aspen's other vision. That sound had been the grinding of broken vertebrae in his neck.

Nearby, Rouge gagged a little. "Oh my *gosh!* What's wrong with that guy's head?"

The dead man's head lolled slightly as he turned his gaze on the girl. As he did, Aspen could see what Rouge had seen. The side of his head was a pulpy mess of hair and blood, leaving no doubts as to the cause of his death.

Aspen instinctively stepped to the side, trying to block Rouge's view of the horrible sight. He knew she was by far the better fighter of the two of them, but his urge to protect her was far stronger than his ability to control it, even if he had wanted to.

As he moved, his body blocked the light from the glowstone held in the possessed man's hand, and he knew his shadow would be falling over his young friend. After a moment, he 'saw' the column of numbers that seemed to be her inner essence fade into near invisibility, and knew that she had taken advantage of it.

"Who, or *what*, are you?" Aspen asked again, drawing the creature's attention back to himself. "You speak as if you know me, but I find that I cannot offer you the same courtesy."

Half of the man's mouth lifted. "Oh, that's all right." He giggled a little. "I don't mind. I'm sure we'll have plenty of time to become reacquainted. Right now, though," he gestured to his companions, "I'm afraid I don't need your little friends anymore. I *could*, however, use a light snack."

With that, his jaw dropped open, revealing that the gap-toothed grin of Millie's horrible but all-too-human parent had become an orifice filled with jagged rows of teeth. He crouched down as long bone claws thrust from his fingers and toes, shredding the flesh around them.

::Aspen, it says he's a Demonic Swineherd!:: Rouge's voice was slightly panicked. ::What's with all the Demonic things? I don't like this!:: But even as she spoke, her faint form was crawling along the floor, staying in the shadow cast by the heavy stone table on which Nekthadt still laid.

The goblin had somehow managed to drag himself to his hands and one foot, though the pain had to be excruciating. His eyes flickered as he glanced down, and Aspen suddenly wondered if one of the goblin's mysterious skills might not allow him to pierce [Stealth]. If, indeed, he could see Rouge, then he would time his own attack for...

Rouge and Nekthadt leapt simultaneously, and Aspen mentally shouted, ::Silus! Go for one of the living men! Disease won't work against someone who's already dead!::

The bat darted down from where she had been hidden above the door lintel, and latched onto Rubico's ear. She bit down as hard as she could, and then flapped away again, though this time she headed straight for Aspen. With her presence revealed, and her most powerful attack now on cooldown, she would be nearly helpless in a head-to-head battle.

Rubico clapped his hand to his ear, howling as much in surprise and indignation as pain. When he pulled his hand back, he stared at the small smear of blood on it. Grimacing, he shook his head and started forward. Halfway through his first step, he staggered, and would have fallen if he hadn't caught himself on the wall. He raised a hand to his nose, and when he pulled it away, it was covered in blood. He tried to speak, and more blood poured from his mouth. As if in slow motion, he fell.

Meanwhile, Nekthadt had sent his blade spinning with lethal precision. The blade sank deep into the eye socket of the unknown man, and the hilt stood out as the man slowly toppled to the side. His body hit the ground before Rubico's.

Rouge, of course, had gone straight for Millie's Pa, swinging her Mambele so that it sank into the soft side of the man's head. Instantly, she flipped backwards, hands thrusting off the floor so she flung her body back to land on her feet beside Nekthadt, dangerously close to hitting him as she landed. The goblin looked as if he wasn't sure if he should applaud or swear at her.

The Demonic Swineherd swayed in place, then slowly turned to look at them. The spike of the Mambele was clearly embedded in his brain, and his tooth-filled sneer was fixed in place by the spike of the blade. When he spoke, the words were nearly unintelligible thanks to his packed dentition and his now-broken jaw.

"I... was... going.... to...," he gestured with his bony claws, and the bodies of his two former companions rose to their feet jerkily, "go... easy..."

Rouge growled, "Oh, stuff it," and called her Mambele back to her hand. It tore through his head, nearly removing the top of his skull, and the moment it touched her hand, she wound up and threw it again. This time it took the Swineherd in the throat, stopping his words in a gurgle.

Aspen felt a tug at his sleeve, and nearly cracked his own neck whipping around to look at the woman who was gripping the cloth. Her black hair was cut in a simple, smooth curve across her forehead, and beneath the bangs two eyes so pale they were almost white met his own. He took in the ritualistic red makeup that covered her face from the bridge of her nose to her hairline, and his mouth went dry. His gaze flicked lower, and he took in the shapeless black robe that covered every bit of her skin from her jawline down, except for graceful dead-white hands.

He gulped.

"I cannot help you fight," said the priestess of Atae, "but I can release those who defy my Lady's rightful claim upon them. The ritual is not quick, however. You must survive until it is complete."

Aspen nodded, unable to speak, and the priestess's red lips turned up in an expression that looked as if it was something she knew should be a reassuring smile, but she wasn't quite sure how to do it properly. "I must not be interrupted, and the spell has a casting time of seven minutes."

He sucked in a breath. That was a major working. Only multi-caster rituals took longer than that. He glanced around. Nekthadt was throwing more blades than it seemed possible that he could have hidden on his small person. Rouge's Mambele was similarly busy, and already both zombies showed deep wounds, none of which slowed them in the slightest.

Manuela was crouched by Struthio, who seemed to have lapsed into unconsciousness again after his initial terror-driven attempts to rise. The Soul Mage met Aspen's eyes and shook her head. "Whatever these things are, demonic or undead," she hissed softly, "they have no souls. I can't affect them. Also, this man is still too close to death. If I stop tying his spirit to his body, it may slip away before the battle is over."

Cursing under his breath, Aspen looked back at the priestess. "Do it," he said softly, and she closed her eyes. Her hands began twisting in front of her, fingers weaving through complex patterns as she murmured what seemed like nonsense words. He could feel something in her life force shift, and tendrils of her power drifted away from her body, reaching toward something he couldn't see.

He looked back at his friends. The goblin and the elf girl were keeping the zombies busy, but the Demonic Swineherd was simply standing, a smile on his torn and twisted face as he flicked his claws in a decidedly creepy manner. He showed no concern for the wounds dealt by Rouge's weapon, though thankfully he had at least stopped trying to speak. When he decided to join the fight, it would end, one way or the other.

Aspen slid some of his magic into Nekthadt and grimaced. While he couldn't see exactly what had happened to the goblin's leg, he could tell that it was badly broken. No doubt Nekthadt was fighting while under the Broken Bone debuff, which would reduce his mobility to practically nothing. When he ran out of blades, he would be, for all intents and purposes, defenseless. Aspen could heal the damage he had taken, but until the limb could be straightened, the debuff couldn't be cleared. Almost absently, Aspen began feeding some mana into Nekthadt, doing what he could for the goblin even as the rest of his mind searched for any other life that could assist them.

Mice in the walls were too few and too weak to do much good, especially against undead who couldn't be frightened and would be effectively immune to the small bites such creatures could deliver.

A very few rats, but they, too, would be ineffective against these creatures.

Voles. Fleas. Flies. Spiders. Moths. Beetles. Moss. A few thin tree roots…

Then, at the edge of his detection range, he caught a flicker of something. An instant later, it returned, steadier, and was joined by others! Some of the lights and numbers he recognized, and others were new. Tessle was on her way, with Flu-flu and two others nearby, though these last were strangers. In the lead, burning brightly as he raced toward his girl, was Codswallop. The brilliant ostrich must have gone for help! Aspen swore he would never again question Rouge's assertions that Codswallop was a genius amongst fowl.

He snapped his attention back to the battle. Nekthadt was wielding a poniard – and *where* had that come from? – against Rubico's zombie. The big man had been whittled down, literally, but was still attempting to snap at the goblin with his teeth and club him with what remained of his arms. Meanwhile, Nekthadt's Stamina was clearly running out, and the Broken Bone debuff would have his regeneration reduced to near zero.

Rouge was focused on her own zombie, but the creature was upon her now, and no matter how she dodged, the room was simply too small to allow her to escape for long. In addition, he could see by the glances she shot at Struthio and Manuela whenever she got too close to them that she was afraid the dead man would turn whatever passed for his attention onto them.

::Help is on the way, Rouge,:: he sent. ::Flu-flu, Tessle, and two others are coming. We just have to let them know where we are.::

Rouge's voice was exhausted, but gleeful. ::That must be Jace! He said he would meet us here.:: She struck out with her knife, then leaned away from the zombie's return swipe. Her back hit the wall, though, and the mob caught her with his jagged claws, ripping open a wound that stretched from her shoulder to her ribs. She cried out and dropped into a roll, though she was far less graceful than usual.

::I don't know how much longer we can make it, though. I tried going for the brain, because that always works in the movies, and that pig farmer is still standing over there grinning at us.:: She sounded overwhelmed. ::I'd use [Repeat] if anything I did actually made a darned bit of difference, but these guys just keep coming!::

Aspen gritted his teeth. He pulled his mana link back from Nekthadt, leaving the goblin to his own devices for a moment as he directed his healing toward Rouge instead. He could see the caramel skin showing through her damaged gear begin to knit, and he focused on the tree roots spreading deep within the earth beneath and around them.

The roots were heavy and dense, and though the tree they grew from seemed willing enough to help, it was a towering eucalyptus, and its hard wood simply couldn't move in any way that would help them inside the house. Outside, however...

He fed power into the tree, and it began to move. The motions were small, at first, just the tops of the most delicate branches shaking as if in a nonexistent wind. Then the slightly larger branches began to shift, and then the tree was waving in slow, ponderous, unnatural movements. Its top, rising nearly two hundred feet above the earth, would be easily visible from where the newcomers had paused not far away. He assumed they were looking for a clue as to where Rouge and the others were, and there was no way they could miss this one.

Sure enough, an instant later they began to move again, now heading straight for the house.

A gurgling snarl was all the warning he had before sharp claws impaled his chest. Gasping at the sudden blinding pain, he looked down. The Demonic Swineherd had finally abandoned his position by the door. Half of his mouth was locked in a sneer, while the sharp teeth in the other side of his jaw were revealed by the slash left by Rouge's Mambele.

::Aspen!:: Rouge and Silus shouted simultaneously, and he looked down.

The claws of the monster's right hand were buried between his ribs. He could almost feel the tip of one scrape against his heart with every beat. The Swineherd's other hand was on his own throat, pinching together the torn flesh to create enough of a seal that he could wheeze out a few words.

"Stop... or he... dies...!"

Aspen drew in an agonizing breath, and pulled something out of his pocket. Echoing Rouge's words of a few minutes earlier, he choked out, "Stuff it..." and put action to words, shoving a trowel deep into the gaping wound on the monster's face.

He left a tiny trickle of power flowing to heal his own wounds, and poured the rest of it, hot and bright, into the metal that had been a chain not long before. The metal melted, pouring in molten rivulets out of the nose and mouth of the Swineherd. A stream even seeped between the clutching fingers at his throat, sizzling as it touched his fingers. A horrible stench filled the room, and the creature staggered back, his claws sliding from Aspen's chest with a sucking sound.

"[Repeat]!" Rouge screamed, leaning back against the stone slab in the center of the room so she could use her powerful legs to catapult her attacker away from her. The undead monster staggered back, slamming into a wall hard enough to crack the stone. Rouge rolled across the table, grabbing Nekthadt as she did, and pulled the two of them back to a more defensible position near Aspen, Manuela, and Struthio.

The rogue's spell, however, had not been aimed at her own opponent, but Aspen's. The Demonic Swineherd threw his head back, silver metal pouring from his ruined throat and overflowing his sinus cavities. His claws, one set red with Aspen's blood, the other gleaming silver and black with cooling iron, clacked open and closed.

Aspen felt an unbearable pressure in his chest and fell to his knees, his vision darkening. Manuela was instantly beside him, her hands pressed to one of the punctures which was frothing with red blood, sealing the wound as best she could. She looked up at Rouge.

"He's dying." His old friend stated the obvious, tears standing in her eyes, and the elf girl blanched. Her fingers flickered, and she tossed something to Manuela. The older woman snatched them from the air with one hand.

"Bandages and my best Healing Potion," Rouge rasped out. *"Don't let him die!"*

Manuela swallowed hard and nodded.

Rouge turned back to the Demonic Swineherd and his minions. Her face was set, but she was noticeably paler than usual. Her greatest strength lay in her dexterity, but she couldn't use it. She had to stand and fight, or the monsters would reach her friends. She raised her blades, Mambele in one hand and Nekthadt's long poniard in the other.

Aspen stared up at Manuela's face, which was fading in and out as the woman worked to patch him up enough that he would survive until the end of the battle. A trickle of fluid, tasting of warm raspberry cordial, flowed into his mouth. He choked, but then managed to swallow, feeling a tiny trickle of health return to him. It was just enough that he could focus his attention on his own wounds.

He swallowed hard, eyes closing, as he saw how close he had come to near instant death. There was no doubt that the Demonic creature could have killed him where he stood if it had wanted to. The claw he had felt against his heart had drawn a thin scratch on the muscle, and that scratch was widening with each frantic beat of his heart.

He shoved the feeble remnants of his power into healing his most vital organ, ignoring the two holes in his left lung for the moment. Manuela had them sealed well enough that he could breathe, barely, so they could wait.

At the edges of his consciousness, he sensed Rouge's life force trickling away. She was taking wounds from all directions, and while she could use her speed and flexibility to avoid some of the damage, she simply wouldn't last for long. Vaguely, he wondered where she would respawn. Then he wondered if he would see Lark in the Chaos Pool, or if his daughter's soul had already been reborn somewhere.

That thought dragged him back from his nearly complete surrender to his inevitable failure. What if Lark *had* been reborn? What kind of world would she have to grow up in? He had thought it would be a peaceful one, but it was clear, now, that the darkness he had thought vanquished had only been licking its wounds, waiting to grow strong enough to attack again.

Even if he wasn't her father any more, she would always be his daughter, and he wouldn't fail her again.

He closed his eyes. *Gina,* he prayed, *if you're listening, if you can, help us! I'll promise you anything you want, just.... Please. Please help me make a world where Lark could be happy.*

A blaze of light burst in his mind, and he felt himself yanked unceremoniously from his nearly dead body. His senses faded, replaced with an emptiness so profound that his mind was momentarily overwhelmed by its vastness.

Then he heard a little sob, and his eyes – or whatever passed for his eyes in this drifting void – blinked open, and he beheld his Goddess.

Gina's rainbow eyes were shining with tears, and showers of shimmering stars drifted around her in a galaxy of light. She held out her hands to him.

"Do you mean it?" she asked. Her voice was simultaneously so quiet that he could barely hear it and also so thunderously loud that it seemed to shake the star-strewn sky that surrounded them. "Are you ready to do what only you can do?"

He looked at her, in her glory, and swallowed hard. "I'm ready to do what I should have done when Birdie was alive. I want to make sure, to the best of my power, that the world she lives in is one that deserves her. One that brings her joy. I'm willing to do whatever it takes, even if it costs my life. Again."

Her mouth quirked, and when she spoke again, her voice was only at the level of normal speech, and filled with sadness. "Always so ready to give your life for your child. Haven't you ever wanted to live for your own sake? I've seen your whole life, you know. You say you wanted power and recognition, and that was true, once. But from the day you looked into your daughter's face, every step you took was for her. You accepted the role forced upon you by circumstance, though it was reviled, because it was the only way you saw to provide for her. You sought riches so you could give her anything her heart desired. You sought power so you could protect her."

She tilted her head, silver streams of stars drifting from her red-gold curls, and a nebula of blues and purples swirling in her depthless gaze. "In struggling to give her everything, you sometimes failed to give her the one thing she really wanted... You." Her face twisted with heartfelt sorrow, and tears flowed like mercury. "Can you, now, find happiness, as well as creating a place where others can find joy? Because I am *absolutely certain* that your daughter wants you to be happy as fervently as you wish that for her."

Something in his chest tightened until he could barely breathe. In that instant, his Goddess and his child blurred together, and his head spun. Then she reached out and touched his chest, and the moment broke. He gasped in a breath, and she smiled, though it was a strange smile, with both more and less truth in it than any expression he had ever seen on her face before.

"What," he swallowed again. "What do I need to do?"

Her small fingers tapped, twice, over his heart. "You'll know."

He nodded, bowing his head in acceptance of the cryptic answer, which was no less than he had expected. Then he looked up, his topaz gaze catching her now blue and green one.

"Can you tell me, though… Do you know, if Birdie has been reborn?" His voice tore at his throat as he asked, and he wasn't sure what answer he wanted. If Lark's soul lived on, in whatever form, there was a minute chance that he would meet her again, but she would be in danger from whatever new evil was emerging. If she was still in the Chaos Pool, she was safe, for the moment, but he would have to die to see her.

Gina closed her eyes. "Has this question not been answered? Are you certain you wish to ask again?" she asked softly.

"…Yes."

The Goddess' eyes blinked open, and they were black, from edge to edge. The inky darkness spilled out, covering her cheeks, then her face, then flowed down to smother her entire body, until she was nothing more than a gleaming patch of absolute night. That patch shrank in on itself, and then bloomed back out in a burst of light.

Aspen blinked.

A woman stood before him, but it wasn't Gina. This woman was slim to the point of androgyny, with short white hair and deep charcoal skin. She wore matte black clothes made of something that was neither cloth nor leather, but something entirely other. Her red eyes glowed softly beneath flat white brows, and only her full, black lips betrayed any of the sensuality of her sister Goddess. Atae herself had come to answer his question.

His former Goddess looked at him with the emotionless mien for which she was so well known. When she spoke, her voice was a familiar cool contralto, and he felt a shudder run down his back.

"Iorgas Penbrooke. New made as Aspen. You have a question. I will answer it, as my sister requests, but in return you must do something for me."

He breathed out slowly, desperately fighting an urge to fall to his knees, as he would have done in the face of this Goddess before she had released her claim on him. "So long as it won't break my covenant with Gina, you will have it, Goddess."

For an instant he thought the corner of her mouth twitched, echoing her sister's familiar smile, but he knew he must be wrong. Atae never smiled, never laughed, never cried. Death was merciful, but also merciless, and no emotion swayed her.

"Someday something precious will come to your hand. You will know, without a doubt, that it is mine. No matter what, you must destroy it. Do this, and you will meet your daughter once again, and she will know she is yours, and no other. Fail me, and her soul is forfeit." Ice cold eyes, red as blood, held his.

Aspen nodded jerkily. "Anything."

Again the most minute motion touched the corner of the dark lips. "Done. Return, then. My priestess needs you."

In his chest, he felt his heart contract. Expand. Contract. And with the next expansion, the vision vanished.

ૐ ૐ ૐ

Aspen gasped, sitting up from where he lay, apparently having collapsed as his life blood drained from his body. He clapped a hand to his chest, amazed to discover that he felt no pain. His mana was still low, but with his retreat from the edge of death, it was now recovering, and he sent a warm flow toward Rouge, who was badly wounded and barely able to continue fighting.

The girl sucked in a surprised breath, and rallied, visibly pushing herself onward. ::Aspen?:: The young elf's mental voice was shocked and relieved. ::I thought you were dying!::

::*Aspen!*:: Silus' tiny form crashed into his chest as she flew down from wherever she had been hiding. ::I prayed and prayed, Aspen! Khor said the gods don't listen to us, but I promised Gina I'd give her the juiciest mosquito from every swarm for ever and ever, and she sent you back!:: The bat's silky head pushed up under his jaw, desperately snuggling into him. His hand shifted up to gently scratch her ears.

::I'm back,:: he said, pushing more mana at Rouge even as he separated off small trickles for each of his other companions, all of whom were injured to some degree. Even Silus was a little bruised from when she'd attacked Rubico.

Aspen cast out with his life sense, once again looking for something he could use to help them, and found something completely unexpected. The priestess of Atae, standing with her eyes closed, her hands flashing in a seamless flow of ritual gestures, her voice quietly intoning her spell, was a towering flame the likes of which he'd never seen before. That flame, though, seemed to be trapped. It swirled up in a tornado of fire, but guttered each time it touched a slick layer of the same greasy slime that seemed to cover the light—the soul?—of the Demonic Swineherd. Somehow, that bastard was blocking her from Atae. She would never be able to complete the ritual, and when it failed, the backlash of all the power she had poured into it would likely kill her. He well knew the pain of a fumbled spell, having suffered through it more than once himself, but he had *never* put as much power into a single casting as this priestess had. There was no way she could survive.

Even as he realized this, he heard shouting from the passage outside the door.

"Rouge? Rouge! Are you here? There was a *big ass tree* dancing around outside, and-"

A boy screeched to a halt in the hallway, mouth gaping. His wavy blonde hair was mussed, and a lute was slung sloppily over one shoulder. His gaily colored garb was mismatched, and he looked even younger than Rouge as his mouth opened and closed in astonishment.

Then the Demonic Swineherd swiped at him with a vicious clawed hand, and crimson stained the bright livery as his chest was slashed open to the bone. Two more swipes, and the boy fell to the ground, his corpse already fading into nothingness, leaving behind a small knife and two acorns.

"Jace!" Rouge shrieked, launching into a fresh round of attacks as she saw her friend die. Her Mambele finally managed to sever the head from Rubico's revenant, and though the body didn't collapse, it was also clearly no longer following instructions. It simply continued in the direction it had been going, ramming into the blank stone wall to the left of the door over and over.

"Bugger! I told that boy he wasn't high enough level to be out of Bright!" A cheerful female voice came from the darkness of the passage, and the second new Traveler came into sight.

This girl was tall and slim, with rich brown hair in a long braid down her back. Her brown eyes twinkled behind an odd contraption made of wires and stacked circles of thick glass. Her eyes were hugely magnified, and Aspen could see every eyelash as she winked at Rouge.

"He'll be right, Rouge. Respawn back in Bright in no time." Her enormous brown eyes blinked. "We may be seein' him there soon, eh? What's a Demonic Swineherd?"

Rouge threw her Mambele in a hard curve toward the other undead minion. "Talk later, kill now, Nina!"

The new girl shrugged. "I'll do my best, eh? I'm a merchie, though, not a fighter." She held out her hand and a large pouch appeared in it. She smacked the bag against her other hand, grinning wickedly. "C'mon, then, you doongi, let's see what you can do." Swinging her money pouch like a blackjack, she leapt into the fray.

Now that the fight was slightly more even, two versus two, though Rouge was still exhausted and injured, and the Demonic Swineherd was still horrifyingly agile and ferocious, Aspen turned back to see what he could do to help the priestess before she exploded.

Staring upward at the greasy bubble that blocked the woman's ability to reach her Goddess, he gritted his teeth, feeling helpless. He didn't even know what that *was*, much less what to do about it. As he watched, another tendril of flickering flame reached up toward the sky, then guttered out again without achieving anything. Nonetheless, the priestess continued with her ritual, seemingly unperturbed or unaware of how quickly she was racing toward a deadly precipice of power.

He blinked hard as he felt a hand touch his arm, and looked down into Manuela's worried brown eyes. "Something is wrong, isn't it? With the ritual." She nodded toward the priestess.

Pressing his lips together, he nodded back. "She needs Atae's power, but he's blocking her somehow. I don't know what to do!"

Forehead creasing, she looked from the priestess to the possessed corpse. "Is he doing it on purpose? Is it a spell? Can we interrupt it?"

Aspen shook his head. "I don't think so. It's the same thing that's keeping his soul in that body, but it's not necromancy. I'd recognize that, and you'd be able to dismiss the soul. It's like," he gestured helplessly, "soap scum or the oil slick that rises up on a road after a rain."

She smiled a little. "Too bad you can't clean it up like Jacinta with her double strength laundry detergent." His mind flashed back to an almost forgotten memory. A giggling, filthy Birdie, covered in tallow and ink from an ill-fated attempt to create a new kind of paint for her latest artistic project, and a long-suffering maid named Jacinta, who had had a nearly magical ability to clean almost anything. The maid's secret weapon had been a concoction that smelled of sunshine and lemons, and seemed to simply push grease and oil away with a single drop.

Sunshine and lemons. Sunshine and fruit. Sunshine and flowers....

Aspen watched the way Atae's priestess reached up with her power with new eyes. The woman wasn't begging. She wasn't pulling. She was stretching like a flower toward the sun, opening herself up to her Goddess in a way he'd never have understood if he couldn't see it with his life sense.

He remembered the words of a woman who had probably died long before he was ever born. *It knew what it was meant to be, Jonny. I just let it go.*

So he let go. He stopped trying to direct his mana, stopped trying to cast a spell. He didn't watch the battle happening behind him. He just remembered the smell of sunshine and lemons, the scent of flowers in a garden that never faded, and opened his soul to his goddess.

Who answered.

A shaft of light pierced the greasy blur like strong soap touching an oil slick, pushing it aside with contemptuous ease. It reached down to him as he felt himself open up to the universe in a way he never would have thought possible when he was a necromancer. For all that he had claimed to be all but a priest of Atae, he suddenly realized that that was no truer than a pebble claiming to be a mountain.

Gina's light touched Aspen's soul, and he felt as if he would burst, he was so full. Power overflowed the little spells he had nearly forgotten, healing Rouge, Manuela, Silus, Struthio, and even clearing Nekthadt's debuff and repairing the shattered bones in his leg. Aspen's vision was filled with the light of every life around him, from his friends to organisms so small they were invisible to his mere human eyes. Then those lights grew, and merged, and filled with numbers...

And then the priestess finished her rite. Rich, powerful darkness flooded down through the hole in the film surrounding them and filled the woman up, overflowing her body like he was overflowing with Gina's light. Atae's power flashed out to touch the Demonic Swineherd, and he staggered.

"Now," said the priestess, in a voice that rang like a bell.

And Struthio, thin as a scarecrow, teeth bared in fury, dug out the heart of the Swineherd with a trowel.

The instant the Demonic Swineherd fell, Struthio and the remaining undead minion fell as well. The minion was nothing more than the shattered ruin of a corpse, but Aspen could see from the rapid rise and fall of Struthio's wasted chest that the man still lived. He rushed to Struthio's side, pouring more healing energy into him, though after absorbing a [Heal] that had been powered by Gina's strength, the man was more exhausted than injured. No doubt he, too, had been kept in a state so near to death that his stamina and health were unable to recover.

Rouge was right behind Aspen, with Manuela, Nekthadt, Silus, and the new Traveler not far behind the girl. They crowded around the figure on the floor, ignoring their defeated foes for the moment, though Aspen caught the brown-haired Traveler eyeing the Demonic Swineherd's corpse thoughtfully.

Notifications popped up in front of Aspen's eyes, and he scanned them quickly before flicking them away impatiently.

Quest: "Find the (S)truth(io)" complete.

Struthio was abducted, and Millie forced into an unwanted engagement. Thanks to you, both of them have been rescued.

Reward: +30 Relationship with Struthio. +30 Relationship with Millie. Cinnamon rolls.

Quest: "Need a Little Help from A Friend" complete.

Success: The magical link between you and any remaining items being used to track you can be broken.

Rouge crouched beside Struthio, picking up the trowel resting on the floor. A sodden black lump that had been cupped in the blade rolled away with a quiet *squelch*. The girl wrinkled her nose and held up the disgusting implement with two fingers. "Where did *this* come from?"

Aspen sat back from Struthio, his life sense assuring him that the man was unconscious but would recover soon. "I, ah, made it. It was the easiest way for me to get Manuela out of her chains."

Manuela arched an eyebrow. "And you were showing off, just a bit."

He grinned a little, picking up his ever more battered hat from the floor and dusting it off before placing it on his head again. "Maybe."

Rouge looked back and forth between the two, eyes narrowing. "Would you like to introduce us, Aspen?"

He felt heat rise in his cheeks, looking between the two females. "Sorry. This is Manuela, my friend from, uh, before. The one we were looking for in Bloodhaven. Apparently, these bast… um, guys thought she could lead them to me, one way or another, so they brought her here. Manuela, this is Rouge the Rogue. She and her fa… *friend*, Motte, have been helping me look for you."

Rouge rolled her eyes, sticking out a hand for Manuela to shake. "Nice to meet you! Yeah, Motte's my dad. Don't worry about the fact that he's human. Travelers are weird like that," the girl said cheerfully. "I guess it doesn't matter that much if everybody knows *all* my business, anyway. You're gonna meet my sister, Doom Bloom, too."

The thief hitched a thumb toward her merchant friend. "This is Wikiwi. She's a friend of mine in, um, our world. Wikiwi, this is Aspen, the tall guy on the floor is Struthio, the gloomy lady is Mai Ley, a priestess of Atae, I guess, and the goblin over there is Ned. He's on our side. And *this*," she snuggled her chin against Silus, who had taken her place on Rouge's shoulder, "little ball of *adorable,* is Silus."

Wikiwi's eyes widened even more behind their odd lenses. "Oh my gosh, Rouge. She's as cute as you said! Can you-"

The rest of the young woman's question was lost as Flu-flu and Tessle burst into the room, staring around wildly. Tessle quickly calmed upon seeing that the battle was over, but Flu-flu, ever searching for more drama, continued to point her loaded bow around the room, shouting, "Hark, we have arrived! If any evil-doers yet remain, we shall fight by your side, dear friends! Ye fiends, submit!"

Everyone else in the room who was conscious simultaneously rolled their eyes, and Tessle reached out to gently press her friend's arms down. "Fluff, it's okay. Put that away before you actually hurt someone." The blond half-dwarf looked over at Aspen and Rouge. "We cleared the rest of the house. No one else is here."

Aspen nodded, glad to have confirmation of what his life sense was telling him. Given that he hadn't sensed Millie's Pa and his two companions until they were practically at the door, he wasn't placing quite as much faith in what his new power was telling him as he had just an hour earlier.

The farmer looked around, noting how tight the space seemed now that ten beings were crammed into it, even though Silus barely took up any space at all. He glanced over at his young friend. "Time for loot?"

She grinned. "You know it!"

Struthio began to come around as Rouge and the other Travelers were finishing up their grim task (though from their behavior, he would have thought they were opening gifts instead of searching thoroughly destroyed corpses), and Aspen and Manuela helped him to his feet.

He swayed, but remained standing, and as soon as he was able to form semi-coherent words, he began asking, "Wheresh Millie? I'she a'right? Wha'happened t'er?"

Aspen pulled the man's arm across his shoulders, amazed to find that the other man was actually slightly taller than he was. Until Motte, that had been quite an uncommon experience, and yet here was another. He was beginning to question whether his ordeal in Akuji's dungeons had actually made him shrink. Though he thought Manuela seemed the same height relative to him as she had been before, so maybe not?

He shook off these pointless thoughts and smiled at Struthio. "Your Millie is fine. She was under the control of another ring like the one you were wearing, but we got it off her, and she's waiting for you. They told her you were dead, so don't worry if she seems overwhelmed when she sees you."

Overwhelmed was an understatement. The tall, muscular woman took a moment to recognize her formerly hefty suitor, but when she did, she leapt on him and swept him up into her arms.

Seeing the blond woman cradling her starved lover like a baby both warmed Aspen's heart and forced him to turn away so they wouldn't see him pinching his cheeks to keep from laughing out loud.

When all the introductions had been sorted out, the thirteen of them – including Jesiqa, who had remained behind in the secluded pool, and Codswallop, who had certainly earned the right to be counted – sat in the small clearing at the center of the brambles, shoulder to shoulder as they exchanged stories.

Millie and Struthio held hands as they recounted their terrifying experiences. Struthio's tale was especially harrowing. "Millie's Pa was right proud'a 'imself, 'e was. He'd come down'n gi'me s'more of th'poison they used to make me sick in the first place. T'keep me too beat down t'heal, y'ken. I kep' tryin' ter escape, an Rubico wanted ter kill me, 'cause I was too much trouble, but Millie's Pa said they could use me ter keep 'er in line as long's I was alive. Then they brung this lady in a bit ago, an' chained 'er on th'table instead o'me. Somethin' happened t'Millie's Pa after that. 'E was real different when we was alone, an' 'e put that ring on me. Testin' it, or summat. Tried it on th'lady, but it din't work, so they 'ad t'make sure it were real. Then t'other lady, the strange lookin' one wi' th' paint, showed up. Just knocked at t'door, they said. Knew what they was doin', though, so they locked 'er up, too."

Mai Ley nodded at this point, and spoke up in her flat and uninflected voice. "My Goddess sent me to that place. She said there were men there making bargains which took them outside of the cycle of life. My sisterhood is sworn to nonviolence, so I could not force them to stop, but I spoke to them at length about the choices they were making. They indicated that they would not cease their wicked ways, and confined me against my will. Atae told me I must stay, and that I would be freed in due course."

Everyone just stared at the priestess for a long moment, unsure how to respond. Then Millie clutched Struthio's hand to her well-padded bosom and smiled through her tears. "We're just so grateful t'all of you for savin' us both. I was bound t'take my own life if I was forced to marry Rubico. I even found some aconis plants and managed t'put it in th' top layer o' the cake. 'E told me t'make it delicious, y'see, but not t'make it safe." Her blue eyes flashed with determination, and Aspen immediately swore to himself that he would never eat anything the formidable lady made for him when she was angry.

Rouge popped to her feet and began brushing off her rear. "*I'm* just glad Wikiwi here came looking for us when she did, and Fluff and Tess were willing to help her find us. I don't want to think what might have happened if you guys had been a minute later."

Wikiwi grinned. "Good timing has always been one of my mad skills. Now poor Lyrec," she shook her head in amusement, "he needs to work on a few things."

Rouge stretched her arms over her head, leaning from side to side. "No doubt. I obviously need to talk to him a little more about his char… uh, avatar? I figured he was higher level than that, since he was almost level 18 when I left Bright months ago. I should have asked him before I said it was okay for him to come meet us. I honestly didn't think we'd be doing anything riskier than facing the Funk of Goose, though."

The other Travelers chuckled, but Millie and Struthio just stared at Rouge, uncomprehending. After a moment, she coughed into her hand, looking slightly embarrassed. "Um, in any case, what are you going to do now, Millie, Struthio? Get married? Take over the, um, piggery?"

Millie's hand tightened on Struthio's until Aspen saw the man wince slightly, though he didn't pull away. "Married, aye, for certain," Millie said. "But I don't think I c'n stay in Nor'Goose after this. Not a person asked me if I was all right, 'cept m'sister Cora. She was too afraid t'do anythin', 'specially after I said I was fine, but that none else e'en asked…" She trailed off, shaking her head sadly.

Struthio shrugged. "I ne'er liked piggins tha'much. S'why I tried th'ostriches in t'first place. I kin work anywhere, an' my Millie, she's brilliant, she is. She kin beat anyone in cookin'."

Aspen and Rouge exchanged glances.

"Would you like to go to Bright, then?" Rouge asked. "We're headed that way, and I'm sure the caravan master wouldn't mind if you wanted to tag along."

Aspen wasn't so sure about that, but if Rouge was right about the quality of Millie's confections, he suspected Restur would come around quickly enough, so he nodded. "It seems to be a bit more dangerous than usual to travel right now. It would likely be wise to travel as part of a group."

Millie and Struthio exchanged glances of their own, and then both nodded enthusiastically, and that was that. Rouge, Codswallop, Flu-flu, Tessle, Wikiwi, Struthio, Millie, Manuela, and Mai Ley all gathered together and began heading for the caravan. The Travelers were already discussing who would 'log off' and who would stay to help protect the caravan as they continued toward Bright in the morning. Aspen was about to follow when he saw Nekthadt lingering at the edge of the group watching him intently. The farmer dropped back as the others set off, until he and the goblin were the only ones remaining at the edge of the pond.

Aspen nodded to Nekthadt, then tilted his head toward Jesiqa, who was strapped to the goblin's thin chest once again. "I remember you mentioned you had your own business near here. I'm guessing it may have to do with your little friend?"

Nekthadt returned the nod solemnly, his expression as serious as ever. "Indeed. There is a small river that runs near here, and Jesiqa believes she can use it to reach her people. I mean to take her there and find out."

Aspen huffed a breath, but inclined his head in acknowledgement. "Then what will you do?"

Nekthadt cast a look to the north, his yellow eyes glowing in the low light of the moons. "You said my sister is beyond the mountains, did you not?"

"She is. If you travel along the widest path through the pass, keeping on the road, you'll come to the house. If you choose to travel that way, would you tell them..." he looked up, eyes caught on the fading stars and the twin moons playing their eternal game of tag across the sky. "Tell them I'm looking forward to coming home."

Nekthadt nodded his agreement, and then sank back into the darkness, taking the shark girl with him. Aspen raised a hand in farewell, and the shift disturbed Silus, who was snoozing against his neck.

Where did everyone go? she asked sleepily, and he scrootched her soft ears.

"Forward," he replied quietly, and set his feet on the path to Bright.

AUTHOR'S NOTE

Thank you for reading book two of the Legendary Farmer series: *Harrowing*! I hope you enjoyed it, and will join us for Zoey, Aspen, and friends further adventures in *Sowing*, *Cultivation*, and *Harvest*, all coming in 2022. What will they find when they reach Bright, and who is their mysterious enemy? What's going on at Veritas Corporation, and will Zoey manage to finish her internship without further incident? Find out soon!

Meanwhile, I'm available on Patreon, Twitter as @AuthorEOswald, on Instagram as authorelizabethoswald, and I check Goodreads regularly. I'd love to hear from you!

I know you've heard it before, but indie authors desperately need your support, so if you love Aspen and Rouge as much as I do, please don't forget to leave a review so other people can find them too.

www.ingramcontent.com/pod-product-compliance
Lightning Source LLC
Chambersburg PA
CBHW070623260626
47161CB00007B/2554